ST. MARTIN'S

MINOTAUR

MYSTERIES

Also by Agatha Christie

AGATHA CHRISTIE

The Witness for the Prosecution
and Other Stories

St. Martin's Paperbacks

THE WITNESS FOR THE PROSECUTION AND OTHER STORIES

Copyright 1924, 1926, 1929, 1933, 1934, 1943, 1948 by Agatha Christie.
Copyright 1932 by The Curtis Pub. Co.
Copyright renewed 1957 by Agatha Christie.
Copyright renewed 1959, 1970 by Agatha Christie Mallowan.
Copyright renewed 1976 by Agatha Christie Limited.

Reprinted by arrangement with G. P. Putnam's Sons, a member of Penguin Putnam Inc.

Cover photo credit: Martin Barraud/Stone

ISBN: 0-312-97973-8

Printed in the United States of America

St. Martin's Paperbacks edition / September 2001

St. Martin's Paperbacks are published by St. Martin's Press, 175 Fifth Avenue, New York, NY 10010.

10 9 8 7 6 5 4 3 2 1

CONTENTS

The Witness for the Prosecution
and Other Stories

THE WITNESS FOR THE PROSECUTION

Mr. Mayherne adjusted his pince-nez and cleared his throat with a little dry-as-dust cough that was wholly typical of him. Then he looked again at the man opposite him, the man charged with willful murder.

Mr. Mayherne was a small man, precise in manner, neatly, not to say foppishly dressed, with a pair of very shrewd and piercing gray eyes. By no means a fool. Indeed, as a solicitor, Mr. Mayherne's reputation stood very high. His voice, when he spoke to his client, was dry but not unsympathetic.

"I must impress upon you again that you are in very grave danger, and that the utmost frankness is necessary."

Leonard Vole, who had been staring in a dazed fashion at the blank wall in front of him, transferred his glance to the solicitor.

"I know," he said hopelessly. "You keep telling me so. But I can't seem to realize yet that I'm charged with murder—*murder*. And such a dastardly crime too."

Mr. Mayherne was practical, not emotional. He coughed again, took off his pince-nez, polished them carefully, and replaced them on his nose. Then he said:

"Yes, yes, yes. Now, my dear Mr. Vole, we're going to make a determined effort to get you off—and we shall succeed—we shall succeed. But I must have all the facts. I must know just how damaging the case against you is likely to be. Then we can fix upon the best line of defense."

Still the young man looked at him in the same dazed, hopeless fashion. To Mr. Mayherne the case had seemed black enough, and the guilt of the prisoner assured. Now, for the first time, he felt a doubt.

"You think I'm guilty," said Leonard Vole, in a low voice. "But, by God, I swear I'm not! It looks pretty black against me, I know that. I'm like a man caught in a net—the meshes of it all round me, entangling me whichever way I turn. But I didn't do it, Mr. Mayherne, I didn't do it!"

In such a position a man was bound to protest his innocence. Mr. Mayherne knew that. Yet, in spite of himself, he was impressed. It might be, after all, that Leonard Vole was innocent.

"You are right, Mr. Vole," he said gravely. "The case does look very black against you. Nevertheless, I accept your assurance. Now, let us get to facts. I want you to tell me in your own words exactly how you came to make the acquaintance of Miss Emily French."

"It was one day in Oxford Street. I saw an elderly lady crossing the road. She was carrying a lot of parcels. In the middle of the street she dropped them, tried to recover them, found a bus was almost on top of her and just managed to reach the curb safely, dazed and bewildered by people having shouted at her. I recovered her parcels, wiped the mud off them as best I could, retied the string of one, and returned them to her."

"There was no question of your having saved her life?"

"Oh, dear me, no! All I did was to perform a common act of courtesy. She was extremely grateful, thanked me warmly, and said something about my manners not being those of most of the younger generation—I can't remember the exact words. Then I lifted my hat and went on. I never expected to see her again. But life is full of coincidences. That very evening I came across her at a party at a friend's house. She recognized me at once and asked that I should be introduced to her. I then found out that she was a Miss Emily French and that she lived at Cricklewood. I talked to her for some time. She was, I imagine, an old lady who took sudden and violent fancies to people. She took one to me on the strength of a perfectly simple action which anyone might have performed. On leaving, she shook me warmly by the hand, and asked me to come and see her. I replied, of course, that I should be very pleased to do so, and she then urged me to name a day. I did not want particularly to go, but it would have seemed churlish to refuse, so I fixed on the following Saturday. After she had gone, I learned something about her from my friends. That she was rich, eccentric, lived alone with one maid and owned no less than eight cats."

"I see," said Mr. Mayherne. "The question of her being well off came up as early as that?"

"If you mean that I inquired——" began Leonard

Vole hotly, but Mr. Mayherne stilled him with a gesture.

"I have to look at the case as it will be presented by the other side. An ordinary observer would not have supposed Miss French to be a lady of means. She lived poorly, almost humbly. Unless you had been told the contrary, you would in all probability have considered her to be in poor circumstances—at any rate to begin with. Who was it exactly who told you that she was well off?"

"My friend, George Harvey, at whose house the party took place."

"Is he likely to remember having done so?"

"I really don't know. Of course it is some time ago now."

"Quite so, Mr. Vole. You see, the first aim of the prosecution will be to establish that you were in low water financially—that is true, is it not?"

Leonard Vole flushed.

"Yes," he said, in a low voice. "I'd been having a run of infernal bad luck just then."

"Quite so," said Mr. Mayherne again. "That being, as I say, in low water financially, you met this rich old lady and cultivated her acquaintance assiduously. Now if we are in a position to say that you had no idea she was well off, and that you visited her out of pure kindness of heart——"

"Which is the case."

"I dare say. I am not disputing the point. I am looking at it from the outside point of view. A great deal depends on the memory of Mr. Harvey. Is he likely to remember that conversation or is he not?

Could he be confused by counsel into believing that it took place later?"

Leonard Vole reflected for some minutes. Then he said steadily enough, but with a rather paler face:

"I do not think that that line would be successful, Mr. Mayherne. Several of those present heard his remark, and one or two of them chaffed me about my conquest of a rich old lady."

The solicitor endeavored to hide his disappointment with a wave of the hand.

"Unfortunate," he said. "But I congratulate you upon your plain speaking, Mr. Vole. It is to you I look to guide me. Your judgment is quite right. To persist in the line I spoke of would have been disastrous. We must leave that point. You made the acquaintance of Miss French, you called upon her, the acquaintanceship progressed. We want a clear reason for all this. Why did you, a young man of thirty-three, good-looking, fond of sport, popular with your friends, devote so much of your time to an elderly woman with whom you could hardly have anything in common?"

Leonard Vole flung out his hands in a nervous gesture.

"I can't tell you—I really can't tell you. After the first visit, she pressed me to come again, spoke of being lonely and unhappy. She made it difficult for me to refuse. She showed so plainly her fondness and affection for me that I was placed in an awkward position. You see, Mr. Mayherne, I've got a weak nature—I drift—I'm one of those people who can't say 'No.' And believe me or not, as you like, after the third or fourth visit I paid her I found myself getting genuinely fond of the old thing. My mother died when I was young, an aunt brought me up, and she too died before I was fifteen. If I told you that I genuinely enjoyed being mothered and pampered, I dare say you'd only laugh."

Mr. Mayherne did not laugh. Instead he took off his pince-nez again and polished them, a sign with him that he was thinking deeply.

"I accept your explanation, Mr. Vole," he said at last. "I believe it to be psychologically probable. Whether a jury would take that view of it is another matter. Please continue your narrative. When was it that Miss French first asked you to look into her business affairs?"

"After my third or fourth visit to her. She understood very little of money matters, and was worried about some investments."

Mr. Mayherne looked up sharply.

"Be careful, Mr. Vole. The maid, Janet Mackenzie, declares that her mistress was a good woman of business and transacted all her own affairs, and this is borne out by the testimony of her bankers."

"I can't help that," said Vole earnestly. "That's what she said to me."

Mr. Mayherne looked at him for a moment or two in silence. Though he had no intention of saying so, his belief in Leonard Vole's innocence was at that moment strengthened. He knew something of the mentality of elderly ladies. He saw Miss French, infatuated with the good-looking young man, hunting about for pretexts that would bring him to the house. What more likely than that she should plead ignorance of business, and beg him to help her with her money affairs? She was enough of a woman of the world to realize that any man is slightly flattered by such an admission of his superiority. Leonard Vole had been flattered. Perhaps, too, she had not been averse to letting this young man know that she was wealthy. Emily French had been a strong-willed old woman, willing to pay her price for what she wanted. All this passed rapidly through Mr. Mayherne's mind, but he gave no indication of it, and asked instead a further question.

"And you did handle her affairs for her at request?"

"I did."

"Mr. Vole," said the solicitor, "I am going to ask you a very serious question, and one to which it is vital I should have a truthful answer. You were in low water financially. You had the handling of an old lady's affairs—an old lady who, according to her own statement, knew little or nothing of business. Did you at any time, or in any manner, convert to your own use the securities which you handled? Did you engage in any transaction for your own pecuniary advantage which will not bear the light of day?" He quelled the other's response. "Wait a minute before you answer. There are two courses open to us. Either we can make a feature of your probity and honesty in conducting her affairs whilst pointing out how unlikely it is that you would commit murder to obtain money which you might have obtained by such infinitely easier means. If, on the other hand, there is anything in your dealings which the prosecution will get hold of—if, to put it baldly, it can be proved that you swindled the old lady in any way, we must take the line that you had no motive for the murder, since she was already a profitable source of income to you. You perceive the distinction. Now, I beg of you, take your time before you reply."

But Leonard Vole took no time at all.

"My dealings with Miss French's affairs were all perfectly fair and above board. I acted for her interests to the very best of my ability, as any one will find who looks into the matter."

"Thank you," said Mr. Mayherne. "You relieve my mind very much. I pay you the compliment of believing that you are far too clever to lie to me over such an important matter."

"Surely," said Vole eagerly, "the strongest point in my favor is the lack of motive. Granted that I cultivated the acquaintanceship of a rich old lady in the hopes of getting money out of her—that, I gather, is the substance of what you have been saying—surely her death frustrates all my hopes?"

The solicitor looked at him steadily. Then, very deliberately, he repeated his unconscious trick with his pince-nez. It was not until they were firmly replaced on his nose that he spoke.

"Are you not aware, Mr. Vole, that Miss French left a will under which you are the principal beneficiary?"

"What?" The prisoner sprang to his feet. His dismay was obvious and unforced. "My God! What are you saying? She left her money to me?"

Mr. Mayherne nodded slowly. Vole sank down again, his head in his hands.

"You pretend you know nothing of this will?"

"Pretend? There's no pretense about it. I knew nothing about it."

"What would you say if I told you that the maid, Janet Mackenzie, swears that you *did* know? That her mistress told her distinctly that she had consulted you in the matter, and told you of her intentions?"

"Say? That she's lying! No, I go too fast. Janet is an elderly woman. She was a faithful watchdog to her mistress, and she didn't like me. She was jealous and suspicious. I should say that Miss French confided her intentions to Janet, and that Janet either mistook something she said, or else was convinced in her own mind that I had persuaded the old lady into doing it. I dare say that she herself believes now that Miss French actually told her so."

"You don't think she dislikes you enough to lie deliberately about the matter?"

Leonard Vole looked shocked and startled.

"No, indeed! Why should she?"

"I don't know," said Mr. Mayherne thoughtfully. "But she's very bitter against you."

The wretched young man groaned again.

"I'm beginning to see," he muttered. "It's frightful. I made up to her, that's what they'll say, I got her to make a will leaving her money to me, and then I go there that night, and there's nobody in the house— they find her the next day—oh! my God, it's awful!"

"You are wrong about there being nobody in the house," said Mr. Mayherne. "Janet, as you remember, was to go out for the evening. She went, but about half-past nine she returned to fetch the pattern of a blouse sleeve which she had promised to a friend. She let herself in by the back door, went upstairs and fetched it, and went out again. She heard voices in the sittingroom, though she could not distinguish what they said, but she will swear that one of them was Miss French's and one was a man's."

"At half-past nine," said Leonard Vole. "At half-past nine. . . ." He sprang to his feet. "But then I'm saved—saved——"

"What do you mean, saved?" cried Mr. Mayherne, astonished.

"By half-past nine I was at home again! My wife can prove that. I left Miss French about five minutes to nine. I arrived home about twenty past nine. My wife was there waiting for me. Oh, thank God—thank God! And bless Janet Mackenzie's sleeve pattern."

In his exuberance, he hardly noticed that the grave expression on the solicitor's face had not altered. But the latter's words brought him down to earth with a bump.

"Who, then, in your opinion, murdered Miss French?"

"Why, a burglar, of course, as was thought at first. The window was forced, you remember. She was killed with a heavy blow from a crowbar, and the crowbar was found lying on the floor beside the body. And several articles were missing. But for Janet's absurd suspicions and dislike of me, the police would never have swerved from the right track."

"That will hardly do, Mr. Vole," said the solicitor. "The things that were missing were mere trifles of no value, taken as a blind. And the marks on the window were not at all conclusive. Besides, think for yourself. You say you were no longer in the house by half-past nine. Who, then, was the man Janet heard talking to Miss French in the sitting-room? She would hardly be having an amicable conversation with a burglar?"

"No," said Vole. "No——" He looked puzzled and discouraged. "But, anyway," he added with reviving spirit, "it lets me out. I've got an alibi. You must see Romaine—my wife—at once."

"Certainly," acquiesced the lawyer. "I should already have seen Mrs. Vole but for her being absent when you were arrested. I wired to Scotland at once, and I understand that she arrives back tonight. I am going to call upon her immediately I leave here."

Vole nodded, a great expression of satisfaction settling down over his face.

"Yes, Romaine will tell you. My God! it's a lucky chance that."

"Excuse me, Mr. Vole, but you are very fond of your wife?"

"Of course."

"And she of you?"

"Romaine is devoted to me. She'd do anything in the world for me."

He spoke enthusiastically, but the solicitor's heart sank a little lower. The testimony of a devoted wife—would it gain credence?

"Was there anyone else who saw you return at nine-twenty. A maid, for instance?"

"We have no maid."

"Did you meet anyone in the street on the way back?"

"Nobody I knew. I rode part of the way in a bus. The conductor might remember."

Mr. Mayherne shook his head doubtfully.

"There is no one, then, who can confirm your wife's testimony?"

"No. But it isn't necessary, surely?"

"I dare say not. I dare say not," said Mr. Mayherne hastily. "Now there's just one thing more. Did Miss French know that you were a married man?"

"Oh, yes."

"Yet you never took your wife to see her. Why was that?"

For the first time, Leonard Vole's answer came halting and uncertain.

"Well—I don't know."

"Are you aware that Janet Mackenzie says her mistress believed you to be single, and contemplated marrying you in the future?"

Vole laughed.

"Absurd! There was forty years' difference in age between us."

"It has been done," said the solicitor drily. "The fact remains. Your wife never met Miss French?"

"No——" Again the constraint.

"You will permit me to say," said the lawyer, "that I hardly understand your attitude in the matter."

Vole flushed, hesitated, and then spoke.

"I'll make a clean breast of it. I was hard up, as you know. I hoped that Miss French might lend me some money. She was fond of me, but she wasn't at all interested in the struggles of a young couple. Early on, I found that she had taken it for granted that my wife and I didn't get on—were living apart. Mr. Mayherne—I wanted the money—for Romaine's sake. I said nothing, and allowed the old lady to think what she chose. She spoke of my being an adopted son to her. There was never any question of marriage—that must be just Janet's imagination."

"And that is all?"

"Yes—that is all."

Was there just a shade of hesitation in the words? The lawyer fancied so. He rose and held out his hand.

"Good-bye, Mr. Vole." He looked into the haggard young face and spoke with an unusual impulse. "I believe in your innocence in spite of the multitude of facts arrayed against you. I hope to prove it and vindicate you completely."

Vole smiled back at him.

"You'll find the alibi is all right," he said cheerfully.

Again he hardly noticed that the other did not respond.

"The whole thing hinges a good deal on the testimony of Janet Mackenzie," said Mr. Mayherne. "She hates you. That much is clear."

"She can hardly hate me," protested the young man.

The solicitor shook his head as he went out.

"Now for Mrs. Vole," he said to himself.

He was seriously disturbed by the way the thing was shaping.

The Voles lived in a small shabby house near Paddington Green. It was to this house that Mr. Mayherne went.

In answer to his ring, a big slatternly woman, obviously a charwoman, answered the door.

"Mrs. Vole? Has she returned yet?"

"Got back an hour ago. But I dunno if you can see her."

"If you will take my card to her," said Mr. Mayherne quietly, "I am quite sure that she will do so."

The woman looked at him doubtfully, wiped her

hand on her apron and took the card. Then she closed the door in his face and left him on the step outside.

In a few minutes, however, she returned with a slightly altered manner.

"Come inside, please."

She ushered him into a tiny drawing-room. Mr. Mayherne, examining a drawing on the wall, started up suddenly to face a tall, pale woman who had entered so quietly that he had not heard her.

"Mr. Mayherne? You are my husband's solicitor, are you not? You have come from him? Will you please sit down?"

Until she spoke he had not realized that she was not English. Now, observing her more closely, he noticed the high cheekbones, the dense blue-black of the hair, and an occasional very slight movement of the hands that was distinctly foreign. A strange woman, very quiet. So quiet as to make one uneasy. From the very first Mr. Mayherne was conscious that he was up against something that he did not understand.

"Now, my dear Mrs. Vole," he began, "you must not give way——"

He stopped. It was so very obvious that Romaine Vole had not the slightest intention of giving way. She was perfectly calm and composed.

"Will you please tell me about it?" she said. "I must know everything. Do not think to spare me. I want to know the worst." She hesitated, then repeated in a lower tone, with a curious emphasis which the lawyer did not understand: "I want to know the worst."

Mr. Mayherne went over his interview with Leonard Vole. She listened attentively, nodding her head now and then.

"I see," she said, when he had finished. "He wants me to say that he came in at twenty minutes past nine that night?"

"He did come in at that time?" said Mr. Mayherne sharply.

"That is not the point," she said coldly. "Will my saying so acquit him? Will they believe me?"

Mr. Mayherne was taken aback. She had gone so quickly to the core of the matter.

"That is what I want to know," she said. "Will it be enough? Is there anyone else who can support my evidence?"

There was a suppressed eagerness in her manner that made him vaguely uneasy.

"So far there is no one else," he said reluctantly.

"I see," said Romaine Vole.

She sat for a minute or two perfectly still. A little smile played over her lips.

The lawyer's feeling of alarm grew stronger and stronger.

"Mrs. Vole——" he began. "I know what you must feel——"

"Do you?" she asked. "I wonder."

"In the circumstances——"

"In the circumstances—I intend to play a lone hand."

He looked at her in dismay.

"But, my dear Mrs. Vole—you are overwrought. Being so devoted to your husband——"

"I beg your pardon?"

The sharpness of her voice made him start. He repeated in a hesitating manner:

"Being so devoted to your husband——"

Romaine Vole nodded slowly, the same strange smile on her lips.

"Did he tell you that I was devoted to him?" she asked softly. "Ah! yes, I can see he did. How stupid men are! Stupid—stupid—stupid——"

She rose suddenly to her feet. All the intense emotion that the lawyer had been conscious of in the atmosphere was now concentrated in her tone.

"I hate him, I tell you! I hate him. I hate him. I hate him! I would like to see him hanged by the neck till he is dead."

The lawyer recoiled before her and the smoldering passion in her eyes.

She advanced a step nearer, and continued vehemently:

"Perhaps I shall see it. Supposing I tell you that he did not come in that night at twenty past nine, but at twenty past ten? You say that he tells you he knew nothing about the money coming to him. Supposing I tell you he knew all about it, and counted on it, and committed murder to get it? Supposing I tell you that he admitted to me that night when he came in what he had done? That there was blood on his coat? What then? Supposing that I stand up in court and say all these things?"

Her eyes seemed to challenge him. With an effort, he concealed his growing dismay, and endeavored to speak in a rational tone.

"You cannot be asked to give evidence against your husband——"

"He is not my husband!"

The words came out so quickly that he fancied he had misunderstood her.

"I beg your pardon? I——"

"He is not my husband."

The silence was so intense that you could have heard a pin drop.

"I was an actress in Vienna. My husband is alive but in a madhouse. So we could not marry. I am glad now."

She nodded defiantly.

"I should like you to tell me one thing," said Mr. Mayherne. He contrived to appear as cool and unemotional as ever. "Why are you so bitter against Leonard Vole?"

She shook her head, smiling a little.

"Yes, you would like to know. But I shall not tell you. I will keep my secret. . . ."

Mr. Mayherne gave his dry little cough and rose.

"There seems no point in prolonging this interview," he remarked. "You will hear from me again after I have communicated with my client."

She came closer to him, looking into his eyes with her own wonderful dark ones.

"Tell me," she said, "did you believe—honestly—that he was innocent when you came here today?"

"I did," said Mr. Mayherne.

"You poor little man," she laughed.

"And I believe so still," finished the lawyer. "Good evening, madam."

He went out of the room, taking with him the memory of her startled face.

"This is going to be the devil of a business," said

Mr. Mayherne to himself as he strode along the street.

Extraordinary, the whole thing. An extraordinary woman. A very dangerous woman. Women were the devil when they got their knife into you.

What was to be done? That wretched young man hadn't a leg to stand upon. Of course, possibly he did commit the crime. . . .

"No," said Mr. Mayherne to himself. "No—there's almost too much evidence against him. I don't believe this woman. She was trumping up the whole story. But she'll never bring it into court."

He wished he felt more conviction on the point.

The police court proceedings were brief and dramatic. The principal witnesses for the prosecution were Janet Mackenzie, maid to the dead woman, and Romaine Heilger, Austrian subject, the mistress of the prisoner.

Mr. Mayherne sat in court and listened to the damning story that the latter told. It was on the lines she had indicated to him in their interview.

The prisoner reserved his defense and was committed for trial.

Mr. Mayherne was at his wits' end. The case against Leonard Vole was black beyond words. Even the famous K. C. who was engaged for the defense held out little hope.

"If we can shake that Austrian woman's testimony, we might do something," he said dubiously. "But it's a bad business."

Mr. Mayherne had concentrated his energies on one single point. Assuming Leonard Vole to be speaking the truth, and to have left the murdered woman's house at nine o'clock, who was the man

Janet heard talking to Miss French at half-past nine?

The only ray of light was in the shape of a scape-grace nephew who had in bygone days cajoled and threatened his aunt out of various sums of money. Janet Mackenzie, the solicitor learned, had always been attached to this young man, and had never ceased urging his claims upon her mistress. It certainly seemed possible that it was this nephew who had been with Miss French after Leonard Vole left, especially as he was not to be found in any of his old haunts.

In all other directions, the lawyer's researches had been negative in their result. No one had seen Leonard Vole entering his own house, or leaving that of Miss French. No one had seen any other man enter or leave the house in Cricklewood. All inquiries drew blank.

It was the eve of the trial when Mr. Mayherne received the letter which was to lead his thoughts in an entirely new direction.

It came by the six o'clock post. An illiterate scrawl, written on common paper and enclosed in a dirty envelope with the stamp stuck on crooked.

Mr. Mayherne read it through once or twice before he grasped its meaning.

DEAR MISTER:
Youre the lawyer chap wot acts for the young feller. If you want that painted foreign hussy showd up for wot she is an her pack of lies you come to 16 Shaw's Rents Stepney to-night It ull cawst you 2 hundred quid Arsk for Misses Mogson.

The solicitor read and reread this strange epistle. It might, of course, be a hoax, but when he thought it over, he became increasingly convinced that it was genuine, and also convinced that it was the one hope for the prisoner. The evidence of Romaine Heilger damned him completely, and the line the defense meant to pursue, the line that the evidence of a woman who had admittedly lived an immoral life was not to be trusted, was at best a weak one.

Mr. Mayherne's mind was made up. It was his duty to save his client at all costs. He must go to Shaw's Rents.

He had some difficulty in finding the place, a ramshackle building in an evil-smelling slum, but at last he did so, and on inquiry for Mrs. Mogson was sent up to a room on the third floor. On this door he knocked, and getting no answer, knocked again.

At this second knock, he heard a shuffling sound inside, and presently the door was opened cautiously half an inch and a bent figure peered out.

Suddenly the woman, for it was a woman, gave a chuckle and opened the door wider.

"So it's you, dearie," she said, in a wheezy voice. "Nobody with you, is there? No playing tricks? That's right. You can come in—you can come in."

With some reluctance the lawyer stepped across the threshold into the small dirty room, with its flickering gas jet. There was an untidy unmade bed in a corner, a plain deal table and two rickety chairs. For the first time Mr. Mayherne had a full view of the tenant of this unsavory apartment. She was a woman of middle age, bent in figure, with a mass of untidy gray hair and a scarf wound tightly round her face.

She saw him looking at this and laughed again, the same curious, toneless chuckle.

"Wondering why I hide my beauty, dear? He, he, he. Afraid it may tempt you, eh? But you shall see— you shall see."

She drew aside the scarf and the lawyer recoiled involuntarily before the almost formless blur of scarlet. She replaced the scarf again.

"So you're not wanting to kiss me, dearie? He, he, I don't wonder. And yet I was a pretty girl once— not so long ago as you'd think, either. Vitriol, dearie, vitriol—that's what did that. Ah! but I'll be even with 'em——"

She burst into a hideous torrent of profanity which Mr. Mayherne tried vainly to quell. She fell silent at last, her hands clenching and unclenching themselves nervously.

"Enough of that," said the lawyer sternly. "I've come here because I have reason to believe you can give me information which will clear my client, Leonard Vole. Is that the case?"

Her eyes leered at him cunningly.

"What about the money, dearie?" she wheezed. "Two hundred quid, you remember."

"It is your duty to give evidence, and you can be called upon to do so."

"That won't do, dearie. I'm an old woman, and I know nothing. But you give me two hundred quid, and perhaps I can give you a hint or two. See?"

"What kind of hint?"

"What should you say to a letter? A letter from *her*. Never mind how I got hold of it. That's my business. It'll do the trick. But I want my two hundred quid."

Mr. Mayherne looked at her coldly, and made up his mind.

"I'll give you ten pounds, nothing more. And only that if this letter is what you say it is."

"Ten pounds?" She screamed and raved at him.

"Twenty," said Mr. Mayherne, "and that's my last word."

He rose as if to go. Then, watching her closely, he drew out a pocketbook, and counted out twenty one-pound notes.

"You see," he said. "That is all I have with me. You can take it or leave it."

But already he knew that the sight of the money was too much for her. She cursed and raved impotently, but at last she gave in. Going over to the bed, she drew something out from beneath the tattered mattress.

"Here you are, damn you!" she snarled. "It's the top one you want."

It was a bundle of letters that she threw to him, and Mr. Mayherne untied them and scanned them in his usual cool, methodical manner. The woman, watching him eagerly, could gain no clue from his impassive face.

He read each letter through, then returned again to the top one and read it a second time. Then he tied the whole bundle up again carefully.

They were love letters, written by Romaine Heilger, and the man they were written to was not Leonard Vole. The top letter was dated the day of the latter's arrest.

"I spoke true, dearie, didn't I?" whined the woman. "It'll do for her, that letter?"

Mr. Mayherne put the letters in his pocket, then he asked a question.

"How did you get hold of this correspondence?"

"That's telling," she said with a leer. "But I know something more. I heard in court what that hussy said. Find out where she was at twenty past ten, the time she says she was at home. Ask at the Lion Road Cinema. They'll remember—a fine upstanding girl like that—curse her!"

"Who is the man?" asked Mr. Mayherne. "There's only a Christian name here."

The other's voice grew thick and hoarse, her hands clenched and unclenched. Finally she lifted one to her face.

"He's the man that did this to me. Many years ago now. She took him away from me—a chit of a girl she was then. And when I went after him—and went for him too—he threw the cursed stuff at me! And she laughed—damn her! I've had it in for her for years. Followed her, I have, spied upon her. And now I've got her! She'll suffer for this, won't she, Mr. Lawyer? She'll suffer?"

"She will probably be sentenced to a term of imprisonment for perjury," said Mr. Mayherne quietly.

"Shut away—that's what I want. You're going, are you? Where's my money? Where's that good money?"

Without a word, Mr. Mayherne put down the notes on the table. Then, drawing a deep breath, he turned and left the squalid room. Looking back, he saw the old woman crooning over the money.

He wasted no time. He found the cinema in Lion Road easily enough, and, shown a photograph of Romaine Heilger, the commissionaire recognized her at once. She had arrived at the cinema with a man some time after ten o'clock on the evening in question. He had not noticed her escort particularly, but he remembered the lady who had spoken to him about the picture that was showing. They stayed until the end, about an hour later.

Mr. Mayherne was satisfied. Romaine Heilger's evidence was a tissue of lies from beginning to end. She had evolved it out of her passionate hatred. The lawyer wondered whether he would ever know what lay behind that hatred. What had Leonard Vole done to her? He had seemed dumbfounded when the solicitor had reported her attitude to him. He had declared earnestly that such a thing was incredible—yet it had seemed to Mr. Mayherne that after the first astonishment his protests had lacked sincerity.

He did know. Mr. Mayherne was convinced of it. He knew, but he had no intention of revealing the fact. The secret between those two remained a secret. Mr. Mayherne wondered if some day he should come to learn what it was.

The solicitor glanced at his watch. It was late, but time was everything. He hailed a taxi and gave an address.

"Sir Charles must know of this at once," he murmured to himself as he got in.

The trial of Leonard Vole for the murder of Emily French aroused widespread interest. In the first place the prisoner was young and good-looking, then he was accused of a particularly dastardly crime, and there was the further interest of Romaine Heilger, the principal witness for the prosecution. There had been pictures of her in many papers, and several fictitious stories as to her origin and history.

The proceedings opened quietly enough. Various technical evidence came first. Then Janet Mackenzie was called. She told substantially the same story as before. In cross-examination counsel for the defense succeeded in getting her to contradict herself once or twice over her account of Vole's association with Miss French; he emphasized the fact that though she had heard a man's voice in the sitting-room that night, there was nothing to show that it was Vole who was there, and he managed to drive home a feeling that jealousy and dislike of the prisoner were at the bottom of a good deal of her evidence.

Then the next witness was called.

"Your name is Romaine Heilger?"

"Yes."

"You are an Austrian subject?"

"Yes."

"For the last three years you have lived with the prisoner and passed yourself off as his wife?"

Just for a moment Romaine Heilger's eyes met those of the man in the dock. Her expression held something curious and unfathomable.

"Yes."

The questions went on. Word by word the damning facts came out. On the night in question the prisoner had taken out a crowbar with him. He had returned at twenty minutes past ten, and had confessed to having killed the old lady. His cuffs had been stained with blood, and he had burned them in the kitchen stove. He had terrorized her into silence by means of threats.

As the story proceeded, the feeling of the court which had, to begin with, been slightly favorable to the prisoner, now set dead against him. He himself sat with downcast head and moody air, as though he knew he were doomed.

Yet it might have been noted that her own counsel sought to restrain Romaine's animosity. He would have preferred her to be more unbiased.

Formidable and ponderous, counsel for the defense arose.

He put it to her that her story was a malicious fabrication from start to finish, that she had not even been in her own house at the time in question, that she was in love with another man and was deliberately seeking to send Vole to his death for a crime he did not commit.

Romaine denied these allegations with superb insolence.

Then came the surprising denouement, the production of the letter. It was read aloud in court in the midst of a breathless stillness.

Max, beloved, the Fates have delivered him into our hands! He has been arrested for murder—but, yes, the murder of an old lady! Leonard, who would not hurt a fly! At last I shall have my revenge. The poor chicken! I shall say that he came in that night with blood upon him—that he confessed to me. I shall hang him, Max—and when he hangs he will know and realize that it was Romaine who sent him to his death. And then—happiness, Beloved! Happiness at last!

There were experts present ready to swear that the handwriting was that of Romaine Heilger, but they were not needed. Confronted with the letter, Romaine broke down utterly and confessed everything. Leonard Vole had returned to the house at the time he said, twenty past nine. She had invented the whole story to ruin him.

With the collapse of Romaine Heilger, the case for the Crown collapsed also. Sir Charles called his few witnesses, the prisoner himself went into the box and told his story in a manly straightforward manner, unshaken by cross-examination.

The prosecution endeavored to rally, but without great success. The judge's summing up was not wholly favorable to the prisoner, but a reaction had set in and the jury needed little time to consider their verdict.

"We find the prisoner not guilty."

Leonard Vole was free!

Little Mr. Mayherne hurried from his seat. He must congratulate his client.

He found himself polishing his pince-nez vigorously, and checked himself. His wife had told him only the night before that he was getting a habit of it. Curious things, habits. People themselves never knew they had them.

An interesting case—a very interesting case. That woman, now, Romaine Heilger.

The case was dominated for him still by the exotic figure of Romaine Heilger. She had seemed a pale, quiet woman in the house at Paddington, but in court she had flamed out against the sober background, flaunting herself like a tropical flower.

If he closed his eyes he could see her now, tall and vehement, her exquisite body bent forward a little, her right hand clenching and unclenching itself uncon-sciously all the time.

Curious things, habits. That gesture of hers with the hand was her habit, he supposed. Yet he had seen someone else do it quite lately. Who was it now? Quite lately——

He drew in his breath with a gasp as it came back to him. The woman in Shaw's Rents. . . .

He stood still, his head whirling. It was impossi-ble—impossible——Yet, Romaine Heilger was an actress.

The K. C. came up behind him and clapped him on the shoulder.

"Congratulated our man yet? He's had a narrow shave, you know. Come along and see him."

But the little lawyer shook off the other's hand.

He wanted one thing only—to see Romaine Heil-ger face to face.

He did not see her until some time later, and the place of their meeting is not relevant.

"So you guessed," she said, when he had told her all that was in his mind. "The face? Oh! that was easy enough, and the light of that gas jet was too bad for you to see the makeup."

"But why—why——"

"Why did I play a lone hand?" She smiled a little, remembering the last time she had used the words.

"Such an elaborate comedy!"

"My friend—I had to save him. The evidence of a woman devoted to him would not have been enough—you hinted as much yourself. But I know something of the psychology of crowds. Let my evidence be wrung from me, as an admission, damning me in the eyes of the law, and a reaction in favor of the prisoner would immediately set in."

"And the bundle of letters?"

"One alone, the vital one, might have seemed like a—what do you call it?—put-up job."

"Then the man called Max?"

"Never existed, my friend."

"I still think," said little Mr. Mayherne, in an aggrieved manner, "that we could have got him off by the—er—normal procedure."

"I dared not risk it. You see you thought he was innocent——"

"And you knew it? I see," said little Mr. Mayherne.

"My dear Mr. Mayherne," said Romaine, "you do not see at all. I knew—he was guilty!"

THE RED SIGNAL

"No, but how too thrilling," said pretty Mrs. Eversleigh, opening her lovely, but slightly vacant, blue eyes very wide. "They always say women have a sixth sense; do you think it's true, Sir Alington?"

The famous alienist smiled sardonically. He had an unbounded contempt for the foolish pretty type, such as his fellow guest. Alington West was the supreme authority on mental disease, and he was fully alive to his own position and importance. A slightly pompous man of full figure.

"A great deal of nonsense is talked, I know that, Mrs. Eversleigh. What does the term mean—a sixth sense?"

"You scientific men are always so severe. And it really is extraordinary the way one seems to positively know things sometimes—just know them, feel them, I mean—quite uncanny—it really is. Claire knows what I mean, don't you, Claire?"

She appealed to her hostess with a slight pout, and a tilted shoulder.

Claire Trent did not reply at once. It was a small dinner party—she and her husband, Violet Eversleigh, Sir Alington West, and his nephew Dermot

West, who was an old friend of Jack Trent's. Jack Trent himself, a somewhat heavy florid man, with a good-humored smile, and a pleasant lazy laugh, took up the thread.

"Bunkum, Violet! Your best friend is killed in a railway accident. Straight away you remember that you dreamed of a black cat last Tuesday—marvelous, you felt all along that something was going to happen!"

"Oh, no, Jack, you're mixing up premonitions with intuition now. Come, now, Sir Alington, you must admit that premonitions are real?"

"To a certain extent, perhaps," admitted the physician cautiously. "But coincidence accounts for a good deal, and then there is the invariable tendency to make the most of a story afterwards."

"I don't think there is any such thing as premonition," said Claire Trent, rather abruptly. "Or intuition, or a sixth sense, or any of the things we talk about so glibly. We go through life like a train rushing through the darkness to an unknown destination."

"That's hardly a good simile, Mrs. Trent," said Dermot West, lifting his head for the first time and taking part in the discussion. There was a curious glitter in the clear gray eyes that shone out rather oddly from the deeply tanned face. "You've forgotten the signals, you see."

"The signals?"

"Yes, green if it's all right, and red—for danger!"

"Red—for danger—how thrilling!" breathed Violet Eversleigh.

Dermot turned from her rather impatiently.

"That's just a way of describing it, of course."

Trent stared at him curiously.

"You speak as though it were an actual experience, Dermot, old boy."

"So it is—has been, I mean."

"Give us the yarn."

"I can give you one instance. Out in Mesopotamia, just after the Armistice, I came into my tent one evening with the feeling strong upon me. Danger! Look out! Hadn't the ghost of a notion what it was all about. I made a round of the camp, fussed unnecessarily, took all precautions against an attack by hostile Arabs. Then I went back to my tent. As soon as I got inside, the feeling popped up again stronger than ever. Danger! In the end I took a blanket outside, rolled myself up in it and slept there."

"Well?"

"The next morning, when I went inside the tent, first thing I saw was a great knife arrangement— about half a yard long—struck down through my bunk, just where I would have lain. I soon found out about it—one of the Arab servants. His son had been shot as a spy. What have you got to say to that, Uncle Alington, as an example of what I call the red signal?"

The specialist smiled noncommittally.

"A very interesting story, my dear Dermot."

"But not one that you accept unreservedly?"

"Yes, yes, I have no doubt but that you had the premonition of danger, just as you state. But it is the origin of the premonition I dispute. According to you, it came from without, impressed by some outside source upon your mentality. But nowadays we find that nearly everything comes from within—from our subconscious self.

"I suggest that by some glance or look this Arab had betrayed himself. Your conscious self did not notice or remember, but with your subconscious self it was otherwise. The subconscious never forgets. We believe, too, that it can reason and deduce quite independently of the higher or conscious will. Your subconscious self, then, believed that an attempt might be made to assassinate you, and succeeded in forcing its fear upon your conscious realization."

"That sounds very convincing, I admit," said Dermot, smiling.

"But not nearly so exciting," pouted Mrs. Eversleigh.

"It is also possible that you may have been subconsciously aware of the hate felt by the man towards you. What in old days used to be called telepathy certainly exists, though the conditions governing it are very little understood."

"Have there been any other instances?" asked Claire of Dermot.

"Oh! yes, but nothing very pictorial—and I suppose they could all be explained under the heading of coincidence. I refused an invitation to a country house once, for no other reason than the 'red signal.' The place was burned out during the week. By the way, Uncle Alington, where does the subconscious come in there?"

"I'm afraid it doesn't," said Sir Alington, smiling.

"But you've got an equally good explanation. Come, now. No need to be tactful with near relatives."

"Well, then, nephew, I venture to suggest that you refused the invitation for the ordinary reason that you didn't much want to go, and that after the fire, you suggested to yourself that you had had a warning of danger, which explanation you now believe implicitly."

"It's hopeless," laughed Dermot. "It's heads you win, tails I lose."

"Never mind, Mr. West," cried Violet Eversleigh. "I believe in your Red Signal. Is the time in Mesopotamia the last time you had it?"

"Yes—until——"

"I beg your pardon?"

"Nothing."

Dermot sat silent. The words which had nearly left his lips were: "Yes, until tonight." They had come quite unbidden to his lips, voicing a thought which had as yet not been consciously realized, but he was aware at once that they were true. The Red Signal was looming up out of the darkness. Danger! Danger close at hand!

But why? What conceivable danger could there be here? Here in the house of his friends? At least—well, yes, there was that kind of danger. He looked at Claire Trent—her whiteness, her slenderness, the exquisite droop of her golden head. But that danger had been there for some time—it was never likely to get acute. For Jack Trent was his best friend, and more than his best friend, the man who had saved his life in Flanders and been recommended for the V.C. for doing so. A good fellow, Jack, one of the best. Damned bad luck that he should have fallen in love with Jack's wife. He'd get over it some day, he supposed. A thing couldn't go on hurting like this forever. One could starve it out—that was it, starve it out. It was not as though she would ever guess—and if she did guess, there was no danger of her caring. A statue, a beautiful statue, a thing of gold and ivory and pale pink coral . . . a toy for a king, not a real woman. . . .

Claire . . . the very thought of her name, uttered silently, hurt him. . . . He must get over it. He'd cared for women before. . . . "But not like this!" said something. "Not like this." Well, there it was. No danger there—heartache, yes, but not danger. Not the danger of the Red Signal. That was for something else.

He looked round the table and it struck him for the first time that it was rather an unusual little gathering. His uncle, for instance, seldom dined out in this small, informal way. It was not as though the Trents were old friends; until this evening Dermot had not been aware that he knew them at all.

To be sure, there was an excuse. A rather notorious medium was coming after dinner to give a séance. Sir Alington professed to be mildly interested in spiritualism. Yes, that was an excuse, certainly.

The word forced itself on his notice. An excuse. Was the séance just an excuse to make the specialist's presence at dinner natural? If so, what was the real object of his being here? A host of details came rushing into Dermot's mind, trifles unnoticed at the time, or, as his uncle would have said, unnoticed by the conscious mind.

The great physician had looked oddly, very oddly, at Claire more than once. He seemed to be watching her. She was uneasy under his scrutiny. She made little twitching motions with her hands. She was nervous, horribly nervous, and was it, could it be, frightened? Why was she frightened?

With a jerk he came back to the conversation round the table. Mrs. Eversleigh had got the great man talking upon his own subject.

"My dear lady," he was saying, "what *is* madness? I can assure you that the more we study the subject, the more difficult we find it to pronounce. We all practice a certain amount of self-deception, and when we carry it so far as to believe we are the Czar of Russia, we are shut up or restrained. But there is a long road before we reach that point. At what particular spot on it shall we erect a post and say, 'On this side sanity, on the other madness'? It can't be done, you know. And I will tell you this: if the man suffering from a delusion happened to hold his tongue about it, in all probability we should never be able to distinguish him from a normal individual. The extraordinary sanity of the insane is an interesting subject."

Sir Alington sipped his wine with appreciation and beamed upon the company.

"I've always heard they are very cunning," remarked Mrs. Eversleigh. "Loonies, I mean."

"Remarkably so. And suppression of one's particular delusion has a disastrous effect very often. All suppressions are dangerous, as psychoanalysis has taught us. The man who has a harmless eccentricity, and can indulge it as such, seldom goes over the border-line. But the man"—he paused—"or woman who is to all appearance perfectly normal, may be in reality a poignant source of danger to the community."

His gaze traveled gently down the table to Claire, and then back again.

A horrible fear shook Dermot. Was that what he meant? Was that what he was driving at? Impossible, but——

"And all from suppressing oneself," sighed Mrs. Eversleigh. "I quite see that one should be very careful always to—to express one's personality. The dangers of the other are frightful."

"My dear Mrs. Eversleigh," expostulated the physician, "you have quite misunderstood me. The cause of the mischief is in the physical matter of the brain—sometimes arising from some outward agency such as a blow; sometimes, alas, congenital."

"Heredity is so sad," sighed the lady vaguely. "Consumption and all that."

"Tuberculosis is not hereditary," said Sir Alington drily.

"Isn't it? I always thought it was. But madness is! How dreadful. What else?"

"Gout," said Sir Alington, smiling. "And color blindness—the latter is rather interesting. It is transmitted direct to males, but is latent in females. So, while there are many color blind men, for a woman to be color blind, it must have been latent in her mother as well as present in her father—rather an unusual state of things to occur. That is what is called sex limited heredity."

"How interesting. But madness is not like that, is it?"

"Madness can be handed down to men or women equally," said the physician gravely.

Claire rose suddenly, pushing back her chair so abruptly that it overturned and fell to the ground. She was very pale and the nervous motions of her fingers were very apparent.

"You—you will not be long, will you?" she begged. "Mrs. Thompson will be here in a few minutes now."

"One glass of port, and I will be with you," declared Sir Alington. "To see this wonderful Mrs. Thompson's performance is what I have come for, is it not? Ha, ha! Not that I needed any inducement." He bowed.

Claire gave a faint smile of acknowledgment and passed out of the room with Mrs. Eversleigh.

"Afraid I've been talking shop," remarked the physician as he resumed his seat. "Forgive me, my dear fellow."

"Not at all," said Trent perfunctorily.

He looked strained and worried. For the first time Dermot felt an outsider in the company of his friend. Between these two was a secret that even an old friend might not share. And yet the whole thing was fantastic and incredible. What had he to go upon? Nothing but a couple of glances and a woman's nervousness.

They lingered over their wine but a very short time, and arrived up in the drawing room just as Mrs. Thompson was announced.

The medium was a plump middle-aged woman, atrociously dressed in magenta velvet, with a loud, rather common voice.

"Hope I'm not late, Mrs. Trent," she said cheerily. "You did say nine o'clock, didn't you?"

"You are quite punctual, Mrs. Thompson," said

Claire in her sweet, slightly husky voice. "This is our little circle."

No further introductions were made, as was evidently the custom. The medium swept them all with a shrewd, penetrating eye.

"I hope we shall get some good results," she remarked briskly. "I can't tell you how I hate it when I go out and I can't give satisfaction, so to speak. It just makes me mad. But I think Shiromako (my Japanese control, you know) will be able to get through all right tonight. I'm feeling ever so fit, and I refused the welsh rarebit, fond of cheese though I am."

Dermot listened, half-amused, half-disgusted. How prosaic the whole thing was! And yet, was he not judging foolishly? Everything, after all, was natural— the powers claimed by mediums were natural powers, as yet imperfectly understood. A great surgeon might be wary of indigestion on the eve of a delicate operation. Why not Mrs. Thompson?

Chairs were arranged in a circle, lights so that they could conveniently be raised and lowered. Dermot noticed that there was no question of tests, or of Sir Alington satisfying himself as to the conditions of the séance. No, this business of Mrs. Thompson was only a blind. Sir Alington was here for quite another purpose. Claire's mother, Dermot remembered, had died abroad. There had been some mystery about her. . . . Hereditary. . . .

With a jerk he forced his mind back to the surroundings of the moment.

Everyone took their places, and the lights were turned out, all but a small red-shaded one on a far table.

For a while nothing was heard but the low, even breathing of the medium. Gradually it grew more and more stertorous. Then, with a suddenness that made Dermot jump, a loud rap came from the far end of the room. It was repeated from the other side. Then a perfect crescendo of raps was heard. They died away, and a sudden high peal of mocking laughter rang through the room.

Then silence, broken by a voice utterly unlike that of Mrs. Thompson, a high-pitched, quaintly inflected voice.

"I am here, gentlemen," it said. "Yess, I am here. You wish ask me things?"

"Who are you? Shiromako?"

"Yess. I Shiromako. I pass over long ago. I work. I very happy."

Further details of Shiromako's life followed. It was all very flat and uninteresting, and Dermot had heard it often before. Everyone was happy, very happy. Messages were given from vaguely described relatives, the description being so loosely worded as to fit almost any contingency. An elderly lady, the mother of someone present, held the floor for some time, imparting copybook maxims with an air of refreshing novelty hardly borne out by her subject matter.

"Someone else want to get through now," announced Shiromako. "Got a very important message for one of the gentlemen."

There was a pause, and then a new voice spoke, prefacing its remarks with an evil demoniacal chuckle.

"Ha, ha! Ha, ha, ha! Better not go home. Take my advice."

"Who are you speaking to?" asked Trent.

"One of you three. I shouldn't go home if I were him. Danger! Blood! Not very much blood—quite enough. No, don't go home." The voice grew fainter. *"Don't go home!"*

It died away completely. Dermot felt his blood tingling. He was convinced that the warning was meant for him. Somehow or other, there was danger abroad tonight.

There was a sigh from the medium, and then a groan. She was coming round. The lights were turned on, and presently she sat upright, her eyes blinking a little.

"Go off well, my dear? I hope so."

"Very good indeed, thank you, Mrs. Thompson."

"Shiromako, I suppose?"

"Yes, and others."

Mrs. Thompson yawned.

"I'm dead beat. Absolutely down and out. Does fairly take it out of you. Well, I'm glad it was a success. I was a bit afraid something disagreeable might happen. There's a queer feel about this room tonight."

She glanced over each ample shoulder in turn, and then shrugged them uncomfortably.

"I don't like it," she said. "Any sudden deaths among any of you people lately?"

"What do you mean—among us?"

"Near relatives—dear friends? No? Well, if I wanted to be melodramatic, I'd say that there was death in the air tonight. There, it's only my nonsense.

Good-bye, Mrs. Trent. I'm glad you've been satisfied."

Mrs. Thompson in her magenta velvet gown went out.

"I hope you've been interested, Sir Alington," murmured Claire.

"A most interesting evening, my dear lady. Many thanks for the opportunity. Let me wish you good night. You are all going on to a dance, are you not?"

"Won't you come with us?"

"No, no. I make it a rule to be in bed by half-past eleven. Good night. Good night, Mrs. Eversleigh. Ah, Dermot, I rather want to have a word with you. Can you come with me now? You can rejoin the others at the Grafton Galleries."

"Certainly, Uncle. I'll meet you there then, Trent."

Very few words were exchanged between uncle and nephew during the short drive to Harley Street. Sir Alington made a semi-apology for dragging Dermot away, and assured him that he would only detain him a few minutes.

"Shall I keep the car for you, my boy?" he asked, as they alighted.

"Oh, don't bother, Uncle. I'll pick up a taxi."

"Very good. I don't like to keep Charlson up later than I can help. Good night, Charlson. Now where the devil did I put my key?"

The car glided away as Sir Alington stood on the steps searching his pockets.

"Must have left it in my other coat," he said at length. "Ring the bell, will you? Johnson is still up, I dare say."

The imperturbable Johnson did indeed open the door within sixty seconds.

"Mislaid my key, Johnson," explained Sir Alington. "Bring a couple of whiskies and sodas into the library."

"Very good, Sir Alington."

The physician strode on into the library and turned on the lights. He motioned to Dermot to close the door.

"I won't keep you long, Dermot, but there's just something I want to say to you. Is it my fancy, or have you a certain—*tendresse*, shall we say, for Mrs. Jack Trent?"

The blood rushed to Dermot's face.

"Jack Trent is my best friend."

"Pardon me, but that is hardly answering my question. I dare say that you consider my views on divorce and such matters highly puritanical, but I must remind you that you are my only near relative and my heir."

"There is no question of a divorce," said Dermot angrily.

"There certainly is not, for a reason which I understand perhaps better than you do. That particular reason I cannot give you now, but I do wish to warn you. She is not for you."

The young man faced his uncle's gaze steadily.

"I do understand—and permit me to say, perhaps better than you think. I know the reason for your presence at dinner tonight."

"Eh?" The physician was clearly startled. "How did you know that?"

"Call it a guess, sir. I am right, am I not, when I

say that you were there in your—professional capacity."

Sir Alington strode up and down.

"You are quite right, Dermot. I could not, of course, have told you so myself, though I am afraid it will soon be common property."

Dermot's heart contracted.

"You mean that you have—made up your mind?"

"Yes, there is insanity in the family—on the mother's side. A sad case—a very sad case."

"I can't believe it, sir."

"I dare say not. To the layman there are few if any signs apparent."

"And to the expert?"

"The evidence is conclusive. In such a case the patient must be placed under restraint as soon as possible."

"My God!" breathed Dermot. "But you can't shut anyone up for nothing at all."

"My dear Dermot! Cases are only placed under restraint when their being at large would result in danger to the community."

"Danger?"

"Very grave danger. In all probability a peculiar form of homicidal mania. It was so in the mother's case."

Dermot turned away with a groan, burying his face in his hands. Claire—white and golden Claire!

"In the circumstances," continued the physician comfortably, "I felt it incumbent on me to warn you."

"Claire," murmured Dermot. "My poor Claire."

"Yes, indeed, we must all pity her."

Suddenly Dermot raised his head.

"I say I don't believe it. Doctors make mistakes. Everyone knows that. And they're always keen on their own specialty."

"My dear Dermot," cried Sir Alington angrily.

"I tell you I don't believe it—and anyway, even if it is so, I don't care. I love Claire. If she will come with me, I shall take her away—far away—out of the reach of meddling physicians. I shall guard her, care for her, shelter her with my love."

"You will do nothing of the sort. Are you mad?" Dermot laughed scornfully.

"*You* would say so."

"Understand me, Dermot." Sir Alington's face was red with suppressed passion. "If you do this thing— this shameful thing—I shall withdraw the allowance I am now making you, and I shall make a new will leaving all I possess to various hospitals."

"Do as you please with your damned money," said Dermot in a low voice. "I shall have the woman I love."

"A woman who——"

"Say a word against her and, by God, I'll kill you!" cried Dermot.

A slight chink of glasses made them both swing round. Unheard by them in the heat of their argument, Johnson had entered with a tray of glasses. His face was the imperturbable one of the good servant, but Dermot wondered just exactly how much he had overheard.

"That'll do, Johnson," said Sir Alington curtly. "You can go to bed."

"Thank you, sir. Good night, sir."

Johnson withdrew.

The two men looked at each other. The momentary interruption had calmed the storm.

"Uncle," said Dermot. "I shouldn't have spoken to you as I did. I can quite see that from your point of view you are perfectly right. But I have loved Claire Trent for a long time. The fact that Jack Trent is my best friend has hitherto stood in the way of my ever speaking of love to Claire herself. But in these circumstances that fact no longer counts. The idea that any monetary conditions can deter me is absurd. I think we've both said all there is to be said. Good night."

"Dermot——"

"It is really no good arguing further. Good night, Uncle Alington."

He went out quickly, shutting the door behind him. The hall was in darkness. He passed through it, opened the front door and emerged into the street, banging the door behind him.

A taxi had just deposited a fare at a house farther along the street and Dermot hailed it, and drove to the Grafton Galleries.

In the door of the ballroom he stood for a minute, bewildered, his head spinning. The raucous jazz music, the smiling women—it was as though he had stepped into another world.

Had he dreamed it all? Impossible that that grim conversation with his uncle should have really taken place. There was Claire floating past, like a lily in her white and silver gown that fitted sheathlike to her slenderness. She smiled at him, her face calm and serene. Surely it was all a dream.

The dance had stopped. Presently she was near

him, smiling up into his face. As in a dream he asked
her to dance. She was in his arms now, the raucous
melodies had begun again.

He felt her flag a little.

"Tired? Do you want to stop?"

"If you don't mind. Can we go somewhere where
we can talk? There is something I want to say to you."

Not a dream. He came back to earth with a bump.
Could he ever have thought her face calm and serene?
It was haunted with anxiety, with dread. How much
did she know?

He found a quiet corner, and they sat down side
by side.

"Well," he said, assuming a lightness he did not
feel, "you said you had something you wanted to say
to me?"

"Yes." Her eyes were cast down. She was playing nervously with the tassel of her gown. "It's difficult——"

"Tell me, Claire."

"It's just this. I want you to—to go away for a
time."

He was astonished. Whatever he had expected, it
was not this.

"You want me to go away? Why?"

"It's best to be honest, isn't it? I know that you
are a—a gentleman and my friend. I want you to go
away because I—I have let myself get fond of you."

"Claire."

Her words left him dumb—tongue-tied.

"Please do not think that I am conceited enough to
fancy that you—would ever be likely to fall in love

with me. It is only that—I am not very happy—and—oh! I would rather you went away."

"Claire, don't you know that I have cared—cared damnably—ever since I met you?"

She lifted startled eyes to his face.

"You cared? You have cared a long time?"

"Since the beginning."

"Oh!" she cried. "Why didn't you tell me? Then? When I could have come to you! Why tell me now when it's too late. No, I'm mad—I don't know what I'm saying. I could never have come to you."

"Claire, what did you mean when you said 'now that it's too late'? Is it—is it because of my uncle? What he knows?"

She nodded, the tears running down her face.

"Listen, Claire, you're not to believe all that. You're not to think about it. Instead, you will come away with me. I will look after you—keep you safe always."

His arms went round her. He drew her to him, felt her tremble at his touch. Then suddenly she wrenched herself free.

"Oh, no, please. Can't you see? I couldn't now. It would be ugly—ugly—ugly. All along I've wanted to be good—and now—it would be ugly as well."

He hesitated, baffled by her words. She looked at him appealingly.

"Please," she said. "I want to be good. . . ."

Without a word, Dermot got up and left her. For the moment he was touched and racked by her words beyond argument. He went for his hat and coat, running into Trent as he did so.

"Hallo, Dermot, you're off early."

"Yes, I'm not in the mood for dancing tonight."

"It's a rotten night," said Trent gloomily. "But you haven't got my worries."

Dermot had a sudden panic that Trent might be going to confide in him. Not that—anything but that!

"Well, so long," he said hurriedly. "I'm off home."

"Home, eh? What about the warning of the spirits?"

"I'll risk that. Good night, Jack."

Dermot's flat was not far away. He walked there, feeling the need of the cool night air to calm his fevered brain. He let himself in with his key and switched on the light in the bedroom.

And all at once, for the second time that night, the feeling of the Red Signal surged over him. So overpowering was it that for the moment it swept even Claire from his mind.

Danger! He was in danger. At this very moment, in this very room!

He tried in vain to ridicule himself free of the fear. Perhaps his efforts were secretly halfhearted. So far, the Red Signal had given him timely warning which had enabled him to avoid disaster. Smiling a little at his own superstition, he made a careful tour of the flat. It was possible that some malefactor had got in and was lying concealed there. But his search revealed nothing. His man, Milson, was away, and the flat was absolutely empty.

He returned to his bedroom and undressed slowly, frowning to himself. The sense of danger was acute as ever. He went to a drawer to get out a handkerchief, and suddenly stood stock still. There was an unfamiliar lump in the middle of the drawer.

His quick nervous fingers tore aside the handkerchiefs and took out the object concealed beneath them.

It was a revolver.

With the utmost astonishment Dermot examined it keenly. It was of a somewhat unfamiliar pattern, and one shot had been fired from it lately. Beyond that he could make nothing of it. Someone had placed it in that drawer that very evening. It had not been there when he dressed for dinner—he was sure of that.

He was about to replace it in the drawer, when he was startled by a bell ringing. It rang again and again, sounding unusually loud in the quietness of the empty flat.

Who could be coming to the front door at this hour? And only one answer came to the question— an answer instinctive and persistent.

Danger—danger—danger.

Led by some instinct for which he did not account, Dermot switched off his light, slipped on an overcoat that lay across a chair, and opened the hall door.

Two men stood outside. Beyond them Dermot caught sight of a blue uniform. A policeman!

"Mr. West?" asked one of the two men.

It seemed to Dermot that ages elapsed before he answered. In reality it was only a few seconds before he replied in a very fair imitation of his servant's expressionless voice:

"Mr. West hasn't come in yet."

"Hasn't come in yet, eh? Very well, then, I think we'd better come in and wait for him."

"No, you don't."

"See here, my man, I'm inspector Verall of Scotland Yard, and I've got a warrant for the arrest of your master. You can see it if you like."

Dermot perused the proffered paper, or pretended to do so, asking in a dazed voice:

"What for? What's he done?"

"Murder. Sir Alington West of Harley Street."

His brain in a whirl, Dermot fell back before his redoubtable visitors. He went into the sitting-room and switched on the light. The inspector followed him.

"Have a search round," he directed the other man. Then he turned to Dermot.

"You stay here, my man. No slipping off to warn your master. What's your name, by the way?"

"Milson, sir."

"What time do you expect your master in, Milson?"

"I don't know, sir, he was going to a dance, I believe. At the Grafton Galleries."

"He left there just under an hour ago. Sure he's not been back here?"

"I don't think so, sir. I fancy I should have heard him come in."

At this moment the second man came in from the adjoining room. In his hand he carried the revolver. He took it across to the inspector in some excitement. An expression of satisfaction flitted across the latter's face.

"That settles it," he remarked. "Must have slipped in and out without your hearing him. He's hooked it by now. I'd better be off. Cawley, you stay here, in case he should come back again, and you can keep an eye on this fellow. He may know more about his master than he pretends."

The inspector bustled off. Dermot endeavored to get the details of the affair from Cawley, who was quite ready to be talkative.

"Pretty clear case," he vouchsafed. "The murder was discovered almost immediately. Johnson, the manservant, had only just gone up to bed when he fancied he heard a shot, and came down again. Found Sir Alington dead, shot through the heart. He rang us up at once and we came along and heard his story."

"Which made it a pretty clear case?" ventured Dermot.

"Absolutely. This young West came in with his uncle and they were quarrelling when Johnson brought in the drinks. The old boy was threatening to make a new will, and your master was talking about shooting him. Not five minutes later the shot was heard. Oh, yes, clear enough."

Clear enough indeed. Dermot's heart sank as he realized the overwhelming evidence against him. And no way out save flight. He set his wits to work. Presently he suggested making a cup of tea. Cawley assented readily enough. He had already searched the flat and knew there was no back entrance.

Dermot was permitted to depart to the kitchen. Once there he put the kettle on, and chinked cups and saucers industriously. Then he stole swiftly to the window and lifted the sash. The flat was on the second floor, and outside the window was the small wire lift used by tradesmen which ran up and down on its steel cable.

Like a flash Dermot was outside the window and

swinging himself down the wire rope. It cut into his hands, making them bleed, but he went on desperately.

A few minutes later he was emerging cautiously from the back of the block. Turning the corner, he cannoned into a figure standing by the sidewalk. To his utter amazement he recognized Jack Trent. Trent was fully alive to the perils of the situation.

"My God! Dermot! Quick, don't hang about here."

Taking him by the arm, he led him down a by street, then down another. A lonely taxi was sighted and hailed and they jumped in, Trent giving the man his own address.

"Safest place for the moment. There we can decide what to do next to put those fools off the track. I came round here, hoping to be able to warn you before the police got here."

"I didn't even know that you had heard of it. Jack, you don't believe——"

"Of course not, old fellow, not for one minute. I know you far too well. All the same, it's a nasty business for you. They came round asking questions—what time you got to the Grafton Galleries, when you left, and so on. Dermot, who could have done the old boy in?"

"I can't imagine. Whoever did it put the revolver in my drawer, I suppose. Must have been watching us pretty closely."

"That séance business was damned funny. 'Don't go home.' Meant for poor old West. He did go home, and got shot."

"It applies to me, too," said Dermot. "I went home and found a planted revolver and a police inspector."

"Well, I hope it doesn't get me, too," said Trent. "Here we are."

He paid the taxi, opened the door with his latchkey, and guided Dermot up the dark stairs to his den, a small room on the first floor.

He threw open the door and Dermot walked in, while Trent switched on the light, and came to join him.

"Pretty safe here for the time being," he remarked. "Now we can get our heads together and decide what is best to be done."

"I've made a fool of myself," said Dermot suddenly. "I ought to have faced it out. I see more clearly now. The whole thing's a plot. What the devil are you laughing at?"

For Trent was leaning back in his chair, shaking with unrestrained mirth. There was something horrible in the sound—something horrible, too, about the man altogether.

There was a curious light in his eyes.

"A damned clever plot," he gasped out. "Dermot, you're done for."

He drew the telephone towards him.

"What are you going to do?" asked Dermot.

"Ring up Scotland Yard. Tell 'em their bird's here—safe under lock and key. Yes, I locked the door when I came in and the key's in my pocket. No good looking at that other door behind me. That leads into Claire's room, and she always locks it on her side. She's afraid of me, you know. Been afraid of me a long time. She always knows when I'm thinking about that knife—a long sharp knife. No, you don't——"

Dermot had been about to make a rush at him, but the other had suddenly produced a revolver.

"That's the second of them," chuckled Trent. "I put the first in your drawer—after shooting old West with it——What are you looking at over my head? That door? It's no use, even if Claire were to open it—and she might to you—I'd shoot you before you got there. Not in the heart—not to kill, just wing you, so that you couldn't get away. I'm a jolly good shot, you know. I saved your life once. More fool I. No, no, I want you hanged—yes, hanged. It isn't you I want the knife for. It's Claire—pretty Claire, so white and soft. Old West knew. That's what he was here for tonight, to see if I were mad or not. He wanted to shut me up—so that I shouldn't get at Claire with a knife. I was very cunning. I took his latchkey and yours, too. I slipped away from the dance as soon as I got there. I saw you come out of his house, and I went in. I shot him and came away at once. Then I went to your place and left the revolver. I was at the Grafton Galleries again almost as soon as you were, and I put the latchkey back in your coat pocket when I was saying good night to you. I don't mind telling you all this. There's no one else to hear, and when you're being hanged I'd like you to know I did it. . . . There's not a loophole of escape. It makes me laugh . . . God, how it makes me laugh! What are you thinking of? What the devil are you looking at?"

"I'm thinking of some words you quoted just now. You'd have done better, Trent, not to come home."

"What do you mean?"

"Look behind you!"

Trent spun round. In the doorway of the communicating room stood Claire—and Inspector Verall. . . .

Trent was quick. The revolver spoke just once—and found its mark. He fell forward across the table. The inspector sprang to his side, as Dermot stared at Claire in a dream. Thoughts flashed through his brain disjointedly. His uncle—their quarrel—the colossal misunderstanding—the divorce laws of England which would never free Claire from an insane husband—"we must all pity her"—the plot between her and Sir Alington which the cunning of Trent had seen through—her cry to him, "Ugly—ugly—ugly!" Yes, but now——

The inspector straightened up.

"Dead," he said vexedly.

"Yes," Dermot heard himself saying, "he was always a good shot. . . ."

THE FOURTH MAN

Canon Parfitt panted a little. Running for trains was not much of a business for a man of his age. For one thing his figure was not what it was and with the loss of his slender silhouette went an increasing tendency to be short of breath. This tendency the Canon himself always referred to, with dignity, as "My heart, you know!"

He sank into the corner of the first-class carriage with a sigh of relief. The warmth of the heated carriage was most agreeable to him. Outside the snow was falling. Lucky to get a corner seat on a long night journey. Miserable business if you didn't. There ought to be a sleeper on this train.

The other three corners were already occupied, and noting this fact Canon Parfitt became aware that the man in the far corner was smiling at him in gentle recognition. He was a clean-shaven man with a quizzical face and hair just turning gray on the temples. His profession was so clearly the law that no one could have mistaken him for anything else for a moment. Sir George Durand was, indeed, a very famous lawyer.

"Well, Parfitt," he remarked genially, "you had a run for it, didn't you?"

"Very bad for my heart, I'm afraid," said the Canon. "Quite a coincidence meeting you, Sir George. Are you going far north?"

"Newcastle," said Sir George laconically. "By the way," he added, "do you know Dr. Campbell Clark?"

The man sitting on the same side of the carriage as the Canon inclined his head pleasantly.

"We met on the platform," continued the lawyer. "Another coincidence."

Canon Parfitt looked at Dr. Campbell Clark with a good deal of interest. It was a name of which he had often heard. Dr. Clark was in the forefront as a physician and mental specialist, and his last book, *The Problem of the Unconscious Mind*, had been the most discussed book of the year.

Canon Parfitt saw a square jaw, very steady blue eyes, and reddish hair untouched by gray, but thinning rapidly. And he received also the impression of a very forceful personality.

By a perfectly natural association of ideas the Canon looked across to the seat opposite him, half-expecting to receive a glance of recognition there also, but the fourth occupant of the carriage proved to be a total stranger—a foreigner, the Canon fancied. He was a slight dark man, rather insignificant in appearance. Hunched in a big overcoat, he appeared to be fast asleep.

"Canon Parfitt of Bradchester?" inquired Dr. Campbell Clark in a pleasant voice.

The Canon looked flattered. Those "scientific sermons" of his had really made a great hit—especially since the press had taken them up. Well, that was what the Church needed—good modern up-to-date stuff.

"I have read your book with great interest, Dr. Campbell Clark," he said. "Though it's a bit too technical here and there for me to follow."

Durand broke in.

"Are you for talking or sleeping, Canon?" he asked. "I'll confess at once that I suffer from insomnia and that therefore I'm in favor of the former."

"Oh, certainly! By all means," said the Canon. "I seldom sleep on these night journeys and the book I have with me is a very dull one."

"We are at any rate a representative gathering," remarked the doctor with a smile. "The Church, the law, the medical profession."

"Not much we couldn't give an opinion on between us, eh?" laughed Durand. "The Church for the spiritual view, myself for the purely worldly and legal view, and you, doctor, with the widest field of all, ranging from the purely pathological to the—super-psychological! Among the three of us we should cover any ground pretty completely, I fancy."

"Not so completely as you imagine, I think," said Dr. Clark. "There's another point of view, you know, that you left out, and that's rather an important one."

"Meaning?" queried the lawyer.

"The point of view of the man in the street."

"Is that so important? Isn't the man in the street usually wrong?"

"Oh, almost always! But he has the thing that all expert opinion must lack—the personal point of view. In the end, you know, you can't get away from personal relationships. I've found that in my profession. For every patient who comes to me genuinely ill, at least five come who have nothing whatever the matter with them except an inability to live happily with the inmates of the same house. They call it everything— from housemaid's knee to writer's cramp, but it's all the same thing, the raw surface produced by mind rubbing against mind."

"You have a lot of patients with 'nerves,' I suppose," the Canon remarked disparagingly. His own nerves were excellent.

"Ah, and what do you mean by that?" The other swung round on him, quick as a flash. "Nerves! People use that word and laugh after it, just as you did. 'Nothing the matter with so and so,' they say. 'Just nerves.' But, good God, man, you've got the crux of everything there! You can get at a mere bodily ailment and heal it. But at this day we know very little more about the obscure causes of the hundred and one forms of nervous disease than we did in—well, the reign of Queen Elizabeth!"

"Dear me," said Canon Parfitt, a little bewildered by this onslaught. "Is that so?"

"Mind you, it's a sign of grace," Dr. Campbell Clark went on. "In the old days we considered man a simple animal, body and soul—with stress laid on the former."

"Body, soul and spirit," corrected the clergyman mildly.

"Spirit?" The doctor smiled oddly. "What do you parsons mean exactly by spirit? You've never been very clear about it, you know. All down the ages you've funked an exact definition."

The Canon cleared his throat in preparation for speech, but to his chagrin he was given no opportunity. The doctor went on.

"Are we even sure the word is spirit—might it not be spirits?"

"Spirits?" Sir George Durand questioned, his eyebrows raised quizzically.

"Yes." Campbell Clark's gaze transferred itself to him. He leaned forward and tapped the other man lightly on the breast. "Are you so sure," he said gravely, "that there is only one occupant of this structure—for that is all it is, you know—this desirable residence to be let furnished—for seven, twenty-one, forty-one, seventy-one—whatever it may be!—years? And in the end the tenant moves his things out—little by little—and then goes out of the house altogether—and down comes the house, a mass of ruin and decay. You're the master of the house, we'll admit that, but aren't you ever conscious of the presence of others—soft-footed servants, hardly noticed, except for the work they do—work that you're not conscious of having done? Or friends—moods that take hold of you and make you, for the time being, a 'different man,' as the saying goes? You're the king of the castle, right enough, but be very sure the 'dirty rascal' is there too."

"My dear Clark," drawled the lawyer, "you make me positively uncomfortable. Is my mind really a battleground of conflicting personalities? Is that Science's latest?"

It was the doctor's turn to shrug his shoulders.

"Your body is," he said drily. "If the body, why not the mind?"

"Very interesting," said Canon Parfitt. "Ah! Wonderful science—wonderful science."

And inwardly he thought to himself: "I can get a most arresting sermon out of the idea."

But Dr. Campbell Clark had leaned back again in his seat, his momentary excitement spent.

"As a matter of fact," he remarked in a dry, professional manner, "it is a case of dual personality that takes me to Newcastle tonight. Very interesting case. Neurotic subject, of course. But quite genuine."

"Dual personality," said Sir George Durand thoughtfully. "It's not so very rare, I believe. There's loss of memory as well, isn't there? I know the matter cropped up in a case in the Probate Court the other day."

Dr. Clark nodded.

"The classic case, of course," he said, "was that of Felicie Bault. You may remember hearing of it?"

"Of course," said Canon Parfitt. "I remember reading about it in the papers—but quite a long time ago—seven years at least."

Dr. Campbell Clark nodded.

"That girl became one of the most famous figures in France. Scientists from all over the world came to see her. She had no less than four distinct personalities. They were known as Felicie 1, Felicie 2, Felicie 3, etc."

"Wasn't there some suggestion of deliberate trickery?" asked Sir George alertly.

"The personalities of Felicie 3 and Felicie 4 were a little open to doubt," admitted the doctor. "But the main facts remain. Felicie Bault was a Brittany peasant girl. She was the third of a family of five, the daughter of a drunken father and a mentally defective mother. In one of his drinking bouts the father strangled the mother and was, if I remember rightly, transported for life. Felicie was then five years of age. Some charitable people interested themselves in the children and Felicie was brought up and educated by an English maiden lady who had a kind of home for destitute children. She could make very little of Felicie, however. She describes the girl as abnormally slow and stupid, taught to read and write only with the greatest difficulty, and clumsy with her hands. This lady, Miss Slater, tried to fit the girl for domestic service, and did indeed find her several places when she was of an age to take them. But she never stayed long anywhere owing to her stupidity and also her intense laziness."

The doctor paused for a minute, and the Canon, recrossing his legs and arranging his traveling rug more closely round him, was suddenly aware that the man opposite him had moved very slightly. His eyes, which had formerly been shut, were now open, and something in them, something mocking and indefinable, startled the worthy Canon. It was as though the man were listening and gloating secretly over what he heard.

"There is a photograph taken of Felicie Bault at the age of seventeen," continued the doctor. "It shows her as a loutish peasant girl, heavy of build. There is nothing in that picture to indicate that she was soon to be one of the most famous persons in France.

"Five years later, when she was 22, Felicie Bault had a severe nervous illness, and on recovery the strange phenomena began to manifest themselves.

The following are facts attested to by many eminent scientists. The personality called Felicie 1 was indistinguishable from the Felicie Bault of the last twenty-two years. Felicie 1 wrote French badly and haltingly, spoke no foreign languages, and was unable to play the piano. Felicie 2, on the contrary, spoke Italian fluently and German moderately. Her handwriting was quite different from that of Felicie 1, and she wrote fluent and expressive French. She could discuss politics and art and she was passionately fond of playing the piano. Felicie 3 had many points in common with Felicie 2. She was intelligent and apparently well educated, but in moral character she was a total contrast. She appeared, in fact, an utterly depraved creature—but depraved in a Parisian and not a provincial way. She knew all the Paris *argot*, and the expressions of the chic *demi monde*. Her language was filthy and she would rail against religion and so-called 'good people' in the most blasphemous terms. Finally there was Felicie 4—a dreamy, almost half-witted creature, distinctly pious and professedly clairvoyant, but this fourth personality was very unsatisfactory and elusive, and has been sometimes thought to be a deliberate trickery on the part of Felicie 3—a kind of joke played by her on a credulous public. I may say that (with the possible exception of Felicie 4) each personality was distinct and separate and had no knowledge of the others. Felicie 2 was undoubtedly the most predominant and would last sometimes for a fortnight at a time, then Felicie 1 would appear abruptly for a day or two. After that, perhaps, Felicie 3 or 4, but the two latter seldom remained in command for more than a few hours. Each change was accompanied by severe headache and heavy sleep, and in each case there was complete loss of memory of the other states, the personality in question taking up life where she had left it, unconscious of the passage of time."

"Remarkable," murmured the Canon. "Very remarkable. As yet we know next to nothing of the marvels of the universe."

"We know that there are some very astute impostors in it," remarked the lawyer dryly.

"The case of Felicie Bault was investigated by lawyers as well as by doctors and scientists," said Dr. Campbell Clark quickly. "Maître Quimbellier, you remember, made the most thorough investigation and confirmed the views of the scientists. And after all, why should it surprise us so much? We come across the double-yolked egg, do we not? And the twin banana? Why not the double soul—or in this case the quadruple soul—in the single body?"

"The double soul?" protested the Canon.

Dr. Campbell Clark turned his piercing blue eyes on him.

"What else can we call it? That is to say—if the personality is the soul?"

"It is a good thing such a state of affairs is only in the nature of a 'freak,' " remarked Sir George. "If the case were common, it would give rise to pretty complications."

"The condition is, of course, quite abnormal," agreed the doctor. "It was a great pity that a longer study could not have been made, but all that was put an end to by Felicie's unexpected death."

"There was something queer about that, if I remember rightly," said the lawyer slowly.

Dr. Campbell Clark nodded.

"A most unaccountable business. The girl was found one morning dead in bed. She had clearly been strangled. But to everyone's stupefaction it was presently proved beyond doubt that she had actually strangled herself. The marks on her neck were those of her own fingers. A method of suicide which, though not physically impossible, must have necessitated terrific muscular strength and almost superhuman will power. What had driven the girl to such straits has never been found out. Of course her mental balance must always have been precarious. Still, there it is. The curtain has been rung down forever on the mystery of Felicie Bault."

It was then that the man in the far corner laughed.

The other three men jumped as though shot. They had totally forgotten the existence of the fourth among them. As they stared towards the place where he sat, still hunched in his overcoat, he laughed again.

"You must excuse me, gentlemen," he said, in perfect English that had, nevertheless, a foreign flavor.

He sat up, displaying a pale face with a small jet-black mustache.

"Yes, you must excuse me," he said, with a mock bow. "But really! in science, is the last word ever said?"

"You know something of the case we have been discussing?" asked the doctor courteously.

"Of the case? No. But I knew her."

"Felicie Bault?"

"Yes. And Annette Ravel also. You have not heard of Annette Ravel, I see? And yet the story of the one is the story of the other. Believe me, you know nothing of Felicie Bault if you do not also know the history of Annette Ravel."

He drew out a watch and looked at it.

"Just half an hour before the next stop. I have time to tell you the story—that is, if you care to hear it?"

"Please tell it to us," said the doctor quietly.

"Delighted," said the Canon. "Delighted."

Sir George Durand merely composed himself in an attitude of keen attention.

"My name, gentlemen," began their strange traveling companion, "is Raoul Letardeau. You have spoken just now of an English lady, Miss Slater, who interested herself in works of charity. I was born in that Brittany fishing village and when my parents were both killed in a railway accident it was Miss Slater who came to the rescue and saved me from the equivalent of your English workhouse. There were some twenty children under her care, girls and boys. Among these children were Felicie Bault and Annette Ravel. If I cannot make you understand the personality of Annette, gentlemen, you will understand nothing. She was the child of what you call a *fille de joie* who had died of consumption abandoned by her lover. The mother had been a dancer, and Annette, too, had the desire to dance. When I saw her first she was eleven years old, a little shrimp of a thing with eyes that alternately mocked and promised—a little creature all fire and life. And at once—yes, at once—she made me her slave. It was 'Raoul, do this for me.' 'Raoul, do that for me.' And me, I obeyed. Already I worshipped her, and she knew it.

"We would go down to the shore together, we

three—for Felicie would come with us. And there Annette would pull off her shoes and stockings and dance on the sand. And then when she sank down breathless, she would tell us of what she meant to do and be.

" 'See you, I shall be famous. Yes, exceedingly famous. I will have hundreds and thousands of silk stockings—the finest silk. And I shall live in an exquisite apartment. All my lovers shall be young and handsome as well as being rich. And when I dance all Paris shall come to see me. They will yell and call and shout and go mad over my dancing. And in the winters I shall not dance, I shall go south to the sunlight. There are villas there with orange trees. I shall have one of them. I shall lie in the sun on silk cushions, eating oranges. As for you, Raoul, I will never forget you, however great and rich and famous I shall be. I will protect you and advance your career. Felicie here shall be my maid—no, her hands are too clumsy. Look at them, how large and coarse they are.'

"Felicie would grow angry at that. And then Annette would go on teasing her.

" 'She is so ladylike, Felicie—so elegant, so refined. She is a princess in disguise—ha, ha.'

" 'My father and mother were married, which is more than yours were,' Felicie would growl out spitefully.

" 'Yes, and your father killed your mother. A pretty thing, to be a murderer's daughter.'

" 'Your father left your mother to rot,' Felicie would rejoin.

" 'Ah! yes.' Annette became thoughtful. '*Pauvre*

Maman. One must keep strong and well. It is everything to keep strong and well.'

" 'I am as strong as a horse,' Felicie boasted.

"And indeed she was. She had twice the strength of any other girl in the Home. And she was never ill.

"But she was stupid, you comprehend, stupid like a brute beast. I often wondered why she followed Annette round as she did. It was, with her, a kind of fascination. Sometimes, I think, she actually hated Annette, and indeed Annette was not kind to her. She jeered at her slowness and stupidity, and baited her in front of the others. I have seen Felicie grow quite white with rage. Sometimes I have thought that she would fasten her fingers round Annette's neck and choke the life out of her. She was not nimble-witted enough to reply to Annette's taunts, but she did learn in time to make one retort which never failed. That was the reference to her own health and strength. She had learned (what I had always known) that Annette envied her her strong physique, and she struck instinctively at the weak spot in her enemy's armor.

"One day Annette came to me in great glee.

" 'Raoul,' she said, 'we shall have fun today with that stupid Felicie.'

" 'What are you going to do?'

" 'Come behind the little shed and I will tell you.'

"It seemed that Annette had got hold of some book. Part of it she did not understand, and indeed the whole thing was much over her head. It was an early work on hypnotism.

" 'A bright object, they say. The brass knob of my bed, it twirls round. I made Felicie look at it last night. "Look at it steadily," I said. "Do not take your

eyes off it." And then I twirled it. Raoul, I was frightened. Her eyes looked so queer—so queer. "Felicie,
you will do what I say always," I said. "I will do
what you say always, Annette," she answered. And
then—and then—I said: "Tomorrow you will bring a
tallow candle out into the playground at twelve
o'clock and start to eat it. And if anyone asks you,
you will say that it is the best *galette* you ever tasted."
Oh! Raoul, think of it!'

" 'But she'll never do such a thing,' I objected.

" 'The book says so. Not that I can quite believe
it—but, oh! Raoul, if the book is all true, how we
shall amuse ourselves!'

"I, too, thought the idea very funny. We passed
word round to the comrades and at twelve o'clock we
were all in the playground. Punctual to the minute,
out came Felicie with a stump of candle in her hand.
Will you believe me, Messieurs, she began solemnly
to nibble at it. We were all in hysterics! Every now
and then one or another of the children would go up
to her and say solemnly: 'It is good, what you eat
there, eh, Felicie?' And she would answer. 'But, yes,
it is the best *galette* I ever tasted.' And then we would
shriek with laughter. We laughed at last so loud that
the noise seemed to wake up Felicie to a realization
of what she was doing. She blinked her eyes in a
puzzled way, looked at the candle, then at us. She
passed her hand over her forehead.

" 'But what is it that I do here?' she muttered.

" 'You are eating a candle,' we screamed.

" '*I* made you do it. *I* made you do it,' cried Annette, dancing about.

"Felicie stared for a moment. Then she went slowly up to Annette.

" 'So it is you—it is you who have made me ridiculous? I seem to remember. Ah! I will kill you for this.'

"She spoke in a very quiet tone, but Annette rushed suddenly away and hid behind me.

" 'Save me, Raoul! I am afraid of Felicie. It was only a joke, Felicie. Only a joke.'

" 'I do not like these jokes,' said Felicie. 'You understand? I hate you. I hate you all.'

"She suddenly burst out crying and rushed away.

"Annette was, I think, scared by the result of her experiment, and did not try to repeat it. But from that day on her ascendancy over Felicie seemed to grow stronger.

"Felicie, I now believe, always hated her, but nevertheless she could not keep away from her. She used to follow Annette around like a dog.

"Soon after that, Messieurs, employment was found for me, and I only came to the Home for occasional holidays. Annette's desire to become a dancer was not taken seriously, but she developed a very pretty singing voice as she grew older and Miss Slater consented to her being trained as a singer.

"She was not lazy, Annette. She worked feverishly, without rest. Miss Slater was obliged to prevent her doing too much. She spoke to me once about her.

" 'You have always been fond of Annette,' she said. 'Persuade her not to work too hard. She has a little cough lately that I do not like.'

"My work took me far afield soon afterwards. I received one or two letters from Annette at first, but then came silence. For five years after that I was abroad.

"Quite by chance, when I returned to Paris, my attention was caught by a poster advertising Annette Ravelli with a picture of the lady. I recognized her at once. That night I went to the theatre in question. Annette sang in French and Italian. On the stage she was wonderful. Afterwards I went to her dressing room. She received me at once.

" 'Why, Raoul,' she cried, stretching out her whitened hands to me. "This is splendid! Where have you been all these years?'

"I would have told her, but she did not really want to listen.

" 'You see, I have very nearly arrived!'

"She waved a triumphant hand round the room filled with bouquets.

" 'The good Miss Slater must be proud of your success.'

" 'That old one? No, indeed. She designed me, you know, for the Conservatoire. Decorous concert singing. But me, I am an artist. It is here, on the variety stage, that I can express myself.'

"Just then a handsome middle-aged man came in. He was very distinguished. By his manner I soon saw that he was Annette's protector. He looked sideways at me, and Annette explained.

" 'A friend of my infancy. He passes through Paris, sees my picture on a poster, *et voilà!'*

"The man was then very affable and courteous. In my presence he produced a ruby and diamond bracelet and clasped it on Annette's wrist. As I rose to go, she threw me a glance of triumph and a whisper.

" 'I arrive, do I not? You see? All the world is before me.'

"But as I left the room, I heard her cough, a sharp dry cough. I knew what it meant, that cough. It was the legacy of her consumptive mother.

"I saw her next two years later. She had gone for refuge to Miss Slater. Her career had broken down. She was in a state of advanced consumption for which the doctors said nothing could be done.

"Ah! I shall never forget her as I saw her then! She was lying in a kind of shelter in the garden. She was kept outdoors night and day. Her cheeks were hollow and flushed, her eyes bright and feverish.

"She greeted me with a kind of desperation that startled me.

" 'It is good to see you, Raoul. You know what they say—that I may not get well? They say it behind my back, you understand. To me they are soothing and consolatory. But it is not true, Raoul, it is not true! I shall not permit myself to die. Die? With beautiful life stretching in front of me? It is the will to live that matters. All the great doctors say that nowadays. I am not one of the feeble ones who let go. Already I feel myself infinitely better—infinitely better, do you hear?'

"She raised herself on her elbow to drive her words home, then fell back, attacked by a fit of coughing that racked her thin body.

" 'The cough—it is nothing,' she gasped. 'And hemorrhages do not frighten me. I shall surprise the doctors. It is the will that counts. Remember, Raoul, I am going to live.'

"It was pitiful, you understand, pitiful.

"Just then, Felicie Bault came out with a tray. A glass of hot milk. She gave it to Annette and watched her drink it with an expression that I could not fathom. There was a kind of smug satisfaction in it.

"Annette, too, caught the look. She flung the glass down angrily, so that it smashed to bits.

" 'You see her? That is how she always looks at me. She is glad I am going to die! Yes, she gloats over it. She who is well and strong. Look at her— never a day's illness, that one! And all for nothing. What good is that great carcass of hers to her? What can she make of it?'

"Felicie stooped and picked up the broken fragments of glass.

" 'I do not mind what she says,' she observed in a singsong voice. 'What does it matter? I am a respectable girl, I am. As for her. She will be knowing the fires of Purgatory before very long. I am a Christian. I say nothing.'

" 'You hate me!' cried Annette. 'You have always hated me. Ah! but I can charm you, all the same. I can make you do what I want. See now, if I asked you to, you would go down on your knees before me now on the grass.'

" 'You are absurd,' said Felicie uneasily.

" 'But, yes, you will do it. You will. To please me. Down on your knees. I ask it of you, I, Annette. Down on your knees, Felicie.'

"Whether it was the wonderful pleading in the voice, or some deeper motive, Felicie obeyed. She sank slowly on to her knees, her arms spread wide, her face vacant and stupid.

"Annette flung back her head and laughed—peal upon peal of laughter.

" 'Look at her, with her stupid face! How ridiculous she looks. You can get up now, Felicie, thank you! It is of no use to scowl at me. I am your mistress. You have to do what I say.'

"She lay back on her pillows exhausted. Felicie picked up the tray and moved slowly away. Once she looked back over her shoulder, and the smoldering resentment in her eyes startled me.

"I was not there when Annette died. But it was terrible, it seems. She clung to life. She fought against death like a madwoman. Again and again she gasped out: 'I will not die—do you hear me? I will not die. I will live—live——'

"Miss Slater told me all this when I came to see her six months later.

" 'My poor Raoul,' she said kindly. 'You loved her, did you not?' "

" 'Always—always. But of what use could I be to her? Let us not talk of it. She is dead—she so brilliant, so full of burning life. . . .'

"Miss Slater was a sympathetic woman. She went on to talk of other things. She was very worried about Felicie, so she told me. The girl had had a queer sort of nervous breakdown and ever since she had been very strange in manner.

" 'You know,' said Miss Slater, after a momentary hesitation, 'that she is learning the piano?'

"I did not know it and was very much surprised to hear it. Felicie—learning the piano! I would have declared the girl would not know one note from another.

" 'She has talent, they say,' continued Miss Slater.

'I can't understand it. I have always put her down as—well, Raoul, you know yourself, she was always a stupid girl.'

"I nodded.

" 'She is so strange in her manner I don't know what to make of it.'

"A few minutes later I entered the Salle de Lecture. Felicie was playing the piano. She was playing the air that I had heard Annette sing in Paris. You understand, Messieurs, it gave me quite a turn. And then, hearing me, she broke off suddenly and looked round at me, her eyes full of mockery and intelligence. For a moment I thought——Well, I will not tell you what I thought.

" *'Tiens!'* she said. 'So it is you—Monsieur Raoul.'

"I cannot describe the way she said it. To Annette I had never ceased to be Raoul. But Felicie, since we had met as grown-ups, always addressed me as Monsieur Raoul. But the way she said it now was different—as though the *Monsieur*, slightly stressed, was somehow amusing.

" 'Why, Felicie,' I stammered, 'you look quite different today.'

" 'Do I?' she said reflectively. 'It is odd, that. But do not be so solemn, Raoul—decidedly I shall call you Raoul—did we not play together as children?— Life was made for laughter. Let us talk of the poor Annette—she who is dead and buried. Is she in Purgatory, I wonder, or where?'

"And she hummed a snatch of song—untunefully enough, but the words caught my attention.

" 'Felicie!' I cried. 'You speak Italian?'

" 'Why not, Raoul? I am not as stupid as I pretend to be, perhaps.' She laughed at my mystification.

" 'I don't understand—' I began.

" 'But I will tell you. I am a very fine actress, though no one suspects it. I can play many parts— and play them very well.'

"She laughed again and ran quickly out of the room before I could stop her.

"I saw her again before I left. She was asleep in an armchair. She was snoring heavily. I stood and watched her, fascinated, yet repelled. Suddenly she woke with a start. Her eyes, dull and lifeless, met mine.

" 'Monsieur Raoul,' she muttered mechanically.

" 'Yes, Felicie. I am going now. Will you play for me again before I go?'

" 'I? Play? You are laughing at me, Monsieur Raoul.'

" 'Don't you remember playing for me this morning?'

"She shook her head.

" 'I play? How can a poor girl like me play?'

"She paused for a minute as though in thought, then beckoned me nearer.

" 'Monsieur Raoul, there are things going on in this house! They play tricks upon you. They alter the clocks. Yes, yes, I know what I am saying. And it is all her doing.'

" 'Whose doing?' I asked, startled.

" 'That Annette's. That wicked one's. When she was alive she always tormented me. Now that she is dead, she comes back from the dead to torment me.'

"I stared at Felicie. I could see now that she was

in an extremity of terror, her eyes starting from her head.

" 'She is bad, that one. She is bad, I tell you. She would take the bread from your mouth, the clothes from your back, the soul from your body. . . .'

"She clutched me suddenly.

" 'I am afraid, I tell you—afraid. I hear her voice—not in my ear—no, not in my ear. Here, in my head——' She tapped her forehead. 'She will drive me away—drive me away altogether, and then what shall I do, what will become of me?'

"Her voice rose almost to a shriek. She had in her eyes the look of the terrified beast at bay. . . .

"Suddenly she smiled, a pleasant smile, full of cunning, with something in it that made me shiver.

" 'If it should come to it, Monsieur Raoul, I am very strong with my hands—very strong with my hands.'

"I had never noticed her hands particularly before. I looked at them now and shuddered in spite of myself. Squat brutal fingers, and as Felicie had said, terribly strong. . . . I cannot explain to you the nausea that swept over me. With hands such as these her father must have strangled her mother. . . .

"That was the last time I ever saw Felicie Bault. Immediately afterwards I went abroad—to South America. I returned from there two years after her death. Something I had read in the newspapers of her life and sudden death. I have heard fuller details tonight—from you. Felicie 3 and Felicie 4—I wonder? She was a good actress, you know!"

The train suddenly slackened speed. The man in

the corner sat erect and buttoned his overcoat more closely.

"What is your theory?" asked the lawyer, leaning forward.

"I can hardly believe——" began Canon Parfitt, and stopped.

The doctor said nothing. He was gazing steadily at Raoul Letardeau.

"The clothes from your back, the soul from your body," quoted the Frenchman lightly. He stood up. "I say to you, Messieurs, that the history of Felicie Bault is the history of Annette Ravel. You did not know her, gentlemen. I did. She was very fond of life. . . ."

His hand on the door, ready to spring out, he turned suddenly and bending down tapped Canon Parfitt on the chest.

"M. le docteur over there, he said just now that all this"—his hand smote the Canon's stomach, and the Canon winced—"was only a residence. Tell me, if you find a burglar in your house what do you do? Shoot him, do you not?"

"No," cried the Canon. "No, indeed—I mean—not in this country."

But he spoke the last words to empty air. The carriage door banged.

The clergyman, the lawyer, and the doctor were alone. The fourth corner was vacant.

S.O.S.

"Ah!" said Mr. Dinsmead appreciatively. He stepped back and surveyed the round table with approval. The firelight gleamed on the coarse white tablecloth, the knives and forks, and the other table appointments.

"Is—is everything ready?" asked Mrs. Dinsmead hesitatingly. She was a little faded woman, with a colorless face, meager hair scraped back from her forehead, and a perpetually nervous manner.

"Everything's ready," said her husband with a kind of ferocious geniality.

He was a big man, with stooping shoulders and a broad red face. He had little pig's eyes that twinkled under his bushy brows, and a big jowl devoid of hair.

"Lemonade?" suggested Mrs. Dinsmead, almost in a whisper.

Her husband shook his head.

"Tea. Much better in every way. Look at the weather, streaming and blowing. A nice cup of hot tea is what's needed for supper on an evening like this."

He winked facetiously, then fell to surveying the table again.

"A good dish of eggs, cold corned beef, and bread

and cheese. That's my order for supper. So come along and get it ready, Mother. Charlotte's in the kitchen waiting to give you a hand."

Mrs. Dinsmead rose, carefully winding up the ball of her knitting.

"She's grown a very good-looking girl," she murmured.

"Ah!" said Mr. Dinsmead. "The mortal image of her ma! So go along with you, and don't let's waste any more time."

He strolled about the room humming to himself for a minute or two. Once he approached the window and looked out.

"Wild weather," he murmured to himself. "Not much likelihood of our having visitors tonight."

Then he too left the room.

About ten minutes later Mrs. Dinsmead entered bearing a dish of fried eggs. Her two daughters followed, bringing the rest of the provisions. Mr. Dinsmead and his son Johnnie brought up the rear. The former seated himself at the head of the table.

"And for what we are to receive, et cetera," he remarked humorously. "And blessings on the man who first thought of tinned foods. What would we do, I should like to know, miles from anywhere, if we hadn't a tin now and then to fall back upon when the butcher forgets his weekly call?"

He proceeded to carve corned beef dexterously.

"I wonder who ever thought of building a house like this, miles from anywhere," said his daughter Magdalen, pettishly. "We never see a soul."

"No," said her father. "Never a soul."

"I can't think what made you take it, Father," said Charlotte.

"Can't you, my girl? Well, I had my reasons—I had my reasons."

His eyes sought his wife's furtively, but she frowned.

"And haunted, too," said Charlotte. "I wouldn't sleep alone here for anything."

"Pack of nonsense," said her father. "Never seen anything, have you?"

"Not seen anything perhaps, but——"

"But what?"

Charlotte did not reply, but she shivered a little. A great surge of rain came driving against the window-pane, and Mrs. Dinsmead dropped a spoon with a tinkle on the tray.

"Not nervous, are you, Mother?" said Mr. Dinsmead. "It's a wild night, that's all. Don't you worry, we're safe here by our fireside, and not a soul from outside likely to disturb us. Why, it would be a miracle if anyone did. And miracles don't happen. No," he added as though to himself, with a kind of peculiar satisfaction, "miracles don't happen."

As the words left his lips there came a sudden knocking at the door. Mr. Dinsmead stayed as though petrified.

"What's that?" he muttered. His jaw fell.

Mrs. Dinsmead gave a little whimpering cry and pulled her shawl up round her. The color came into Magdalen's face and she leaned forward and spoke to her father.

"The miracle has happened," she said. "You'd better go and let whoever it is in."

*   *   *

Twenty minutes earlier Mortimer Cleveland had stood in the driving rain and mist surveying his car. It was really cursed bad luck. Two punctures within ten minutes of each other, and here he was, stranded, miles from anywhere, in the midst of these bare Wiltshire downs with night coming on and no prospect of shelter. Serve him right for trying to take a short cut. If only he had stuck to the main road! Now he was lost on what seemed a mere cart-track on the hillside, with no possibility of getting the car farther, and with no idea if there were even a village anywhere near.

He looked round him perplexedly, and his eye was caught by a gleam of light on the hillside above him. A second later the mist obscured it once more but, waiting patiently, he presently got a second glimpse of it. After a moment's cogitation, he left the car and struck up the side of the hill.

Soon he was out of the mist, and he recognized the light as shining from the lighted window of a small cottage. Here, at any rate, was shelter. Mortimer Cleveland quickened his pace, bending his head to meet the furious onslaught of wind and rain trying its best to drive him back.

Cleveland was, in his own way, something of a celebrity though doubtless the majority of folks would have displayed complete ignorance of his name and achievements. He was an authority on mental science and had written two excellent text books on the subconscious. He was also a member of the Psychical Research Society and a student of the occult in so far as it affected his own conclusions and line of research.

He was by nature peculiarly susceptible to atmosphere, and by deliberate training he had increased his own natural gift. When he had at last reached the cottage and rapped at the door, he was conscious of an excitement, a quickening of interest, as though all his faculties had suddenly been sharpened.

The murmur of voices within had been plainly audible to him. Upon his knock there came a sudden silence, then the sound of a chair being pushed back along the floor. In another minute the door was flung open by a boy of about fifteen. Cleveland could look straight over his shoulder upon the scene within.

It reminded him of an interior by some Dutch painter. A round table spread for a meal, a family party sitting round it, one or two flickering candles and the firelight's glow over all. The father, a big man, sat at one side of the table, a little gray woman with a frightened face sat opposite him. Facing the door, looking straight at Cleveland, was a girl. Her startled eyes looked straight into his, her hand with a cup in it was arrested halfway to her lips.

She was, Cleveland saw at once, a beautiful girl of an extremely uncommon type. Her hair, red gold, stood out round her face like a mist; her eyes, very far apart, were a pure gray. She had the mouth and chin of an early Italian Madonna.

There was a moment's dead silence. Then Cleveland stepped into the room and explained his predicament. He brought his trite story to a close, and there was another pause harder to understand. At last, as though with an effort, the father rose.

"Come in, sir—Mr. Cleveland, did you say?"

"That is my name," said Mortimer, smiling.

"Ah, yes. Come in, Mr. Cleveland. Not weather for a dog outside, is it? Come in by the fire. Shut the door, can't you, Johnnie? Don't stand there half the night."

Cleveland came forward and sat on a wooden stool by the fire. The boy Johnnie shut the door.

"Dinsmead, that's my name," said the other man. He was all geniality now. "This is the Missus, and these are my two daughters, Charlotte and Magdalen."

For the first time, Cleveland saw the face of the girl who had been sitting with her back to him, and saw that, in a totally different way, she was quite as beautiful as her sister. Very dark, with a face of marble pallor, a delicate aquiline nose, and a grave mouth. It was a kind of frozen beauty, austere and almost forbidding. She acknowledged her father's introduction by bending her head, and she looked at him with an intent gaze that was searching in character. It was as though she were summing him up, weighing him in the balance of her clear young judgement.

"A drop of something to drink, eh, Mr. Cleveland?"

"Thank you," said Mortimer. "A cup of tea will meet the case admirably."

Mr. Dinsmead hesitated a minute, then he picked up the five cups, one after another, from the table and emptied them into the slop bowl.

"This tea's cold," he said brusquely. "Make us some more, will you, Mother?"

Mrs. Dinsmead got up quickly and hurried off with the teapot. Mortimer had an idea that she was glad to get out of the room.

The fresh tea soon came, and the unexpected guest was plied with viands.

Mr. Dinsmead talked and talked. He was expansive, genial, loquacious. He told the stranger all about himself. He'd lately retired from the building trade—yes, made quite a good thing out of it. He and the Missus thought they'd like a bit of country air—never lived in the country before. Wrong time of year to choose, of course, October and November, but they didn't want to wait. "Life's uncertain, you know, sir." So they had taken this cottage. Eight miles from anywhere, and nineteen miles from anything you could call a town. No, they didn't complain. The girls found it a bit dull, but he and Mother enjoyed the quiet.

So he talked on, leaving Mortimer almost hypnotized by the easy flow. Nothing here, surely, but rather commonplace domesticity. And yet, at that first glimpse of the interior, he had diagnosed something else, some tension, some strain, emanating from one of those four people—he didn't know which. Mere foolishness, his nerves were all awry! They were startled by his sudden appearance—that was all.

He broached the question of a night's lodging, and was met with a ready response.

"You'll have to stop with us, Mr. Cleveland. Nothing else for miles around. We can give you a bedroom, and though my pajamas may be a bit roomy, why, they're better than nothing, and your own clothes will be dry by morning."

"It's very good of you."

"Not at all," said the other genially. "As I said just now, one couldn't turn away a dog on a night like this. Magdalen, Charlotte, go up and see to the room."

The two girls left the room. Presently Mortimer heard them moving about overhead.

"I can quite understand that two attractive young ladies like your daughters might find it dull here," said Cleveland.

"Good lookers, aren't they?" said Mr. Dinsmead with fatherly pride. "Not much like their mother or myself. We're a homely pair, but much attached to each other, I'll tell you that, Mr. Cleveland. Eh, Maggie, isn't that so?"

Mrs. Dinsmead smiled primly. She had started knitting again. The needles clicked busily. She was a fast knitter.

Presently the room was announced ready, and Mortimer, expressing thanks once more, declared his intention of turning in.

"Did you put a hot-water bottle in the bed?" demanded Mrs. Dinsmead, suddenly mindful of her house pride.

"Yes, Mother, two."

"That's right," said Dinsmead. "Go up with him, girls, and see that every thing is all right."

Magdalen preceded him up the staircase, her candle held aloft. Charlotte came behind.

The room was quite a pleasant one, small and with a sloping roof, but the bed looked comfortable, and the few pieces of somewhat dusty furniture were of old mahogany. A large can of hot water stood in the basin, a pair of pink pajamas of ample proportions were laid over a chair, and the bed was made and turned down.

Magdalen went over to the window and saw that the fastenings were secure. Charlotte cast a final eye over the washstand appointments. Then they both lingered by the door.

"Good night, Mr. Cleveland. You are sure there is everything?"

"Yes, thank you, Miss Magdalen. I am sorry to have given you both so much trouble. Good night."

"Good night."

They went out, shutting the door behind them. Mortimer Cleveland was alone. He undressed slowly and thoughtfully. When he had donned Mr. Dinsmead's pink pajamas, he gathered up his own wet clothes and put them outside the door as his host had bade him. From downstairs he could hear the rumble of Dinsmead's voice.

What a talker the man was! Altogether an odd personality—but indeed there was something odd about the whole family, or was it his imagination?

He went slowly back into his room and shut the door. He stood by the bed lost in thought. And then he started——

The mahogany table by the bed was smothered in dust. Written in the dust were three letters, clearly visible. *S.O.S.*

Mortimer stared as if he could hardly believe his eyes. It was a confirmation of all his vague surmises and forebodings. He was right, then. Something was wrong in this house.

S.O.S. A call for help. But whose finger had written it in the dust? Magdalen's or Charlotte's? They had both stood there, he remembered, for a moment or two, before going out of the room. Whose hand had secretly dropped to the table and traced out those three letters?

The faces of the two girls came up before him. Magdalen's, dark and aloof, and Charlotte's, as he had seen it first, wide-eyed, startled, with an unfathomable something in her glance.

He went again to the door and opened it. The boom of Mr. Dinsmead's voice was no longer to be heard. The house was silent.

He thought to himself.

"I can do nothing tonight. Tomorrow—well, we shall see."

Cleveland woke early. He went down through the living room, and out into the garden. The morning was fresh and beautiful after the rain. Someone else was up early, too. At the bottom of the garden Charlotte was leaning on the fence staring out over the Downs. His pulses quickened a little as he went down to join her. All along he had been secretly convinced that it was Charlotte who had written the message. As he came up to her, she turned and wished him "Good morning." Her eyes were direct and childlike, with no hint of a secret understanding in them.

"A very good morning," said Mortimer, smiling. "The weather this morning is a contrast to last night's."

"It is indeed."

Mortimer broke off a twig from a tree near by. With it he began idly to draw on the smooth, sandy patch at his feet. He traced an S, then an O, then an S, watching the girl narrowly as he did so. But again he could detect no gleam of comprehension.

"Do you know what these letters represent?" he said abruptly.

Charlotte frowned a little. "Aren't they what boats send out when they are in distress?" she asked.

Mortimer nodded. "Someone wrote that on the table by my bed last night," he said quietly. "I thought perhaps you might have done so."

She looked at him in wide-eyed astonishment.

"I? Oh, no."

He was wrong then. A sharp pang of disappointment shot through him. He had been so sure—so sure. It was not often that his intuitions led him astray.

"You are quite certain?" he persisted.

"Oh, yes."

They turned and went slowly together toward the house. Charlotte seemed preoccupied about something. She replied at random to the few observations he made. Suddenly she burst out in a low, hurried voice.

"It—it's odd your asking that about those letters, S.O.S. I didn't write them, of course, but—I so easily might have."

He stopped and looked at her, and she went on quickly: "It sounds silly, I know, but I have been so frightened, so dreadfully frightened, and when you came in last night, it seemed like an—an answer to something."

"What are you frightened of?" he asked quickly.

"I don't know."

"You don't know?"

"I think—it's the house. Ever since we came here it has been growing and growing. Everyone seems different somehow. Father, Mother, and Magdalen, they all seem different."

Mortimer did not speak at once, and before he could do so, Charlotte went on again.

"You know this house is supposed to be haunted?"

"What?" All his interest was quickened.

"Yes, a man murdered his wife in it, oh, some years ago now. We only found out about it after we got here. Father says ghosts are all nonsense, but I—don't know."

Mortimer was thinking rapidly.

"Tell me," he said in a businesslike tone, "was this murder committed in the room I had last night?"

"I don't know anything about that," said Charlotte.

"I wonder now," said Mortimer half to himself, "yes, that may be it."

Charlotte looked at him uncomprehendingly.

"Miss Dinsmead," said Mortimer, gently, "Have you ever had any reason to believe that you are mediumistic?"

She stared at him.

"I think you know that you did write S.O.S. last night," he said quietly. "Oh! quite unconsciously, of course. A crime stains the atmosphere, so to speak. A sensitive mind such as yours might be acted upon in such a manner. You have been reproducing the sensations and impressions of the victim. Many years ago *she* may have written S.O.S. on that table, and you unconsciously reproduced her act last night."

Charlotte's face brightened.

"I see," she said. "You think that is the explanation?"

A voice called her from the house, and she went in, leaving Mortimer to pace up and down the garden paths. Was he satisfied with his own explanation? Did it cover the facts as he knew them? Did it account for the tension he had felt on entering the house last night?

Perhaps, and yet he still had the odd feeling that his sudden appearance had produced something very like consternation. He thought to himself.

"I must not be carried away by the psychic explanation. It might account for Charlotte—but not for the others. My coming as I did upset them horribly, all except Johnnie. Whatever it is that's the matter, Johnnie is out of it."

He was quite sure of that; strange that he should be so positive, but there it was.

At that minute Johnnie himself came out of the cottage and approached the guest.

"Breakfast's ready," he said awkwardly. "Will you come in?"

Mortimer noticed that the lad's fingers were much stained. Johnnie felt his glance and laughed ruefully.

"I'm always messing about with chemicals, you know," he said. "It makes Dad awfully wild sometimes. He wants me to go into building, but I want to do chemistry and research work."

Mr. Dinsmead appeared at the window ahead of them, broad, jovial, smiling, and at sight of him all Mortimer's distrust and antagonism reawakened. Mrs. Dinsmead was already seated at the table. She wished him "Good morning" in her colorless voice, and he had again the impression that for some reason or other, she was afraid of him.

Magdalen came in last. She gave him a brief nod and took her seat opposite him.

"Did you sleep well?" she asked abruptly. "Was your bed comfortable?"

She looked at him very earnestly, and when he replied courteously in the affirmative he noticed something very like a flicker of disappointment pass over her face. What had she expected him to say, he wondered?

He turned to his host.

"This lad of yours is interested in chemistry, it seems," he said pleasantly.

There was a crash. Mrs. Dinsmead had dropped her tea cup.

"Now then, Maggie, now then," said her husband.

It seemed to Mortimer that there was admonition, warning, in his voice. He turned to his guest and spoke fluently of the advantages of the building trade, and of not letting young boys get above themselves.

After breakfast he went out in the garden by himself, and smoked. The time was clearly at hand when he must leave the cottage. A night's shelter was one thing; to prolong it was difficult without an excuse, and what possible excuse could he offer? And yet he was singularly loath to depart.

Turning the thing over and over in his mind, he took a path that led round the other side of the house. His shoes were soled with crepe rubber, and made little or no noise. He was passing the kitchen window when he heard Dinsmead's words from within, and the words attracted his attention immediately.

"It's a fair lump of money, it is."

Mrs. Dinsmead's voice answered. It was too faint in tone for Mortimer to hear the words, but Dinsmead replied:

"Nigh on £60,000, the lawyer said."

Mortimer had no intention of eavesdropping, but he retraced his steps very thoughtfully. The mention of money seemed to crystallize the situation. Somewhere or other there was a question of £60,000. It made the thing clearer—and uglier.

Magdalen came out of the house, but her father's voice called her almost immediately, and she went in again. Presently Dinsmead himself joined his guest.

"Rare good morning," he said genially. "I hope your car will be none the worse."

"Wants to find out when I'm going," thought Mortimer to himself.

Aloud he thanked Mr. Dinsmead once more for his timely hospitality.

"Not at all, not at all," said the other.

Magdalen and Charlotte came together out of the house and strolled arm in arm to a rustic seat some little distance away. The dark head and the golden one made a pleasant contrast together and on an impulse Mortimer said:

"Your daughters are very unlike, Mr. Dinsmead."

The other who was just lighting his pipe gave a sharp jerk of the wrist and dropped the match.

"Do you think so?" he asked. "Yes, well, I suppose they are."

Mortimer had a flash of intuition.

"But of course they are not both your daughters," he said smoothly.

He saw Dinsmead look at him, hesitate for a moment, and then make up his mind.

"That's very clever of you, sir," he said. "No, one of them is a foundling; we took her in as a baby and we have brought her up as our own. She herself has not the least idea of the truth, but she'll have to know soon." He sighed.

"A question of inheritance?" suggested Mortimer quietly.

The other flashed a suspicious look at him.

Then he decided that frankness was best; his manner became almost aggressively frank and open.

"It's odd you should say that, sir."

"A case of telepathy, eh?" said Mortimer, and smiled.

"It is like this, sir. We took her in to oblige the mother—for a consideration, as at the time I was just starting in the building trade. A few months ago I noticed an advertisement in the papers, and it seemed to me that the child in question must be our Magdalen. I went to see the lawyers, and there has been a lot of talk one way and another. They were suspicious—naturally, as you might say—but everything is cleared up now. I am taking the girl herself to London next week—she doesn't know anything about it so far. Her father, it seems, was a very rich man. He only learned of the child's existence a few months before his death. He hired agents to try and trace her, and left all his money to her when she should be found."

Mortimer listened with close attention. He had no reason to doubt Mr. Dinsmead's story. It explained Magdalen's dark beauty; explained too, perhaps, her aloof manner. Nevertheless, though the story itself might be true, something lay undivulged behind it.

But Mortimer had no intention of rousing the

other's suspicions. Instead, he must go out of his way to allay them.

"A very interesting story, Mr. Dinsmead," he said. "I congratulate Miss Magdalen. An heiress and a beauty, she has a great future ahead."

"She has that," agreed her father warmly, "and she's a rare good girl too, Mr. Cleveland."

There was every evidence of hearty warmth in his manner.

"Well," said Mortimer, "I must be pushing along now, I suppose. I have got to thank you once more, Mr. Dinsmead, for your singularly well-timed hospitality."

Accompanied by his host, he went into the house to bid farewell to Mrs. Dinsmead. She was standing by the window with her back to them, and did not hear them enter. At her husband's jovial, "Here's Mr. Cleveland come to say good-bye," she started nervously and swung round, dropping something which she held in her hand. Mortimer picked it up for her. It was a miniature of Charlotte done in the style of some twenty-five years ago. Mortimer repeated to her the thanks he had already proffered to her husband. He noticed again her look of fear and the furtive glances that she shot at him beneath her eyelids.

The two girls were not in evidence, but it was not part of Mortimer's policy to seem anxious to see them; also he had his own idea, which was shortly to prove correct.

He had gone about half a mile from the house on his way down to where he had left the car the night before, when the bushes on one side of the path were thrust aside, and Magdalen came out on the track ahead of him.

"I had to see you," she said.

"I expected you," said Mortimer. "It was you who wrote S.O.S. on the table in my room last night, wasn't it?"

Magdalen nodded.

"Why?" asked Mortimer gently.

The girl turned aside and began pulling off leaves from a bush.

"I don't know," she said. "Honestly, I don't know."

"Tell me," said Mortimer.

Magdalen drew a deep breath.

"I am a practical person," she said, "not the kind of person who imagines things or fancies them. You, I think, believe in ghosts and spirits. I don't, and when I tell you that there is something very wrong in that house," she pointed up the hill, "I mean that there is something tangibly wrong—it's not just an echo of the past. It has been coming on ever since we've been there. Every day it grows worse. Father is different, Mother is different, Charlotte is different."

Mortimer interposed. "Is Johnnie different?" he asked.

Magdalen looked at him, a dawning appreciation in her eyes. "No," she said, "now I come to think of it. Johnnie is not different. He is the only one who's— who's untouched by it all. He was untouched last night at tea."

"And you?" asked Mortimer.

"I was afraid—horribly afraid, just like a child— without knowing what it was I was afraid of. And

Father was—queer, there's no other word for it. He talked about miracles and then I prayed—actually prayed for a miracle, and *you* knocked on the door."

She stopped abruptly, staring at him. "I seem mad to you, I suppose," she said defiantly.

"No," said Mortimer, "on the contrary you seem extremely sane. All sane people have a premonition of danger if it is near them."

"You don't understand," said Magdalen. "I was not afraid—for myself."

"For whom, then?"

But again Magdalen shook her head in a puzzled fashion. "I don't know."

She went on: "I wrote S.O.S. on an impulse. I had an idea—absurd, no doubt—that they would not let me speak to you—the rest of them, I mean. I don't know what it was I meant to ask you to do. I don't know now."

"Never mind," said Mortimer. "I shall do it."

"What can you do?"

Mortimer smiled a little.

"I can think."

She looked at him doubtfully.

"Yes," said Mortimer, "a lot can be done that way, more than you would ever believe. Tell me, was there any chance word or phrase that attracted your attention just before that meal last evening?"

Magdalen frowned. "I don't think so," she said.

"At least I heard Father saying something to Mother about Charlotte being the living image of her, and he laughed in a very queer way, but—there's nothing odd in that, is there?"

"No," said Mortimer slowly, "except that Charlotte is not like your mother."

He remained lost in thought for a minute or two, then looked up to find Magdalen watching him uncertainly.

"Go home, child," he said, "and don't worry. Leave it in my hands."

She went obediently up the path towards the cottage. Mortimer strolled on a little farther, then threw himself from conscious thought or effort, and let a series of pictures flit at will across the surface of his mind.

Johnnie! He always came back to Johnnie. Johnnie, completely innocent, utterly free from all the network of suspicion and intrigue, but nevertheless the pivot around which everything turned. He remembered the crash of Mrs. Dinsmead's cup on her saucer at breakfast that morning. What had caused her agitation? A chance reference on his part to the lad's fondness for chemicals? At the moment he had not been conscious of Mr. Dinsmead, but he saw him now clearly, as he sat, his teacup poised halfway to his lips.

That took him back to Charlotte, as he had seen her when the door opened last night. She had sat staring at him over the rim of her teacup. And swiftly on that followed another memory. Mr. Dinsmead emptying teacups one after the other, and saying, "This tea's cold."

He remembered the steam that went up. Surely the tea had not been so very cold after all?

Something began to stir in his brain. A memory of something read not so very long ago, within a month perhaps. Some account of a whole family poisoned by a lad's carelessness. A packet of arsenic left in the larder had sifted through to the bread below. He had read it in the paper. Probably Mr. Dinsmead had read it too.

Things began to grow clearer. . . .

Half an hour later, Mortimer Cleveland rose briskly to his feet.

It was evening once more in the cottage. The eggs were poached tonight and there was a tin of brawn. Presently Mrs. Dinsmead came in from the kitchen bearing the big teapot. The family took their places round the table.

Mrs. Dinsmead filled the cups and handed them round the table. Then, as she put the teapot down, she gave a sudden little cry and pressed her hand to her throat. Mr. Dinsmead swung round in his chair, following the direction of her terrified eyes. Mortimer Cleveland was standing in the doorway.

He came forward. His manner was pleasant and apologetic.

"I'm afraid I startled you," he said. "I had to come back for something."

"Back for something," cried Mr. Dinsmead. His face was purple, his veins swelling. "Back for what, I should like to know?"

"Some tea," said Mortimer.

With a swift gesture he took something from his pocket and taking up one of the teacups from the table, emptied some of its contents into a little test-tube he held in his left hand.

"What—what are you doing?" gasped Mr. Dinsmead. His face had gone chalky-white, the purple dying out as if by magic. Mrs. Dinsmead gave a thin, high, frightened cry.

"You read the papers, Mr. Dinsmead? I am sure you do. Sometimes one reads accounts of a whole family being poisoned—some of them recover, some do not. In this case, one would not. The first explanation would be the tinned brawn you were eating, but supposing the doctor to be a suspicious man, not easily taken in by the tinned food theory? There is a packet of arsenic in your larder. On the shelf below it is a packet of tea. There is a convenient hole in the top shelf. What more natural to suppose than that the arsenic found its way into the tea by accident? Your son Johnnie might be blamed for carelessness, nothing more."

"I—I don't know what you mean," gasped Dinsmead.

"I think you do." Mortimer took up a second teacup and filled a second test-tube. He fixed a red label to one and a blue label to the other.

"The red-labeled one," he said, "contains tea from your daughter Charlotte's cup, the other from your daughter Magdalen's. I am prepared to swear that in the first I shall find four or five times the amount of arsenic than in the latter."

"You are mad!" said Dinsmead.

"Oh, dear me, no. I am nothing of the kind. You told me today, Mr. Dinsmead, that Magdalen was not your own daughter. You lied to me. Magdalen *is* your daughter. Charlotte was the child you adopted, the child who was so like her mother that when I held a miniature of that mother in my hand today I mistook it for one of Charlotte herself. You wanted your own

daughter to inherit the fortune, and since it might be
impossible to keep Charlotte out of sight, and someone who knew her mother might have realized the
truth of the resemblance, you decided on, well—sufficient white arsenic at the bottom of a teacup."

Mrs. Dinsmead gave a sudden high cackle, rocking
herself to and fro in violent hysterics.

"Tea," she squeaked, "that's what he said, tea, not
lemonade."

"Hold your tongue, can't you?" roared her husband
wrathfully.

Mortimer saw Charlotte looking at him, wide-eyed,
wondering, across the table. Then he felt a hand on
his arm, and Magdalen dragged him out of earshot.

"Those," she pointed at the phials—"Daddy. You
won't——"

Mortimer laid his hand on her shoulder. "My
child," he said, "you don't believe in the past. I do. I
believe in the atmosphere of this house. If he had not
come to this particular house, perhaps—I say *perhaps*—your father might not have conceived the plan
he did. I will keep these two test-tubes to safeguard
Charlotte now and in the future. Apart from that, I
shall do nothing—in gratitude, if you will, to the hand
that wrote S.O.S."

WHERE THERE'S A WILL

"Above all, avoid worry and excitement," said Dr. Meynell, in the comfortable fashion affected by doctors.

Mrs. Harter, as is often the case with people hearing these soothing but meaningless words, seemed more doubtful than relieved.

"There is a certain cardiac weakness," continued the doctor fluently, "but nothing to be alarmed about. I can assure you of that. All the same," he added, "it might be as well to have an elevator installed. Eh? What about it?"

Mrs. Harter looked worried.

Dr. Meynell, on the contrary, looked pleased with himself. The reason he liked attending rich patients rather than poor ones was that he could exercise his active imagination in prescribing for their ailments.

"Yes, an elevator," said Dr. Meynell, trying to think of something else even more dashing—and failing. "Then we shall avoid all undue exertion. Daily exercise on the level on a fine day, but avoid walking up hills. And, above all, plenty of distraction for the mind. Don't dwell on your health."

To the old lady's nephew, Charles Ridgeway, the doctor was slightly more explicit.

"Do not misunderstand me," he said. "Your aunt may live for years, probably will. At the same time, shock or overexertion might carry her off like that!" He snapped his fingers. "She must lead a very quiet life. No exertion. No fatigue. But, of course, she must not be allowed to brood. She must be kept cheerful and the mind well distracted."

"Distracted," said Charles Ridgeway thoughtfully.

Charles was a thoughtful young man. He was also a young man who believed in furthering his own inclinations whenever possible.

That evening he suggested the installation of a radio set.

Mrs. Harter, already seriously upset at the thought of the elevator, was disturbed and unwilling. Charles was persuasive.

"I do not know that I care for these new-fangled things," said Mrs. Harter piteously. "The waves, you know—the electric waves. They might affect me."

Charles, in a superior and kindly fashion, pointed out the futility of this idea.

Mrs. Harter, whose knowledge of the subject was of the vaguest but who was tenacious of her own opinion, remained unconvinced.

"All that electricity," she murmured timorously. "You may say what you like, Charles, but some people are affected by electricity. I always have a terrible headache before a thunderstorm. I know that."

She nodded her head triumphantly.

Charles was a patient young man. He was also persistent.

"My dear Aunt Mary," he said, "let me make the thing clear to you."

He was something of an authority on the subject. He delivered quite a lecture on the theme; warming to his task, he spoke of bright-emitter tubes, of dull-emitter tubes, of high frequency and low frequency, of amplification and of condensers.

Mrs. Harter, submerged in a sea of words that she did not understand, surrendered.

"Of course, Charles," she murmured, "if you really think——"

"My dear Aunt Mary," said Charles enthusiastically, "it is the very thing for you, to keep you from moping and all that."

The elevator prescribed by Dr. Meynell was installed shortly afterwards and was very nearly the death of Mrs. Harter since, like many other old ladies, she had a rooted objection to strange men in the house. She suspected them one and all of having designs on her old silver.

After the elevator the radio set arrived. Mrs. Harter was left to contemplate the, to her, repellent object—a large, ungainly-looking box, studded with knobs.

It took all Charles's enthusiasm to reconcile her to it, but Charles was in his element, turning knobs and discoursing eloquently.

Mrs. Harter sat in her high-backed chair, patient and polite, with a rooted conviction in her own mind that these new-fangled notions were neither more nor less than unmitigated nuisances.

"Listen, Aunt Mary, we are on to Berlin! Isn't that splendid? Can you hear the fellow?"

"I can't hear anything except a good deal of buzzing and clicking," said Mrs. Harter.

Charles continued to twirl knobs. "Brussels," he announced with enthusiasm.

"It is really?" said Mrs. Harter with no more than a trace of interest.

Charles again turned knobs and an unearthly howl echoed forth into the room.

"Now we seem to be on to the Dogs' Home," said Mrs. Harter, who was an old lady with a certain amount of spirit.

"Ha, ha!" said Charles, "you will have your joke, won't you, Aunt Mary? Very good that!"

Mrs. Harter could not help smiling at him. She was very fond of Charles. For some years a niece, Miriam Harter, had lived with her. She had intended to make the girl her heiress, but Miriam had not been a success. She was impatient and obviously bored by her aunt's society. She was always out, "gadding about" as Mrs. Harter called it. In the end she had entangled herself with a young man of whom her aunt thoroughly disapproved. Miriam had been returned to her mother with a curt note much as if she had been goods on approval. She had married the young man in question and Mrs. Harter usually sent her a handkerchief case or a table center at Christmas.

Having found nieces disappointing, Mrs. Harter turned her attention to nephews. Charles, from the first, had been an unqualified success. He was always pleasantly deferential to his aunt and listened with an appearance of intense interest to the reminiscences of her youth. In this he was a great contrast to Miriam who had been frankly bored and showed it. Charles was never bored; he was always good-tempered, always gay. He told his aunt many times a day that she was a perfectly marvelous old lady.

Highly satisfied with her new acquisition, Mrs. Harter had written to her lawyer with instructions as to the making of a new will. This was sent to her, duly approved by her, and signed.

And now even in the matter of the radio, Charles was soon proved to have won fresh laurels.

Mrs. Harter, at first antagonistic, became tolerant and finally fascinated. She enjoyed it very much better when Charles was out. The trouble with Charles was that he could not leave the thing alone. Mrs. Harter would be seated in her chair comfortably listening to a symphony concert or a lecture on Lucrezia Borgia or Pond Life, quite happy and at peace with the world. Not so Charles. The harmony would be shattered by discordant shrieks while he enthusiastically attempted to get foreign stations. But on those evenings when Charles was dining out with friends, Mrs. Harter enjoyed the radio very much indeed. She would turn on two switches, sit in her high-backed chair, and enjoy the program of the evening.

It was about three months after the radio had been installed that the first eerie happening occurred. Charles was absent at a bridge party.

The program for that evening was a ballad concert. A well-known soprano was singing *Annie Laurie*, and in the middle of *Annie Laurie* a strange thing happened. There was a sudden break, the music ceased for a moment, the buzzing, clicking noise continued, and then that too died away. There was silence, and then very faintly a low buzzing sound was heard.

Mrs. Harter got the impression, why she did not know, that the machine was tuned into somewhere very far away, and then, clearly and distinctly, a voice spoke, a man's voice with a faint Irish accent.

"Mary—can you hear me, Mary? It is Patrick speaking. . . . I am coming for you soon. You will be ready, won't you, Mary?"

Then, almost immediately, the strains of *Annie Laurie* once more filled the room.

Mrs. Harter sat rigid in her chair, her hands clenched on each arm of it. Had she been dreaming? Patrick! Patrick's voice! Patrick's voice in this very room, speaking to her. No, it must be a dream, a hallucination perhaps. She must just have dropped off to sleep for a minute or two. A curious thing to have dreamed—that her dead husband's voice should speak to her over the ether. It frightened her just a little. What were the words he had said?

"I am coming for you soon. You will be ready, won't you, Mary?"

Was it, could it be a premonition? Cardiac weakness. Her heart. After all, she was getting on in years.

"It's a warning—that's what it is," said Mrs. Harter, rising slowly and painfully from her chair, and added characteristically, "All that money wasted on putting in an elevator!"

She said nothing of her experience to anyone, but for the next day or two she was thoughtful and a little preoccupied.

And then came the second occasion. Again she was alone in the room. The radio, which had been playing an orchestral selection, died away with the same suddenness as before. Again there was silence, the sense of distance, and finally Patrick's voice, not as it had been in life—but a voice rarefied, far-away, with a strange unearthly quality.

"Patrick speaking to you, Mary. I will be coming for you very soon now. . . ."

Then click, buzz, and the orchestral selection was in full swing again.

Mrs. Harter glanced at the clock. No, she had not been asleep this time. Awake and in full possession of her faculties, she had heard Patrick's voice speaking. It was no hallucination, she was sure of that. In a confused way she tried to think over all that Charles had explained to her of the theory of ether waves.

Could it be that Patrick had really spoken to her? That his actual voice had been wafted through space? There were missing wave lengths or something of that kind. She remembered Charles speaking of "gaps in the scale." Perhaps the missing waves explained all the so-called psychological phenomena? No, there was nothing inherently impossible in the idea. Patrick had spoken to her. He had availed himself of modern science to prepare her for what must soon be coming.

Mrs. Harter rang the bell for her maid, Elizabeth.

Elizabeth was a tall, gaunt woman of sixty. Beneath an unbending exterior she concealed a wealth of affection and tenderness for her mistress.

"Elizabeth," said Mrs. Harter when her faithful retainer had appeared, "you remember what I told you? The top left-hand drawer of my bureau. It is locked—the long key with the white label. Everything there is ready."

"Ready, ma'am?"

"For my burial," snorted Mrs. Harter. "You know

perfectly well what I mean, Elizabeth. You helped me to put the things there yourself."

Elizabeth's face began to work strangely.

"Oh, ma'am," she wailed, "don't dwell on such things. I thought you was a sight better."

"We have all got to go sometime or another," said Mrs. Harter practically. "I am over my three score years and ten, Elizabeth. There, there, don't make a fool of yourself. If you must cry, go and cry somewhere else."

Elizabeth retired, still sniffing.

Mrs. Harter looked after her with a good deal of affection.

"Silly old fool, but faithful," she said, "very faithful. Let me see, was it a hundred pounds, or only fifty I left her? It ought to be a hundred."

The point worried the old lady and the next day she sat down and wrote to her lawyer asking if he would send her her will so that she might look it over. It was that same day that Charles startled her by something he said at lunch.

"By the way, Aunt Mary," he said, "who is that funny old josser up in the spare room? The picture over the mantelpiece, I mean. The old johnny with the beaver and sidewhiskers?"

Mrs. Harter looked at him austerely.

"That is your Uncle Patrick as a young man," she said.

"Oh, I say, Aunt Mary, I am awfully sorry. I didn't mean to be rude."

Mrs. Harter accepted the apology with a dignified bend of the head.

Charles went on rather uncertainly, "I just wondered. You see——"

He stopped undecidedly and Mrs. Harter said sharply:

"Well? What were you going to say?"

"Nothing," said Charles hastily. "Nothing that makes sense, I mean."

For the moment the old lady said nothing more, but later that day, when they were alone together, she returned to the subject.

"I wish you would tell me, Charles, what it was that made you ask me about the picture of your uncle."

Charles looked embarrassed.

"I told you, Aunt Mary. It was nothing but a silly fancy of mine—quite absurd."

"Charles," said Mrs. Harter in her most autocratic voice, "I insist upon knowing."

"Well, my dear aunt, if you will have it, I fancied I saw him—the man in the picture, I mean—looking out of the end window when I was coming up the drive last night. Some effect of the light, I suppose. I wondered who on earth he could be, the face so— early Victorian, if you know what I mean. And then Elizabeth said there was no one, no visitor or stranger in the house, and later in the evening I happened to drift into the spare room, and there was the picture over the mantelpiece. My man to the life! It is quite easily explained, really, I expect. Subconscious and all that. Must have noticed the picture before without realizing that I had noticed it, and then just fancied the face at the window."

"The end window?" said Mrs. Harter sharply.

"Yes, why?"

"Nothing," said Mrs. Harter.

But she was startled all the same. That room had been her husband's dressing room.

That same evening, Charles again being absent, Mrs. Harter sat listening to the wireless with feverish impatience. If for the third time she heard the mysterious voice, it would prove to her finally and without a shadow of doubt that she was really in communication with some other world.

Although her heart beat faster, she was not surprised when the same break occurred, and after the usual interval of deathly silence the faint far-away Irish voice spoke once more.

"Mary—you are prepared now. . . . On Friday I shall come for you. . . . Friday at half-past nine. . . . Do not be afraid—there will be no pain. . . . Be ready. . . ."

Then, almost cutting short the last word, the music of the orchestra broke out again, clamorous and discordant.

Mrs. Harter sat very still for a minute or two. Her face had gone white and she looked blue and pinched round the lips.

Presently she got up and sat down at her writing-desk. In a somewhat shaky hand she wrote the following lines:

Tonight, at 9:15, I have distinctly heard the voice of my dead husband. He told me that he would come for me on Friday night at 9:30. If I should die on that day and at that hour I should like the facts made known so as to prove beyond question

the possibility of communicating with the spirit
world.

—MARY HARTER

Mrs. Harter read over what she had written, enclosed it in an envelope, and addressed the envelope.
Then she rang the bell, which was promptly answered
by Elizabeth. Mrs. Harter got up from her desk and
gave the note she had just written to the old woman.

"Elizabeth," she said, "if I should die on Friday
night I should like that note given to Dr. Meynell.
No"—as Elizabeth appeared about to protest—"do
not argue with me. You have often told me you believe in premonitions. I have a premonition now.
There is one thing more. I have left you in my will
£50. I should like you to have £100. If I am not able
to go to the bank myself before I die, Mr. Charles
will see to it."

As before, Mrs. Harter cut short Elizabeth's tearful
protests. In pursuance of her determination the old
lady spoke to her nephew on the subject the following
morning.

"Remember, Charles, that if anything should happen to me, Elizabeth is to have an extra £50."

"You are very gloomy these days, Aunt Mary,"
said Charles cheerfully. "What is going to happen to
you? According to Dr. Meynell, we shall be cele-
brating your hundredth birthday in twenty years or
so!"

Mrs. Harter smiled affectionately at him but did
not answer. After a minute or two she said:

"What are you doing on Friday evening, Charles?"
Charles looked a trifle surprised.

"As a matter of fact, the Ewings asked me to go in and play bridge, but if you would rather I stayed at home——"

"No," said Mrs. Harter with determination. "Certainly not. I mean it, Charles. On that night of all nights I should much rather be alone."

Charles looked at her curiously, but Mrs. Harter vouchsafed no further information. She was an old lady of courage and determination. She felt that she must go through with her strange experience single-handed.

Friday evening found the house very silent. Mrs. Harter sat as usual in her straight-backed chair drawn up to the fireplace. All her preparations were made. That morning she had been to the bank, had drawn out £50 in notes, and had handed them over to Elizabeth despite the latter's tearful protests. She had sorted and arranged all her personal belongings and had labeled one or two pieces of jewelry with the names of friends or relations. She had also written out a list of instructions for Charles. The Worcester tea service was to go to Cousin Emma, the Sèvres jars to young William, and so on.

Now she looked at the long envelope she held in her hand and drew from it a folded document. This was her will sent to her by Mr. Hopkinson in accordance with her instructions. She had already read it carefully, but now she looked over it once more to refresh her memory. It was a short, concise document. A bequest of £50 to Elizabeth Marshall in consideration of faithful service; two bequests of £500 to a sister and a first cousin; and the remainder to her beloved nephew Charles Ridgeway.

Mrs. Harter nodded her head several times. Charles would be a very rich man when she was dead. Well, he had been a dear good boy to her. Always kind, always affectionate, and with a merry tongue which never failed to please her.

She looked at the clock. Three minutes to the half-hour. Well, she was ready. And she was calm—quite calm. Although she repeated these last words to herself several times, her heart beat strangely and unevenly. She hardly realized it herself, but she was strung up to a fine point of over-wrought nerves.

Half-past nine. The wireless was switched on. What would she hear? A familiar voice announcing the weather forecast or that far-away voice belonging to a man who had died twenty-five years before?

But she heard neither. Instead there came a familiar sound, a sound she knew well but which tonight made her feel as though an icy hand were laid on her heart. A fumbling at the front door. . . .

It came again. And then a cold blast seemed to sweep through the room. Mrs. Harter had now no doubt what her sensations were. She was afraid. . . . She was more than afraid—she was terrified. . . .

And suddenly there came to her the thought: *"Twenty-five years is a long time. Patrick is a stranger to me now."*

Terror! That was what was invading her.

A soft step outside the door—a soft halting footstep. Then the door swung silently open. . . .

Mrs. Harter staggered to her feet, swaying slightly from side to side, her eyes fixed on the open doorway. Something slipped from her fingers into the grate.

She gave a strangled cry which died in her throat.

In the dim light of the doorway stood a familiar figure with chestnut beard and whiskers and an old-fashioned Victorian coat.

Patrick had come for her!

Her heart gave one terrified leap and stood still. She slipped to the ground in a crumpled heap.

There Elizabeth found her, an hour later.

Dr. Meynell was called at once and Charles Ridgeway was hastily summoned from his bridge party. But nothing could be done. Mrs. Harter was beyond human aid.

It was not until two days later that Elizabeth remembered the note given to her by her mistress. Dr. Meynell read it with great interest and showed it to Charles Ridgeway.

"A very curious coincidence," he said. "It seems clear that your aunt had been having hallucinations about her dead husband's voice. She must have strung herself up to such a point that the excitement was fatal, and when the time actually came she died of the shock."

"Auto-suggestion?" asked Charles.

"Something of the sort. I will let you know the result of the autopsy as soon as possible, though I have no doubt of it myself. In the circumstances an autopsy is desirable, though purely as a matter of form."

Charles nodded comprehendingly.

On the preceding night, when the household was in bed, he had removed a certain wire which ran from the back of the radio cabinet to his bedroom on the floor above. Also, since the evening had been a chilly one, he had asked Elizabeth to light a fire in his room, and in that fire he had burned a chestnut beard and whiskers. Some Victorian clothing belonging to his late uncle he replaced in the camphor-scented chest in the attic.

As far as he could see, he was perfectly safe. His plan, the shadowy outline of which had first formed in his brain when Doctor Meynell had told him that his aunt might with due care live for many years, had succeeded admirably. A sudden shock, Dr. Meynell had said. Charles, that affectionate young man, beloved of old ladies, smiled to himself.

When the doctor had departed, Charles went about his duties mechanically. Certain funeral arrangements had to be finally settled. Relatives coming from a distance had to have trains looked out for them. In one or two cases they would have to stay the night. Charles went about it all efficiently and methodically, to the accompaniment of an undercurrent of his own thoughts.

A very good stroke of business! That was the burden of them. Nobody, least of all his dead aunt, had known in what perilous straits Charles stood. His activities, carefully concealed from the world, had landed him where the shadow of a prison loomed ahead.

Exposure and ruin had stared him in the face unless he could in a few short months raise a considerable sum of money. Well—that was all right now. Charles smiled to himself. Thanks to—yes, call it a practical joke—nothing criminal about *that*—he was saved. He was now a very rich man. He had no anxieties on the subject, for Mrs. Harter had never made any secret of her intentions.

Chiming in very appositely with these thoughts, Elizabeth put her head round the door and informed him that Mr. Hopkinson was here and would like to see him.

About time, too, Charles thought. Repressing a tendency to whistle, he composed his face to one of suitable gravity and went to the library. There he greeted the precise old gentleman who had been for over a quarter of a century the late Mrs. Harter's legal adviser.

The lawyer seated himself at Charles's invitation and with a dry little cough entered upon business matters.

"I did not quite understand your letter to me, Mr. Ridgeway. You seemed to be under the impression that the late Mrs. Harter's will was in our keeping?"

Charles stared at him.

"But surely—I've heard my aunt say as much."

"Oh! quite so, quite so. It *was* in our keeping."

"Was?"

"That is what I said. Mrs. Harter wrote to us, asking that it might be forwarded to her on Tuesday last."

An uneasy feeling crept over Charles. He felt a far-off premonition of unpleasantness.

"Doubtless it will come to light among her papers," continued the lawyer smoothly.

Charles said nothing. He was afraid to trust his tongue. He had already been through Mrs. Harter's papers pretty thoroughly, well enough to be quite certain that no will was among them. In a minute or two, when he had regained control of himself, he said so.

His voice sounded unreal to himself, and he had a sensation as of cold water trickling down his back.

"Has anyone been through her personal effects?" asked the lawyer.

Charles replied that the maid, Elizabeth, had done so. At Mr. Hopkinson's suggestion Elizabeth was sent for. She came promptly, grim and upright, and answered the questions put to her.

She had been through all her mistress's clothes and personal belongings. She was quite sure that there had been no legal document such as a will among them. She knew what the will looked like—her poor mistress had had it in her hand only the morning of her death.

"You are sure of that?" asked the lawyer sharply.

"Yes, sir. She told me so. And she made me take fifty pounds in notes. The will was in a long blue envelope."

"Quite right," said Mr. Hopkinson.

"Now I come to think of it," continued Elizabeth, "that same blue envelope was lying on this table the morning after—but empty. I laid it on the desk."

"I remember seeing it there," said Charles.

He got up and went over to the desk. In a minute or two he turned round with an envelope in his hand which he handed to Mr. Hopkinson. The latter examined it and nodded his head.

"That is the envelope in which I dispatched the will on Tuesday last."

Both men looked hard at Elizabeth.

"Is there anything more, sir?" she inquired respectfully.

"Not at present, thank you."

Elizabeth went towards the door.

"One minute," said the lawyer. "Was there a fire in the grate that evening?"

"Yes, sir, there was always a fire."

"Thank you, that will do."

Elizabeth went out. Charles leaned forward, resting a shaking hand on the table.

"What do you think? What are you driving at?"

Mr. Hopkinson shook his head.

"We must still hope the will may turn up. If it does not——"

"Well, if it does not?"

"I am afraid there is only one conclusion possible. Your aunt sent for that will in order to destroy it. Not wishing Elizabeth to lose by that, she gave her the amount of her legacy in cash."

"But why?" cried Charles wildly. "Why?"

Mr. Hopkinson coughed. A dry cough.

"You have had no—er—disagreement with your aunt, Mr. Ridgeway?" he murmured.

Charles gasped.

"No, indeed," he cried warmly. "We were on the kindliest, most affectionate terms, right up to the end."

"Ah!" said Mr. Hopkinson, not looking at him.

It came to Charles with a shock that the lawyer did not believe him. Who knew what this dry old stick might not have heard? Rumors of Charles's doings might have come round to him. What more natural than that he should suppose that these same rumors had come to Mrs. Harter, and that aunt and nephew should have had an altercation on the subject?

But it wasn't so! Charles knew one of the bitterest

moments of his career. His lies had been believed. Now that he spoke the truth, belief was withheld. The irony of it!

Of course his aunt had never burned the will! Of course——

His thoughts came to a sudden check. What was that picture rising before his eyes? An old lady with one hand clasped to her heart . . . something slipping . . . a paper . . . falling on the red-hot embers. . . .

Charles's face grew livid. He heard a hoarse voice—his own—asking:

"If that will's never found——?"

"There is a former will of Mrs. Harter's still extant. Dated September, 1920. By it Mrs. Harter leaves everything to her niece, Miriam Harter, now Miriam Robinson."

What was the old fool saying? Miriam? Miriam with her nondescript husband, and her four whining brats. All his cleverness—for Miriam!

The telephone rang sharply at his elbow. He took up the receiver. It was the doctor's voice, hearty and kindly.

"That you, Ridgeway? Thought you'd like to know. The autopsy's just concluded. Cause of death as I surmised. But as a matter of fact the cardiac trouble was much more serious than I suspected when she was alive. With the utmost care she couldn't have lived longer than two months at the outside. Thought you'd like to know. Might console you more or less."

"Excuse me," said Charles, "would you mind saying that again?"

"She couldn't have lived longer than two months,"

said the doctor in a slightly louder tone. "All things work out for the best, you know, my dear fellow——"

But Charles had slammed back the receiver on its hook. He was conscious of the lawyer's voice speaking from a long way off.

"Dear me, Mr. Ridgeway, are you ill?"

Damn them all! The smug-faced lawyer. That poisonous old ass Meynell. No hope in front of him—only the shadow of the prison wall. . . .

He felt that Somebody had been playing with him—playing with him like a cat with a mouse. Somebody must be laughing. . . .

The Mystery of the Blue Jar

Jack Hartington surveyed his topped drive ruefully. Standing by the ball, he looked back to the tee, measuring the distance. His face was eloquent of the disgusted contempt which he felt. With a sigh he drew out his iron, executed two vicious swings with it, annihilating in turn a dandelion and a tuft of grass, and then addressed himself firmly to the ball.

It is hard when you are twenty-four years of age, and your one ambition in life is to reduce your handicap at golf, to be forced to give time and attention to the problem of earning your living. Five and a half days out of the seven saw Jack imprisoned in a kind of mahogany tomb in the city. Saturday afternoon and Sunday were religiously devoted to the real business of life, and in an excess of zeal he had taken rooms at the small hotel near Stourton Heath links, and rose daily at the hour of six a.m. to get in an hour's practice before catching the 8.46 to town.

The only disadvantage to the plan was that he seemed constitutionally unable to hit anything at that hour in the morning. A foozled iron succeeded a muffed drive. His mashie shots ran merrily along the ground, and four putts seemed to be the minimum on any green.

Jack sighed, grasped his iron firmly, and repeated to himself the magic words, "Left arm right through, and don't look up."

He swung back—and then stopped, petrified, as a shrill cry rent the silence of the summer's morning.

"Murder," it called. "Help! Murder!"

It was a woman's voice, and it died away at the end into a sort of gurgling sigh.

Jack flung down his club and ran in the direction of the sound. It had come from somewhere quite near at hand. This particular part of the course was quite wild country, and there were few houses about. In fact, there was only one near at hand, a small pictur-esque cottage, which Jack had often noticed for its air of Old World daintiness. It was towards this cottage that he ran. It was hidden from him by a heather-covered slope, but he rounded this and in less than a minute was standing with his hand on the small latched gate.

There was a girl standing in the garden, and for a moment Jack jumped to the natural conclusion that it was she who had uttered the cry for help. But he quickly changed his mind.

She had a little basket in her hand, half-full of weeds, and had evidently just straightened herself up from weeding a wide border of pansies. Her eyes, Jack noticed, were just like pansies themselves, vel-vety and soft and dark, and more violet than blue. She was like a pansy altogether, in her straight purple linen gown.

The girl was looking at Jack with an expression

midway between annoyance and surprise.

"I beg your pardon," said the young man. "But did you cry out just now?"

"I? No, indeed."

Her surprise was so genuine that Jack felt confused. Her voice was very soft and pretty with a slight foreign inflection.

"But you must have heard it," he exclaimed. "It came from somewhere just near here."

She stared at him.

"I heard nothing at all."

Jack in his turn stared at her. It was perfectly incredible that she should not have heard that agonized appeal for help. And yet her calmness was so evident that he could not believe she was lying to him.

"It came from somewhere close at hand," he insisted.

She was looking at him suspiciously now.

"What did it say?" she asked.

"Murder—help! Murder!"

"Murder—help, murder," repeated the girl. "Somebody has played a trick on you, Monsieur. Who could be murdered here?"

Jack looked about him with a confused idea of discovering a dead body upon a garden path. Yet he was still perfectly sure that the cry he had heard was real and not a product of his imagination. He looked up at the cottage windows. Everything seemed perfectly still and peaceful.

"Do you want to search our house?" asked the girl dryly.

She was so clearly sceptical that Jack's confusion grew deeper than ever. He turned away.

"I'm sorry," he said. "It must have come from higher up in the woods."

He raised his cap and retreated. Glancing back over his shoulder, he saw that the girl had calmly resumed her weeding.

For some time he hunted through the woods, but could find no sign of anything unusual having occurred. Yet he was as positive as ever that he had really heard the cry. In the end, he gave up the search and hurried home to bolt his breakfast and catch the 8.46 by the usual narrow margin of a second or so. His conscience pricked him a little as he sat in the train. Ought he not to have immediately reported what he had heard to the police? That he had not done so was solely owing to the pansy girl's incredulity. She had clearly suspected him of romancing—possibly the police might do the same. Was he absolutely certain that he had heard the cry?

By now he was not nearly so positive as he had been—the natural result of trying to recapture a lost sensation. Was it some bird's cry in the distance that he had twisted into the resemblance of a woman's voice?

But he rejected the suggestion angrily. It was a woman's voice, and he had heard it. He remembered looking at his watch just before the cry had come. As nearly as possible it must have been five and twenty minutes past seven when he had heard the call. That might be a fact useful to the police if—if anything should be discovered.

Going home that evening, he scanned the evening papers anxiously to see if there were any mention of a crime having been committed. But there was nothing, and he hardly knew whether to be relieved or disappointed.

The following morning was wet—so wet that even the most ardent golfer might have his enthusiasm damped. Jack rose at the last possible moment, gulped his breakfast, ran for the train, and again eagerly scanned the papers. Still no mention of any gruesome discovery having been made. The evening papers told the same tale.

"Queer," said Jack to himself, "but there it is. Probably some blinking little boys having a game together up in the woods."

He was out early the following morning. As he passed the cottage, he noted out of the tail of his eye that the girl was out in the garden again weeding. Evidently a habit of hers. He did a particularly good approach shot, and hoped that she had noticed it. As he teed up on the next tee, he glanced at his watch.

"Just five and twenty past seven," he murmured. "I wonder——"

The words were frozen on his lips. From behind him came the same cry which had so startled him before. A woman's voice, in dire distress.

"Murder—help, murder!"

Jack raced back. The pansy girl was standing by the gate. She looked startled, and Jack ran up to her triumphantly, crying out:

"You heard it this time, anyway."

Her eyes were wide with some emotion he could not fathom but he noticed that she shrank back from him as he approached, and even glanced back at the house, as though she meditated running to it for shelter.

She shook her head, staring at him.

"I heard nothing at all," she said wonderingly.

It was as though she had struck him a blow between the eyes. Her sincerity was so evident that he could not disbelieve her. Yet he couldn't have imagined it—he couldn't—he couldn't——

He heard her voice speaking gently—almost with sympathy.

"You have had the shell-shock, yes?"

In a flash he understood her look of fear, her glance back at the house. She thought that he suffered from delusions. . . .

And then, like a douche of cold water, came the horrible thought, was she right? Did he suffer from delusions? Obsessed by the horror of the thought, he turned and stumbled away without vouchsafing a word. The girl watched him go, sighed, shook her head, and bent down to her weeding again.

Jack endeavored to reason matters out with himself. "If I hear the damned thing again, at twenty-five minutes past seven," he said to himself, "it's clear that I've got hold of a hallucination of some sort. But I won't hear it."

He was nervous all day, and went to bed early, determined to put the matter to the proof the following morning.

As was perhaps natural in such a case, he remained awake half the night and finally overslept himself. It was twenty past seven by the time he was clear of the hotel and running towards the links. He realized that he would not be able to get to the fatal spot by twenty-five past, but surely, if the voice were a hallucination pure and simple, he would hear it anywhere. He ran on, his eyes fixed on the hands of his watch.

Twenty-five past. From far off came the echo of a woman's voice, calling. The words could not be distinguished, but he was convinced that it was the same cry he had heard before, and that it came from the same spot, somewhere in the neighborhood of the cottage.

Strangely enough, that fact reassured him. It might, after all, be a hoax. Unlikely as it seemed, the girl herself might be playing a trick on him. He set his shoulders resolutely, and took out a club from his golf bag. He would play the few holes up to the cottage.

The girl was in the garden as usual. She looked up this morning, and when he raised his cap to her, said good morning rather shyly. . . . She looked, he thought, lovelier than ever.

"Nice day, isn't it?" Jack called out cheerily, cursing the unavoidable banality of the observation.

"Yes, indeed, it is lovely."

"Good for the garden, I expect?"

The girl smiled a little, disclosing a fascinating dimple.

"Alas, no! For my flowers the rain is needed. See, they are all dried up."

Jack accepted the invitation of her gesture, and came up to the low hedge dividing the garden from the course, looking over it into the garden.

"They seem all right," he remarked awkwardly, conscious as he spoke of the girl's slightly pitying glance running over him.

"The sun is good, is it not?" she said. "For the flowers one can always water them. But the sun gives strength and repairs the health. Monsieur is much better today, I can see."

Her encouraging tone annoyed Jack intensely.

"Curse it all," he said to himself. "I believe she's trying to cure me by suggestion.

"I'm perfectly well," he said irritably.

"That is good then," returned the girl, quickly and soothingly.

Jack had the irritating feeling that she didn't believe him.

He played a few more holes and hurried back to breakfast. As he ate it, he was conscious, not for the first time, of the close scrutiny of a man who sat at the table next to him. He was a man of middle-age, with a powerful, forceful face. He had a small dark beard and very piercing gray eyes, and an ease and assurance of manner which placed him among the higher ranks of the professional classes. His name, Jack knew, was Lavington, and he had heard vague rumors as to his being a well-known medical specialist, but as Jack was not a frequenter of Harley Street, the name had conveyed little or nothing to him.

But this morning he was very conscious of the quiet observation under which he was being kept, and it frightened him a little. Was his secret written plainly in his face for all to see? Did this man, by reason of his professional calling, know that there was something amiss in the hidden gray matter?

Jack shivered at the thought. Was it true? Was he really going mad? Was the whole thing a hallucination, or was it a gigantic hoax?

And suddenly a very simple way of testing the solution occurred to him. He had hitherto been alone on his round. Supposing someone else was with him? Then one out of three things might happen. The voice might be silent. They might both hear it. Or—he only might hear it.

That evening he proceeded to carry his plan into effect. Lavington was the man he wanted with him. They fell into conversation easily enough—the older man might have been waiting for such an opening. It was clear that for some reason or other Jack interested him. The latter was able to come quite easily and naturally to the suggestion that they might play a few holes together before breakfast. The arrangement was made for the following morning.

They started out a little before seven. It was a perfect day, still and cloudless, but not too warm. The doctor was playing well, Jack wretchedly. His whole mind was intent on the forthcoming crisis. He kept glancing surreptitiously at his watch. They reached the seventh tee, between which and the hole the cottage was situated, about twenty past seven.

The girl, as usual, was in the garden as they passed. She did not look up as they passed.

The two balls lay on the green, Jack's near the hole, the doctor's some little distance away.

"I've got this for it," said Lavington. "I must go for it, I suppose."

He bent down, judging the line he should take. Jack stood rigid, his eyes glued on his watch. It was exactly twenty-five minutes past seven.

The ball ran swiftly along the grass, stopped on the edge of the hole, hesitated, and dropped in.

"Good putt," said Jack. His voice sounded hoarse

and unlike himself. . . . He shoved his wrist watch farther up his arm with a sigh of overwhelming relief.
Nothing had happened. The spell was broken.

"If you don't mind waiting a minute," he said, "I
think I'll have a pipe."

They paused a while on the eighth tee. Jack filled
and lit the pipe with fingers that trembled a little in
spite of himself. An enormous weight seemed to have
lifted from his mind.

"Lord, what a good day it is," he remarked, staring
at the prospect ahead of him with great contentment.

"Go on, Lavington, your swipe."

And then it came. Just at the very instant the doctor
was hitting. A woman's voice, high and agonized.

"Murder—Help! Murder!"

The pipe fell from Jack's nerveless hand, as he
spun round in the direction of the sound, and then,
remembering, gazed breathlessly at his companion.

Lavington was looking down the course, shading
his eyes.

"A bit short—just cleared the bunker, though, I
think."

He had heard nothing.

The world seemed to spin round with Jack. He
took a step or two, lurching heavily. When he recovered himself, he was lying on the short turf, and Lavington was bending over him.

"There, take it easy now, take it easy."

"What did I do?"

"You fainted, young man—or gave a very good
try at it."

"My God!" said Jack, and groaned.

"What's the trouble? Something on your mind?"

"I'll tell you in one minute, but I'd like to ask you something first."

The doctor lit his own pipe and settled himself on the bank.

"Ask anything you like," he said comfortably.

"You've been watching me for the last day or two. Why?"

Lavington's eyes twinkled a little.

"That's rather an awkward question. A cat can look at a king, you know."

"Don't put me off. I'm in earnest. Why was it? I've a vital reason for asking."

Lavington's face grew serious.

"I'll answer you quite honestly. I recognized in you all the signs of a man laboring under a sense of acute strain, and it intrigued me what that strain could be."

"I can tell you that easily enough," said Jack bitterly. "I'm going mad."

He stopped dramatically, but his statement not seeming to arouse the interest and consternation he expected, he repeated it.

"I tell you I'm going mad."

"Very curious," murmured Lavington. "Very curious indeed."

Jack felt indignant.

"I suppose that's all it does seem to you. Doctors are so damned callous."

"Come, come, my young friend, you're talking at random. To begin with, although I have taken my degree, I do not practice medicine. Strictly speaking, I am not a doctor—not a doctor of the body, that is."

Jack looked at him keenly.

"Of the mind?"

"Yes, in a sense, but more truly I call myself a doctor of the soul."

"Oh!"

"I perceive the disparagement in your tone, and yet we must use some word to denote the active principle which can be separated and exist independently of its fleshy home, the body. You've got to come to terms with the soul, you know, young man; it isn't just a religious term invented by clergymen. But we'll call it the mind, or the subconscious self, or any term that suits you better. You took offense at my tone just now, but I can assure you that it really did strike me as very curious that such a well-balanced and perfectly normal young man as yourself should suffer from the delusion that he was going out of his mind."

"I'm out of my mind all right. Absolutely balmy."

"You will forgive me for saying so, but I don't believe it."

"I suffer from delusions."

"After dinner?"

"No, in the morning."

"Can't be done," said the doctor, relighting his pipe which had gone out.

"I tell you I hear things that no one else hears."

"One man in a thousand can see the moons of Jupiter. Because the other nine hundred and ninety-nine can't see them there's no reason to doubt that the moons of Jupiter exist, and certainly no reason for calling the thousandth man a lunatic."

"The moons of Jupiter are a proved scientific fact."

"It's quite possible that the delusions of today may be the proved scientific facts of tomorrow."

In spite of himself, Lavington's matter-of-fact

manner was having its effect upon Jack. He felt immeasurably soothed and cheered. The doctor looked at him attentively for a minute or two and then nodded.

"That's better," he said. "The trouble with you young fellows is that you're so cocksure nothing can exist outside your own philosophy that you get the wind up when something occurs to jolt you out of that opinion. Let's hear your grounds for believing that you're going mad, and we'll decide whether or not to lock you up afterwards."

As faithfully as he could, Jack narrated the whole series of occurrences.

"But what I can't understand," he ended, "is why this morning it should come at half-past seven—five minutes late."

Lavington thought for a minute or two. Then——

"What's the time now by your watch?" he asked.

"Quarter to eight," replied Jack, consulting it.

"That's simple enough, then. Mine says twenty to eight. Your watch is five minutes fast. That's a very interesting and important point—to me. In fact, it's invaluable."

"In what way?"

Jack was beginning to get interested.

"Well, the obvious explanation is that on the first morning you *did* hear some such cry—may have been a joke, may not. On the following mornings, you suggestioned yourself to hear it exactly the same time."

"I'm sure I didn't."

"Not consciously, of course, but the subconscious plays us some funny tricks, you know. But, anyway, that explanation won't wash. If it were a case of suggestion, you would have heard the cry at twenty-five minutes past seven by your watch, and you could never have heard it when the time, as you thought, was past."

"Well, then?"

"Well—it's obvious, isn't it? This cry for help occupies a perfectly definite place and time in space. The place is the vicinity of that cottage and the time is twenty-five minutes past seven."

"Yes, but why should I be the one to hear it? I don't believe in ghosts and all that spook stuff—spirits rapping and all the rest of it. Why should I hear the damned thing?"

"Ah! that we can't tell at present. It's a curious thing that many of the best mediums are made out of confirmed sceptics. It isn't the people who are interested in occult phenomena who get the manifestations. Some people see and hear things that other people don't—we don't know why, and nine times out of ten they don't want to see or hear them, and are convinced that they are suffering from delusions—just as you were. It's like electricity. Some substances are good conductors, and for a long time we didn't know why, and had to be content just to accept the fact. Nowadays we do know why. Some day, no doubt, we shall know why you hear this thing and I and the girl don't. Everything's governed by natural law, you know—there's no such thing really as the supernatural. Finding out the laws that govern so-called psychic phenomena is going to be a tough job—but every little helps."

"But what am I going to do?" asked Jack.

Lavington chuckled.

"Practical, I see. Well, my young friend, you are going to have a good breakfast and get off to the city without worrying your head further about things you don't understand. I, on the other hand, am going to poke about, and see what I can find out about that cottage back there. That's where the mystery centers, I dare swear."

Jack rose to his feet.

"Right, sir. I'm on, but, I say——"

"Yes?"

Jack flushed awkwardly.

"I'm sure the girl's all right," he muttered.

Lavington looked amused.

"You didn't tell me she was a pretty girl! Well, cheer up, I think the mystery started before her time."

Jack arrived home that evening in a perfect fever of curiosity. He was by now pinning his faith blindly to Lavington. The doctor had accepted the matter so naturally, had been so matter-of-fact and unperturbed by it, that Jack was impressed.

He found his new friend waiting for him in the hall when he came down for dinner, and the doctor suggested that they should dine together at the same table.

"Any news, sir?" asked Jack anxiously.

"I've collected the life history of Heather Cottage all right. It was tenanted first by an old gardener and his wife. The old man died, and the old woman went to her daughter. Then a builder got hold of it, and modernized it with great success, selling it to a city gentleman who used it for week ends. About a year ago, he sold it to some people called Turner—Mr. and Mrs. Turner. They seem to have been rather a curious couple from all I can make out. He was an Englishman, his wife was popularly supposed to be partly Russian, and was a very handsome, exotic-looking woman. They lived very quietly, seeing no one, and hardly ever going outside the cottage garden. The local rumor goes that they were afraid of something—but I don't think we ought to rely on that.

"And then suddenly one day they departed, cleared out one morning early, and never came back. The agents here got a letter from Mr. Turner, written from London, instructing him to sell the place as quickly as possible. The furniture was sold off, and the house itself was sold to a Mr. Mauleverer. He only actually lived in it a fortnight—then he advertised it to be let furnished. The people who have it now are a consumptive French professor and his daughter. They have been there just ten days."

Jack digested this in silence.

"I don't see that that gets us any forrader," he said at last. "Do you?"

"I rather want to know more about the Turners," said Lavington quietly. "They left very early in the morning, you remember. As far as I can make out, nobody actually saw them go. Mr. Turner has been seen since—but I can't find anybody who has seen Mrs. Turner."

Jack paled.

"It can't be—you don't mean——"

"Don't excite yourself, young man. The influence of anyone at the point of death—and especially of violent death—upon their surroundings is very strong. Those surroundings might conceivably absorb that influence, transmitting it in turn to a suitably tuned receiver—in this case yourself."

"But why me?" murmured Jack rebelliously. "Why not someone who could do some good?"

"You are regarding the force as intelligent and purposeful, instead of blind and mechanical. I do not believe myself in earth-bound spirits, haunting a spot for one particular purpose. But the thing I have seen, again and again, until I can hardly believe it to be pure coincidence, is a kind of blind groping towards justice—a subterranean moving of blind forces, always working obscurely towards that end. . . ."

He shook himself, as though casting off some obsession that preoccupied him, and turned to Jack with a ready smile.

"Let us banish the subject—for tonight at all events," he suggested.

Jack agreed readily enough, but did not find it so easy to banish the subject from his own mind.

During the week end, he made vigorous inquiries of his own, but succeeded in eliciting little more than the doctor had done. He had definitely given up playing golf before breakfast.

The next link in the chain came from an unexpected quarter. On getting back one day, Jack was informed that a young lady was waiting to see him. To his intense surprise it proved to be the girl of the garden—the pansy girl, as he always called her in his own mind. She was very nervous and confused.

"You will forgive me, Monsieur, for coming to seek you like this? But there is something I want to tell you—I——"

She looked around uncertainly.

"Come in here," said Jack promptly, leading the way into the now deserted "Ladies' Drawing-room" of the hotel, a dreary apartment, with a good deal of red plush about it. "Now, sit down, Miss, Miss——"

"Marchaud, Monsieur. Felise Marchaud."

"Sit down, Mademoiselle Marchaud, and tell me all about it."

Felise sat down obediently. She was dressed in dark green today, and the beauty and charm of the proud little face was more evident than ever. Jack's heart beat faster as he sat down beside her.

"It is like this," explained Felise. "We have been here but a short time, and from the beginning we hear the house—our so sweet little house—is haunted. No servant will stay in it. That does not matter so much— me, I can do the *ménage* and cook easily enough."

"Angel," thought the infatuated young man. "She's wonderful."

But he maintained an outward semblance of business-like attention.

"This talk of ghosts, I think it is all folly—that is until four days ago. Monsieur, four nights running, I have had the same dream. A lady stands there—she is beautiful, tall and very fair. In her hands she holds a blue china jar. She is distressed—very distressed, and continually she holds out the jar to me, as though imploring me to do something with it. But alas! she cannot speak, and I—I do not know what she asks. That was the dream for the first two nights—but the night before last, there was more of it. She and the blue jar faded away, and suddenly I heard her voice crying out—I know it is her voice, you comprehend— and, oh! Monsieur, the words she says are those you spoke to me that morning. 'Murder—help! Murder!' I awoke in terror. I say to myself—it is a nightmare, the words you heard are an accident. But last night the dream came again. Monsieur, what is it? You too have heard. What shall we do?"

Felise's face was terrified. Her small hands clasped themselves together, and she gazed appealingly at Jack. The latter affected an unconcern he did not feel.

"That's all right, Mademoiselle Marchaud. You mustn't worry. I tell you what I'd like you to do, if you don't mind. Repeat the whole story to a friend of mine who is staying here, a Dr. Lavington."

Felise signified her willingness to adopt this course, and Jack went off in search of Lavington. He returned with him a few minutes later.

Lavington gave the girl a keen scrutiny as he acknowledged Jack's hurried introductions. With a few reassuring words, he soon put the girl at her ease, and he, in his turn, listened attentively to her story.

"Very curious," he said, when she had finished. "You have told your father this?"

Felise shook her head.

"I have not liked to worry him. He is very ill still"—her eyes filled with tears—"I keep from him anything that might excite or agitate him."

"I understand," said Lavington kindly. "And I am glad you came to us, Mademoiselle Marchaud. Hartington here, as you know, had an experience something similar to yours. I think I may say that we are well on the track now. There is nothing else that you can think of?"

Felise gave a quick movement.

"Of course! How stupid I am. It is the point of the

whole story. Look, Monsieur, at what I found at the back of one of the cupboards where it had slipped behind the shelf."

She held out to them a dirty piece of drawing-paper on which was executed roughly in water colors a sketch of a woman. It was a mere daub, but the likeness was probably good enough. It represented a tall fair woman, with something subtly un-English in her face. She was standing by a table on which was standing a blue china jar.

"I only found it this morning," explained Felise. "Monsieur le docteur, that is the face of the woman I saw in my dream, and that is the identical blue jar."

"Extraordinary," commented Lavington. "The key to the mystery is evidently the blue jar. It looks like a Chinese jar to me, probably an old one. It seems to have a curious raised pattern over it."

"It is Chinese," declared Jack. "I have seen an exactly similar one in my uncle's collection—he is a great collector of Chinese porcelain, you know, and I remember noticing a jar just like this a short time ago."

"The Chinese jar," mused Lavington. He remained a minute or two lost in thought, then raised his head suddenly, a curious light shining in his eyes. "Hartington, how long has your uncle had that jar?"

"How long? I really don't know."

"Think. Did he buy it lately?"

"I don't know—yes, I believe he did, now I come to think of it. I'm not very interested in porcelain myself, but I remember his showing me his 'recent acquisitions,' and this was one of them."

"Less than two months ago? The Turners left Heather Cottage just two months ago."

"Yes, I believe it was."

"Your uncle attends country sales sometimes?"

"He's always tooling round to sales."

"Then there is no inherent improbability in our assuming that he bought this particular piece of porcelain at the sale of the Turners' things. A curious coincidence—or perhaps what I call the groping of blind justice. Hartington, you must find out from your uncle at once where he bought this jar."

Jack's face fell.

"I'm afraid that's impossible. Uncle George is away on the Continent. I don't even know where to write to him."

"How long will he be away?"

"Three weeks to a month at least."

There was a silence. Felise sat looking anxiously from one man to the other.

"Is there nothing that we can do?" she asked timidly.

"Yes, there is one thing," said Lavington, in a tone of suppressed excitement. "It is unusual, perhaps, but I believe that it will succeed. Hartington, you must get hold of that jar. Bring it down here and, if Mademoiselle permits, we will spend a night in Heather Cottage, taking the blue jar with us."

Jack felt his skin creep uncomfortably.

"What do you think will happen?" he asked uneasily.

"I have not the slightest idea—but I honestly believe that the mystery will be solved and the ghost laid. Quite possibly there may be a false bottom to the jar and something is concealed inside it. If no phenomenon occurs, we must use our own ingenuity."

Felise clasped her hands.

"It is a wonderful idea," she exclaimed.

Her eyes were alight with enthusiasm. Jack did not feel nearly so enthusiastic—in fact, he was inwardly funking it badly, but nothing would have induced him to admit the fact before Felise. The doctor acted as though his suggestion were the most natural one in the world.

"When can you get the jar?" asked Felise, turning to Jack.

"Tomorrow," said the latter, unwillingly.

He had to go through with it now, but the memory of that frenzied cry for help that had haunted him each morning was something to be ruthlessly thrust down and not thought about more than could be helped.

He went to his uncle's house the following evening, and took away the jar in question. He was more than ever convinced when he saw it again that it was the identical one pictured in the water color sketch, but carefully as he looked it over he could see no sign that it contained a secret receptacle of any kind.

It was eleven o'clock when he and Lavington arrived at Heather Cottage. Felise was on the lookout for them, and opened the door softly before they had time to knock.

"Come in," she whispered. "My father is asleep upstairs, and we must not wake him. I have made coffee for you in here."

She led the way into a small cosy sitting-room. A spirit lamp stood in the grate, and bending over it, she brewed them both some fragrant coffee.

Then Jack unfastened the Chinese jar from its many wrappings. Felise gasped as her eyes fell on it.

"But yes, but yes," she cried eagerly. "That is it—I would know it anywhere."

Meanwhile Lavington was making his own preparations. He removed all the ornaments from a small table and set it in the middle of the room. Round it he placed three chairs. Then, taking the blue jar from Jack, he placed it in the center of the table.

"Now," he said, "we are ready. Turn off the lights, and let us sit round the table in the darkness."

The others obeyed him. Lavington's voice spoke again out of the darkness.

"Think of nothing—or of everything. Do not force the mind. It is possible that one of us has mediumistic powers. If so, that person will go into a trance. Remember, there is nothing to fear. Cast out fear from your hearts, and drift—drift——"

His voice died away and there was silence. Minute by minute, the silence seemed to grow more pregnant with possibilities. It was all very well for Lavington to say "Cast out fear." It was not fear that Jack felt— it was panic. And he was almost certain that Felise felt the same way. Suddenly he heard her voice, low and terrified.

"Something terrible is going to happen. I feel it."

"Cast out fear," said Lavington. "Do not fight against the influence."

The darkness seemed to get darker and the silence more acute. And nearer and nearer came that indefinable sense of menace.

Jack felt himself choking—stifling—the evil thing was very near. . . .

And then the moment of conflict passed. He was drifting—drifting downstream—his lids closed—peace—darkness. . . .

Jack stirred slightly. His head was heavy—heavy as lead. Where was he?

Sunshine . . . birds. . . . He lay staring up at the sky.

Then it all came back to him. The sitting. The little room. Felise and the doctor. What had happened?

He sat up, his head throbbing unpleasantly, and looked round him. He was lying in a little copse not far from the cottage. No one else was near him. He took out his watch. To his amazement it registered half-past twelve.

Jack struggled to his feet, and ran as fast as he could in the direction of the cottage. They must have been alarmed by his failure to come out of the trance, and carried him out into the open air.

Arrived at the cottage, he knocked loudly on the door. But there was no answer, and no signs of life about it. They must have gone off to get help. Or else—Jack felt an indefinable fear invade him. What had happened last night?

He made his way back to the hotel as quickly as possible. He was about to make some inquiries at the office, when he was diverted by a colossal punch in the ribs which nearly knocked him off his feet. Turning in some indignation, he beheld a white-haired old gentleman wheezing with mirth.

"Didn't expect me, my boy. Didn't expect me, hey?" said this individual.

"Why, Uncle George, I thought you were miles away—in Italy somewhere."

"Ah! but I wasn't. Landed at Dover last night. Thought I'd motor up to town and stop here to see you on the way. And what did I find. Out all night, hey? Nice goings on——"

"Uncle George," Jack checked him firmly. "I've got the most extraordinary story to tell you. I dare say you won't believe it."

He narrated the whole story.

"And God knows what's become of them," he ended.

His uncle seemed on the verge of apoplexy.

"The jar," he managed to ejaculate at last. "THE BLUE JAR! What's become of that?"

Jack stared at him in non-comprehension, but submerged in the torrent of words that followed he began to understand.

It came with a rush: "Ming—unique—gem of my collection—worth ten thousand pounds at least—offer from Hoggenheimer, the American millionaire—only one of its kind in the world.—Confound it, sir, what have you done with my BLUE JAR?"

Jack rushed to the office. He must find Lavington. The young lady in the office eyed him coldly.

"Dr. Lavington left late last night—by motor. He left a note for you."

Jack tore it open. It was short and to the point.

MY DEAR YOUNG FRIEND:
Is the day of the supernatural over? Not quite—especially when tricked out in new scientific lan-

guage. Kindest regards from Felise, invalid father,
and myself. We have twelve hours start, which
ought to be ample.

> Yours ever,
> Ambrose Lavington,
> Doctor of the Soul

SING A SONG OF SIXPENCE

Sir Edward Palliser, K. C., lived at No. 9 Queen Anne's Close. Queen Anne's Close is a cul-de-sac. In the very heart of Westminster it manages to have a peaceful Old World atmosphere far removed from the turmoil of the twentieth century. It suited Sir Edward Palliser admirably.

Sir Edward had been one of the most eminent criminal barristers of his day and now that he no longer practiced at the bar he had amused himself by amassing a very fine criminological library. He was also the author of a volume of Reminiscences of Eminent Criminals.

On this particular evening Sir Edward was sitting in front of his library fire, sipping some very excellent black coffee and shaking his head over a volume of Lombroso. Such ingenious theories and so completely out of date!

The door opened almost noiselessly and his well-trained manservant approached over the thick pile carpet, and murmured discreetly:

"A young lady wishes to see you, sir."

"A young lady?"

Sir Edward was surprised. Here was something

quite out of the usual course of events. Then he reflected that it might be his niece, Ethel—but no, in that case Armour would have said so.

He inquired cautiously. "The lady did not give her name?"

"No, sir, but she said she was quite sure you would wish to see her."

"Show her in," said Sir Edward Palliser. He felt pleasurably intrigued.

A tall, dark girl of close on thirty, wearing a black coat and skirt, well cut, and a little black hat, came to Sir Edward with outstretched hand and a look of eager recognition on her face. Armour withdrew, closing the door noiselessly behind him.

"Sir Edward—you do know me, don't you? I'm Magdalen Vaughan."

"Why, of course." He pressed the outstretched hand warmly.

He remembered her perfectly now. That trip home from America on the *Siluric!* This charming child—for she had been little more than a child. He had made love to her, he remembered, in a discreet, elderly man-of-the-world fashion. She had been so adorably young—so eager—so full of admiration and hero-worship—just made to captivate the heart of a man near sixty. The remembrance brought additional warmth into the pressure of his hand.

"This is most delightful of you. Sit down, won't you." He arranged an armchair for her, talking easily and evenly, wondering all the time why she had come. When at last he brought the easy flow of small talk to an end, there was a silence.

Her hand closed and unclosed on the arm of the

chair, she moistened her lips. Suddenly she spoke—abruptly.

"Sir Edward—I want you to help me."

He was surprised and murmured mechanically: "Yes?"

She went on, speaking more intensely: "You said that if ever I needed help—that if there were anything in the world you could do for me—you would do it."

Yes, he had said that. It was the sort of thing one did say—particularly at the moment of parting. He could recall the break in his voice—the way he had raised her hand to his lips.

"If there is ever anything I can do—remember, I mean it. . . ."

Yes, one said that sort of thing. . . . But very, very rarely did one have to fulfil one's words! And certainly not after—how many?—nine or ten years. He flashed a quick glance at her—she was still a very good-looking girl, but she had lost what had been to him her charm—that look of dewy untouched youth. It was a more interesting face now, perhaps—a younger man might have thought so—but Sir Edward was far from feeling the tide of warmth and emotion that had been his at the end of that Atlantic voyage.

His face became legal and cautious. He said in a rather brisk way: "Certainly, my dear young lady, I shall be delighted to do anything in my power—though I doubt if I can be very helpful to anyone in these days."

If he were preparing his way of retreat she did not notice it. She was of the type that can only see one thing at a time and what she was seeing at this moment was her own need. She took Sir Edward's willingness to help for granted.

"We are in terrible trouble, Sir Edward."

"We? You are married?"

"No—I meant my brother and I. Oh, and William and Emily, too, for that matter. But I must explain. I have—I had an aunt—Miss Crabtree. You may have read about her in the papers? It was horrible. She was killed—murdered."

"Ah!" A flash of interest lit up Sir Edward's face. "About a month ago, wasn't it?"

The girl nodded. "Rather less than that—three weeks."

"Yes, I remember. She was hit on the head in her own house. They didn't get the fellow who did it."

Again Magdalen Vaughan nodded. "They didn't get the man—I don't believe they ever will get the man. You see—there mightn't be any man to get."

"What?"

"Yes—it's awful. Nothing's come out about it in the papers. But that's what the police think. They know nobody came to the house that night."

"You mean—?"

"That it's one of us four. It must be. They don't know which—and we don't know which. . . . We don't know. And we sit there every day looking at each other surreptitiously and wondering. Oh! if only it could have been someone from outside—but I don't see how it can . . ."

Sir Edward stared at her, his interest rising.

"You mean that the members of the family are under suspicion?"

"Yes, that's what I mean. The police haven't said

so, of course. They've been quite polite and nice. But they've ransacked the house, they've questioned us all, and Martha again and again. . . . And because they don't know which, they're holding their hand. I'm so frightened—so horribly frightened. . . ."

"My dear child. Come now, surely you are exaggerating."

"I'm not. It's one of us four—it must be."

"Who are the four to whom you refer?"

Magdalen sat up straight and spoke more composedly.

"There's myself and Matthew. Aunt Lily was our great aunt. She was my grandmother's sister. We've lived with her ever since we were fourteen (we're twins, you know). Then there was William Crabtree. He was her nephew—her brother's child. He lived there, too, with his wife, Emily."

"She supported them?"

"More or less. He has a little money of his own, but he's not strong and has to live at home. He's a quiet, dreamy sort of man. I'm sure it would have been impossible for him to have—oh! it's awful of me to think of it even!"

"I am still very far from understanding the position. Perhaps you would not mind running over the facts—if it does not distress you too much."

"Oh, no! I want to tell you. And it's all quite clear in my mind still—horribly clear. We'd had tea, you understand, and we'd all gone off to do things of our own. I to do some dressmaking, Matthew to type an article—he does a little journalism; William to do his stamps. Emily hadn't been down to tea. She'd taken a headache powder and was lying down. So there we were, all of us, busy and occupied. And when Martha went in to lay supper at half-past seven, there Aunt Lily was—dead. Her head—oh, it's horrible!—all crushed in."

"The weapon was found, I think?"

"Yes. It was a heavy paper weight that always lay on the table by the door. The police tested it for fingerprints, but there were none. It had been wiped clean."

"And your first surmise?"

"We thought, of course, it was a burglar. There were two or three drawers of the bureau pulled out, as though a thief had been looking for something. Of course we thought it was a burglar! And then the police came—and they said she had been dead at least an hour, and asked Martha who had been to the house, and Martha said nobody. And all the windows were fastened on the inside, and there seemed no signs of anything having been tampered with. And then they began to ask us questions . . ."

She stopped. Her breast heaved. Her eyes, frightened and imploring, sought Sir Edward's in search of reassurance.

"For instance, who benefited by your aunt's death?"

"That's simple. We all benefit equally. She left her money to be divided in equal shares among the four of us."

"And what was the value of her estate?"

"The lawyer told us it will come to about eighty thousand pounds after the death duties are paid."

Sir Edward opened his eyes in some slight surprise.

"That is quite a considerable sum. You knew, I

suppose, the total of your aunt's fortune?"

Magdalen shook her head.

"No—it came quite as a surprise to us. Aunt Lily was always terribly careful about money. She kept just the one servant and always talked a lot about economy."

Sir Edward nodded thoughtfully. Magdalen leaned forward a little in her chair.

"You will help me—you will?"

Her words came to Sir Edward as an unpleasant shock just at the moment when he was becoming interested in her story for its own sake.

"My dear young lady—what can I possibly do? If you want good legal advice, I can give you the name—"

She interrupted him. "Oh! I don't want that sort of thing! I want you to help me personally—as a friend."

"That's very charming of you, but—"

"I want you to come to our house. I want you to ask questions. I want you to see and judge for yourself."

"But my dear young—"

"Remember, you promised. Anywhere—any time— you said, if I wanted help . . ."

Her eyes, pleading yet confident, looked into his. He felt ashamed and strangely touched. That terrific sincerity of hers, that absolute belief in an idle promise, ten years old, as a sacred binding thing. How many men had not said those self-same words—a cliché almost!—and how few of them had ever been called upon to make good.

He said rather weakly: "I'm sure there are many people who would advise you better than I could."

"I've got lots of friends—naturally." (He was amused by the naive self-assurance of that.) "But, you see, none of them are clever. Not like you. You're used to questioning people. And with all your experience you must know."

"Know what?"

"Whether they're innocent or guilty."

He smiled rather grimly to himself. He flattered himself that, on the whole, he usually had known! Though, on many occasions, his private opinion had not been that of the jury.

Magdalen pushed back her hat from her forehead with a nervous gesture, looked round the room, and said: "How quiet it is here. Don't you sometimes long for some noise?"

The cul-de-sac! All unwittingly her words, spoken at random, touched him on the raw. A cul-de-sac. Yes, but there was always a way out—the way you had come—the way back into the world. . . . Something impetuous and youthful stirred in him. Her simple trust appealed to the best side of his nature—and the condition of her problem appealed to something else—the innate criminologist in him. He wanted to see these people of whom she spoke. He wanted to form his own judgment.

He said: "If you are really convinced I can be of any use. . . . Mind, I guarantee nothing."

He expected her to be overwhelmed with delight, but she took it very calmly.

"I knew you would do it. I've always thought of you as a real friend. Will you come back with me now?"

"No. I think if I pay you a visit tomorrow it will

be more satisfactory. Will you give me the name and address of Miss Crabtree's lawyer? I may want to ask him a few questions."

She wrote it down and handed it to him. Then she got up and said rather shyly: "I—I'm really most awfully grateful. Good-bye."

"And your own address?"

"How stupid of me. 18 Palatine Walk, Chelsea."

It was three o'clock on the following afternoon when Sir Edward Palliser approached the 18 Palatine Walk with a sober, measured tread. In the interval he had found out several things. He had paid a visit that morning to Scotland Yard, where the Assistant Commissioner was an old friend of his, and he had also had an interview with the late Miss Crabtree's lawyer. As a result he had a clearer vision of the circumstances. Miss Crabtree's arrangements in regard to money had been somewhat peculiar. She never made use of a check book. Instead she was in the habit of writing to her lawyer and asking him to have a certain sum in five-pound notes waiting for her. It was nearly always the same sum. Three hundred pounds four times a year. She came to fetch it herself in a four-wheeler, which she regarded as the only safe means of conveyance. At other times she never left the house.

At Scotland Yard Sir Edward learned that the question of finance had been gone into very carefully. Miss Crabtree had been almost due for her next instalment of money. Presumably the previous three hundred had been spent—or almost spent. But this was exactly the point that had not been easy to ascertain. By checking the household expenditure, it was soon evident that Miss Crabtree's expenditure per quarter fell a good deal short of the three hundred. On the other hand, she was in the habit of sending five-pound notes to needy friends and relatives. Whether there had been much or little money in the house at the time of her death was a debatable point. None had been found.

It was this particular point which Sir Edward was revolving in his mind as he approached Palatine Walk.

The door of the house (which was a non-basement one) was opened to him by a small elderly woman with an alert gaze. He was shown into a big double room on the left of the small hallway and there Magdalen came to him. More clearly than before, he saw the traces of nervous strain in her face.

"You told me to ask questions, and I have come to do so," said Sir Edward, smiling as he shook hands. "First of all, I want to know who last saw your aunt and exactly what time that was?"

"It was after tea—five o'clock. Martha was the last person with her. She had been paying the books that afternoon, and brought Aunt Lily the change and the accounts."

"You trust Martha?"

"Oh, absolutely. She was with Aunt Lily for—oh, thirty years, I suppose. She's honest as the day."

Sir Edward nodded.

"Another question. Why did your cousin, Mrs. Crabtree, take a headache powder?"

"Well, because she had a headache."

"Naturally, but was there any particular reason why she should have a headache?"

"Well, yes, in a way. There was rather a scene at lunch. Emily is very excitable and highly strung. She and Aunt Lily used to have rows sometimes."

"And they had one at lunch?"

"Yes. Aunt Lily was rather trying about little things. It all started out of nothing—and then they were at it hammer and tongs—with Emily saying all sorts of things she couldn't possibly have meant— that she'd leave the house and never come back— that she was grudged every mouthful she ate—oh, all sorts of silly things. And Aunt Lily said the sooner she and her husband packed their boxes and went the better. But it all meant nothing, really."

"Because Mr. and Mrs. Crabtree couldn't afford to pack up and go?"

"Oh, not only that. William was fond of Aunt Emily. He really was."

"It wasn't a day of quarrels, by any chance?"

Magdalen's color heightened.

"You mean me? The fuss about my wanting to be a manikin?"

"Your aunt wouldn't agree?"

"No."

"Why did you want to be a manikin, Miss Magdalen? Does the life strike you as a very attractive one?"

"No, but anything would be better than going on living here."

"Yes, then. But now you will have a comfortable income, won't you?"

"Oh, yes, it's quite different now."

She made the admission with the utmost simplicity.

He smiled but pursued the subject no further. Instead he said: "And your brother? Did he have a quarrel, too?"

"Matthew? Oh, no."

"Then no one can say he had a motive for wishing his aunt out of the way?"

He was quick to seize on the momentary dismay that showed in her face.

"I forgot," he said casually. "He owed a good deal of money, didn't he?"

"Yes; poor old Matthew."

"Still, that will be all right now."

"Yes—" She sighed. "It is a relief."

And still she saw nothing! He changed the subject hastily.

"Your cousins and your brother are at home?"

"Yes; I told them you were coming. They are all so anxious to help. Oh, Sir Edward—I feel, somehow, that you are going to find out that everything is all right—that none of us had anything to do with it— that, after all, it was an outsider."

"I can't do miracles. I may be able to find out the truth, but I can't make the truth be what you want it to be."

"Can't you? I feel that you could do anything— anything."

She left the room. He thought, disturbed, "What did she mean by that? Does she want me to suggest a line of defense? For whom?"

His meditations were interrupted by the entrance of a man about fifty years of age. He had a naturally powerful frame, but stooped slightly. His clothes were untidy and his hair carelessly brushed. He looked good-natured but vague.

"Sir Edward Palliser? Oh, how do you do? Magdalen sent me along, It's very good of you, I'm sure, to wish to help us, though I don't think anybody will ever be really discovered. I mean, they won't catch the fellow.

"You think it was a burglar, then—someone from outside?"

"Well, it must have been. It couldn't be one of the family. These fellows are very clever nowadays, they climb like cats and they get in and out as they like."

"Where were you, Mr. Crabtree, when the tragedy occurred?"

"I was busy with my stamps—in my little sitting-room upstairs."

"You didn't hear anything?"

"No—but then I never do hear anything when I'm absorbed. Very foolish of me, but there it is."

"Is the sitting-room you refer to over this room?"

"No, it's at the back."

Again the door opened. A small, fair woman entered. Her hands were twitching nervously. She looked fretful and excited.

"William, why didn't you wait for me? I said 'wait.' "

"Sorry, my dear, I forgot. Sir Edward Palliser—my wife."

"How do you do, Mrs. Crabtree? I hope you don't mind my coming here to ask a few questions. I know how anxious you must all be to have things cleared up."

"Naturally. But I can't tell you anything—can I, William? I was asleep—on my bed—I only woke up when Martha screamed."

Her hands continued to twitch.

"Where is your room, Mrs. Crabtree?"

"It's over this. But I didn't hear anything—how could I? I was asleep."

He could get nothing out of her but that. She knew nothing—she had heard nothing—she had been asleep. She reiterated it with the obstinacy of a frightened woman. Yet Sir Edward knew very well that it might easily be—probably was—the bare truth.

He excused himself at last—said he would like to put a few questions to Martha. William Crabtree volunteered to take him to the kitchen. In the hall Sir Edward nearly collided with a tall, dark young man who was striding towards the front door.

"Mr. Matthew Vaughan?"

"Yes—but, look here, I can't wait. I've got an appointment."

"Matthew!" It was his sister's voice from the stairs. "Oh, Matthew, you promised—"

"I know, sis. But I can't. Got to meet a fellow. And, anyway, what's the good of talking about the damned thing over and over again. We have enough of that with the police. I'm fed up with the whole show."

The front door banged. Mr. Matthew Vaughan had made his exit.

Sir Edward was introduced into the kitchen. Martha was ironing. She paused, iron in hand. Sir Edward shut the door behind him.

"Miss Vaughan has asked me to help her," he said.

"I hope you won't object to my asking you a few questions."

She looked at him, then shook her head.

"None of them did it, sir. I know what you're thinking, but it isn't so. As nice a set of ladies and gentlemen as you could wish to see."

"I've no doubt of it. But their niceness isn't what we call evidence, you know."

"Perhaps not, sir. The law's a funny thing. But there is evidence—as you call it, sir. None of them could have done it without my knowing."

"But surely—"

"I know what I'm talking about, sir. There, listen to that—"

"That" was a creaking sound above their heads.

"The stairs, sir. Every time anyone goes up or down, the stairs creak something awful. It doesn't matter how quiet you go. Mrs. Crabtree, she was lying on her bed, and Mr. Crabtree was fiddling about with them wretched stamps of his, and Miss Magdalen she was up above, working her sewing machine, and if any one of those three had come down the stairs I should have known it. And they didn't!"

She spoke with a positive assurance which impressed the barrister. He thought: "A good witness. She'd carry weight."

"You mightn't have noticed."

"Yes, I would. I'd have noticed without noticing, so to speak. Like you notice when a door shuts and somebody goes out."

Sir Edward shifted his ground.

"That is three of them accounted for, but there is a fourth. Was Mr. Matthew Vaughan upstairs also?"

"No, but he was in the little room downstairs. Next door. And he was typewriting. You can hear it plain in here. His machine never stopped for a moment. Not for a moment, sir. I can swear to it. A nasty, irritating tap-tapping noise it is, too."

Sir Edward paused a minute.

"It was you who found her, wasn't it?"

"Yes, sir, it was. Lying there with blood on her poor hair. And no one hearing a sound on account of the tap-tapping of Mr. Matthew's typewriter."

"I understand you are positive that no one came to the house?"

"How could they, sir, without my knowing? The bell rings in here. And there's only the one door."

He looked at her straight in the face.

"You were attached to Miss Crabtree?"

A warm glow—genuine—unmistakable—came into her face.

"Yes, indeed, I was, sir. But for Miss Crabtree— well, I'm getting on and I don't mind speaking of it now. I got into trouble, sir, when I was a girl, and Miss Crabtree stood by me—took me back into her service, she did, when it was all over. I'd have died for her—I would indeed."

Sir Edward knew sincerity when he heard it. Martha was sincere.

"As far as you know, no one came to the door—?"

"No one could have come."

"I said as far as you know. But if Miss Crabtree had been expecting someone—if she opened the door to that someone herself . . ."

"Oh!" Martha seemed taken back.

"That's possible, I suppose?" Sir Edward urged.

"It's possible—yes—but it isn't very likely. I mean . . ."

She was clearly taken aback. She couldn't deny and yet she wanted to do so. Why? Because she knew that the truth lay elsewhere. Was that it? The four people in the house—one of them guilty? Did Martha want to shield that guilty party? Had the stairs creaked? Had someone come stealthily down and did Martha know who that someone was?

She herself was honest—Sir Edward was convinced of that.

He pressed his point, watching her.

"Miss Crabtree might have done that, I suppose? The window of that room faces the street. She might have seen whoever it was she was waiting for from the window and gone out into the hall and let him—or her—in. She might even have wished that no one should see the person."

Martha looked troubled. She said at last reluctantly:

"Yes, you may be right, sir. I never thought of that. That she was expecting a gentleman—yes, it well might be."

It was as though she began to perceive advantages in the idea.

"You were the last person to see her, were you not?"

"Yes, sir. After I'd cleared away the tea. I took the receipted books to her and the change from the money she'd given me."

"Had she given the money to you in five-pound notes?"

"A five-pound note, sir," said Martha in a shocked voice. "The books never came up as high as five pounds. I'm very careful."

"Where did she keep her money?"

"I don't rightly know, sir. I should say that she carried it about with her—in her black velvet bag. But of course she may have kept it in one of the drawers in her bedroom that were locked. She was very fond of locking up things, though prone to lose her keys."

Sir Edward nodded. "You don't know how much money she had—in five-pound notes, I mean?"

"No, sir, I couldn't say what the exact amount was."

"And she said nothing to you that could lead you to believe that she was expecting anybody?"

"No, sir."

"You're quite sure? What exactly did she say?"

"Well," Martha considered, "she said the butcher was nothing more than a rogue and a cheat, and she said I'd had in a quarter of a pound of tea more than I ought, and she said Mrs. Crabtree was full of nonsense for not liking to eat margarine, and she didn't like one of the sixpences I'd brought her back—one of the new ones with oak leaves on it—she said it was bad, and I had a lot of trouble to convince her. And she said—oh, that the fishmonger had sent haddocks instead of whitings, and had I told him about it, and I said I had—and, really, I think that's all, sir."

Martha's speech had made the deceased lady loom clear to Sir Edward as a detailed description would never have done. He said casually: "Rather a difficult mistress to please, eh?"

"A bit fussy, but there, poor dear, she didn't often get out, and staying cooped up she had to have something to amuse herself like. She was pernickety but kindhearted—never a beggar sent away from the door without something. Fussy she may have been, but a real charitable lady."

"I am glad, Martha, that she leaves one person to regret her."

The old servant caught her breath.

"You mean—oh, but they were all fond of her—really—underneath. They all had words with her now and again, but it didn't mean anything."

Sir Edward lifted his head. There was a crack above.

"That's Miss Magdalen coming down."

"How do you know?" he shot at her.

The old woman flushed. "I know her step," she muttered.

Sir Edward left the kitchen rapidly. Martha had been right. Magdalen had just reached the bottom stair. She looked at him hopefully.

"Not very far on as yet," said Sir Edward, answering her look, and added, "You don't happen to know what letters your aunt received on the day of her death?"

"They are all together. The police have been through them, of course."

She led the way to the big double drawing-room and, unlocking a drawer, took out a large black velvet bag with an old-fashioned silver clasp.

"This is Aunt's bag. Everything is in here just as it was on the day of her death. I've kept it like that."

Sir Edward thanked her and proceeded to turn out

the contents of the bag on the table. It was, he fancied, a fair specimen of an eccentric elderly lady's handbag.

There were some odd silver change, two ginger nuts, three newspaper cuttings about Joanna Southcott's box, a trashy, printed poem about the unemployed, an *Old Moore's Almanack*, a large piece of camphor, some spectacles, and three letters. A spidery one from someone called "Cousin Lucy," a bill for mending a watch, and an appeal from a charitable institution.

Sir Edward went through everything very carefully, then repacked the bag and handed it to Magdalen with a sigh.

"Thank you, Miss Magdalen. I'm afraid there isn't much there."

He rose, observed that the window commanded a good view of the front door steps, then took Magdalen's hand in his.

"You are going?"

"Yes."

"But it's—it's going to be all right?"

"Nobody connected with the law ever commits himself to a rash statement like that," said Sir Edward solemnly, and made his escape.

He walked along the street, lost in thought. The puzzle was there under his hand—and he had not solved it. It needed something—some little thing. Just to point the way.

A hand fell on his shoulder and he started. It was Matthew Vaughan, somewhat out of breath.

"I've been chasing you, Sir Edward. I want to apologize. For my rotten manners half an hour ago. But

I've not got the best temper in the world, I'm afraid. It's awfully good of you to bother about this business. Please ask me whatever you like. If there's anything I can do to help—"

Suddenly Sir Edward stiffened. His glance was fixed—not on Matthew—but across the street. Somewhat bewildered, Matthew repeated: "If there's anything I can do to help—"

"You have already done it, my dear young man," said Sir Edward. "By stopping me at this particular spot and so fixing my attention on something I might otherwise have missed."

He pointed across the street to a small restaurant opposite.

"The Four and Twenty Blackbirds?" asked Matthew in a puzzled voice.

"Exactly."

"It's an odd name—but you get quite decent food there, I believe."

"I shall not take the risk of experimenting," said Sir Edward. "Being further from my nursery days than you are, my young friend, I probably remember my nursery rhymes better. There is a classic that runs thus, if I remember rightly: *Sing a song of sixpence, a pocket full of rye, Four and twenty blackbirds baked in a pie*—and so on. The rest of it does not concern us."

He wheeled round sharply.

"Where are you going?" asked Matthew Vaughan.

"Back to your house, my friend."

They walked there in silence, Matthew Vaughan shooting puzzled glances at his companion. Sir Edward entered, strode to a drawer, lifted out a velvet bag, and opened it. He looked at Matthew and the young man reluctantly left the room.

Sir Edward tumbled out the silver change on the table. Then he nodded. His memory had not been at fault.

He got up and rang the bell, slipping something into the palm of his hand as he did so.

Martha answered the bell.

"You told me, Martha, if I remember rightly, that you had a slight altercation with your late mistress over one of the new sixpences."

"Yes, sir."

"Ah! but the curious thing is, Martha, that among this loose change, there is no new sixpence. There are two sixpences, but they are both old ones."

She stared at him in a puzzled fashion.

"You see what that means? Someone did come to the house that evening—someone to whom your mistress gave sixpence. . . . I think she gave it to him in exchange for this. . . ."

With a swift movement he shot his hand forward, holding out the doggerel verse about unemployment.

One glance at her face was enough.

"The game is up, Martha—you see, I know. You may as well tell me everything."

She sank down on a chair—the tears raced down her face.

"It's true—it's true—the bell didn't ring properly—I wasn't sure, and then I thought I'd better go and see. I got to the door just as he struck her down. The roll of five-pound notes was on the table in front of her—it was the sight of them as made him do it—that and thinking she was alone in the house as she'd let him in. I couldn't scream. I was too paralyzed and then he turned—and I saw it was my boy. . . .

"Oh, he's been a bad one always. I gave him all the money I could. He's been in jail twice. He must have come around to see me, and then Miss Crabtree, seeing as I didn't answer the door, went to answer it herself, and he was taken aback and pulled out one of those unemployment leaflets, and the mistress being kind of charitable, told him to come in, and got out a sixpence. And all the time that roll of notes was lying on the table where it had been when I was giving her the change. And the devil got into my Ben and he got behind her and struck her down."

"And then?" asked Sir Edward.

"Oh, sir, what could I do? My own flesh and blood. His father was a bad one, and Ben takes after him— but he was my own son. I hustled him out, and I went back to the kitchen, and I went to lay for supper at the usual time. Do you think it was very wicked of me, sir? I tried to tell you no lies when you was asking me questions."

Sir Edward rose.

"My poor woman," he said with feeling in his voice. "I am very sorry for you. All the same, the law will have to take its course, you know."

"He's fled the country, sir. I don't know where he is."

"There's a chance, then, that he may escape the gallows, but don't build upon it. Will you send Miss Magdalen to me?"

"Oh, Sir Edward. How wonderful of you—how wonderful you are," said Magdalen when he had finished his brief recital. "You've saved us all. How can I ever thank you?"

Sir Edward smiled down at her and patted her hand gently. He was very much the great man. Little Magdalen had been very charming on the *Siluric*. That bloom of seventeen—wonderful! She had completely lost it now, of course.

"Next time you need a friend—" he said.

"I'll come straight to you."

"No, no," cried Sir Edward in alarm. "That's just what I don't want you to do. Go to a younger man."

He extricated himself with dexterity from the grateful household and hailing a taxi sank into it with a sigh of relief. Even the charm of a dewy seventeen seemed doubtful.

It could not really compare with a really well-stocked library on criminology.

The taxi turned into Queen Anne's Close.

His cul-de-sac.

THE MYSTERY OF THE SPANISH SHAWL

Mr. Eastwood looked at the ceiling. Then he looked down at the floor. From the floor his gaze traveled slowly up the right-hand wall. Then, with a sudden stern effort, he focused his gaze once more upon the typewriter before him.

The virgin white of the sheet of paper was defaced by a title written in capital letters.

"THE MYSTERY OF THE SECOND CUCUMBER," so it ran. A pleasing title. Anthony Eastwood felt that anyone reading that title would be at once intrigued and arrested by it. "The Mystery of the Second Cucumber," they would say. "What can that be about? A cucumber? The second cucumber? I must certainly read that story." And they would be thrilled and charmed by the consummate ease with which this master of detective fiction had woven an exciting plot round this simple vegetable.

That was all very well. Anthony Eastwood knew as well as anyone what the story ought to be like—the bother was that somehow or other he couldn't get on with it. The two essentials for a story were a title and a plot—the rest was mere spade-work; sometimes the title led to a plot all by itself, as it were, and then all was plain sailing—but in this case the title continued to adorn the top of the page, and not the vestige of a plot was forthcoming.

Again Anthony Eastwood's gaze sought inspiration from the ceiling, the floor, and the wallpaper, and still nothing materialized.

"I shall call the heroine Sonia," said Anthony, to urge himself on. "Sonia or possibly Dolores—she shall have a skin of ivory pallor—the kind that's not due to ill-health, and eyes like fathomless pools. The hero shall be called George, or possibly John—something short and British. Then the gardener—I suppose there will have to be a gardener, we've got to drag that beastly cucumber in somehow or other—the gardener might be Scottish, and amusingly pessimistic about the early frosts."

This method sometimes worked, but it didn't seem to be going to this morning. Although Anthony could see Sonia and George and the comic gardener quite clearly, they didn't show any willingness to be active and do things.

"I could make it a banana, of course," thought Anthony desperately. "Or a lettuce, or a Brussels sprout—Brussels sprout, now, how about that? Really a cryptogram for Brussels—stolen bearer bonds—sinister Belgian baron."

For a moment a gleam of light seemed to show, but it died down again. The Belgian baron wouldn't materialize, and Anthony suddenly remembered that early frosts and cucumbers were incompatible, which seemed to put the lid on the amusing remarks of the Scottish gardener.

"Oh! Damn!" said Mr. Eastwood.

He rose and seized the *Daily Mail*. It was just possible that someone or other had been done to death in such a way as to lend inspiration to a perspiring author. But the news this morning was mainly political and foreign. Mr. Eastwood cast down the paper in disgust.

Next seizing a novel from the table, he closed his eyes and dabbed his finger down on one of the pages. The word thus indicated by fate was "sheep." Immediately, with startling brilliance, a whole story unrolled itself in Mr. Eastwood's brain. Lovely girl— lover killed in the war, her brain unhinged—tends sheep on the Scottish mountains—mystic meeting with dead lover, final effect of sheep and moonlight like Academy picture, with girl lying dead in the snow, and two trails of footsteps. . . .

It was a beautiful story. Anthony came out of its conception with a sigh and a sad shake of the head. He knew only too well that the editor in question did not want that kind of story—beautiful though it might be. The kind of story he wanted, and insisted on having (and incidentally paid handsomely for getting), was all about mysterious dark women, stabbed to the heart, a young hero unjustly suspected, and the sudden unraveling of the mystery and fixing of the guilt on the least likely person, by means of wholly inadequate clues—in fact, "THE MYSTERY OF THE SECOND CUCUMBER."

"Although," reflected Anthony, "ten to one he'll alter the title and call it something rotten, like '*Murder Most Foul*,' without so much as asking me! Oh, curse that telephone."

He strode angrily to it, and took down the receiver.

Twice already in the last hour he had been summoned to it—once for a wrong number, and once to be roped in for dinner by a skittish society dame whom he hated bitterly, but who had been too pertinacious to defeat.

"Hallo!" he growled into the receiver.

A woman's voice answered him, a soft, caressing voice with a trace of foreign accent.

"Is that you, beloved?" it said.

"Well—er—I don't know," said Mr. Eastwood cautiously. "Who's speaking?"

"It is I. Carmen. Listen, beloved. I am pursued— in danger—you must come at once. It is life or death now."

"I beg your pardon," said Mr. Eastwood politely. "I'm afraid you've got the wrong——"

She broke in before he could complete the sentence.

"Madre de Dios! They are coming. If they find out what I am doing, they will kill me. Do not fail me. Come at once. It is death for me if you don't come. You know, 320 Kirk Street. The word is cucumber. . . . Hush. . . ."

He heard the faint click as she hung up the receiver at the other end. "Well, I'm damned," said Mr. Eastwood, very much astonished. He crossed over to his tobacco jar, and filled his pipe carefully.

"I suppose," he mused, "that that was some curious effect of my subconscious self. She can't have said cucumber. The whole thing is very extraordinary. Did she say cucumber, or didn't she?"

He strolled up and down irresolutely.

"320 Kirk Street. I wonder what it's all about?

She'll be expecting the other man to turn up. I wish I could have explained. 320 Kirk Street. The word is cucumber—oh, impossible, absurd—hallucination of a busy brain."

He glanced malevolently at the typewriter.

"What good are you, I should like to know? I've been looking at you all the morning, and a lot of good it's done me. An author should get his plots from life—from life, do you hear? I'm going out to get one now."

He clapped a hat on his head, gazed affectionately at his priceless collection of old enamels, and left the flat.

Kirk Street, as most Londoners know, is a long, straggling thoroughfare, chiefly devoted to antique shops, where all kinds of spurious goods are offered at fancy prices. There are also old brass shops, glass shops, decayed second-hand shops, and second-hand clothes dealers.

No. 320 was devoted to the sale of old glass. Glassware of all kinds filled it to overflowing. It was necessary for Anthony to move gingerly as he advanced up a center aisle flanked by wine glasses and with lusters and chandeliers swaying and twinkling over his head.

A very old lady was sitting at the back of the shop. She had a budding mustache that many an undergraduate might have envied, and a truculent manner.

She looked at Anthony and said, "Well?" in a forbidding voice.

Anthony was a young man somewhat easily discomposed. He immediately inquired the price of some hock glasses.

"Forty-five shillings for half a dozen."

"Oh, really," said Anthony. "Rather nice, aren't they? How much are these things?"

"Beautiful, they are, old Waterford. Let you have the pair for eighteen guineas."

Mr. Eastwood felt that he was laying up trouble for himself. In another minute he would be buying something, hypnotized by this fierce old woman's eye. And yet he could not bring himself to leave the shop.

"What about that?" he asked, and pointed to a chandelier.

"Thirty-five guineas."

"Ah!" said Mr. Eastwood regretfully. "That's rather more than I can afford."

"What do you want?" asked the old lady. "Something for a wedding present?"

"That's it," said Anthony, snatching at the explanation. "But they're very difficult to suit."

"Ah, well," said the lady, rising with an air of determination. "A nice piece of old glass comes amiss to nobody. I've got a couple of old decanters here—and there's a nice little liqueur set, just the thing for a bride——"

For the next ten minutes Anthony endured agonies. The lady had him firmly in hand. Every conceivable specimen of the glass maker's art was paraded before his eyes. He became desperate.

"Beautiful, beautiful," he exclaimed in a perfunctory manner, as he put down a large goblet that was being forced on his attention. Then blurted out hurriedly, "I say, are you on the telephone here?"

"No, we're not. There's a call office at the post

office just opposite. Now, what do you say, the goblet—or these fine old rummers?"

Not being a woman, Anthony was quite unversed in the gentle art of getting out of a shop without buying anything.

"I'd better have the liqueur set," he said gloomily. It seemed the smallest thing. He was terrified of being landed with the chandelier.

With bitterness in his heart he paid for his purchase. And then, as the old lady was wrapping up the parcel, courage suddenly returned to him. After all, she would only think him eccentric, and, anyway, what the devil did it matter what she thought?

"Cucumber," he said, clearly and firmly.

The old crone paused abruptly in her wrapping operations.

"Eh? What did you say?"

"Nothing," lied Anthony hastily.

"Oh! I thought you said cucumber."

"So I did," said Anthony defiantly.

"Well," said the old lady. "Why ever didn't you say that before? Wasting my time. Through that door there and upstairs. She's waiting for you."

As though in a dream, Anthony passed through the door indicated, and climbed some extremely dirty stairs. At the top of them a door stood ajar displaying a tiny sitting-room.

Sitting on a chair, her eyes fixed on the door, and an expression of eager expectancy on her face, was a girl.

Such a girl! She really had the ivory pallor that Anthony had so often written about. And her eyes! Such eyes! She was not English, that could be seen at a glance. She had a foreign exotic quality which showed itself even in the costly simplicity of her dress.

Anthony paused in the doorway, somewhat abashed. The moment of explanations seemed to have arrived. But with a cry of delight the girl rose and flew into his arms.

"You have come," she cried. "You have come. Oh, the saints and the Holy Madonna be praised."

Anthony, never one to miss opportunities, echoed her fervently. She drew away at last, and looked up in his face with a charming shyness.

"I should never have known you," she declared. "Indeed I should not."

"Wouldn't you?" said Anthony feebly.

"No, even your eyes seem different—and you are ten times handsomer than I ever thought you would be."

"Am I?"

To himself Anthony was saying, "Keep calm, my boy, keep calm. The situation is developing very nicely, but don't lose your head."

"I may kiss you again, yes?"

"Of course you can," said Anthony heartily. "As often as you like."

There was a very pleasant interlude.

"I wonder who the devil I am?" thought Anthony. "I hope to goodness the real fellow won't turn up. What a perfect darling she is."

Suddenly the girl drew away from him, and terror showed in her face.

"You were not followed here?"

"Lord, no."

"Ah, but they are very cunning. You do not know them as I do. Boris, he is a fiend."

"I'll soon settle Boris for you."

"You are a lion—yes, but a lion. As for them, they are *canaille*—all of them. Listen, I have *it!* They would have killed me had they known. I was afraid— I did not know what to do, and then I thought of you. . . . Hush, what was that?"

It was a sound in the shop below. Motioning to him to remain where he was, she tiptoed out on to the stairs. She returned with a white face and staring eyes.

"*Madre de Dios!* It is the police. They are coming up here. You have a knife? A revolver? Which?"

"My dear girl, you don't seriously expect me to murder a policeman?"

"Oh, but you are mad—mad! They will take you away and hang you by the neck until you're dead."

"They'll what?" said Mr. Eastwood, with a very unpleasant feeling going up and down his spine.

Steps sounded on the stair.

"Here they come," whispered the girl. "Deny everything. It is the only hope."

"That's easy enough," muttered Mr. Eastwood, *sotto voce.*

In another minute two men had entered the room. They were in plain clothes, but they had an official bearing that spoke of long training. The smaller of the two, a little dark man with quiet gray eyes, was the spokesman.

"I arrest you, Conrad Fleckman," he said, "for the murder of Anna Rosenberg. Anything you say will be used in evidence against you. Here is my warrant and you will do well to come quietly."

A half-strangled scream burst from the girl's lips. Anthony stepped forward with a composed smile.

"You are making a mistake, officer," he said pleasantly. "My name is Anthony Eastwood."

The two detectives seemed completely unimpressed by his statement.

"We'll see about that later," said one of them, the one who had not spoken before. "In the meantime, you come along with us."

"Conrad," wailed the girl. "Conrad, do not let them take you."

Anthony looked at the detectives.

"You will permit me, I am sure, to say good-bye to this young lady?"

With more decency of feeling than he had expected, the two men moved towards the door. Anthony drew the girl into the corner by the window, and spoke to her in a rapid undertone.

"Listen to me. What I said was true. I am not Conrad Fleckman. When you rang up this morning, they must have given you the wrong number. My name is Anthony Eastwood. I came in answer to your appeal because—well, I came."

She stared at him incredulously.

"You are not Conrad Fleckman?"

"No."

"Oh!" she cried, with a deep accent of distress. "And I kissed you!"

"That's all right," Mr. Eastwood assured her. "The early Christians made a practice of that sort of thing. Jolly sensible. Now, look here. I'll tool off these people. I shall soon prove my identity. In the meantime, they won't worry you, and you can warn this precious Conrad of yours. Afterwards——"

"Yes?"

"Well—just this. My telephone number is North-western 1743—and mind they don't give you the wrong one."

She gave him an enchanting glance, half-tears, half a smile.

"I shall not forget—indeed, I shall not forget."

"That's all right then. Good-bye. I say——"

"Yes?"

"Talking of the early Christians—once more wouldn't matter, would it?"

She flung her arms round his neck. Her lips just touched his.

"I do like you—yes, I do like you. You will re-member that, whatever happens, won't you?"

Anthony disengaged himself reluctantly and ap-proached his captors.

"I am ready to come with you. You don't want to detain this young lady, I suppose?"

"No, sir, that will be quite all right," said the small man civilly.

"Decent fellows, these Scotland Yard men," thought Anthony to himself, as he followed them down the narrow stairway.

There was no sign of the old woman in the shop, but Anthony caught a heavy breathing from a door at the rear, and guessed that she stood behind it, cau-tiously observing events.

Once out in the dinginess of Kirk Street, Anthony

drew a long breath, and addressed the smaller of the two men.

"Now, then, Inspector—you are an inspector, I suppose?"

"Yes, sir. Detective-Inspector Verrall. This is Detective-Sergeant Carter."

"Well, Inspector Verrall, the time has come to talk sense—and to listen to it, too. I'm not Conrad What's-his-name. My name is Anthony Eastwood, as I told you, and I am a writer by profession. If you will accompany me to my flat, I think that I shall be able to satisfy you of my identity."

Something in the matter-of-fact way Anthony spoke seemed to impress the detectives. For the first time an expression of doubt passed over Verrall's face.

Carter, apparently, was harder to convince.

"I dare say," he sneered. "But you'll remember the young lady was calling you 'Conrad' all right."

"Ah! that's another matter. I don't mind admitting to you both that for—er—reasons of my own, I was passing myself off upon that lady as a person called Conrad. A private matter, you understand."

"Likely story, isn't it?" observed Carter. "No, sir, you come along with us. Hail that taxi, Joe."

A passing taxi was stopped, and the three men got inside. Anthony made a last attempt, addressing himself to Verrall as the more easily convinced of the two.

"Look here, my dear Inspector, what harm is it going to do you to come along to my flat and see if I'm speaking the truth? You can keep the taxi if you like—there's a generous offer! It won't make five minutes difference either way."

Verall looked at him searchingly.

"I'll do it," he said suddenly. "Strange as it appears, I believe you're speaking the truth. We don't want to make fools of ourselves at the station by arresting the wrong man. What's the address?"

"Forty-eight Brandenburg Mansions."

Verrall leaned out and shouted the address to the taxi driver. All three sat in silence until they arrived at their destination, when Carter sprang out, and Verrall motioned to Anthony to follow him.

"No need for any unpleasantness," he explained, as he too descended. "We'll go in friendly like, as though Mr. Eastwood was bringing a couple of pals home."

Anthony felt extremely grateful for the suggestion and his opinion of the Criminal Investigation Department rose every minute.

In the hallway they were fortunate enough to meet Rogers, the porter. Anthony stopped.

"Ah! Good evening, Rogers," he remarked casually.

"Good evening, Mr. Eastwood," replied the porter respectfully.

He was attached to Anthony, who set an example of liberality not always followed by his neighbors.

Anthony paused with his foot on the bottom step of the stairs.

"By the way, Rogers," he said casually, "how long have I been living here? I was just having a little discussion about it with these friends of mine."

"Let me see, sir, it must be getting on for close on four years now."

"Just what I thought."

Anthony flung a glance of triumph at the two detectives. Carter grunted, but Verrall was smiling broadly.

"Good, but not good enough, sir," he remarked. "Shall we go up?"

Anthony opened the door of the flat with his latchkey. He was thankful to remember that Seamark, his man, was out. The fewer witnesses of this catastrophe the better.

The typewriter was as he had left it. Carter strode across to the table and read the headline on the paper.

"THE MYSTERY OF THE SECOND CUCUMBER?" he announced in a gloomy voice.

"A story of mine," exclaimed Anthony nonchalantly.

"That's another good point, sir," said Verall nodding his head, his eyes twinkling. "By the way, sir, what was it about? What was the mystery of the second cucumber?"

"Ah, there you have me," said Anthony. "It's that second cucumber that's at the bottom of this trouble."

Carter was looking at him intently. Suddenly he shook his head and tapped his forehead significantly.

"Balmy, poor young fellow," he murmured in an audible aside.

"Now, gentlemen," said Mr. Eastwood briskly, "to business. Here are letters addressed to me, my bankbook, communications from editors. What more do you want?"

Verrall examined the papers that Anthony thrust upon him.

"Speaking for myself, sir," he said respectfully, "I want nothing more. I'm quite convinced. But I can't take the responsibility of releasing you upon myself. You see, although it seems positive that you have been residing here as Mr. Eastwood for some years, yet it is possible that Conrad Fleckman and Anthony Eastwood are one and the same person. I must make a thorough search of the flat, take your fingerprints, and telephone to headquarters."

"That seems a comprehensive program," remarked Anthony. "I can assure you that you're welcome to any guilty secrets of mine you may lay your hands on."

The inspector grinned. For a detective he was a singularly human person.

"Will you go into the little end room, sir, with Carter, while I'm getting busy?"

"All right," said Anthony unwillingly. "I suppose it couldn't be the other way about, could it?"

"Meaning?"

"That you and I and a couple of whiskies and sodas should occupy the end room while our friend, the sergeant, does the heavy searching."

"If you prefer it, sir?"

"I do prefer it."

They left Carter investigating the contents of the desk with business-like dexterity. As they passed out of the room, they heard him take down the telephone and call up Scotland Yard.

"This isn't so bad," said Anthony, settling himself with a whisky and soda by his side, having hospitably attended to the wants of Inspector Verrall. "Shall I drink first, just to show you that the whisky isn't poisoned?"

The inspector smiled.

"Very irregular, all this," he remarked. "But we know a thing or two in our profession. I realized right from the start that we'd made a mistake. But of course one had to observe all the usual forms. You can't get away from red tape, can you, sir?"

"I suppose not," said Anthony regretfully. "The sergeant doesn't seem very matey yet, though, does he?"

"Ah, he's a fine man, Detective-Sergeant Carter. You wouldn't find it easy to put anything over on him."

"I've noticed that," said Anthony. "By the way, Inspector," he added, "is there any objection to my hearing something about myself?"

"In what way, sir?"

"Come, now, don't you realize that I'm devoured by curiosity? Who was Anna Rosenberg, and why did I murder her?"

"You'll read all about it in the newspapers tomorrow, sir."

" 'Tomorrow I may be Myself with Yesterday's ten thousand years,' " quoted Anthony. "I really think you might satisfy my perfectly legitimate curiosity, Inspector. Cast aside your official reticence, and tell me all."

"It's quite irregular, sir."

"My dear Inspector, when we are becoming such fast friends?"

"Well, sir, Anna Rosenberg was a German who

lived at Hampstead. With no visible means of livelihood, she grew yearly richer and richer."

"I'm just the opposite," commented Anthony. "I
have a visible means of livelihood and I get yearly
poorer and poorer. Perhaps I should do better if I lived
in Hampstead. I've always heard Hampstead is very
bracing."

"At one time," continued Verrall, "she was a
second-hand clothes dealer——"

"That explains it," interrupted Anthony. "I remember selling my uniform after the war—not khaki, the
other stuff. The whole flat was full of red trousers and
gold lace, spread out to best advantage. A fat man in
a check suit arrived in a Rolls Royce with a factotum
complete with bag. He bid one pound ten for the lot.
In the end I threw in a hunting coat and some Zeiss
glasses and at a given signal the factotum opened the
bag and shoveled the goods inside, and the fat man
tendered me a ten-pound note and asked me for
change."

"About ten years ago," continued the inspector,
"there were several Spanish political refugees in London—among them a certain Don Fernando Ferrarez
with his young wife and child. They were very poor,
and the wife was ill. Anna Rosenberg visited the place
where they were lodging and asked if they had anything to sell. Don Fernando was out, and his wife
decided to part with a very wonderful Spanish shawl,
embroidered in a marvelous manner, which had been
one of her husband's last presents to her before flying
from Spain. When Don Fernando returned, he flew
into a terrible rage on hearing the shawl had been
sold, and tried vainly to recover it. When he at last

succeeded in finding the second-hand clothes woman in question, she declared that she had resold the shawl to a woman whose name she did not know. Don Fernando was in despair. Two months later he was stabbed in the street and died as a result of his wounds. From that time onward, Anna Rosenberg seemed suspiciously flush of money. In the ten years that followed, her house at Hampstead was burgled no less than eight times. Four of the attempts were frustrated and nothing was taken; on the other four occasions, an embroidered shawl of some kind was among the booty."

The inspector paused, and then went on in obedience to an urgent gesture from Anthony.

"A week ago, Carmen Ferrarez, the young daughter of Don Fernando, arrived in this country from a convent in France. Her first action was to seek out Anna Rosenberg at Hampstead. There she is reported to have had a violent scene with the old woman, and her words at leaving were overheard by one of the servants.

" 'You have it still,' she cried. 'All these years you have grown rich on it—but I say to you solemnly that in the end it will bring you bad luck. You have no moral right to it, and the day will come when you will wish you had never seen the Shawl of the Thousand Flowers.'

"Three days after that, Carmen Ferrarez, disappeared mysteriously from the hotel where she was staying. In her room was found a name and address— the name of Conrad Fleckman, and also a note from a man purporting to be an antique dealer asking if she were disposed to part with a certain embroidered shawl which he believed she had in her possession. The address given on the note was a false one.

"It is clear that the shawl is the center of the whole mystery. Yesterday morning Conrad Fleckman called upon Anna Rosenberg. She was shut up with him for an hour or more, and when he left she was obliged to go to bed, so white and shaken was she by the interview. But she gave orders that if he came to see her again he was always to be admitted. Last night she got up and went out about nine o'clock, and did not return. She was found this morning in the house occupied by Conrad Fleckman, stabbed through the heart. On the floor beside her was—what do you think?"

"The shawl?" breathed Anthony. "The Shawl of a Thousand Flowers."

"Something far more gruesome than that. Something which explained the whole mysterious business of the shawl and made its hidden value clear. . . . Excuse me, I fancy that's the chief——"

There had indeed been a ring at the bell. Anthony contained his impatience as best he could, and waited for the inspector to return. He was pretty well at ease about his own position now. As soon as they took his fingerprints they would realize their mistake.

And then, perhaps, Carmen would ring up. . . .

The Shawl of a Thousand Flowers! What a strange story—just the kind of story to make an appropriate setting for the girl's exquisite dark beauty.

Carmen Ferrarez. . . .

He jerked himself back from day dreaming. What a time that inspector fellow was. He rose and pulled the door open. The flat was strangely silent. Could they have gone? Surely not without a word to him.

He strode out into the next room. It was empty—so was the sitting-room. Strangely empty! It had a bare, dishevelled appearance. Good heavens! His enamels—the silver!

He rushed wildly through the flat. It was the same tale everywhere. The place had been denuded. Every single thing of value, and Anthony had a very pretty collector's taste in small things, had been taken.

With a groan Anthony staggered to a chair, his head in his hands. He was aroused by the ringing of the front door bell. He opened it to confront Rogers.

"You'll excuse me, sir," said Rogers. "But the gentlemen fancied you might be wanting something."

"The gentlemen?"

"Those two friends of yours, sir. I helped them with the packing as best I could. Very fortunately I happened to have them two good cases in the basement." His eyes dropped to the floor. "I've swept up the straw as best I could, sir."

"You packed the things in here?" groaned Anthony.

"Yes, sir. Was that not your wishes, sir? It was the tall gentlemen told me to do so, sir, and seeing as you were busy talking to the other gentleman in the little end room, I didn't like to disturb you."

"I wasn't talking to him," said Anthony. "He was talking to me—curse him."

Rogers coughed.

"I'm sure I'm very sorry for the necessity, sir," he murmured.

"Necessity?"

"Of parting with your little treasures, sir."

"Eh? Oh, yes. Ha, ha!" He gave a mirthless laugh. "They've driven off by now, I suppose. Those—those friends of mine, I mean?"

"Oh, yes, sir, some time ago. I put the cases on the taxi and the tall gentleman went upstairs again, and then they both came running down and drove off at once. . . . Excuse me, sir, but is anything wrong, sir?"

Rogers might well ask. The hollow groan which Anthony emitted would have aroused surmise anywhere.

"Everything is wrong, thank you, Rogers. But I see clearly that you were not to blame. Leave me, I would commune a while with my telephone."

Five minutes later saw Anthony pouring his tale into the ears of Inspector Driver, who sat opposite to him, notebook in hand. An unsympathetic man, Inspector Driver, and not (Anthony reflected) nearly so like a real inspector! Distinctly stagey, in fact. Another striking example of the superiority of Art over Nature.

Anthony reached the end of his tale. The inspector shut up his notebook.

"Well?" said Anthony anxiously.

"Clear as paint," said the inspector. "It's the Patterson gang. They've done a lot of smart work lately. Big fair man, small dark man, and the girl."

"The girl?"

"Yes, dark and mighty good-looking. Acts as decoy usually."

"A—a Spanish girl?"

"She might call herself that. She was born in Hampstead."

"I said it was a bracing place," murmured Anthony.

"Yes, it's clear enough," said the inspector, rising to depart. "She got you on the phone and pitched you a tale—she guessed you'd come along all right. Then she goes along to old Mother Gibson's, who isn't above accepting a tip for the use of her room for them as finds it awkward to meet in public—lovers, you understand, nothing criminal. You fall for it all right, they get you back here, and while one of them pitches you a tale, the other gets away with the swag. It's the Pattersons all right—just their touch."

"And my things?" asked Anthony anxiously.

"We'll do what we can, sir. But the Pattersons are uncommon sharp."

"They seem to be," said Anthony bitterly.

The inspector departed, and scarcely had he gone before there came a ring at the door. Anthony opened it. A small boy stood there, holding a package.

"Parcel for you, sir."

Anthony took it with some surprise. He was not expecting a parcel of any kind. Returning to the sitting-room with it, he cut the string.

It was a liqueur set!

"Damn!" said Anthony.

Then he noticed that at the bottom of one of the glasses there was a tiny artificial rose. His mind flew back to the upper room in Kirk Street.

"I do like you—yes, I do like you. You will remember that whatever happens, won't you?"

That was what she had said. Whatever happens. . . . Did she mean——

Anthony took hold of himself sternly.

"This won't do," he admonished himself.

His eye fell on the typewriter, and he sat down with a resolute face.

THE MYSTERY OF THE SECOND CUCUMBER

His face grew dreamy again. The Shawl of a Thousand Flowers. What was it that was found on the floor beside the dead body? The gruesome thing that explained the whole mystery?

Nothing, of course, since it was only a trumped-up tale to hold his attention, and the teller had used the old Arabian Nights' trick of breaking off at the most interesting point. But couldn't there be a gruesome thing that explained the whole mystery? Couldn't there? If one gave one's mind to it?

Anthony tore the sheet of paper from his typewriter and substituted another. He typed a headline:

THE MYSTERY OF THE SPANISH SHAWL

He surveyed it for a moment or two in silence. Then he began to type rapidly. . . .

PHILOMEL COTTAGE

"Good-bye, darling."

"Good-bye, sweetheart."

Alix Martin stood leaning over the small rustic gate, watching the retreating figure of her husband, as he walked down the road in the direction of the village.

Presently he turned a bend and was lost to sight, but Alix still stayed in the same position, absent-mindedly smoothing a lock of the rich brown hair which had blown across her face, her eyes far-away and dreamy.

Alix Martin was not beautiful, nor even, strictly speaking, pretty. But her face, the face of a woman no longer in her first youth, was irradiated and softened until her former colleagues of the old office days would hardly have recognized her. Miss Alix King had been a trim business-like young woman, efficient, slightly brusque in manner, obviously capable and matter-of-fact. She had made the least, not the most, of her beautiful brown hair. Her mouth, not ungenerous in its lines, had always been severely compressed. Her clothes had been neat and suitable, without a hint of coquetry.

Alix had graduated in a hard school. For fifteen years, from the age of eighteen until she was thirty-three, she had kept herself (and for seven years of the time, an invalid mother) by her work as a shorthand-typist. It was the struggle for existence which had hardened the soft lines of her girlish face.

True, there had been romance—of a kind. Dick Windyford, a fellow clerk. Very much of a woman at heart, Alix had always known without seeming to know that he cared. Outwardly they had been friends, nothing more. Out of his slender salary, Dick had been hard put to it to provide for the schooling of a younger brother. For the moment, he could not think of marriage. Nevertheless, when Alix envisaged the future, it was with the half acknowledged certainty that she would one day be Dick's wife. They cared for one another, so she would have put it, but they were both sensible people. Plenty of time, no need to do anything rash. So the years had gone on.

And then suddenly deliverance from daily toil had come to the girl in the most unexpected manner. A distant cousin had died leaving her money to Alix. A few thousand pounds, enough to bring in a couple of hundred a year. To Alix, it was freedom, life, independence. Now she and Dick need wait no longer.

But Dick reacted unexpectedly. He had never directly spoken of his love to Alix, now he seemed less inclined to do so than ever. He avoided her, became morose and gloomy. Alix was quick to realize the truth. She had become a woman of means. Delicacy and pride stood in the way of Dick's asking her to be his wife.

She liked him none the worse for it and was indeed

deliberating as to whether she herself might not take the first step when for the second time the unexpected descended upon her.

She met Gerald Martin at a friend's house. He fell violently in love with her and within a week they were engaged. Alix, who had always considered herself "not the falling-in-love kind," was swept clean off her feet.

Unwittingly she had found the way to arouse her former lover. Dick Windyford had come to her stammering with rage and anger.

"The man's a perfect stranger to you. You know nothing about him."

"I know that I love him."

"How can you know—in a week?"

"It doesn't take everyone eleven years to find out that they're in love with a girl," cried Alix angrily.

His face went white.

"I've cared for you ever since I met you. I thought that you cared also."

Alix was truthful.

"I thought so, too," she admitted. "But that was because I didn't know what love was."

Then Dick had burst out again. Prayers, entreaties, even threats. Threats against the man who had supplanted him. It was amazing to Alix to see the volcano that existed beneath the reserved exterior of the man she thought she knew so well. Also, it frightened her a little. . . . Dick, of course, couldn't possibly mean the things he was saying, the threats of vengeance against Gerald Martin. He was angry, that was all. . . .

Her thoughts had gone back to that interview now,

on this sunny morning, as she leaned on the gate of the cottage. She had been married a month, and she was idyllically happy. Yet, in the momentary absence of the husband who was everything to her, a tinge of anxiety invaded her perfect happiness, and the cause of that anxiety was Dick Windyford.

Three times since her marriage she had dreamed the same dream. The environment differed, but the main facts were always the same. She saw her husband lying dead and Dick Windyford standing over him, and she knew clearly and distinctly that his was the hand which had dealt the fatal blow.

But horrible though that was, there was something more horrible still—horrible that was, on awakening, for in the dream it seemed perfectly natural and inevitable. *She, Alix Martin, was glad that her husband was dead*—she stretched out grateful hands to the murderer, sometimes she thanked him. The dream always ended the same way, with herself clasped in Dick Windyford's arms.

She had said nothing of this dream to her husband, but secretly it had perturbed her more than she liked to admit. Was it a warning—a warning against Dick Windyford? Had he some secret power which he was trying to establish over her at a distance? She did not know much about hypnotism, but surely she had always heard that persons could not be hypnotized against their will.

Alix was roused from her thoughts by the sharp ringing of the telephone bell from within the house. She entered the cottage, and picked up the receiver. Suddenly she swayed, and put out a hand to keep herself from falling.

"Who did you say was speaking?"

"Why, Alix, what's the matter with your voice? I wouldn't have known it. It's Dick."

"Oh!" said Alix——"Oh! Where are you?"

"At the Travelers Arms—that's the right name, isn't it? Or don't you even know of the existence of your village pub? I'm on my holiday—doing a bit of fishing here. Any objection to my looking you two good people up this evening after dinner?"

"No," said Alix sharply. "You mustn't come."

There was a pause, and Dick's voice, with a subtle alteration in it, spoke again.

"I beg your pardon," he said formally. "Of course I won't bother you——"

Alix broke in hastily. Of course he must think her behavior too extraordinary. It was extraordinary. Her nerves must be all to pieces. It wasn't Dick's fault that she had these dreams.

"I only meant that we were—engaged tonight," she explained, trying to make her voice sound as natural as possible. "Won't you—won't you come to dinner tomorrow night?"

But Dick evidently noticed the lack of cordiality in her tone.

"Thanks very much," he said, in the same formal voice. "But I may be moving on any time. Depends upon whether a pal of mine turns up or not. Goodbye, Alix." He paused, and then added hastily, in a different tone, "Best of luck to you, my dear."

Alix hung up the receiver with a feeling of relief.

"He mustn't come here," she repeated to herself. "He mustn't come here. Oh! what a fool I am! To imagine myself into a state like this. All the same, I'm glad he's not coming."

She caught up a rustic rush hat from a table, and passed out into the garden again, pausing to look up at the name carved over the porch, Philomel Cottage.

"Isn't it a very fanciful name?" she had said to Gerald once before they were married. He had laughed.

"You little Cockney," he had said, affectionately. "I don't believe you have ever heard a nightingale. I'm glad you haven't. Nightingales should sing only for lovers. We'll hear them together on a summer's evening outside our own home."

And at the remembrance of how they had indeed heard them, Alix, standing in the doorway of her home, blushed happily.

It was Gerald who had found Philomel Cottage. He had come to Alix bursting with excitement. He had found the very spot for them—unique—a gem—the chance of a lifetime. And when Alix had seen it, she too was captivated. It was true that the situation was rather lonely—they were two miles from the nearest village—but the cottage itself was so exquisite with its Old World appearance, and its solid comfort of bathrooms, hot-water system, electric light and telephone, that she fell a victim to its charm immediately. And then a hitch occurred. The owner, a rich man who had made it his whim, declined to rent it. He would only sell.

Gerald Martin, though possessed of a good income, was unable to touch his capital. He could raise at most a thousand pounds. The owner was asking three. But Alix, who had set her heart on the place, came to the rescue. Her own capital was easily realized, being in bearer bonds. She would contribute half of it to the purchase of the home. So Philomel Cottage became their very own, and never for a minute had Alix regretted the choice. It was true that servants did not appreciate the rural solitude—indeed at the moment they had none at all—but Alix, who had been starved of domestic life, thoroughly enjoyed cooking dainty little meals and looking after the house.

The garden which was magnificently stocked with flowers was attended to by an old man from the village who came twice a week, and Gerald Martin, who was keen on gardening, spent most of his time there.

As she rounded the corner of the house, Alix was surprised to see the old gardener in question busy over the flower beds. She was surprised because his days for work were Mondays and Fridays, and today was Wednesday.

"Why, George, what are you doing here?" she asked, as she came towards him.

The old man straightened up with a chuckle, touching the brim of an aged cap.

"I thought as how you'd be surprised, ma'am. But 'tis this way. There be a fête over to Squire's on Friday, and I sez to myself, I sez, neith Mr. Martin nor yet his good lady won't take it amiss if I comes for once on a Wednesday instead of a Friday."

"That's quite all right," said Alix. "I hope you'll enjoy yourself at the fête."

"I reckon to," said George simply. "It's a fine thing to be able to eat your fill and know all the time as it's not you as is paying for it. Squire allus has a proper sit-down tea for 'is tenants. Then I thought too, ma'am, as I might as well see you before you goes away so as to learn your wishes for the borders. You'll have no idea when you'll be back, ma'am, I suppose?"

"But I'm not going away."

George stared at her.

"Bain't you going to Lunnon tomorrow?"

"No. What put such an idea into your head?"

George jerked his head over his shoulder.

"Met Maister down to village yesterday. He told me you was both going away to Lunnon tomorrow, and it was uncertain when you'd be back again."

"Nonsense," said Alix, laughing. "You must have misunderstood him."

All the same, she wondered exactly what it could have been that Gerald had said to lead the old man into such a curious mistake. Going to London? She never wanted to go to London again.

"I hate London," she said suddenly and harshly.

"Ah!" said George placidly. "I must have been mistook somehow, and yet he said it plain enough it seemed to me. I'm glad you're stopping on here—I don't hold with all this gallivanting about, and I don't think nothing of Lunnon. I've never needed to go there. Too many moty cars—that's the trouble nowadays. Once people have got a moty car, blessed if they can stay still anywheres. Mr. Ames, wot used to have this house—nice peaceful sort of gentleman he was until he bought one of them things. Hadn't 'ad it a month before he put up this cottage for sale. A tidy lot he'd spent on it, too, with taps in all the bedrooms, and the electric light and all. 'You'll never see your money back,' I sez to him. 'It's not everyone as'll have your fad for washing themselves in every room in the house, in a manner of speaking.' But 'George,' he sez to me, 'I'll get every penny of two thousand pounds for this house.' And sure enough, he did."

"He got three thousand," said Alix, smiling.

"Two thousand," repeated George. "The sum he was asking was talked of at the time. And a very high figure it was thought to be."

"It really was three thousand," said Alix.

"Women never understand figures," said George, unconvinced. "You'll not tell me that Mr. Ames had the face to stand up to you, and say three thousand brazen like in a loud voice."

"He didn't say it to me," said Alix. "He said it to my husband."

George stooped again to his flower bed.

"The price was two thousand," he said obstinately.

Alix did not trouble to argue with him. Moving to one of the further beds, she began to pick an armful of flowers. The sunshine, the scent of the flowers, the faint hum of hurrying bees, all conspired to make the day a perfect thing.

As she moved with her fragrant posy towards the house, Alix noticed a small dark green object, peeping from between some leaves in one of the beds. She stooped and picked it up, recognizing it for her husband's pocket diary. It must have fallen from his pocket when he was weeding.

She opened it, scanning the entries with some amusement. Almost from the beginning of their married life, she had realized that the impulsive and emotional Gerald had the uncharacteristic virtues of neatness and method. He was extremely fussy about meals being punctual, and always planned his day ahead with the accuracy of a time table. This morning, for instance, he had announced that he should start for the village after breakfast—at 10:15. And at 10:15 to the minute he had left the house.

Looking through the diary, she was amused to notice the entry on the date of May 14th. "Marry Alix St. Peter's 2:30."

"The big silly," murmured Alix to herself, turning the pages.

Suddenly she stopped.

"Thursday, June 18th—why that's today."

In the space for that day was written in Gerald's neat precise hand: "9 p.m." Nothing else. What had Gerald planned to do at 9 p.m. Alix wondered. She smiled to herself as she realized that had this been a story, like those she had so often read, the diary would doubtless have furnished her with some sensational revelation. It would have had in it for certain the name of another woman. She fluttered the back pages idly. There were dates, appointments, cryptic references to business deals, but only one woman's name—her own.

Yet as she slipped the book into her pocket and went on with her flowers to the house, she was aware of a vague uneasiness. Those words of Dick Windyford's recurred to her, almost as though he had been at her elbow repeating them: "The man's a perfect stranger to you. You know nothing about him."

It was true. What did she know about him. After all, Gerald was forty. In forty years there must have been women in his life. . . .

Alix shook herself impatiently. She must not give

way to these thoughts. She had a far more instant preoccupation to deal with. Should she, or should she not, tell her husband that Dick Windyford had rung her up?

There was the possibility to be considered that Gerald might have already run across him in the village. But in that case he would be sure to mention it to her immediately upon his return and matters would be taken out of her hands. Otherwise—what? Alix was aware of a distinct desire to say nothing about it. Gerald had always shown himself kindly disposed towards the other. "Poor devil," he had said once, "I believe he's just as keen on you as I am. Hard luck on him to be shelved." He had had no doubts of Alix's own feelings.

If she told him, he was sure to suggest asking Dick Windyford to Philomel Cottage. Then she would have to explain that Dick had proposed it himself, and that she had made an excuse to prevent his coming. And when he asked her why she had done so, what could she say? Tell him her dream? But he would only laugh—or worse, see that she attached an importance to it which he did not. Then he would think—oh! he might think anything!

In the end, rather shamefacedly, Alix decided to say nothing. It was the first secret she had ever kept from her husband, and the consciousness of it made her feel ill at ease.

When she heard Gerald returning from the village shortly before lunch, she hurried into the kitchen and pretended to be busy with the cooking so as to hide her confusion.

It was evident at once that Gerald had seen nothing

of Dick Windyford. Alix felt at once relieved and embarrassed. She was definitely committed now to a policy of concealment. For the rest of the day she was nervous and absentminded, starting at every sound, but her husband seemed to notice nothing. He himself seemed to have his thoughts far away, and once or twice she had to speak a second time before he answered some trivial remark of hers.

It was not until after their simple evening meal, when they were sitting in the oak beamed living room with the windows thrown open to let in the sweet night air scented with the perfume of the mauve and white stocks that grew outside, that Alix remembered the pocket diary, and seized upon it gladly to distract her thoughts from their doubt and perplexity.

"Here's something you've been watering the flowers with," she said, and threw it into his lap.

"Dropped it in the border, did I?"

"Yes, I know all your secrets now."

"Not guilty," said Gerald, shaking his head.

"What about your assignation at nine o'clock tonight?"

"Oh! that——" he seemed taken back for a moment, then he smiled as though something afforded him particular amusement. "It's an assignation with a particularly nice girl, Alix. She's got brown hair and blue eyes and she's particularly like you."

"I don't understand," said Alix, with mock severity. "You're evading the point."

"No, I'm not. As a matter of fact, that's a reminder that I'm going to develop some negatives tonight, and I want you to help me."

Gerald Martin was an enthusiastic photographer.

He had a somewhat old-fashioned camera, but with an excellent lens, and he developed his own plates in a small cellar which he had fitted up as a dark room. He was never tired of posing Alix in different positions.

"And it must be done at nine o'clock precisely," said Alix teasingly.

Gerald looked a little vexed.

"My dear girl," he said, with a shade of testiness in his manner, "one should always plan a thing for a definite time. Then one gets through one's work properly."

Alix sat for a minute or two in silence watching her husband as he lay in his chair smoking, his dark head flung back and the clear-cut lines of his clean-shaven face showing up against the somber background. And suddenly, from some unknown source, a wave of panic surged over her, so that she cried out before she could stop herself. "Oh! Gerald, I wish I knew more about you."

Her husband turned an astonished face upon her.

"But, my dear Alix, you do know all about me. I've told you of my boyhood in Northumberland, of my life in South Africa, and these last ten years in Canada which have brought me success."

"Oh, business!"

Gerald laughed suddenly.

"I know what you mean—love affairs. You women are all the same. Nothing interests you but the personal element."

Alix felt her throat go dry, as she muttered indistinctly: "Well, but there must have been—love affairs. I mean——If I only knew——"

There was silence again for a minute or two. Gerald Martin was frowning, a look of indecision on his face. When he spoke, it was gravely, without a trace of his former bantering manner.

"Do you think it wise, Alix—this Bluebeard's chamber business? There have been women in my life, yes. I don't deny it. You wouldn't believe me if I did deny it. But I can swear to you truthfully that not one of them meant anything to me."

There was a ring of sincerity in his voice which comforted the listening wife.

"Satisfied, Alix?" he asked, with a smile. Then he looked at her with a shade of curiosity.

"What has turned your mind onto these unpleasant subjects tonight of all nights? You never mentioned them before."

Alix got up and began to walk about restlessly.

"Oh! I don't know," she said. "I've been nervy all day."

"That's odd," said Gerald, in a low voice, as though speaking to himself. "That's very odd."

"Why is it odd?"

"Oh, my dear girl, don't flash out at me so. I only said it was odd because as a rule you're so sweet and serene."

Alix forced a smile.

"Everything's conspired to annoy me today," she confessed. "Even old George had got some ridiculous idea into his head that we were going away to London. He said you had told him so."

"Where did you see him?" asked Gerald sharply.

"He came to work today instead of Friday."

"The old fool," said Gerald angrily.

Alix stared in surprise. Her husband's face was convulsed with rage. She had never seen him so angry. Seeing her astonishment, Gerald made an effort to regain control of himself.

"Well, he *is* a stupid old fool," he protested.

"What can you have said to make him think that?"

"I? I never said anything. At least——Oh, yes, I remember. I made some weak joke about being 'off to London in the morning' and I suppose he took it seriously. Or else he didn't hear properly. You undeceived him, of course?"

He waited anxiously for her reply.

"Of course, but he's the sort of old man who if once he gets an idea in his head—well, it isn't so easy to get it out again."

Then she told him of the gardener's insistence on the sum asked for the cottage.

Gerald was silent for a minute or two, then he said slowly:

"Ames was willing to take two thousand in cash and the remaining thousand on mortgage. That's the origin of that mistake, I fancy."

"Very likely," agreed Alix.

Then she looked up at the clock, and pointed to it with a mischievous finger.

"We ought to be getting down to it, Gerald. Five minutes behind schedule."

A very peculiar smile came over Gerald Martin's face.

"I've changed my mind," he said quietly. "I shall not do any photography tonight."

*   *   *

A woman's mind is a curious thing. When she went to bed that Thursday night, Alix's mind was contented and at rest. Her momentarily assailed happiness reasserted itself, triumphant as of yore.

But by the evening of the following day, she realized that some subtle forces were at work undermining it. Dick Windyford had not rung up again, nevertheless she felt what she supposed to be his influence at work. Again and again those words of his recurred to her. "The man's a perfect stranger. You know nothing about him." And with them came the memory of her husband's face, photographed clearly on her brain as he said: "Do you think it wise, Alix, this Bluebeard's chamber business?" Why had he said that? What had he meant by those words?

There had been warning in them—a hint of menace. It was as though he had said in effect—"You had better not pry into my life, Alix. You may get a nasty shock if you do." True, a few minutes later, he had sworn to her that there had been no woman in his life that mattered—but Alix tried in vain to recapture her sense of his sincerity. Was he not bound to swear that?

By Friday morning, Alix had convinced herself that there had been a woman in Gerald's life—a Bluebeard's chamber that he had sedulously sought to conceal from her. Her jealousy, slow to awaken, was now rampant.

Was it a woman he had been going to meet that night, at 9 p.m.? Was his story of photographs to develop a lie invented upon the spur of the moment? With a queer sense of shock Alix realized that ever since she had found that pocket diary she had been in torment. And there had been nothing in it? That was the irony of the whole thing.

Three days ago she would have sworn that she knew her husband through and through. Now it seemed to her that he was a stranger of whom she knew nothing. She remembered his unreasonable anger against old George, so at variance with his usual good-tempered manner. A small thing, perhaps, but it showed her that she did not really know the man who was her husband.

There were several little things required on Friday from the village to carry them over the week-end. In the afternoon Alix suggested that she should go for them whilst Gerald remained in the garden, but somewhat to her surprise he opposed this plan vehemently, and insisted on going himself whilst she remained at home. Alix was forced to give way to him, but his insistence surprised and alarmed her. Why was he so anxious to prevent her going to the village?

Suddenly an explanation suggested itself to her which made the whole thing clear. Was it not possible that, whilst saying nothing to her, Gerald had indeed come across Dick Windyford? Her own jealousy, entirely dormant at the time of their marriage, had only developed afterwards. Might it not be the same with Gerald? Might he not be anxious to prevent her seeing Dick Windyford again? This explanation was so consistent with the facts, and so comforting to Alix's perturbed mind, that she embraced it eagerly.

Yet when tea time had come and past, she was restless and ill at ease. She was struggling with a temptation that had assailed her ever since Gerald's departure. Finally, pacifying her conscience with the assurance that the room did need a thorough tidying, she went upstairs to her husband's dressing room. She took a duster with her to keep up the pretense of housewifery.

"If I were only sure," she repeated to herself. "If I could only be sure."

In vain she told herself that anything compromising would have been destroyed ages ago. Against that she argued that men do sometimes keep the most damning piece of evidence through an exaggerated sentimentality.

In the end Alix succumbed. Her cheeks burning with the shame of her action, she hunted breathlessly through packets of letters and documents, turned out the drawers, even went through the pockets of her husband's clothes. Only two drawers eluded her—the lower drawer of the chest of drawers and the small right-hand drawer of the writing desk were both locked. But Alix was by now lost to all shame. In one of those drawers she was convinced that she would find evidence of this imaginary woman of the past who obsessed her.

She remembered that Gerald had left his keys lying carelessly on the sideboard downstairs. She fetched them and tried them one by one. The third key fitted the writing table drawer. Alix pulled it open eagerly. There was a check book and a wallet well stuffed with notes, and at the back of the drawer a packet of letters tied up with a piece of tape.

Her breath coming unevenly, Alix untied the tape. Then a deep burning blush overspread her face, and she dropped the letters back into the drawer, closing and relocking it. For the letters were her own, written to Gerald Martin before she married him.

She turned now to the chest of drawers, more with a wish to feel that she had left nothing undone, than from any expectation of finding what she sought. She was ashamed and almost convinced of the madness of her obsession.

To her annoyance none of the keys on Gerald's bunch fitted the drawer in question. Not to be defeated, Alix went into the other rooms and brought back a selection of keys with her. To her satisfaction, the key of the spare room wardrobe also fitted the chest of drawers. She unlocked the drawer and pulled it open. But there was nothing in it but a roll of newspaper clippings already dirty and discolored with age.

Alix breathed a sigh of relief. Nevertheless she glanced at the clippings, curious to know what subject had interested Gerald so much that he had taken the trouble to keep the dusty roll. They were nearly all American papers, dated some seven years ago, and dealing with the trail of the notorious swindler and bigamist, Charles LeMaitre. LeMaitre had been suspected of doing away with his women victims. A skeleton had been found beneath the floor of one of the houses he had rented, and most of the women he had "married" had never been heard of again.

He had defended himself from the charge with consummate skill, aided by some of the best legal talent in the United States. The Scottish verdict of "Non proven" might perhaps have stated the case best. In its absence, he was found Not Guilty on the capital charge, though sentenced to a long term of imprisonment on the other charges preferred against him.

Alix remembered the excitement caused by the case at the time, and also the sensation aroused by the escape of LeMaitre some three years later. He had never been recaptured. The personality of the man and his extraordinary power over women had been discussed at great length in the English papers at the time, together with an account of his excitability in court, his passionate protestations, and his occasional sudden physical collapses, due to the fact that he had a weak heart, though the ignorant accredited it to his dramatic powers.

There was a picture of him in one of the clippings Alix held, and she studied it with some interest—a long-bearded, scholarly looking gentleman. It reminded her of someone, but for the moment she could not tell who that someone was. She had never known that Gerald took an interest in crime and famous trials, though she knew that it was a hobby with many men.

Who was it the face reminded her of? Suddenly, with a shock, she realized that it was Gerald himself. The eyes and brows bore a strong resemblance to him. Perhaps he had kept the cutting for that reason. Her eyes went on to the paragraph beside the picture. Certain dates, it seemed, had been entered in the accused's pocketbook, and it was contended that these were dates when he had done away with his victims. Then a woman gave evidence and identified the prisoner positively by the fact that he had a mole on his left wrist, just below the palm of the left hand.

Alix dropped the papers from a nerveless hand, and swayed as she stood. *On his left wrist, just below the palm, Gerald had a small scar. . . .*

The room whirled round her. . . . Afterwards it struck her as strange that she should have leaped at once to such absolute certainty. Gerald Martin was Charles LeMaitre! She knew it and accepted it in a flash. Disjointed fragments whirled through her brain, like pieces of a jigsaw puzzle fitting into place.

The money paid for the house—her money—her money only. The Bearer bonds she had entrusted to his keeping. Even her dream appeared in its true significance. Deep down in her, her subconscious self had always feared Gerald Martin and wished to escape from him. And it was to Dick Windyford this self of hers had looked for help. That, too, was why she was able to accept the truth so easily, without doubt or hesitation. She was to have been another of LeMaitre's victims. Very soon, perhaps.

A half cry escaped her as she remembered something. Thursday 9 p.m. The cellar, with the flagstones that were so easily raised. Once before, he had buried one of his victims in a cellar. It had been all planned for Thursday night. But to write it down beforehand in that methodical manner—insanity! No, it was logical. Gerald always made a memorandum of his engagements—murder was, to him, a business proposition like any other.

But what had saved her? What could possibly have saved her? Had he relented at the last minute? No—in a flash the answer came to her. Old George. She understood now her husband's uncontrollable anger. Doubtless he had paved the way by telling everyone he met that they were going to London the next day. Then George had come to work unexpectedly, had mentioned London to her, and she had contradicted the story. Too risky to do away with her that night, with old George repeating that conversation. But what an escape! If she had not happened to mention that trivial matter—Alix shuddered.

But there was no time to be lost. She must get away at once—before he came back. For nothing on earth would she spend another night under the same roof with him. She hurriedly replaced the roll of clippings in the drawer, shut it to and locked it.

And then she stayed motionless as though frozen to stone. She had heard the creak of the gate into the road. Her husband had returned.

For a moment Alix stayed as though petrified, then she crept on tiptoe to the window, looking out from behind the shelter of the curtain.

Yes, it was her husband. He was smiling to himself and humming a little tune. In his hand he held an object which almost made the terrified girl's heart stop beating. It was a brand new spade.

Alix leaped to a knowledge born of instinct. *It was to be tonight. . . .*

But there was still a chance. Gerald, still humming his little tune, went round to the back of the house.

"He's going to put it in the cellar—ready," thought Alix with a shiver.

Without hesitating a moment, she ran down the stairs and out of the cottage. But just as she emerged from the door, her husband came round the other side of the house.

"Hullo," he said. "Where are you running off to in such a hurry?"

Alix strove desperately to appear calm and as usual. Her chance was gone for the moment, but if she was careful not to arouse his suspicions, it would come again later. Even now, perhaps. . . .

"I was going to walk to the end of the lane and back," she said, in a voice that sounded weak and uncertain to her own ears.

"Right," said Gerald, "I'll come with you."

"No—please, Gerald. I'm—nervy, headachy—I'd rather go alone."

He looked at her attentively. She fancied a momentary suspicion gleamed in his eye.

"What's the matter with you, Alix? You're pale—trembling."

"Nothing," she forced herself to be brusque—smiling. "I've got a headache, that's all. A walk will do me good."

"Well, it's no good you're saying you don't want me," declared Gerald with his easy laugh. "I'm coming whether you want me or not."

She dared not protest further. If he suspected that she knew——

With an effort she managed to regain something of her normal manner. Yet she had an uneasy feeling that he looked at her sideways every now and then, as though not quite satisfied. She felt that his suspicions were not completely allayed.

When they returned to the house, he insisted on her lying down, and brought some eau de cologne to bathe her temples. He was, as ever, the devoted husband, yet Alix felt herself as helpless as though bound hand and foot in a trap.

Not for a minute would he leave her alone. He went with her into the kitchen and helped her to bring in the simple cold dishes she had already prepared.

Supper was a meal that choked her, yet she forced herself to eat, and even to appear gay and natural. She knew now that she was fighting for her life. She was alone with this man, miles from help, absolutely at his mercy. Her only chance was so to lull his suspicions that he would leave her alone for a few moments—long enough for her to get to the telephone in the hall and summon assistance. That was her only hope now. He would overtake her if she took to flight long before she could reach assistance.

A momentary hope flashed over her as she remembered how he had abandoned his plan before. Suppose she told him that Dick Windyford was coming up to see them that evening?

The words trembled on her lips—then she rejected them hastily. This man would not be balked a second time. There was a determination, an elation underneath his calm bearing that sickened her. She would only precipitate the crime. He would murder her there and then, and calmly ring up Dick Windyford with a tale of having been suddenly called away. Oh! if only Dick Windyford were coming to the house this evening. If Dick——

A sudden idea flashed into her mind. She looked sharply sideways at her husband as though she feared that he might read her mind. With the forming of a plan, her courage was reinforced. She became so completely natural in manner that she marveled at herself. She felt that Gerald now was completely reassured.

She made the coffee and took it out to the porch where they often sat on fine evenings.

"By the way," said Gerald suddenly, "we'll do those photographs later."

Alix felt a shiver run through her, but she replied nonchalantly:

"Can't you manage alone? I'm rather tired to-night."

"It won't take long." He smiled to himself. "And I can promise you you won't be tired afterwards."

The words seemed to amuse him. Alix shuddered. Now or never was the time to carry out her plan.

She rose to her feet.

"I'm just going to telephone to the butcher," she announced nonchalantly. "Don't you bother to move."

"To the butcher? At this time of night?"

"His shop's shut, of course, silly. But he's in his house all right. And tomorrow's Saturday, and I want him to bring me some veal cutlets early, before some-one else grabs them from him. The old dear will do anything for me."

She passed quickly into the house, closing the door behind her. She heard Gerald say, "Don't shut the door," and was quick with her light reply. "It keeps the moths out. I hate moths. Are you afraid I'm going to make love to the butcher, silly?"

Once inside she snatched down the telephone receiver and gave the number of the Travelers Arms. She was put through at once.

"Mr. Windyford? Is he still there? May I speak to him?"

Then her heart gave a sickening thump. The door was pushed open and her husband came into the hall.

"Do go away, Gerald," she said pettishly. "I hate

anyone listening when I'm telephoning."

He merely laughed and threw himself into a chair.

"Sure it really is the butcher you're telephoning to?" he quizzed.

Alix was in despair. Her plan had failed. In a minute Dick Windyford would come to the phone. Should she risk all and cry out an appeal for help. Would he grasp what she meant before Gerald wrenched her away from the phone. Or would he merely treat it as a practical joke.

And then as she nervously depressed and released the little key in the receiver she was holding, which permits the voice to be heard or not heard at the other end, another plan flashed into her head.

"It will be difficult," she thought. "It means keeping my head, and thinking of the right words, and not faltering for a moment, but I believe I could do it. I *must* do it."

And at that minute she heard Dick Windyford's voice at the other end of the phone.

Alix drew a deep breath. Then she depressed the key firmly and spoke.

"Mrs. Martin speaking—from Philomel Cottage. *Please come* (she released the key) tomorrow morning with six nice veal cutlets (she depressed the key again) *It's very important* (she released the key) Thank you so much, Mr. Hexworthy, you don't mind my ringing you up so late, I hope, but those veal cutlets are really a matter of (she depressed the key again) *life or death* . . . (she released it) Very well— tomorrow morning—(she depressed it) *as soon as possible* . . ."

She replaced the receiver on the hook and turned to face her husband, breathing hard.

"So that's how you talk to your butcher, is it?" said Gerald.

"It's the feminine touch," said Alix lightly.

She was simmering with excitement. He had suspected nothing. Surely Dick, even if he didn't understand, would come.

She passed into the sitting room and switched on the electric light. Gerald followed her.

"You seem very full of spirits now," he said, watching her curiously.

"Yes," said Alix, "my headache's gone."

She sat down in her usual seat and smiled at her husband, as he sank into his own chair opposite her. She was saved. It was only five and twenty past eight. Long before nine o'clock Dick would have arrived.

"I didn't think much of that coffee you gave me," complained Gerald. "It tasted very bitter."

"It's a new kind I was trying. We won't have it again if you don't like it, dear."

Alix took up a piece of needlework and began to stitch. She felt complete confidence in her own ability to keep up the part of the devoted wife. Gerald read a few pages of his book. Then he glanced up at the clock and tossed the book away.

"Half-past eight. Time to go down to the cellar and start work."

The work slipped from Alix's fingers.

"Oh! not yet. Let us wait until nine o'clock."

"No, my girl, half-past eight. That's the time I fixed. You'll be able to get to bed all the earlier."

"But I'd rather wait until nine."

"Half-past eight," said Gerald obstinately. "You know when I fix a time, I always stick to it. Come along, Alix. I'm not going to wait a minute longer."

Alix looked up at him, and in spite of herself she felt a wave of terror slide over her. The mask had been lifted; Gerald's hands were twitching; his eyes were shining with excitement; he was continually passing his tongue over his dry lips. He no longer cared to conceal his excitement.

Alix thought: "It's true—he can't wait—he's like a madman."

He strode over to her, and jerked her onto her feet with a hand on her shoulder.

"Come on, my girl—or I'll carry you there."

His tone was gay, but there was an undisguised ferocity behind it that appalled her. With a supreme effort she jerked herself free and clung cowering against the wall. She was powerless. She couldn't get away—she couldn't do anything—and he was coming towards her.

"Now, Alix——"

"No—no."

She screamed, her hands held out impotently to ward him off.

"Gerald—stop—I've got something to tell you, something to confess . . ."

He did stop.

"To confess?" he said curiously.

"Yes, to confess." She went on desperately, seeking to hold his arrested attention. "Something I ought to have told you before."

A look of contempt swept over his face. The spell was broken.

"A former lover, I suppose," he sneered.

"No," said Alix. "Something else. You'd call it, I expect—yes, you'd call it a crime."

And at once she saw that she had struck the right note. Again his attention was arrested, held. Seeing that, her nerve came back to her. She felt mistress of the situation once more.

"You had better sit down again," she said quietly.

She herself crossed the room to her old chair and sat down. She even stooped and picked up her needlework. But behind her calmness she was thinking and inventing feverishly. For the story she invented must hold his interest until help arrived.

"I told you," she said, "that I had been a shorthand typist for fifteen years. That was not entirely true. There were two intervals. The first occurred when I was twenty-two. I came across a man, an elderly man with a little property. He fell in love with me and asked me to marry him. I accepted. We were married." She paused. "I induced him to insure his life in my favor."

She saw a sudden keen interest spring up in her husband's face, and went on with renewed assurance.

"During the war I worked for a time in a Hospital Dispensary. There I had the handling of all kinds of rare drugs and poisons. Yes, poisons."

She paused reflectively. He was keenly interested now, not a doubt of it. The murderer is bound to have an interest in murder. She had gambled on that, and succeeded. She stole a glance at the clock. It was five and twenty to nine.

"There is one poison—it is a little white powder.

A pinch of it means death. You know something about poisons perhaps?"

She put the question in some trepidation. If he did, she would have to be careful.

"No," said Gerald, "I know very little about them."

She drew a breath of relief. This made her task easier.

"You have heard of hyoscine, of course? This is a drug that acts much the same way, but it is absolutely untraceable. Any doctor would give a certificate of heart failure. I stole a small quantity of this drug and kept it by me."

She paused, marshaling her forces.

"Go on," said Gerald.

"No. I'm afraid. I can't tell you. Another time."

"Now," he said impatiently. "I want to hear."

"We had been married a month. I was very good to my elderly husband, very kind and devoted. He spoke in praise of me to all the neighbors. Everyone knew what a devoted wife I was. I always made his coffee myself every evening. One evening, when we were alone together, I put a pinch of the deadly alkaloid in his cup."

Alix paused, and carefully rethreaded her needle. She, who had never acted in her life, rivaled the greatest actress in the world at this moment. She was actually living the part of the cold-blooded poisoner.

"It was very peaceful. I sat watching him. Once he gasped a little and asked for air. I opened the window. Then he said he could not move from his chair. Presently he died."

She stopped, smiling. It was a quarter to nine. Surely they would come soon.

"How much," said Gerald, "was the insurance money?"

"About two thousand pounds. I speculated with it, and lost it. I went back to my office work. But I never meant to remain there long. Then I met another man. I had stuck to my maiden name at the office. He didn't know I had been married before. He was a younger man, rather good-looking, and quite well off. We were married quietly in Sussex. He didn't want to insure his life, but of course he made a will in my favor. He liked me to make his coffee myself also, just as my first husband had done."

Alix smiled reflectively, and added simply:

"I make very good coffee."

Then she went on.

"I had several friends in the village where we were living. They were very sorry for me, with my husband dying suddenly of heart failure one evening after dinner. I didn't quite like the doctor. I don't think he suspected me, but he was certainly very surprised at my husband's sudden death. I don't quite know why I drifted back to the office again. Habit, I suppose. My second husband left about four thousand pounds. I didn't speculate with it this time. I invested it. Then, you see——"

But she was interrupted. Gerald Martin, his face suffused with blood, half choking, was pointing a shaking forefinger at her.

"The coffee—my God! the coffee!"

She stared at him.

"I understand now why it was bitter. You devil. You've poisoned me."

His hands gripped the arms of his chair. He was ready to spring upon her.

"You've poisoned me."

Alix had retreated from him to the fireplace. Now, terrified, she opened her lips to deny—and then paused. In another minute he would spring upon her. She summoned all her strength. Her eyes held his steadily, compellingly.

"Yes," she said, "I poisoned you. Already the poison is working. At this minute you can't move from your chair—you can't move——"

If she could keep him there—even a few minutes——

Ah! what was that? Footsteps on the road. The creak of the gate. Then footsteps on the path outside. The door of the hall opened——

"You can't move," she said again.

Then she slipped past him and fled headlong from the room to fall, half fainting, into Dick Windyford's arms.

"My God! Alix!" he cried.

Then he turned to the man with him, a tall stalwart figure in policeman's uniform.

"Go and see what's been happening in that room."

He laid Alix carefully down on a couch and bent over her.

"My little girl," he murmured. "My poor little girl. What have they been doing to you?"

Her eyelids fluttered and her lips just murmured his name.

Dick was aroused from tumultuous thoughts by the policeman's touching him on the arm.

"There's nothing in that room, sir, but a man sitting

in a chair. Looks as though he'd had some kind of bad fright, and——"

"Yes?"

"Well, sir, he's—dead."

They were startled by hearing Alix's voice. She spoke as though in some kind of dream.

"And presently," she said, almost as though she were quoting from something, "he died. . . ."

ACCIDENT

"And I tell you this—it's the same woman—not a doubt of it!" Captain Haydock looked into the eager, vehement face of his friend and sighed. He wished Evans would not be so positive and so jubilant. In the course of a career spent at sea, the old sea captain had learned to leave things that did not concern him well alone. His friend Evans, late C.I.D. Inspector, had a different philosophy of life. "Acting on information received—" had been his motto in early days, and he had improved upon it to the extent of finding out his own information. Inspector Evans had been a very smart, wide-awake officer, and had justly earned the promotion which had been his. Even now, when he had retired from the force, and had settled down in the country cottage of his dreams, his professional instinct was still active.

"Don't often forget a face," he reiterated complacently. "Mrs. Anthony—yes, it's Mrs. Anthony right enough. When you said Mrs. Merrowdene—I knew her at once."

Captain Haydock stirred uneasily. The Merrowdenes were his nearest neighbors, barring Evans himself, and this identifying of Mrs. Merrowdene with a former heroine of a *cause célèbre* distressed him.

"It's a long time ago," he said rather weakly.

"Nine years," said Evans, accurate as ever. "Nine years and three months. You remember the case?"

"In a vague sort of way."

"Anthony turned out to be an arsenic eater," said Evans, "so they acquitted her."

"Well, why shouldn't they?"

"No reason in the world. Only verdict they could give on the evidence. Absolutely correct."

"Then, that's all right," said Haydock. "And I don't see what we're bothering about."

"Who's bothering?"

"I thought you were."

"Not at all."

"The thing's over and done with," summed up the Captain. "If Mrs. Merrowdene at one time of her life was unfortunate enough to be tried and acquitted of murder——"

"It's not usually considered unfortunate to be acquitted," put in Evans.

"You know what I mean," said Captain Haydock, irritably. "If the poor lady has been through that harrowing experience, it's no business of ours to rake it up, is it?"

Evans did not answer.

"Come now, Evans. The lady was innocent—you've just said so."

"I didn't say she was innocent. I said she was acquitted."

"It's the same thing."

"Not always."

Captain Haydock, who had commenced to tap his

pipe out against the side of his chair, stopped, and sat up with a very alert expression:

"Hullo-ullo-ullo," he said. "The wind's in that quarter, is it? You think she wasn't innocent?"

"I wouldn't say that. I just—don't know. Anthony was in the habit of taking arsenic. His wife got it for him. One day, by mistake, he takes far too much. Was the mistake his or his wife's? Nobody could tell, and the jury very properly gave her the benefit of the doubt. That's all quite right and I'm not finding fault with it. All the same—I'd like to know."

Captain Haydock transferred his attention to his pipe once more.

"Well," he said comfortably, "it's none of our business."

"I'm not so sure. . . ."

"But, surely——"

"Listen to me a minute. This man, Merrowdene—in his laboratory this evening, fiddling round with tests—you remember——"

"Yes. He mentioned Marsh's test for arsenic. Said you would know all about it—it was in your line—and chuckled. He wouldn't have said that if he'd thought for one moment——"

Evans interrupted him.

"You mean he wouldn't have said that if he knew. They've been married how long—six years, you told me? I bet you anything he has no idea his wife is the once notorious Mrs. Anthony."

"And he will certainly not know it from me," said Captain Haydock stiffly.

Evans paid no attention, but went on.

"You interrupted me just now. After Marsh's test,

Merrowdene heated a substance in a test tube, the metallic residue he dissolved in water and then precipitated it by adding silver nitrate. That was a test for chlorates. A neat, unassuming little test. But I chanced to read these words in a book that stood open on the table. *H_2SO_4 decomposes chlorates with evolution of Cl_2O_4. If heated, violent explosions occur, the mixture ought therefore to be kept cool and only very small quantities used.*"

Haydock stared at his friend.

"Well, what about it?"

"Just this. In my profession we've got tests, too— tests for murder. There's adding up the facts—weighing them, dissecting the residue when you've allowed for prejudice and the general inaccuracy of witnesses. But there's another test for murder—one that is fairly accurate, but rather—dangerous! A murderer is seldom content with one crime. Give him time and a lack of suspicion and he'll commit another. You catch a man—has he murdered his wife or hasn't he?— perhaps the case isn't very black against him. Look into his past—if you find that he's had several wives—and that they've all died, shall we say— rather curiously?—then you know! I'm not speaking legally, you understand. I'm speaking of moral certainty. Once you know, you can go ahead looking for evidence."

"Well?"

"I'm coming to the point. That's all right if there is a past to look into. But suppose you catch your murderer at his or her first crime? Then that test will be one from which you get no reaction. But the prisoner acquitted—starting life under another name.

Will or will not the murderer repeat the crime?"

"That's a horrible idea."

"Do you still say it's none of our business?"

"Yes, I do. You've no reason to think that Mrs. Merrowdene is anything but a perfectly innocent woman."

The ex-Inspector was silent for a moment. Then he said slowly:

"I told you that we looked into her past and found nothing. That's not quite true. There was a stepfather. As a girl of eighteen she had a fancy for some young man—and her stepfather exerted his authority to keep them apart. She and her stepfather went for a walk along a rather dangerous part of the cliff. There was an accident—the stepfather went too near the edge—it gave way and he went over and was killed."

"You don't think——"

"It was an accident. Accident! Anthony's overdose of arsenic was an accident. She'd never have been tried if it hadn't transpired that there was another man—he sheered off, by the way. Looked as though he weren't satisfied even if the jury were. I tell you, Haydock, where that woman is concerned I'm afraid of another—accident!"

The old Captain shrugged his shoulders.

"Well, I don't know how you're going to guard against that."

"Neither do I," said Evans ruefully.

"I should leave well enough alone," said Captain Haydock. "No good ever came of butting into other people's affairs."

But that advice was not palatable to the ex-Inspector. He was a man of patience but determination. Taking leave of his friend, he sauntered down to the village, revolving in his mind the possibilities of some kind of successful action.

Turning into the post office to buy some stamps, he ran into the object of his solicitude, George Merrowdene. The ex-chemistry professor was a small, dreamy-looking man, gentle and kindly in manner, and usually completely absent-minded. He recognized the other and greeted him amicably, stooping to recover the letters that the impact had caused him to drop on the ground. Evans stooped also and, more rapid in his movements than the other, secured them first, handing them back to their owner with an apology.

He glanced down at them in doing so, and the address on the topmost suddenly awakened all his suspicions anew. It bore the name of a well-known insurance firm.

Instantly his mind was made up. The guileless George Merrowdene hardly realized how it came about that he and the ex-Inspector were strolling down the village together, and still less could he have said how it came about that the conversation should come round to the subject of life insurance.

Evans had no difficulty in attaining his object. Merrowdene of his own accord volunteered the information that he had just insured his life for his wife's benefit, and asked Evans's opinion of the company in question.

"I made some rather unwise investments," he explained. "As a result, my income has diminished. If anything were to happen to me, my wife would be left very badly off. This insurance will put things right."

"She didn't object to the idea?" inquired Evans casually. "Some ladies do, you know. Feel it's unlucky—that sort of thing."

"Oh, Margaret is very practical," said Merrowdene, smiling. "Not at all superstitious. In fact, I believe it was her idea originally. She didn't like my being so worried."

Evans had got the information he wanted. He left the other shortly afterwards, and his lips were set in a grim line. The late Mr. Anthony had insured his life in his wife's favor a few weeks before his death.

Accustomed to rely on his instincts, he was perfectly sure in his own mind. But how to act was another matter. He wanted, not to arrest a criminal red-handed, but to prevent a crime being committed and that was a very different and a very much more difficult thing.

All day he was very thoughtful. There was a Primrose League Fête that afternoon held in the grounds of the local squire, and he went to it, indulging in the penny dip, guessing the weight of a pig, and shying at coconuts, all with the same look of abstracted concentration on his face. He even indulged in half a crown's worth of Zara the Crystal Gazer, smiling a little to himself as he did so, remembering his own activities against fortune-tellers in his official days.

He did not pay very much heed to her singsong, droning voice till the end of a sentence held his attention.

"—and you will very shortly—very shortly indeed—be engaged on a matter of life or death—life or death to one person."

"Eh—what's that?" he asked abruptly.

"A decision—you have a decision to make. You must be very careful—very, very careful. . . . If you were to make a mistake—the smallest mistake—-"

"Yes?"

The fortune-teller shivered. Inspector Evans knew it was all nonsense, but he was nevertheless impressed.

"I warn you—you must not make a mistake. If you do, I see the result clearly, a death. . . ."

Odd, damned odd! A death. Fancy her lighting upon that!

"If I make a mistake a death will result? Is that it?"

"Yes."

"In that case," said Evans, rising to his feet and handing over half a crown, "I mustn't make a mistake, eh?"

He spoke lightly enough, but as he went out of the tent, his jaw set determinedly. Easy to say—not so easy to be sure of doing. He mustn't make a slip. A life, a valuable human life depended on it.

And there was no one to help him. He looked across at the figure of his friend Haydock in the distance. No help there. "Leave things alone," was Haydock's motto. And that wouldn't do here.

Haydock was talking to a woman. She moved away from him and came towards Evans, and the Inspector recognized her. It was Mrs. Merrowdene. On an impulse he put himself deliberately in her path.

Mrs. Merrowdene was rather a fine-looking

woman. She had a broad serene brow, very beautiful brown eyes, and a placid expression. She had the look of an Italian Madonna which she heightened by parting her hair in the middle and looping it over her ears. She had a deep, rather sleepy voice.

She smiled up at Evans, a contented, welcoming smile.

"I thought it was you, Mrs. Anthony—I mean Mrs. Merrowdene," he said glibly.

He made the slip deliberately, watching her without seeming to do so. He saw her eyes widen, heard the quick intake of her breath. But her eyes did not falter. She gazed at him steadily and proudly.

"I was looking for my husband," she said quietly. "Have you seen him anywhere about?"

"He was over in that direction when I last saw him."

They went side by side in the direction indicated, chatting quietly and pleasantly. The Inspector felt his admiration mounting. What a woman! What self-command! What wonderful poise! A remarkable woman—and a very dangerous one. He felt sure—a very dangerous one.

He still felt very uneasy, though he was satisfied with his initial step. He had let her know that he recognized her. That would put her on her guard. She would not dare attempt anything rash. There was the question of Merrowdene. If he could be warned. . . .

They found the little man absently contemplating a china doll which had fallen to his share in the penny dip. His wife suggested home and he agreed eagerly. Mrs. Merrowdene turned to the Inspector.

"Won't you come back with us and have a quiet cup of tea, Mr. Evans?"

Was there a faint note of challenge in her voice? He thought there was.

"Thank you, Mrs. Merrowdene. I should like to very much."

They walked there, talking together of pleasant ordinary things. The sun shone, a breeze blew gently, everything around them was pleasant and ordinary.

Their maid was out at the Fête, Mrs. Merrowdene explained, when they arrived at the charming Old World cottage. She went into her room to remove her hat, returning to set out tea and boil the kettle on a little silver lamp. From a shelf near the fireplace she took three small bowls and saucers.

"We have some very special Chinese tea," she explained. "And we always drink it in the Chinese manner—out of bowls, not cups."

She broke off, peered into a cup, and exchanged it for another, with an exclamation of annoyance.

"George—it's too bad of you. You've been taking these bowls again."

"I'm sorry, dear," said the professor apologetically. "They're such a convenient size. The ones I ordered haven't come."

"One of these days you'll poison us all," said his wife with a half laugh. "Mary finds them in the laboratory and brings them back here and never troubles to wash them out unless they've something very noticeable in them. Why, you were using one of them for potassium cyanide the other day;. Really, George, it's frightfully dangerous."

Merrowdene looked a little irritated.

"Mary's no business to remove things from the laboratory. She's not to touch anything there."

"But we often leave our teacups there after tea. How is she to know? Be reasonable, dear."

The professor went into his laboratory, murmuring to himself, and with a smile. Mrs. Merrowdene poured boiling water on the tea and blew out the flame of the little silver lamp.

Evans was puzzled. Yet a glimmering of light penetrated to him. For some reason or other, Mrs. Merrowdene was showing her hand. Was this to be the "accident"? Was she speaking of all this so as deliberately to prepare her alibi beforehand. So that when, one day, the "accident" happened, he would be forced to give evidence in her favor. Stupid of her, if so, because before that——

Suddenly he drew in his breath. She had poured the tea into the three bowls. One she set before him, one before herself, the other she placed on a little table by the fire near the chair her husband usually sat in, and it was as she placed this last one on the table that a little strange smile curved round her lips. It was the smile that did it.

He knew!

A remarkable woman—a dangerous woman. No waiting—no preparation. This afternoon—this very afternoon—with him here as witness. The boldness of it took his breath away.

It was clever—it was damnably clever. He would be able to prove nothing. She counted on his not suspecting—simply because it was "so soon." A woman of lightning rapidity of thought and action.

He drew a deep breath and leaned forward.

"Mrs. Merrowdene, I'm a man of queer whims. Will you be very kind and indulge me in one of them?"

She looked inquiring but unsuspicious.

He rose, took the bowl from in front of her, and crossed to the little table, where he substituted it for the other. This other he brought back and placed in front of her.

"I want to see you drink this."

Her eyes met his. They were steady, unfathomable. The color slowly drained from her face.

She stretched out her hand, raised the cup. He held his breath.

Supposing all along he had made a mistake.

She raised it to her lips—at the last moment, with a shudder she leaned forward and quickly poured it into a pot containing a fern. Then she sat back and gazed at him defiantly.

He drew a long sigh of relief, and sat down again.

"Well?" she said.

Her voice had altered. It was slightly mocking—defiant.

He answered her soberly and quietly.

"You are a very clever woman, Mrs. Merrowdene. I think you understand me. There must be no—repetition. You know what I mean?"

"I know what you mean."

Her voice was even, devoid of expression. He nodded his head, satisfied. She was a clever woman, and she didn't want to be hanged.

"To your long life and to that of your husband," he said significantly and raised his tea to his lips.

Then his face changed. It contorted horribly . . . he

tried to rise—to cry out. . . . His body stiffened—his face went purple. He fell back sprawling over the chair—his limbs convulsed.

Mrs. Merrowdene leaned forward, watching him. A little smile crossed her lips. She spoke to him— very softly and gently.

"You made a mistake, Mr. Evans. You thought I wanted to kill George. . . . How stupid of you—how very stupid."

She sat there a min ute longer looking at the dead man, the third man who had threatened to cross her path and separate her from the man she loved. . . .

Her smile broadened. She looked more than ever like a Madonna. Then she raised her voice and called.

"George—George. . . . Oh! Do come here. I'm afraid there's been the most dreadful accident. . . . Poor Mr. Evans. . . ."

THE SECOND GONG

Joan Ashby came out of her bedroom and stood a moment on the landing outside her door. She was half turning as if to go back into the room when, below her feet as it seemed, a gong boomed out.

Immediately Joan started forward almost at a run. So great was her hurry that at the top of the big staircase she collided with a young man arriving from the opposite direction.

"Hullo, Joan! Why the wild hurry?"

"Sorry, Harry. I didn't see you."

"So I gathered," said Harry Dalehouse dryly. "But as I say, why the wild haste?"

"It was the gong."

"I know. But it's only the first gong."

"No, it's the second."

"First."

"Second."

Thus arguing they had been descending the stairs. They were now in the hall, where the butler, having replaced the gongstick, was advancing toward them at a grave and dignified pace.

"It is the second," persisted Joan. "I know it is. Well, for one thing, look at the time."

Harry Dalehouse glanced up at the grandfather clock.

"Just twelve minutes past eight," he remarked. "Joan, I believe you're right, but I never heard the first one. Digby," he addressed the butler, "is this the first gong or the second?"

"The first, sir."

"At twelve minutes past eight? Digby, somebody will get the sack for this."

A faint smile showed for a minute on the butler's face.

"Dinner is being served ten minutes later tonight, sir. The master's orders."

"Incredible!" cried Harry Dalehouse. "Tut, tut! Upon my word, things are coming to a pretty pass! Wonders will never cease. What ails my revered uncle?"

"The seven o'clock train, sir, was half an hour late, and as——"

The butler broke off, as a sound like the crack of a whip was heard.

"What on earth——" said Harry. "Why, that sounded exactly like a shot."

A dark handsome man of thirty-five came out of the drawing-room on their left.

"What was that?" he asked. "It sounded exactly like a shot."

"It must have been a car backfiring, sir," said the butler. "The road runs quite close to the house this side and the upstairs windows are open."

"Perhaps," said Joan doubtfully. "But that would be over there." She waved a hand to the right. "And

I thought the noise came from here." She pointed to the left.

The dark man shook his head.

"I don't think so. I was in the drawing-room. I came out here because I thought the noise came from this direction." He nodded his head in front of him in the direction of the gong and the front door.

"East, west, and south, eh?" said the irrepressible Harry. "Well, I'll make it complete, Keene. North for me. I thought it came from behind us. Any solutions offered?"

"Well, there's always murder," said Geoffrey Keene, smiling. "I beg your pardon, Miss Ashby."

"Only a shiver," said Joan. "It's nothing. A what-do-you-call-it walking over my grave."

"A good thought—murder," said Harry. "But, alas! No groans, no blood. I fear the solution is a poacher after a rabbit."

"Seems tame, but I suppose that's it," agreed the other. "But it sounded so near. However, let's come into the drawing-room."

"Thank goodness, we're not late," said Joan fervently. "I was simply hareing it down the stairs thinking that was the second gong."

All laughing, they went into the big drawing-room.

Lytcham Close was one of the most famous old houses in England. Its owner, Hubert Lytcham Roche, was the last of a long line, and his more distant relatives were apt to remark that "Old Hubert, you know, really ought to be certified. Mad as a hatter, poor old bird."

Allowing for the exaggeration natural to friends and relatives, some truth remained. Hubert Lytcham

Roche was certainly eccentric. Though a very fine musician, he was a man of ungovernable temper and had an almost abnormal sense of his own importance. People staying in the house had to respect his prejudices or else they were never asked again.

One such prejudice was his music. If he played to his guests, as he often did in the evening, absolute silence must obtain. A whispered comment, a rustle of a dress, a movement even—and he would turn round scowling fiercely, and good-bye to the unlucky guest's chances of being asked again.

Another point was absolute punctuality for the crowning meal of the day. Breakfast was immaterial—you might come down at noon if you wished. Lunch also—a simple meal of cold meats and stewed fruit. But dinner was a rite, a festival, prepared by a *cordon bleu* whom he had tempted from a big hotel by the payment of a fabulous salary.

A first gong was sounded at five minutes past eight. At a quarter-past eight a second gong was heard, and immediately after the door was flung open, dinner announced to the assembled guests, and a solemn procession wended its way to the dining room. Anyone who had the temerity to be late for the second gong was henceforth excommunicated—and Lytcham Close shut to the unlucky diner forever.

Hence the anxiety of Joan Ashby, and also the astonishment of Harry Dalehouse, at hearing that the sacred function was to be delayed ten minutes on this particular evening. Though not very intimate with his uncle, he had been to Lytcham Close often enough to know what a very unusual occurrence that was.

Geoffrey Keene, who was Lytcham Roche's secretary, was also very much surprised.

"Extraordinary," he commented. "I've never known such a thing happen. Are you sure?"

"Digby said so."

"He said something about a train," said Joan Ashby. "At least I think so."

"Queer," said Keene thoughtfully. "We shall hear all about it in due course, I suppose. But it's very odd."

Both men were silent for a moment or two, watching the girl. Joan Ashby was a charming creature, blue-eyed and golden-haired, with an impish glance. This was her first visit to Lytcham Close and her invitation was at Harry's prompting.

The door opened and Diana Cleves, the Lytcham Roches' adopted daughter, came into the room.

There was a daredevil grace about Diana, a witchery in her dark eyes and her mocking tongue. Nearly all men fell for Diana and she enjoyed her conquests. A strange creature, with her alluring suggestion of warmth and her complete coldness.

"Beaten the Old Man for once," she remarked. "First time for weeks he hasn't been here first, looking at his watch and tramping up and down like a tiger at feeding time."

The young men had sprung forward. She smiled entrancingly at them both—then turned to Harry. Geoffrey Keene's dark cheek flushed as he dropped back.

He recovered himself, however, a moment later as Mrs. Lytcham Roche came in. She was a tall, dark woman, naturally vague in manner, wearing floating draperies of an indeterminate shade of green. With her was a middle-aged man with a beaklike nose and a determined chin—Gregory Barling. He was a somewhat prominent figure in the financial world and, well bred on his mother's side, he had for some years been an intimate friend of Hubert Lytcham Roche.

Boom!

The gong resounded imposingly. As it died away, the door was flung open and Digby announced:

"Dinner is served."

Then, well-trained servant though he was, a look of complete astonishment flashed over his impassive face. For the first time in his memory, his master was not in the room!

That his astonishment was shared by everybody was evident. Mrs. Lytcham Roche gave a little uncertain laugh.

"Most amazing. Really—I don't know what to do. . . ."

Everybody was taken aback. The whole tradition of Lytcham Close was undermined. What could have happened? Conversation ceased. There was a strained sense of waiting.

At last the door opened once more; a sigh of relief went round only tempered by a slight anxiety as to how to treat the situation. Nothing must be said to emphasize the fact that the host had himself transgressed the stringent rule of the house.

But the newcomer was not Lytcham Roche. Instead of the big, bearded, vikinglike figure, there advanced into the long drawing-room a very small man, palpably a foreigner, with an egg-shaped head, a flamboyant mustache, and most irreproachable evening clothes.

His eyes twinkling, the newcomer advanced toward Mrs. Lytcham Roche.

"My apologies, madame," he said. "I am, I fear, a few minutes late."

"Oh, not at all!" murmured Mrs. Lytcham Roche vaguely. "Not at all, Mr.——" She paused.

"Poirot, madame. Hercule Poirot."

He heard behind him a very soft "Oh"—a gasp rather than an articulate word—a woman's ejaculation. Perhaps he was flattered.

"You knew I was coming?" he murmured gently. "*N'est-ce pas, madame?* your husband told you."

"Oh—oh, yes," said Mrs. Lytcham Roche, her manner unconvincing in the extreme. "I mean, I suppose so. I am so terribly unpractical, M. Poirot. I never remember anything. But fortunately Digby sees to everything."

"My train, I fear, was late," said M. Poirot. "An accident on the line in front of us."

"Oh," cried Joan, "so that's why dinner was put off."

His eye came quickly round to her—a most uncannily discerning eye.

"That is something out of the usual—eh?"

"I really can't think——" began Mrs. Lytcham Roche, and then stopped. "I mean," she went on confusedly, "it's so odd. Hubert never——"

Poirot's eyes swept rapidly round the group.

"M. Lytcham Roche is not down yet?"

"No, and it's so extraordinary——" She looked appealingly at Geoffrey Keene.

"Mr. Lytcham Roche is the soul of punctuality," explained Keene. "He has not been late for dinner for—well, I don't know that he was ever late before."

To a stranger the situation must have been ludicrous—the perturbed faces and the general consternation.

"I know," said Mrs. Lytcham Roche with the air of one solving a problem; "I shall ring for Digby."

She suited the action to the word.

The butler came promptly.

"Digby," said Mrs. Lytcham Roche, "your master. Is he——"

As was customary with her, she did not finish her sentence. It was clear that the butler did not expect her to do so. He replied promptly and with understanding.

"Mr. Lytcham Roche came down at five minutes to eight and went into the study, madam."

"Oh!" She paused. "You don't think—I mean—he heard the gong?"

"I think he must have—the gong is immediately outside the study door."

"Yes, of course, of course," said Mrs. Lytcham Roche more vaguely than ever.

"Shall I inform him, madam, that dinner is ready?"

"Oh, thank you, Digby. Yes, I think—yes, yes, I should."

"I don't know," said Mrs. Lytcham Roche to her guests as the butler withdrew, "what I would do without Digby!"

A pause followed.

Then Digby reëntered the room. His breath was

coming a little faster than is considered good form in a butler.

"Excuse me, madam—the study door is locked."

It was then that M. Hercule Poirot took command of the situation.

"I think," he said, "that we had better go to the study."

He led the way and everyone followed. His assumption of authority seemed perfectly natural. He was no longer a rather comic-looking guest. He was a personality and master of the situation.

He led the way out into the hall, past the staircase, past the great clock, past the recess in which stood the gong. Exactly opposite that recess was a closed door.

He tapped on it, first gently, then with increasing violence. But there was no reply. Very nimbly he dropped to his knees and applied his eye to the keyhole. He rose and looked round.

"Messieurs," he said, "we must break open this door. Immediately!"

As before no one questioned his authority. Geoffrey Keene and Gregory Barling were the two biggest men. They attacked the door under Poirot's directions. It was no easy matter. The doors of Lytcham Close were solid affairs—no modern jerry-building here. It resisted the attack valiantly, but at last it gave before the united attack of the men and crashed inward.

The house party hesitated in the doorway. They saw what they had subconsciously feared to see. Facing them was the window. On the left, between the door and the window, was a big writing table. Sitting, not at the table, but sideways to it, was a man—a big man—slouched forward in the chair. His back was to them and his face to the window, but his position told the tale. His right hand hung limply down and below it, on the carpet, was a small shining pistol.

Poirot spoke sharply to Gregory Barling:

"Take Mrs. Lytcham Roche away—and the other two ladies."

The other nodded comprehendingly. He laid a hand on his hostess' arm. She shivered.

"He has shot himself," she murmured. "Horrible!" With another shiver she permitted him to lead her away. The two girls followed.

Poirot came forward into the room, the two young men behind him.

He knelt down by the body, motioning them to keep back a little.

He found the bullet hole on the right side of the head. It had passed out the other side and had evidently struck a mirror hanging on the left-hand wall, since this was shivered. On the writing table was a sheet of paper, blank save for the word "SORRY" scrawled across it in hesitating, shaky writing.

Poirot's eyes darted back to the door.

"The key is not in the lock," he said. "I wonder——"

His hand slid into the dead man's pocket.

"Here it is," he said. "At least I think so. Have the goodness to try it, monsieur?"

Geoffrey Keene took it from him and tried it in the lock.

"That's it, all right."

"And the window?"

Harry Dalehouse strode across to it.

"Shut."

"You permit?" Very swiftly, Poirot scrambled to his feet and joined the other at the window. It was a long French window. Poirot opened it, stood a minute scrutinizing the grass just in front of it, then closed it again.

"My friends," he said, "we must telephone for the police. Until they have come and satisfied themselves that it is truly suicide nothing must be touched. Death can only have occurred about a quarter of an hour ago."

"I know," said Harry hoarsely. "We heard the shot."

"*Comment?* What is that you say?"

Harry explained with the help of Geoffrey Keene. As he finished speaking, Barling reappeared.

Poirot repeated what he had said before, and while Keene went off to telephone, Poirot requested Barling to give him a few minutes' interview.

They went into a small morning room, leaving Digby on guard outside the study door, while Harry went off to find the ladies.

"You were, I understand, an intimate friend of M. Lytcham Roche," began Poirot. "It is for that reason that I address myself to you primarily. In etiquette, perhaps, I should have spoken first to madame, but at the moment I do not think that is *pratique*."

He paused.

"I am, see you, in a delicate situation. I will lay the facts plainly before you. I am, by profession, a private detective."

The financier smiled a little.

"It is not necessary to tell me that, M. Poirot. Your name is, by now, a household word."

"Monsieur is too amiable," said Poirot, bowing. "Let us, then, proceed. I receive, at my London address, a letter from this M. Lytcham Roche. In it he says that he has reason to believe that he is being swindled of large sums of money. For family reasons, so he puts it, he does not wish to call in the police, but he desires that I should come down and look into the matter for him. Well, I agree. I come. Not quite so soon as M. Lytcham Roche wishes—for after all I have other affairs, and M. Lytcham Roche, he is not quite the King of England, though he seems to think he is."

Barling gave a wry smile.

"He did think of himself that way."

"Exactly. Oh, you comprehend—his letter showed plainly enough that he was what one calls an eccentric. He was not insane, but he was unbalanced, *n'est-ce pas?*"

"What he's just done ought to show that."

"Oh, monsieur, but suicide is not always the act of the unbalanced. The coroner's jury, they say so, yes, but that is to spare the feelings of those left behind."

"Hubert was not a normal individual," said Barling decisively. "He was given to ungovernable rages, was a monomaniac on the subject of family pride, and had a bee in his bonnet in more ways than one. But for all that he was a shrewd man."

"Precisely. He was sufficiently shrewd to discover that he was being robbed."

"Does a man commit suicide because he's being robbed?" Barling asked.

"As you say, monsieur. Ridiculous. And that brings me to the need for haste in the matter. For family reasons—that was the phrase he used in his letter. *Eh, bien*, monsieur, you are a man of the world, you know that it is for precisely that—family reasons—that a man does commit suicide."

"You mean?"

"That it looks—on the face of it—as if *ce pauvre* monsieur had found out something further—and was unable to face what he had found out. But you perceive, I have a duty. I am already employed—commissioned—I have accepted the task. This 'family reason,' the dead man did not want it to get to the police. So I must act quickly. I must learn the truth."

"And when you have learned it?"

"Then—I must use my discretion. I must do what I can."

"I see," said Barling. He smoked for a minute or two in silence, then he said: "All the same I'm afraid I can't help you. Hubert never confided anything to me. I know nothing."

"But tell me, monsieur, who, should you say, had a chance of robbing this poor gentleman?"

"Difficult to say. Of course, there's the agent for the estate. He's a new man."

"The agent?"

"Yes. Marshall. Captain Marshall. Very nice fellow, lost an arm in the war. He came here a year ago. But Hubert liked him, I know, and trusted him too."

"If it were Captain Marshall who was playing him false, there would be no family reasons for silence."

"N-no."

The hesitation did not escape Poirot.

"Speak, monsieur. Speak plainly, I beg of you."

"It may be gossip."

"I implore you, speak."

"Very well, then, I will. Did you notice a very attractive-looking young woman in the drawing-room?"

"I noticed two very attractive-looking young women."

"Oh, yes, Miss Ashby. Pretty little thing. Her first visit. Harry Dalehouse got Mrs. Lytcham Roche to ask her. No, I mean a dark girl—Diana Cleves."

"I noticed her," said Poirot. "She is one that all men would notice, I think."

"She's a little devil," burst out Barling. "She's played fast and loose with every man for twenty miles round. Someone will murder her one of these days."

He wiped his brow with a handkerchief, oblivious of the keen interest with which the other was regarding him.

"And this young lady is——"

"She's Lytcham Roche's adopted daughter. A great disappointment when he and his wife had no children. They adopted Diana Cleves—she was some kind of cousin. Hubert was devoted to her, simply worshiped her."

"Doubtless he would dislike the idea of her marrying?" suggested Poirot.

"Not if she married the right person."

"And the right person was—you, monsieur?"

Barling started and flushed.

"I never said——"

"*Mais, non, mais non!* You said nothing. But it was so, was it not?"

"I fell in love with her—yes. Lytcham Roche was pleased about it. It fitted in with his ideas for her."

"And mademoiselle herself?"

"I told you—she's the devil incarnate."

"I comprehend. She has her own ideas of amusement, is it not so? But Captain Marshall, where does he come in?"

"Well, she's been seeing a lot of him. People talked. Not that I think there's anything in it. Another scalp, that's all."

Poirot nodded.

"But supposing that there had been something in it—well, then, it might explain why M. Lytcham Roche wanted to proceed cautiously."

"You do understand, don't you, that there's no earthly reason for suspecting Marshall of defalcation."

"*Oh, parfaitement, parfaitement!* It might be an affair of a forged check with someone in the household involved. This young Mr. Dalehouse, who is he?"

"A nephew."

"He will inherit, yes?"

"He's a sister's son. Of course he might take the name—there's not a Lytcham Roche left."

"I see."

"The place isn't actually entailed, though it's always gone from father to son. I've always imagined that he'd leave the place to his wife for her lifetime and then perhaps to Diana if he approved of her marriage. You see, her husband could take the name."

"I comprehend," said Poirot. "You have been most kind and helpful to me, monsieur. May I ask of you one thing further—to explain to Madame Lytcham

Roche all that I have told you, and to beg of her that she accord me a minute?"

Sooner than he had thought likely, the door opened and Mrs. Lytcham Roche entered. She floated to a chair.

"Mr. Barling has explained everything to me," she said. "We mustn't have any scandal, of course. Though I do feel really it's fate, don't you? I mean with the mirror and everything."

"*Comment*—the mirror?"

"The moment I saw it—it seemed a symbol. Of Hubert! A curse, you know. I think old families have a curse very often. Hubert was always very strange. Lately he has been stranger than ever."

"You will forgive me for asking, madame, but you are not in any way short of money?"

"Money? I never think of money."

"Do you know what they say, madame? Those who never think of money need a great deal of it."

He ventured a tiny laugh. She did not respond. Her eyes were far away.

"I thank you, madame," he said, and the interview came to an end.

Poirot rang and Digby answered.

"I shall require you to answer a few questions," said Poirot. "I am a private detective sent for by your master before he died."

"A detective!" the butler gasped. "Why?"

"You will please answer my questions. As to the shot now——"

He listened to the butler's account.

"So there were four of you in the hall?"

"Yes, sir; Mr. Dalehouse and Miss Ashby and Mr. Keene came from the drawing-room."

"Where were the others?"

"The others, sir?"

"Yes, Mrs. Lytcham Roche, Miss Cleves, and Mr. Barling."

"Mrs. Lytcham Roche and Mr. Barling came down later, sir."

"And Miss Cleves?"

"I think Miss Cleves was in the drawing-room, sir."

Poirot asked a few more questions, then dismissed the butler with the command to request Miss Cleves to come to him.

She came immediately, and he studied her attentively in view of Barling's revelations. She was certainly beautiful in her white satin frock with the rosebud on the shoulder.

He explained the circumstances which had brought him to Lytcham Close, eyeing her very closely, but she showed only what seemed to be genuine astonishment, with no signs of uneasiness. She spoke of Marshall indifferently with tepid approval. Only at mention of Barling did she approach animation.

"That man's a crook," she said sharply. "I told the Old Man so, but he wouldn't listen—went on putting money into his rotten concerns."

"Are you sorry, mademoiselle, that your—father is dead?"

She stared at him.

"Of course. I'm modern, you know, M. Poirot. I don't indulge in sob stuff. But I was fond of the Old Man. Though, of course, it's best for him."

"Best for him?"

"Yes. One of these days he would have had to be locked up. It was growing on him—this belief that the last Lytcham Roche of Lytcham Close was omnipotent."

Poirot nodded thoughtfully.

"I see, I see—yes, decided signs of mental trouble. By the way, you permit that I examine your little bag? It is charming—all these silk rosebuds. . . . What was I saying? Oh, yes, did you hear the shot?"

"Oh, yes! But I thought it was a car or a poacher, or something."

"You were in the drawing-room?"

"No. I was out in the garden."

"I see. Thank you, mademoiselle. Next I would like to see M. Keene, is it not?"

"Geoffrey? I'll send him along."

Keene came in, alert and interested.

"Mr. Barling has been telling me of the reason for your being down here. I don't know that there's anything I can tell you, but if I can——"

Poirot interrupted him.

"I only want to know one thing, Monsieur Keene. What was it that you stooped and picked up just before we got to the study door this evening?"

"I——" Keene half sprang up from his chair, then subsided again. "I don't know what you mean," he said lightly.

"Oh, I think you do, monsieur. You were behind me, I know, but a friend of mine he says I have eyes in the back of my head. You picked up something and you put it in the right-hand pocket of your dinner jacket."

There was a pause. Indecision was written plainly on Keene's handsome face. At last he made up his mind.

"Take your choice, M. Poirot," he said, and leaning forward he turned his pockets inside out. There was a cigarette holder, a handkerchief, a tiny silk rosebud, and a little gold match box.

A moment's silence and then Keene said, "As a matter of fact it was this." He picked up the match box. "I must have dropped it earlier in the evening."

"I think not," said Poirot.

"What do you mean?"

"What I say. I, monsieur, am a man of tidiness, of method, of order. A match box on the ground, I should see it and pick it up—a match box of this size, assuredly I should see it! No, monsieur, I think it was something very much smaller—such as this, perhaps."

He picked up the little silk rosebud.

"From Miss Cleves' bag, I think?"

There was a moment's pause, then Keene admitted it with a laugh.

"Yes, that's so. She—gave it to me last night."

"I see," said Poirot, and at the moment the door opened and a tall fair-haired man in a lounge suit strode into the room.

"Keene—what's all this? Lytcham Roche shot himself? Man, I can't believe it. It's incredible."

"Let me introduce you," said Keene, "to M. Hercule Poirot." The other started. "He will tell you all about it." And he left the room, banging the door.

"M. Poirot"—John Marshall was all eagerness—"I'm most awfully pleased to meet you. It is a bit of luck your being down here. Lytcham Roche never told me you were coming. I'm a most frightful admirer of yours, sir."

A disarming young man, thought Poirot—not so young, either, for there was gray hair at the temples and lines in the forehead. It was the voice and manner that gave the impression of boyishness.

"The police——"

"They are here now, sir. I came up with them on hearing the news. They don't seem particularly surprised. Of course he was mad as a hatter, but even then——"

"Even then you are surprised at his committing suicide?"

"Frankly, yes. I shouldn't have thought that—well, that Lytcham Roche could have imagined the world getting on without him."

"He has had money troubles of late, I understand?" Marshall nodded.

"He speculated. Wildcat schemes of Barling's."

Poirot said quietly: "I will be very frank. Had you any reason to suppose that Mr. Lytcham Roche suspected you of tampering with your accounts?"

Marshall stared at Poirot in a kind of ludicrous bewilderment. So ludicrous was it that Poirot was forced to smile.

"I see that you are utterly taken aback, Captain Marshall."

"Yes, indeed. The idea's ridiculous."

"Ah! Another question. He did not suspect you of robbing him of his adopted daughter?"

"Oh, so you know about me and Di?" He laughed in an embarrassed fashion.

"It is so, then?"

Marshall nodded.

"But the old man didn't know anything about it. Di wouldn't have him told. I suppose she was right. He'd have gone up like a—a basketful of rockets. I should have been chucked out of a job, and that would have been that."

"And instead what was your plan?"

"Well, upon my word, sir, I hardly know. I left things to Di. She said she'd fix it. As a matter of fact I was looking out for a job. If I could have got one I would have chucked this up."

"And mademoiselle would have married you? But M. Lytcham Roche might have stopped her allowance. Mademoiselle Diana is, I should say, fond of money."

Marshall looked rather uncomfortable.

"I'd have tried to make it up to her, sir."

Geoffrey Keene came into the room. "The police are just going and would like to see you, M. Poirot."

"*Merci*. I will come."

In the study were a stalwart inspector and the police surgeon.

"Mr. Poirot?" said the inspector. "We've heard of you, sir. I'm Inspector Reeves."

"You are most amiable," said Poirot, shaking hands. "You do not need my co-operation, no?" He gave a little laugh.

"Not this time, sir. All plain sailing."

"The case is perfectly straightforward, then?" demanded Poirot.

"Absolutely. Door and window locked, key of door

in dead man's pocket. Manner very strange the past few days. No doubt about it."

"Everything quite—natural?"

The doctor grunted.

"Must have been sitting at a damned queer angle for the bullet to have hit that mirror. But suicide's a queer business."

"You found the bullet?"

"Yes, here." The doctor held it out. "Near the wall below the mirror. Pistol was Mr. Roche's own. Kept it in the drawer of the desk always. Something behind it all, I daresay, but what that is we shall never know."

Poirot nodded.

The body had been carried to a bedroom. The police now took their leave. Poirot stood at the front door looking after them. A sound made him turn. Harry Dalehouse was close behind him.

"Have you, by any chance, a strong flashlight, my friend?" asked Poirot.

"Yes, I'll get it for you."

When he returned with it Joan Ashby was with him.

"You may accompany me if you like," said Poirot graciously.

He stepped out of the front door and turned to the right, stopping before the study window. About six feet of grass separated it from the path. Poirot bent down, playing the flashlight on the grass. He straightened himself and shook his head.

"No," he said, "not there."

Then he paused and slowly his figure stiffened. On either side of the grass was a deep flower border. Poirot's attention was focused on the right-hand border, full of Michaelmas-daisies and dahlias. His torch was directed on the front of the bed. Distinct on the soft mold were footprints.

"Four of them," murmured Poirot. "Two going toward the window, two coming from it."

"A gardener," suggested Joan.

"But no, mademoiselle, but no. Employ your eyes. These shoes are small, dainty, high-heeled, the shoes of a woman. Mademoiselle Diana mentioned having been out in the garden. Do you know if she went downstairs before you did, mademoiselle?"

Joan shook her head.

"I can't remember. I was in such a hurry because the gong went, and I thought I'd heard the first one. I do seem to remember that her room door was open as I went past, but I'm not sure. Mrs. Lytcham Roche's was shut, I know."

"I see," said Poirot.

Something in his voice made Harry look up sharply, but Poirot was merely frowning gently to himself.

In the doorway they met Diana Cleves.

"The police have gone," she said. "It's all—over."

She gave a deep sigh.

"May I request one little word with you, mademoiselle?"

She led the way into the morning room and Poirot followed, shutting the door.

"Well?" She looked a little surprised.

"One little question, mademoiselle. Were you tonight at any time in the flower border outside the study window?"

"Yes." She nodded. "About seven o'clock and again just before dinner."

"I do not understand," he said.

"I can't see that there is anything to 'understand,' as you call it," she said coldly. "I was picking Michaelmas-daisies—for the table. I always do the flowers. That was about seven o'clock."

"And afterwards—later?"

"Oh, that! As a matter of fact I dropped a spot of hair oil on my dress—just on the shoulder here. It was just as I was ready to come down. I didn't want to change the dress. I remembered I'd seen a late rose in bud in the border. I ran out and picked it and pinned it in. See——" She came close to him and lifted the head of the rose. Poirot saw the minute grease spot. She remained close to him, her shoulder almost brushing his.

"And what time was this?"

"Oh, about ten minutes past eight, I suppose."

"You did not—try the window?"

"I believe I did. Yes, I thought it would be quicker to go in that way. But it was fastened."

"I see." Poirot drew a deep breath. "And the shot," he said, "where were you when you heard that? Still in the flower border?"

"Oh, no; it was two or three minutes later, just before I came in by the side door."

"Do you know what this is, mademoiselle?"

On the palm of his hand he held out the tiny silk rosebud. She examined it coolly.

"It looks like a rosebud off my little evening bag. Where did you find it?"

"It was in Mr. Keene's pocket," said Poirot dryly.

"Did you give it to him, mademoiselle?"

"Did he tell you I gave it to him?"

Poirot smiled.

"When did you give it to him, mademoiselle?"

"Last night."

"Did he warn you to say that, mademoiselle?"

"What do you mean?" she asked angrily.

But Poirot did not answer. He strode out of the room and into the drawing-room. Barling, Keene, and Marshall were there. He went straight up to them.

"Messieurs," he said brusquely, "will you follow me to the study?"

He passed out into the hall and addressed Joan and Harry.

"You, too, I pray of you. And will somebody request madame to come? I thank you. Ah! and here is the excellent Digby. Digby, a little question, a very important little question. Did Miss Cleves arrange some Michaelmas-daisies before dinner?"

The butler looked bewildered.

"Yes, sir, she did."

"You are sure?"

"Quite sure, sir."

"*Très bien*. Now—come, all of you."

Inside the study he faced them.

"I have asked you to come here for a reason. The case is over, the police have come and gone. They say Mr. Lytcham Roche has shot himself. All is finished." He paused. "But I, Hercule Poirot, say that it is not finished."

As startled eyes turned to him the door opened and Mrs. Lytcham Roche floated into the room.

"I was saying, madame, that this case is not finished. It is a matter of the psychology. Mr. Lytcham Roche, he had the *manie de grandeur*, he was a king. Such a man does not kill himself. No, no, he may go mad, but he does not kill himself. Mr. Lytcham Roche did not kill himself." He paused. "He was killed."

"Killed?" Marshall gave a short laugh. "Alone in a room with the door and window locked?"

"All the same," said Poirot stubbornly, "he was killed."

"And got up and locked the door or shut the window afterwards, I suppose," said Diana cuttingly.

"I will show you something," said Poirot, going to the window. He turned the handle of the French windows and then pulled gently.

"See, they are open. Now I close them, but without turning the handle. Now the window is closed but not fastened. Now!"

He gave a short jarring blow and the handle turned, shooting the bolt down into its socket.

"You see?" said Poirot softly. "It is very loose, this mechanism. It could be done from outside quite easily."

He turned, his manner grim.

"When that shot was fired at twelve minutes past eight, there were four people in the hall. Four people have an alibi. Where were the other three? You, madame? In your room. You, Monsieur Barling. Were you, too, in your room?"

"I was."

"And you, mademoiselle, were in the garden. So you have admitted."

"I don't see——" began Diana.

"Wait." He turned to Mrs. Lytcham Roche. "Tell

me, madame, have you any idea of how your husband
left his money?"

"Hubert read me his will. He said I ought to know.
He left me three thousand a year chargeable on the
estate, and the dower house or the town house, whichever I preferred. Everything else he left to Diana, on
condition that if she married her husband must take
the name."

"Ah!"

"But then he made a codicil thing—a few weeks
ago, that was."

"Yes, madame?"

"He still left it all to Diana, but on condition that
she married Mr. Barling. If she married anyone else,
it was all to go to his nephew, Harry Dalehouse."

"But the codicil was only made a few weeks ago,"
purred Poirot. "Mademoiselle may not have known of
that." He stepped forward accusingly. "Mademoiselle
Diana, you want to marry Captain Marshall, do you
not? Or is it Mr. Keene?"

She walked across the room and put her arm
through Marshall's sound one.

"Go on," she said.

"I will put the case against you, mademoiselle.
You loved Captain Marshall. You also loved money.
Your adopted father he would never have consented
to your marrying Captain Marshall, but if he dies you
are fairly sure that you get everything. So you go out,
you step over the flower border to the window which
is open, you have with you the pistol which you have
taken from the writing-table drawer. You go up to
your victim talking amiably. You fire. You drop the
pistol by his hand, having wiped it and then pressed

his fingers on it. You go out again, shaking the window till the bolt drops. You come into the house. Is that how it happened? I am asking you, mademoiselle?"

"No," Diana screamed. "No—no!"

He looked at her, then he smiled.

"No," he said, "it was not like that. It might have been so—it is plausible—it is possible—but it cannot have been like that for two reasons. The first reason is that you picked Michaelmas-daisies at seven o'clock, the second arises from something that mademoiselle here told me." He turned toward Joan, who stared at him in bewilderment. He nodded encouragement.

"But yes, mademoiselle. You told me that you hurried downstairs because you thought it was the second gong sounding, having already heard the first."

He shot a rapid glance round the room.

"You do not see what that means?" he cried. "You do not see. Look! Look!" He sprang forward to the chair where the victim had sat. "Did you notice how the body was? Not sitting square to the desk—no, sitting sideways to the desk, facing the window. Is that a natural way to commit suicide? *Jamais, jamais!* You write your apologia 'sorry' on a piece of paper—you open the drawer, you take out the pistol, you hold it to your head and you fire. That is the way of suicide. But now consider murder! The victim sits at his desk, the murderer stands beside him—talking. And talking still—fires. Where does the bullet go then?" He paused. "Straight through the head, through the door if it is open, and so—hits the gong.

"Ah! you begin to see? That was the first gong—

heard only by mademoiselle, since her room is above.

"What does our murderer do next? Shuts the door, locks it, puts the key in the dead man's pocket, then turns the body sideways in the chair, presses the dead man's fingers on the pistol and then drops it by his side, cracks the mirror on the wall as a final spectacular touch—in short, 'arranges' his suicide. Then out through the window, the bolt is shaken home, the murderer steps not on the grass, where footprints must show, but on the flower bed, where they can be smoothed out behind him, leaving no trace. Then back into the house, and at twelve minutes past eight, when he is alone in the drawing-room, he fires a service revolver out of the drawing-room window and dashes out into the hall. Is that how you did it, Mr. Geoffrey Keene?"

Fascinated, the secretary stared at the accusing figure drawing nearer to him. Then, with a gurgling cry, he fell to the ground.

"I think I am answered," said Poirot. "Captain Marshall, will you ring up the police?" He bent over the prostrate form. "I fancy he will be still unconscious when they come."

"Geoffrey Keene," murmured Diana. "But what motive had he?"

"I fancy that as secretary he had certain opportunities—accounts—checks. Something awakened Mr. Lytcham Roche's suspicions. He sent for me."

"Why for you? Why not for the police?"

"I think, mademoiselle, you can answer that question. Monsieur suspected that there was something between you and that young man. To divert his mind from Captain Marshall, you had flirted shamelessly with Mr. Keene. But yes, you need not deny! Mr. Keene gets wind of my coming and acts promptly. The essence of his scheme is that the crime must seem to take place at 8:12, when he has an alibi. His one danger is the bullet, which must be lying somewhere near the gong and which he has not had time to retrieve. When we are all on our way to the study he picks that up. At such a tense moment he thinks no one will notice. But me, I notice everything! I question him. He reflects a little minute and then he plays the comedy! He insinuates that what he picked up was the silk rosebud, he plays the part of the young man in love shielding the lady he loves. Oh, it was very clever, and if you had not picked Michaelmas-daisies——"

"I don't understand what they have to do with it."

"You do not? Listen—there were only four footprints in the bed, but when you were picking the flowers you must have made many more than that. So in between your picking the flowers and your coming to get the rosebud someone must have smoothed over the bed. Not a gardener—no gardener works after seven. Then it must be someone guilty—it must be the murderer . . . the murder was committed before the shot was heard."

"But why did nobody hear the real shot?" asked Harry.

"A silencer. They will find that and the revolver thrown into the shrubbery."

"What a risk!"

"Why a risk? Everyone was upstairs dressing for dinner. It was a very good moment. The bullet was the only contretemps, and even that, as he thought, passed off well."

Poirot picked it up. "He threw it under the mirror when I was examining the window with Mr. Dalehouse."

"Oh!" Diana wheeled on Marshall. "Marry me, John, and take me away."

Barling coughed. "My dear Diana, under the terms of my friend's will——"

"I don't care," the girl cried. "We can draw pictures on pavements."

"There's no need to do that," said Harry. "We'll go halves, Di. I'm not going to bag things because Uncle had a bee in his bonnet."

Suddenly there was a cry. Mrs. Lytcham Roche had sprung to her feet.

"M. Poirot—the mirror—he—he must have deliberately smashed it."

"Yes, madame."

"Oh!" she stared at him. "But it is unlucky to break a mirror."

"It has proved very unlucky for Mr. Geoffrey Keene," said Poirot cheerfully.

Mystery's #1 Bestselling Author

AGATHA CHRISTIE

Three Blind Mice
AND OTHER STORIES

(Also published as *The Mousetrap and Other Stories*)

A BLINDING SNOWSTORM—and a homicidal maniac—traps a small party of friends in an isolated estate. Out of this deceptively simple set-up, Agatha Christie fashioned one of her most ingenious puzzlers, which, in turn, would provide the basis for *The Mousetrap*, the longest-running play in history. From this classic title novella to the deliciously clever gems on its tail (solved to perfection by Hercule Poirot and Miss Jane Marple), this rare collection of murder most foul showcases the inimitable Christie at her inventive best, proving her reputation as "the champion deceiver of our time." (*The New York Times*)

3BM 4/01

BANTAM
KNOWLEDGE
THROUGH
COLOR

WILD CATS

BY MICHAEL BOORER
ILLUSTRATED BY PETER WARNER

BANTAM BOOKS
TORONTO NEW YORK LONDON
A NATIONAL GENERAL COMPANY

FOREWORD

Probably the most popular of all the animals in the zoo are the big cats and their relatives. This book is a general account of all the living species and their habits. Besides descriptions of the cats and their natural environments, ways in which man has used these animals are also described, such as hunting with cheetahs and tiger-hunting using elephants. The cat family is introduced with its ancestors, including sabertoothed 'tigers,' and is followed through its various developments to the wild cats we know today.

WILD CATS

*A Bantam Book / published by arrangement with
Grosset & Dunlap, Inc.*

PRINTING HISTORY
*Grosset & Dunlap edition published September 1970
Bantam edition published October 1971*

*Bantam Books are published by Bantam Books, Inc., a National
General company. Its trade-mark, consisting of the words "Bantam
Books" and the portrayal of a bantam, is registered in the United
States Patent Office and in other countries. Marca Registrada.
Bantam Books, Inc., 666 Fifth Avenue, New York, N.Y. 10019.*

CONTENTS

INTRODUCTION

The Cats—Fiercest of Hunters

No one is indifferent to cats. People either love them or hate them. If questioned about his feelings, the average cat-lover would probably talk of the graceful movements and the endearing and friendly, yet independent ways of the domestic cat, but this is only part of the story. It is only necessary to visit a lion house in any zoo to see that most people also find wild cats fascinating and that these cats are by no means friendly. If most are graceful, some, such as the jaguar, are clumsy by comparison. That another explanation exists becomes very clear when the excited crowd throngs around the lion's cage at feeding time. The fascination that cats exert has a great deal to do with the fact that they are meat eaters, or carnivores.

Only plants manufacture food from simple raw materials: water and carbon dioxide from the air are combined through the energy of sunlight into sugar and other complex food molecules. Once this has been done, animals obtain their food by eating plants. But soon after the origin of simple plants and plant-eating animals some 2½ billion years ago—there was an alternative. Some animals could now feed on other animals. The carnivorous way of life is therefore almost as old as life on this planet. As the herbivorous or plant-eating animals have developed defenses, the carnivores in their turn have developed more efficient weapons and hunting methods.

Animals with backbones first evolved where life began—in the sea. Being larger and more active than most other animals they became successful. During the past few hundred million years some fishes invaded the land as the first amphibians, some of which later became reptiles. These animals all had cold blood, which was adequate for an aquatic life, but not ideal for active life in varied climates on land. The warm-blooded mammals evolved from the reptiles, and within the last 70 million years they have become the most important active land animals.

Like all other animals, the mammals show a range of specializations. Some of them are herbivorous and others are hunters. There are other carnivorous mammals, but the real specialists are the members of the order Carnivora. The most

4

Two extremes of the cat family—the lion and the domestic cat.

highly developed of these, in a sense the pinnacle of mammalian carnivore evolution, are the cats.

In the same way, the hunting methods of the cats are highly developed. Most cats hunt by stealth, creeping up on their prey unobserved, and then pouncing rapidly on their victims. This behavior can be observed in domestic cats, as they lie in wait in the garden for mice or birds. The cheetah hunts more like a dog, running swiftly after its prey. But whatever the method, the cat's perfect coordination of mind and limb makes it a successful hunter. Hunting is always an exciting subject, and perfection must demand respect. No wonder that man, himself a mammal, finds the cats—from the tabby to the lion—fascinating.

5

EVOLUTION OF THE CAT

The Origin of the Carnivora

Like many other groups of living mammals, the Carnivora are descended from small, furry, insect-eating animals that flourished about 70 million years ago. Some descendants of this group, such as the shrews, have changed very little while others, including the hoofed herbivorous mammals and man himself, have changed a great deal. The Carnivora, too, have undergone considerable change, but in a very understandable way.

The first really successful group of animals within the order Carnivora flourished between 40 and 50 million years ago. We know this because their fossilized remains are common in rocks formed at that time. The creodonts, as this early group are called, have been extinct for millions of years, but we know that they were once successful because a whole range of them existed, adapted for a number of different carnivorous modes of life.

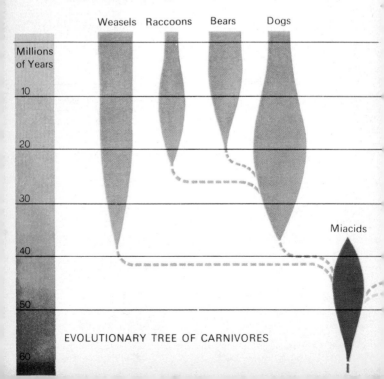

EVOLUTIONARY TREE OF CARNIVORES

The earliest of them were quite small—about the size of a weasel—and had very small brains. None of the teeth in either the upper or the lower jaw were enlarged for the purpose of shearing through meat. Their bodies and limbs were slender, and they moved on flat feet with their heels touching the ground as they walked.

From these early creodonts a host of more highly developed animals evolved. These animals had as shearing teeth the first or second upper molars and the second or third lower molars. Exactly which teeth were used for this purpose may seem unimportant, but small details can be important in science. Shearing teeth have also been developed by the modern successful carnivores, but in a slightly different part of the jaw.

At the height of their success the creodonts included medium-sized, wolf-like animals, and huge bear-like creatures, but by 10 million years ago the last lingering line of them had died out. The descendants of the miacids, another early group within the Carnivora, had come to rule the roost.

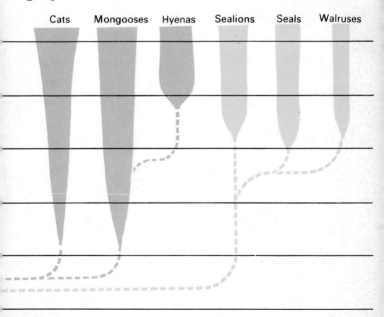

Cats   Mongooses   Hyenas   Sealions   Seals   Walruses

A miacid, a prehistoric forebear of the cats.

The Beginnings of the Modern Carnivora

The miacids sprang from the same stock as the creodonts. At first they were overshadowed by their more numerous cousins, although they flourished as forest dwellers, climbing easily and often hunting among the branches of trees. As befits climbers they were not large, being perhaps the size of a small cat. They had long bodies and tails, and short but flexible limbs. Each foot bore five toes which were probably armed with retractile claws, not unlike those of modern cats. Their brains were larger than those of the creodonts and, significantly, the shearing teeth they developed were formed from the last premolar tooth of the upper jaw and the first molar of the lower.

About 40 million years ago, a time when the creodonts were dwindling, a whole range of hunters of different kinds were evolving from the miacid stock. At this time the groups which we know today as the families of modern Carnivora became recognizable. The miacids themselves died out, but their more highly developed descendants grew in numbers and importance as they adopted the modes of life left vacant by the creodonts.

Marine Carnivores

One surpising development was the evolution, from normal land animals, of a group of excellent swimmers capable of spending much of their time at sea. Seals, sea lions and walruses used to be grouped together under the name pinnipeds ('fin-footed'). New research indicates, however, that the seals were derived from otter-like weasels, while the sea lions and walruses descended from bears. In all tails became shorter and limbs became powerfully webbed for swimming. They kept their fur, but as wet fur is useless for heat retention, the fat beneath the skin became the most important means of keeping the body warm. Today there are several groups of aquatic carnivores.

The Sea Lions still retain the ear-flaps typical of mammals and swim mainly by using their long forelimbs. Out of the water they can use their hind feet to move in a clumsy gallop. **The Walruses** lack ear-flaps and move clumsily on land or in water. They feed on shellfish and have teeth that are adapted for this purpose. They are an offshoot of the eared seals. **The Seals** are the most aquatic of the carnivores. They lack ear-flaps and swim well using their hind feet, which are of no use out of water. Like the sea lions, most of them feed on fish and have sharply pointed teeth.

Sea lions evolved from the same miacid stock as did the cats. Both in their different ways are fierce and able hunters.

The remaining modern Carnivora are known as the fissipeds—a name which means 'split-footed ones' and refers to the fact that they do not have webbed feet. As the majority of the Carnivora are fissipeds it is most convenient to classify them into two main groups.

The Dog-like Group of Families

The oldest of the fissipeds are closer to the dogs than they are to the cats. These carnivores have retained the long jaw of the miacids and have a relatively large number of teeth. It might appear that numerous teeth ought to be an asset to a hunter, but this is not so. A long jaw does not bite as hard as a short jaw and, as long as there are enough teeth left to do the job, a short jaw is therefore best. However, the dog-like carnivores have one advantage. Above their long mouths they have room for large and most efficient noses. Their sense of smell is unequaled. There are four families in this group:

The Brown Bear, like the cats, is descended from the miacids and has their long jaw and large number of teeth.

The Dog Family consists of running hunters, always moving on tiptoe, such as wolves and foxes.

The Bear Family contains a few heavyweight, flat-footed species.

The Raccoon Family, like the bears, consist of flat-footed animals, but being smaller, they are mostly excellent climbers.

The Weasel Family has retained something of the original miacid shape, but its members—martens, otters and skunks—have a wide range of hunting methods.

Other, descendants of the miacids include the raccoon (*top*), the marten (*center*), which resembles a miacid more than other dog-like mammals, and the wolf (*bottom*).

The Indian Mongoose, like the cat, is an agile hunter and is known for its practice of killing snakes.

The Cat-like Group of Families

Apart from the cats themselves, two other families of the Carnivora have short jaws and hence improved biting power. **The Mongoose and Civet Family** contains many species which have a superficial resemblance to the weasels. This resemblance exists partly because both families have retained something of the appearance of the miacid ancestors they share, but mainly because some members of each family have separately become adapted for the same forms of hunting. Mongooses and weasels rarely compete for the same food, however, for most weasels come from the cool climates of Europe, northern Asia and North America, while mongooses typically inhabit the warmer parts of Asia and Africa.

The mongoose family contains about eighty different species. Some of them, like the Indian Mongoose, are fierce hunters, capable of working through quick cover and diving into burrows, but others, such as the equally short-legged Meerkat of Africa, feed mainly on insects and eat quite a lot of plant food as well. The genets and civets have slightly longer legs and are more cat-like in appearance. They are expert climbers, and various species inhabit the forests of Africa and Asia feeding on small mammals and birds, as well as invertebrates and fruit.

The Hyena Family contains only four species. At a quick glance the hyenas look more like dogs than cats, but with their weak-looking, sloping backs they could never undertake the strenuous running and hunting typical of the dogs, and neither do they need to. With their shorter jaws the hyenas have, in relation to their size, a more powerful bite than any other living mammal, and for this reason they rarely lack food. Once the lion has killed its prey, and the vultures and such mammalian scavengers as the jackals have eaten their fill, then there is always food for the hyena. Coming last to the banquet, they are able to crack bones which no other mammal can deal with, and are thus able to dine on bone marrow. This is the mode of life of both the Striped Hyena of Africa and Asia and the bigger Spotted Hyena of East Africa.

The other two species are less formidable. The Brown Hyena of southern Africa mainly feeds on carrion which it finds on seashores, while the aardwolf of eastern and southern Africa has unusually weak jaws and eats insects.

The Striped Hyena of Africa and Asia. Although it resembles a dog, it is closely related to the cat.

Cats of the Past

The first cats were descended from the same ancestors as the mongooses and civets, but 35 million years ago the cats were clearly distinguishable as a distinct type. Perhaps it would be better to say two types, for right from the beginning there were two types of cat, not one, and this state of affairs lasted until only a few thousand years ago. One of these lines became adapted for hunting active animals, and this stock eventually gave rise to all of the cats we know today. The other line, successful until times which must be regarded as recent when considered against the long perspective of geological time, consisted of the saber-tooths, often mistakenly called 'tigers'.

All the Carnivora have well-developed canine teeth, but in the saber-tooths these weapons became phenomenal. Even the early forms, which were cats of medium size, had remarkably large canines, but the trend reached its peak in the Saber-toothed 'Tiger' (Smilodon), which was as large as a tiger and had fangs seven or eight inches in length.

It is always difficult to be sure exactly how extinct animals lived, for we know them only as fossils and a certain amount of guesswork is involved. However, almost certainly the saber-tooths were adapted to hunt animals such as rhinoceroses and elephants, whose chief defenses were their size and their thick skins. The Saber-toothed 'Tiger' could open its mouth very widely, so that the teeth were exposed for use like daggers, and inflict a slashing, stabbing wound even upon the most thick-skinned of prey.

Saber-tooths mostly inhabited the northern hemisphere — North America, Europe and Asia — but at one stage within the past million years they also invaded South America, a continent which has been cut off by the sea, and therefore difficult for land animals to reach, for most of its history. While the mammoths and the mastodons flourished, so did the saber-tooths that hunted them. When the giant land mammals dwindled in numbers the saber-tooths died out. They were specialists, creatures unable to adopt other forms of hunting.

Their cousins, the ancestors of the modern cats, lived on. Chance plays a large part in these matters, and by chance they had not blundered into an evolutionary cul-de-sac.

Saber-toothed 'Tigers' had fangs seven or eight inches long, and the shape of the skull (*below*) enabled them to open their mouths very widely. The normal jaw muscles were not especially large, so that the strength of the bite itself could have been nothing remarkable. The muscles of the neck, however, were very strong so that the whole head, with the jaws gaping, could be jerked powerfully downward. In this way, a savage wound was inflicted on the prey.

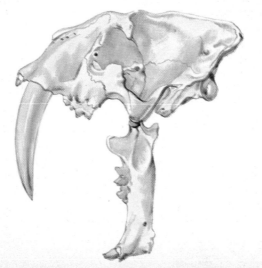

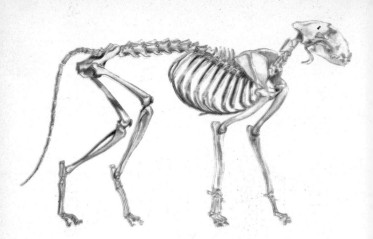

THE CAT'S BODY

Modern Cats

Even before the remarkable killing spree in which man has indulged during the past few hundred years, there were far more kinds of animals extinct than still living. At any stage in the history of life on earth the species alive were the lucky survivors from times past—lucky because they were adapted to conditions that still continued to exist. The modern cats are stealthy hunters, capable of sudden bursts of power. This is what they are adapted for from the front of their short jaws to the sharp ends of their claws.

Cats hunt animals which are wary and which are well able to escape if they perceive danger. A stealthy, silent approach is essential, and for this a cat must have a supple and freely moving body. Once within range—and cats of most kinds get very close before launching the final attack—stealth is abandoned and speed replaces it. Over the last few feet or yards the cat pounces. Over slightly longer distances a cat may sprint for a few strides, but cats never run while hunting in the way that wild dogs such as wolves do. An exception is the cheetah, which will often launch itself at full speed in pursuit of its prey, rather in the way that dogs hunt.

Cat-style hunting calls for a strong but flexible body, yet

The cat's skeleton (*left*) has a flexible backbone and leg bones connected to powerful muscles (*above*), enabling the animal to spring and move with agility.

no great powers of endurance. Basically, the only parts of the skeleton which have changed greatly from the original shrew-like mammal pattern in the course of evolution are the skull (including the teeth) and, to a slightly lesser degree, the limbs. The backbone is very flexible, especially in the lumbar (or waist) region, and it is from the back, together with the hind legs, which can be bent and then straightened in a strong kick, that the cats derive their power in pouncing. The ease with which the legs can move, even in a crouching position, is due to their ability to bend freely at the shoulder, elbow, wrist, knee and ankle, and this explains the skill with which a cat creeps toward its prey.

Graceful movement calls for a well-developed system of muscles, for the best of skeletons is useless without muscle to power it, and this cats certainly possess. The grace with which they move is proverbial. As might be expected, the strongest muscles are to be found in the lumbar region and hind legs (for springing) and the shoulder region and neck (for power in striking), but it is only necessary to watch a kitten playing with a ping-pong ball to see that cats are capable of delicate movements as well.

17

The Limbs

The first mammals had *plantigrade* limbs—that is to say that they walked on flat feet with the wrist and heel making contact with the ground during each stride. This form of limb was ideal for a small mammal clambering about among vegetation which was large in relation to its size. The flat part of the foot could make contact with the rounded plant stem, giving an efficient grip. Some mammals have retained this sort of limb because they are still climbers. Examples are the monkeys and their relation, man. Other mammals, like the bears, retain plantigrade limbs because they are useful in spreading the animal's heavy weight over the ground.

But this type of limb is not perfect for all purposes. We are plantigrade when we walk, but when we run we rise on tiptoe to effectively make the legs longer so that we can travel farther with each stride. Where running or springing are important, animals become adapted to move in this way all the time. Because such animals move on their toes, or digits, they are said to have *digitigrade* limbs. Cats are digitigrade.

To understand the cat's limbs in relation to our own it is only necessary to appreciate that the bend which appears to be in the position of a knee in a cat's hind leg but which

A cat's feet are digitigrade, meaning that the animal walks on tiptoe, enabling it to run with long strides and to spring.

A cat's claws are retractile and are drawn into the openings in the feet when they are not being used.

bends the same way as the human ankle, really *is* an ankle. The soft pads upon which the hunting cat can move so quietly are not on the sole of the foot, but are on the toes or at the base of them.

Cats have five toes on their front feet. The digit which corresponds to the human thumb is shorter than the others but is useful when the forelimb is used for manipulation. On the hind foot there are only four toes, the digit corresponding to the human big toe being absent.

The limbs of vertebrates normally end in claws and have done so almost ever since limbs evolved on the first amphibians. Almost certainly the original function of claws was to protect the ends of the digits from wear. Claws were adapted to take the wear, growing as fast as they were worn away. However, once structures have come into existence they often acquire new functions and this is true of the claws of many animals. Cats' claws have developed to become so useful in other ways that they are now useless for their original purpose.

Cats have retractile claws. This means that the claws are normally hidden in special openings on the ends of the digits. Thus, when a cat walks the claws do not scrape on the ground, which is a great advantage during stealthy movement. Because the claws are retracted they remain sharp until they are really needed, when they can be pulled out by special muscles and be ready for action. Sharp claws make excellent weapons and are also useful for climbing trees. Most cats climb well.

The cat's skull contains powerful jaws and a comparatively large brain cavity.

The Head

As is the case in most animals, invertebrate or vertebrate, the head of a cat contains several of the most important sense organs: the brain which is, in a sense, the chief information and executive center of the body, and also the mouth. Cats require keen senses to detect the tiny clues that may be useful to a hunter, and the eyes, ears and nose of a cat are all large and very highly developed.

As a group the mammals are the most intelligent animals in existence. The cats are not the most intelligent of mammals—that place is reserved for man and his closest relations—but compared to the mammals as a whole the cats must be regarded as reasonably bright. Their brains and, in particular, their cerebral hemispheres, which have to do with intelligent behavior, are large.

Nevertheless much of their behavior is not the product of reason, but of instinct. Instinctive behavior is automatic, inborn behavior which happens as a result of the way in which the nerve messages pass through fixed circuits by way of the brain to the muscles or glands, which are responsible for activity. Once a certain group of circumstances occurs, an appropriate response is made without pause for cogitation.

Behavior of this kind, although rather inflexible, is adequate for most of the situations that a cat encounters.

The Jaws and Teeth

As we have seen, the jaws of a cat are short, and this makes for power in biting. The large muscles which power the jaws extend from the lower jaw itself and, passing over the sides of the head, are joined to the roof of the skull where there is a bony ridge ideal for the purpose.

Mammals are unique in having various types of teeth in different parts of their mouths. At the front are the incisors, which are often chisel-shaped as they are in man, although those of the Carnivora are more pointed. Immediately behind these teeth come the sharply pointed eye teeth or canines. The teeth at the sides of the mouth are sometimes grouped together as cheek teeth, but are of two types. Those immediately behind the canines are the premolars, and these are usually simpler in structure than the molars that come behind them. A mammal has two sets of teeth during its lifetime—the milk teeth, which are lost quite early, and the adult teeth. The milk teeth do not form a complete set as molars are never present at this stage. The molars in all mammals only come in as part of the adult set.

Different kinds of mammals have not only teeth of different shapes, adapted according to their diet, but also different numbers of teeth of the various kinds. The number of teeth typically possessed by a species is conveniently expressed in a dental formula. This gives, for one side of the jaws only, the numbers of teeth of each type present, figures for the upper and lower jaws being given separately. Thus the dental formula of the cats, which altogether have six incisors in the upper jaw (three on each side), and six more below, one canine on each side in both the upper and lower jaws, three premolars on each side of the upper jaw and two below, and one molar on each side above and below is:

$$I\frac{3}{3}C\frac{1}{1}P\frac{3}{2}M\frac{1}{1}$$

This means that there is a total of thirty teeth altogether in the full adult set.

The first of the premolars of the upper jaw is small and

may in some cases be absent. As is the case in all of the modern Carnivora, the hindmost of the upper premolars and the first of the lower molars (and the only lower molar in the case of the cats) are large. These teeth, known as the carnassials, are of great importance in shearing through meat.

The shortening of the jaw typical of the cats and their closer relatives goes together with a reduction in the number of cheek teeth. As a comparison, the dogs have the dental formula:

$$I\frac{3}{3}C\frac{1}{1}P\frac{4}{4}M\frac{2}{3}$$

The cat's incisor teeth are of little importance in hunting or feeding, although they are sometimes used to nibble small tidbits from a carcass. The rasping action of the rough tongue is more important in this respect, however. The incisors are more often used for grooming the fur, the upper lip being curled back to expose them for this purpose.

The canines are of great importance for they, together with the claws, are the weapons used in making a kill. They are in use again immediately afterwards, ripping and tearing at the prey so as to reduce the feast to manageable proportions. Once this has been accomplished, the carnassial teeth come into play.

Cats have large, grinning mouths, and because of this it is

easy for them to use the teeth at the sides of their mouths in feeding. The meat is taken between the crowns of the carnassial teeth which, as the lower jaw moves straight upward, approach and pass close to each other like the blades of a pair of shears, cutting through the food. Once this has been done, the morsel in the mouth is swallowed at once. Cats have no teeth suitable for grinding food, and in any case meat is easy to digest and does not need to be pulverized first.

Cats' teeth are ideal for their purpose, but if used in other ways would be almost useless, as anyone who has ever watched a cat trying to take a morning snack of grass (presumably for health reasons) will know.

A cat bites its food in various ways. The front *canine* teeth act like a pair of daggers (*left*) to kill and tear the prey. The side *carnassial* teeth act with a shearing action (*right*) to cut through pieces of meat, which are then swallowed whole.

23

At night, a cat's pupils
open wide.

The Eyes

A cat's eyes are on the front of the head rather than at the side. This means that cats do not have all-round vision, a feature which would not be important to them for they are fierce enough not to fear surprise attacks. But they are able to judge distance, an ability which is important when pouncing on other animals who will not allow a second attempt if it can be avoided. Like most other mammals, cats are color blind and do not see in such sharp detail as human beings do. Nevertheless, their eyesight is good when compared to that of almost any mammal other than man.

The night vision of cats is proverbial. In fact not all kinds of cats have equally good vision in this respect, and none of them equal mammals like the bushbabies, which are completely nocturnal animals.

Cats of many species are adapted to hunt both by day and

by night as opportunity offers, and the design of the eyes is therefore a compromise. The most obvious sign of this adaptation appears in the shape of the pupils. In the domestic cat and many other species the pupil is not round, but forms a vertical slit. A pupil of this shape can be opened more widely and closed more narrowly than a pupil of the conventional round shape, and is therefore more useful in an eye which must work under a wide variety of light. A vertical slit is of more use than a horizontal one because in bright light the amount of light entering the eye is still further reduced when the eyelids are partly closed, thus reducing the functional part of the pupil slit to a mere pinpoint.

Because their eyes glow at night, cats were regarded as sacred by the ancient Egyptians. The cat, it was thought, has eyes which reflect the sun when it is hidden from mere man. The true explanation is only a little less remarkable. Beneath the sensitive nerve cells inside a cat's eye there is a reflecting layer, so that in dim light each ray of light has two chances of affecting the nerve cells, one on the way into the eye and the other on the way out again.

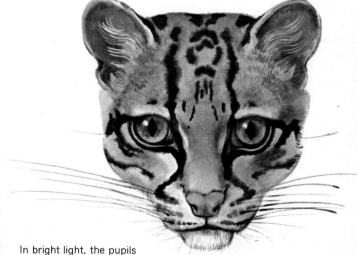

In bright light, the pupils narrow to a slit.

25

The Ears

The ears of a cat are even larger than they appear to be at first, for the fur growing round their base conceals their true size. They are, in fact, huge ear-trumpets and serve to funnel even tiny sounds into the internal ears, from which the information passes to the brain. The external ears are also useful in locating the source of the sound, and this is partly explained by the fact that they can be moved on the head, swiveling around like direction-finders until they point in the direction in which the sound is loudest. In general, cats have the largest ears possible, bearing in mind that there are other factors involved.

Large ears, although efficient, can have disadvantages. For example, extremely long ears might be damaged by prickly undergrowth and would be a mixed blessing to a cat which inhabits dense bush country. A more important

An example of Allen's Rule among the cats. The marbled cat living in a warm climate has longer ears than the cold-adapted snow leopard.

consideration, however, has to do with temperature. We ourselves know only too well that on chilly days our ears quickly become cold. This is because they are well shaped for losing heat; flat, thin structures have a large surface through which heat can be lost. Despite their thin covering of fur, a cat's ears are liable to get cold almost as much as human ears.

For this reason the size of the ears found on a species of cat depends in part upon the climate in which the species lives. Cats from warm places, such as the marbled cat, have relatively large ears, while the snow leopard, which inhabits cold mountainous parts of central Asia, has relatively small ears.

Of course, the climate does not only affect cats' ears. Any flattened and long, thin appendages on the bodies of all warm-blooded animals will be equally affected. A rough, but more or less accurate summary of the situation is made by Allen's Rule, which states that species or varieties from cool climates will, in general, tend to have smaller appendages than will related species from warmer climates. If a smaller organ would not, for one reason or another, be good enough for the task for which it is required another answer must be found. This is the main reason why Allen's Rule is not always accurate. It is not only a snow leopard's ears which will feel the cold; the long tail will also be subject to frostbite. However, although a shorter tail would be easier to keep warm, it apparently would not be of much use to the animal for some other important function. Thus snow leopards have very long tails which are, however, covered with remarkably long, thick fur.

The Nose

It is sometimes said that cats have no sense of smell, but this is most certainly untrue. Like most mammals, they have very efficient noses. However, it is true that they have smaller noses and a less perfect sense of smell than their distant cousins, the wild dogs. This is understandable, for wolves mainly hunt by scent, running tirelessly for mile after mile with nothing to guide them but the scent of their quarry, until at last they begin to catch up with it. Cats locate their prey by means of sight, sound or smell, and stalk by sight.

27

Special glands evolved for the purpose of secreting scents exist in all cat species. These odors serve as aids in various social relationships, particularly at mating time.

The Whiskers

Whiskers, or *vibrissae* to give them their technical name, are simple large, specially adapted hairs. But while the function of ordinary mammalian hair is to trap a blanket of air and thus conserve heat, cat whiskers are useful for another purpose.

They are dead, of course. All hairs are. A hair consists of a dead rod of a substance called *keratin* which is produced by a living root. But although hair is dead tissue, if it is touched it passes on the pressure, and this can be picked up by living nerve endings in the skin. This is true of all hairs, but it is especially true of whiskers. They are extra strong and have a large number of nerves clustered around their

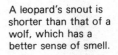

A leopard's snout is shorter than that of a wolf, which has a better sense of smell.

A cat's whiskers help it to find its way in very dim light.

roots. Above all, they are situated on the head of the animal, and on a four-legged animal which moves head first this is the most useful place to have extra organs of touch.

Stories about domestic cats using their whiskers as a sort of gauge, used to test gaps to see if they are wide enough for the body to pass through, are untrue. One has only to look at some overfed pets to see that the idea is laughable. Nevertheless, when moving in dim light—even with specially adapted eyes—the sense of touch can be valuable, performing the same sort of service that a walking stick does for a blind man.

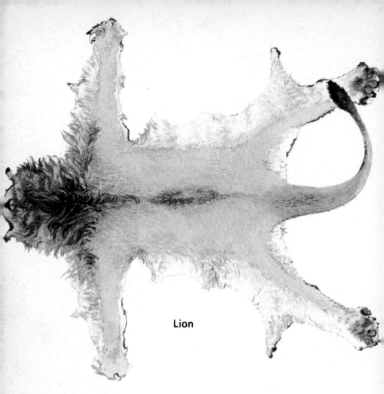

Lion

The Fur and Markings

Cats of all kinds have beautiful coats. Naturally, the fur is longest in those species which live in cool climates, but even tropical cats are well wrapped up. In the tropics it can be cold at night.

A stealthy hunter must be able to approach its prey unseen, and the most important function of the coat color is to provide camouflage. Cats that hunt in the open, as lions do, are therefore brownish to match their surroundings, while cats which keep to thicker cover have patterns of spots or stripes which blend with the shadows cast by the leaves.

Not all of a cat's markings have to do with camouflage. Some are concerned with making the animal's signaling systems more efficient, such as dark tassels on lions' tails.

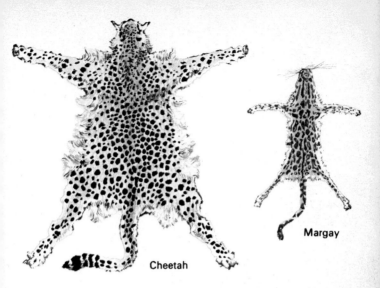

The markings of a wild cat may provide camouflage or improve social signals.

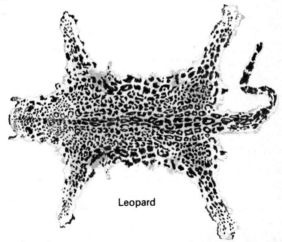

CAT BEHAVIOR

Territory

Like the cat in *The Jungle Book* who 'walked by himself', cats are solitary creatures on the whole. The reason for this is obvious enough. It suits their way of getting a living. For success in hunting, a cat must be able to get really close to its prey without being observed, and surprise is much more easily achieved if the hunter works on his own.

There is also another reason for the cat's unsociable ways. In the wild, hunters can never be as common as the animals they feed on. If they were they would soon run out of food and starve. Cats therefore tend to space themselves out, each one defending an area—called a *territory*—that is big enough to support it. Each animal gets to know its own territory, with the advantage that on its home ground an animal is never at a loss when it comes to finding anything it needs for survival.

The territories of different individuals of the same species do not overlap, but around each territory there may be a neutral area, known as the home range, where neighbors can meet on more or less equal terms. Territorial defense may take the form of fighting, but more often bluff is sufficient.

The pattern of territorial behavior described so far is common to many animals. How far it applies to wild cats is far from clear. Wild cats are furtive by nature, and the difficulty of studying the movements and behavior of, say, an ocelot in its native jungles will be apparent. Such observations as have been made are sketchy and do not form a clear picture. However, domestic cats are easier to watch, and recent observations of this species are of great interest.

For much of the time domestic cats behave as territorial animals, keeping apart as each individual stalks around its own territory, keeping to favored paths along the tops of garden walls or through shrubberies. However, sometimes this pattern breaks down, and the proprietors of several adjoining territories congregate together. This is a form of social behavior, even if vocal exchanges do sound distinctly unfriendly when heard through a bedroom window.

Lions and Tigers

The idea that typical cat behavior includes both solitary and social phases may be of value in interpreting the known facts about the behavior of the big cats.

Lions are quite closely related to the other big cats. In zoos, for example, they can cross-breed with tigers. Nevertheless, at first sight the behavior of these two species appears to be very different. Large gatherings of tigers are unknown, but lions, in part of their range at least, are the only cats which normally live together in social groups at all times. Only for the lions is there a special name for a group, and we speak of a *pride* of lions.

Behavior, like any other feature of an animal, is adaptive and aids survival. Like the form of the body itself, it is derived through combination and reconstruction of its ancestors' heredities. If the ancestors which both lions and tigers share were both solitary and social at different times, then, by varying modifications of this pattern, the behavior of the different kinds of modern big cats could come into being.

The tiger's behavior has probably changed least in the course of evolution. They hunt in thick cover—the traditional hunting-ground of the cats, in fact—and have continued to be solitary for most of this time. Whether their normal behavior also includes an occasional social gathering is not clear. Their social instincts may have become reduced in the course of time, but men who have made a point of stalking wild tigers have usually not had scientific observation in mind, being more concerned with their own predatory instincts.

How lions behave depends upon where they live. In western Africa, where lions are no longer common, there were never the large herds of game which occurred in other parts of the continent. The lions which lived there stalked single animals, and solitary behavior was best for this purpose. In eastern and southern Africa, on the other hand, the lions' prey lives in herds, and these are very difficult for a single lion to approach. Collectively, a herd has many eyes, ears and nostrils, and for a predator to approach undetected by one of these keen sense organs is impossible. Under these conditions, the lions must use teamwork to overcome the vigilance of their prey, and the social aspects of the lions' behavior have perhaps become exaggerated.

Lions live together in groups, or *prides,* in eastern and southern Africa. They help each other in hunting the herds of animals on which they prey.

35

Social Signals

All animals need some sort of language. Not a complicated one like English or Chinese—these human languages are a by-product of intelligence and we have to learn them. But there is a basic human language which all men speak. A smile or a scream of fear can be understood by an American as well as a Chinese man. The ability to understand communication at this level is born in us. It is at this instinctive level that the communication systems of other animal species operate.

Notice that the basic human language does not only consist of sounds. We can also make faces and if the mouth moves, as it does when we smile, then this signal is the more obvious if our lips are naturally pink and our teeth are white. Moving a part of the body—it does not have to be the face—is as useful a form of signaling as any other if the species concerned has sharp eyesight. If the human sense of smell were better we should make more use of scent in signaling. Most mammal species do. Signals which can be heard, seen or smelled can all play a part.

As we have already seen, cats make use of scent signals, but we are far from sure exactly what this part of their vocabulary means to them. It is difficult for us to appreciate the subtleties of smells.

Cats also use sounds. They roar, yowl, spit and miaow. All cats purr to show that they are pleased. Small differences occur. The big cats—the lion, tiger, leopard, jaguar and snow leopard—all roar, while the smaller cats have more high-pitched voices. The big cats pause for breath between each purr, but the small cats purr almost continuously.

Cats also use visual signals. They wave their tails as a sign of unpleasurable excitement. Stripes, or in the case of the lion a tassel, on the tail make this signal more obvious. This is a very deep-rooted signal among the Carnivora. Dogs wag their tails as a sign of excitement which is usually pleasurable, but the theme of excitement is common to both groups. Even with dogs one can never be quite sure that pleasure is the emotion invloved—excitement is the only certain feature. This may be why people are sometimes bitten by 'treacherous' dogs that were wagging their tails at the time.

A cat's ears are among its most effective signals. If they are laid back then one mood is indicated, but if they are right forward, and especially if the teeth are exposed in a snarl at the same time, this indicates quite another frame of mind. The big cats have special markings on the backs of their ears to emphasize these signals, but all cats use the ears in this way. The lynxes have long tassels of hair on their ears. This may be because they have short tails and must be able to compensate for their lack of ability to signal with the tail.

A cat's ears are particularly indicative of its moods. These can easily be seen in a domestic cat. When it is contented and lying still, the ears are usually laid back. But if the animal's attention is attracted by calling to it, the ears will rise up in awareness. The same kind of social signals may be observed in wild cats such as tigers (*above*).

Cats in Nature

The part played by predators such as the cats in maintaining the balance of nature may appear to be a purely destructive one, but in fact this is not the case. They are not simply destroyers, but play a vital part in maintaining a balance. Without them the very species that they hunt would be worse off, paradoxical though this may be.

Animal food begins with plants. Any given area, with its climate and its soil, can support a certain amount of plant life. The plants will grow and, over the years, the type of vegetation may tend to change—from grassland to bushy scrub and then to forest, for example—but this does not always happen, because plant growth is kept in check by the herbivorous animals that consume the increase in plants.

As a result of the food they eat, the herbivores in their turn thrive, grow and breed. Breeding will tend to increase their numbers, and this will mean that there are more mouths to be fed. Soon a situation could easily arise in which the plants are eaten faster than they can grow, so that the whole area becomes a denuded desert. That this does not happen is entirely due to hunters like the wild cats.

Predatory animals must kill off just enough of the herbivores to keep the population steady. This is not achieved by accident. If there are too many hunters their prey will become scarce and some of them may starve. If there are too few hunters, then hunting will be easy, and the hunters will breed well, building up their numbers. The balance is a delicate one but, although there are bound to be minor fluctuations in animal populations due to disease and such natural disasters as bush fires and locusts, on the whole a balance is achieved over the years.

The carnivores are thus at the top of a pyramid of life with the more numerous herbivores upon which they feed below them and the still more numerous plants at the base. Food passes from the bottom to the top. The actual numbers concerned are bound to vary with the conditions, but in one count made in the African grassland, for every lion that was counted, there were well over a hundred herbivorous mammals of the kind that provide lions with food.

Man, depending on the kind of interference he undertakes, strongly influences, for good or bad, this balance of nature.

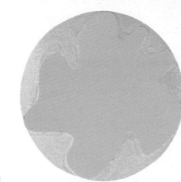

Without control, vegetation eventually overgrows a given area of land.

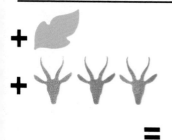

Herbivorous animals alone wil multiply and consume almost all the vegetation.

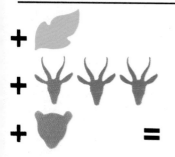

A few carnivores check the increase in herbivores and maintain a balance.

39

Conservation

During most of his million years or so of existence, man has killed other animals whenever the opportunity was presented. He has mostly been a hunter like any other, and the effects of his hunting were not unduly severe. Within the last few hundred years, however, a change has taken place. Man has produced firearms which make hunting much easier. Animals which would previously have escaped have been slaughtered in the millions.

Man's technical triumphs have also had other effects. The spread of agriculture has meant that there is less room for wild animals. The elimination of disease from man's domesticated herds of cattle has sometimes meant that the wild animals, which also harbor the disease, must be slain. All over the world the large stocks of wild animals have dwindled, as man has sought more and more to control his environment.

Almost too late man has come to realize the danger. If the untimely extinction of many species is not to occur, special reserves must be set up where wild animals can survive unmolested.

In nature reserves, game wardens keep an eye on wild cats and other animals to make sure that the balance of nature is being conserved.

To be truly successful, a game reserve must provide a complete environment for its occupants. There must be a sufficient variety of vegetation for the herbivorous animals and room for them to move around with the seasons as they normally do. There must also be enough carnivores to prevent the numbers of herbivores from getting out of hand.

Conservation does not mean that all the carnivores in the reserve must be destroyed. Apart from the fact that they must be conserved, too, they must play their natural part in maintaining the balance. Ideally, in a reserve, life should go on just as it did before man started to interfere. This is not always the case, for not all reserves provide a complete environment. In cases like this it may be necessary for man to step in and, by providing additional facilities or even by killing off some members of a species that has got out of hand, set things right again.

Game reserves can be a big tourist attraction, and in some African reserves herbivores such as antelopes have been shot as lion food by game wardens, who are careful to weed out the specimens which can be spared. Lions can thus be induced to feed in places where they can be seen.

ZOOGEOGRAPHICAL REGIONS

Palearctic
Nearctic
} Holarctic

Neotropical

Ethiopian

Oriental

Australasian

THE CAT FAMILY

Animal Geography

So far as is known the earliest members of the cat family
lived in the Palearctic region. From here representatives of
the family easily reached the Nearctic region. Even today
Asia is separated from Alaska by less than a hundred miles
of sea, and often animals of the same species are found on
either side of the gap. In the past, too, this gap was frequently above water. Other early cats reached the Ethiopian
and Oriental regions. The Neotropical region was reached
with more difficulty, as for much of the time South America

has been an island continent. The Australasian region proved too inaccessible. The cats, like most other highly developed mammals, never got there until they were taken there by man.

Once each region was colonized, the cats there, being more or less isolated from others of their kind, tended to diverge in appearance and habits, forming new species. However, it is possible for animals of the same species to colonize more than one region, as pumas do the Nearctic and Neotropical regions. Nevertheless, these *zoogeographical* regions provide an excellent basis for understanding the distribution of the cat species, as well as other land animals.

Classification

Carolus Linnaeus, a Swedish naturalist who lived from 1707 to 1778, originated the method by means of which living things are classified. His observation of plants and animals led him to see that sometimes two organisms of different kinds resemble each other quite closely in structure, while differing to a lesser or greater degree from others. He therefore proposed that animals of the same kind should be placed in the same *species,* and that this species should be in the same *genus* with other very similar species. Broadly similar *genera* (the plural of genus) were placed in the same *order,* orders were grouped in *classes,* and so on. The cats were part of the class Mammalia, and Linnaeus thought that all cats were so much alike that they could be put into a single genus, *Felis.*

The tenth edition of Linnaeus' book *Systema Naturae,* published in 1758, began the system which is still, with modifications, in use today. Animals are no longer classified purely on the basis of similarity of structure. The important factor nowadays is that animals within the same group must be related to each other, sharing the same ancestors. However, as related animals tend to look alike it very often comes to the same thing. To make the system more flexible some new groups have been introduced. Species are still placed in genera, but these are now sorted into *families*—a grouping not used by Linnaeus—which in their turn are placed in orders and classes.

Within the classification used today, the cats are thought to form a family, the Felidae, within the order Carnivora. Once the cats were placed in a single family it became possible to be fussier about the genus. Within Linnaeus' genus *Felis* there were obviously cats of several broad types, and zoologists began to sort these out, forming new genera in the process. At one time no fewer than twenty-three genera of cats were recognized. At this point there arose a feeling that the splitting process had gone too far—that not all of the named genera were really as distinct as their status made them out to be. A process of grouping them together again, so as to reduce their number, began. When this trend ground to a halt it was generally accepted by most authorities that the cat family in fact contained three genera.

The big cats, actually distinguished by the structure of their larynges rather than their size, formed the genus *Leo* (sometimes called *Panthera*). The small cats remained in the old genus *Felis*. The Cheetah, which is distinct in a number of ways—it cannot retract its claws, for example—is alone in the genus *Acinonyx*. Recently zoologists have tended to agree that the clouded leopard, intermediate between the big and small cats, belongs in the genus it once had before, *Neofelis*, and that the distinctive snow leopard should be *Uncia*.

At the present time there are thought to be thirty-six species of cats forming five genera.

Carolus Linnaeus originated the system of classifying living things in 1758. He placed all cats in a single group or *genus* called *Felis*. Nowadays, zoologists classify cats into five such groups.

CATS OF THE GENUS FELIS AND GENUS NEOFELIS

The Domestic Cat

It is difficult to be certain exactly when the association between the domestic cat and man began. Archeologists have unearthed the bones of cats near remains left by early man, but the bones of wild and domestic cats are very similar, and the bones of wild animals are often found near the remains of human dwellings. Wild cats may not have made such good eating as some other game, but perhaps our ancestors could not afford to be fussy.

Even the identity of the wild species from which the domestic cat sprang is a matter for doubt. It is not unlike the European wild cat, but neither is it unlike some of the other wild cats of Africa and Asia, which are closely related. Wild cats of all these types may be descended from *Felis lunensis,* which flourished in Europe just over a million years ago, and they all resemble each other closely in structure, differing mainly in the color and pattern of their fur.

The best guess is that the cat was first domesticated by the Egyptians some time before 1600 B.C. Perhaps African wild cats, *Felis libyca,* found that small rodents were common and easily caught near man's dwellings and eventually, emboldened by their success, even began to enter the houses, where they were tolerated as destroyers of vermin. Once the Egyptians had accepted the cat it rapidly rose in esteem, being regarded as sacred to the goddess Ubasti or Pasht. Her name, it is thought, has been associated with the cat ever since, although by now in the corrupted form—'Puss'. Those who killed a cat in Egypt were severely punished, and when a cat died its owners went into mourning. Dead cats were mummified and buried with great reverence.

From Egypt, cats spread along the trade routes to Greece and Italy. This was a slow process, for Egyptians were reluctant to part with them. By the time of Christ, cats had become popular pets amongst the Romans. They were thus introduced to all parts of the Roman Empire. They have been popular ever since, although by the Middle Ages they had long since ceased being regarded as sacred in any way.

On the contrary, the cat was sometimes thought of as the familiar of witches. This idea has just lingered on into our own time, when some people think of cats as sinister, while others regard them as lucky, especially black cats.

Domestic cats usually weigh about seven pounds, although very fat specimens can weigh over twice as much. They are fully grown at about a year old and normally have a lifespan of up to twelve years, although exceptional individuals live to more than twenty. The females usually give birth to from four to six kittens and can breed two or three times a year. They are generally devoted mothers and the father takes no part in rearing the young.

Some domestic cats are self-supporting and are easily able to catch their own food.

The tabby is just one of the many varieties of domestic cats. Becoming domesticated must have entailed undergoing profound psychological changes, for all the wild cats of the present day are shy and retiring. Domestication was probably a gradual process that took several hundreds of years to complete.

47

Domestic Varieties

In the wild, members of the same species from the same part of the world usually resemble each other closely. The average animal is very well adapted for its life and if, during the normal course of breeding, young of a different color or shape should appear, then the chances are that these freaks will be less well adapted than the parents, and will have little chance of survival. 'Freaks' do occur in the wild, but are usually eliminated by natural selection. Sometimes, however, they provide the stock from which a new species or variety could evolve.

When man domesticates animals and controls their choice of mates, all this is changed. Human beings are fascinated by novelty. When freaks occur they are carefully reared and, if it is possible, bred to others that resemble them so as to produce more of their kind. In domesticated animals 'abnormal' shapes and colors become almost the rule rather than the exception.

As everyone knows, domestic cats come in a wide variety and mixture of colors—black, white, gray and ginger. The tabby pattern is the least changed, although even tabbies often show blotches rather than the stripes of wild cats.

The dark points of Siamese cats are the result of an ususual hereditary factor which determines the colors of their coats. On the warmer parts of the body this produces light-colored hairs, but on the cooler extremities it produces a darker coloring.

The length of the fur also varies in different breeds of domesticated cats; Persian Cats have long hair. There is some variation in body shape, too, although less than with some other domestic animals. Domestic dogs vary in size from the Chihuahua to the Great Dane and show an almost equally varied range of shapes. They almost form a living catalogue of the genetic disasters which can be thrown up by a stock of animals. The dwarf legs of the Dachshund and the stunted head of the Bulldog are examples. Domestic cats show less variety perhaps, partly because they are more difficult to keep in confinement. Breeders have therefore been unable to keep stocks pure for many generations, in-breeding until the line becomes 'pure' and the real oddities appear. Cats' heredity probably contains as much variation as that of dogs, but the variations that occur are not always readily apparent.

Domestic cats show great variety in fur and marking. The Siamese cat (*left*) has unusual dark points in its coat and startling blue eyes. The Persian cat (*right*) is well known for its beautiful long-haired coat.

The European Wild Cat

The English name of the European wild cat (*Felis silvestris*) is a little misleading, for the range of this species extends from Britain, through Europe, into western Asia, although it is now found only in out-of-the-way forested and mountainous areas.

At a quick glance it may not be easy to distinguish a wild cat from a domestic tabby which has run wild, as often happens. Besides this, there is always the possibility that a 'wild cat' which is reported is not pure-bred, but is the result of a misalliance between a domestic cat and a true wild cat, for the two species interbreed readily. However, wild cats have black stripes rather than the black blotches usually seen on domestic tabbies, and the black tip of their tails is rounded rather than pointed. It is reasonably easy to identify dead specimens, for wild cats have larger skulls and teeth than tame cats, although surprisingly their intestines are considerably shorter. Both wild and domestic cats are about the same size.

Wild cats usually hunt on their own, each animal keeping to an area of about 150 acres which is crossed by paths and punctuated by resting places and trees upon which the claws are regularly sharpened. This habit of sharpening the claws may also be a means of marking out the territory. Wild cats are most active when it is dry, and dawn and dusk are the most favored times for hunting.

They do not ignore small, tasty morsels like grasshoppers and beetles, but small mammals such as mice and voles make up the bulk of their food. They also hunt birds and sometimes tackle mammals the size of a small deer or a lamb. If they do, they usually content themselves with tearing off the head and eating the brains.

In the spring the males wander more widely than usual, calling noisily. Mating takes place, and after a gestation period of 63 days, the kittens are born in a den beneath the roots of a fallen tree or among rocks. This compares with an average of 58 days for the domestic cat. There are usually from two to four kittens, and their father plays no part in bringing them up. They leave their mother in the autumn and are fully grown at about a year. If they survive the first few dangerous months they may live for a number of years, for apart from man they have no enemies.

The European wild cat was once widely distributed in Britain and Europe. It now survives only in sparsely settled forested areas of its former range.

The African Wild Cat

The African wild cat (*Felis libyca*) is obviously closely related to the Euopean Wild Cat, and some experts regard the two as different varieties of the same species. It has a wide range in Africa, being found in all areas apart from the great deserts and the equatorial forests. Like many other African mammals, it is also found in Arabia (which forms part of the Ethiopian region), and from there its range extends to Syria and eastward to India. The cats that inhabit the Mediterranean islands of Sardinia and Corsica also belong to this species.

This cat is a little larger than the domestic cat, the average weight being about eight pounds, but African wild cats and domestic cats interbreed freely when the opportunity occurs. In appearance the African wild cat is not unlike its European cousin, but the stripes on the body are not so distinct, and the underside of the body sometimes has a yellowish tinge. The backs of the ears are always reddish-yellow.

It is usually active at night, but it sometimes can be seen in daylight on cool, cloudy days. It prefers thinly forested country where it makes a den under the ground or among bushes. It hunts birds and small mammals.

The Sand Cat

The sand cat (*Felis margarita*) inhabits semidesert areas of North Africa (although its range does not extend into the Sahara Desert), Arabia and parts of the Middle East, ex-

The African wild cat resembles a long-legged large domestic tabby.

The sand cat hunts jerboas and other small mammals.

tending as far north as southern Russia. It is about the size of the domestic cat and is plain-colored with few signs of stripes, except on the legs. The color varies from yellow-brown to gray-brown, but the backs of the ears always have a black patch, and there are three dark rings at the end of the tail, one extending to the tip. Like some other desert mammals, such as the desert foxes, it has large ears which are widely spaced and situated rather toward the sides of the head. Although seldom seen, this species is easily identified by its footprints, as the pads of the feet are almost covered by hair.

In southern Russia, sand cats hide during the day among bushes, where they dig shallow burrows in the sand between the roots. They hunt ground squirrels, hares, sand voles and jerboas. The young, about four in number, are born in April.

The Jungle Cat

The jungle cat (*Felis chaus*) is rather larger than the cats so far considered, and may weigh up to twenty pounds. It occurs in Egypt, the Middle East and Asia Minor, Russia just east of the Caspian Sea, India, Ceylon, Nepal, Burma, the Indo-Chinese region and Thailand. It is gray-brown with faintly striped markings, except for the tail, which has prominent black rings. The underside is white. The short tail and the presence of small tufts on the ears suggest that this species may have some affinity with the lynxes.

The jungle cat usually keeps to thick bushes and almost impenetrable reeds, often in low-lying, swampy forests, but if these are not available, cornfields or tall grass seem to suit it just as well. Although it is most often active at night, it is not exclusively nocturnal and is quite often about in the daytime. It climbs well and, although it sometimes hunts mammals such as hares, birds are its main quarry. It kills water-fowl, pheasants, francolins, partridges and even—in India—peacocks. If human dwellings are nearby, it boldly raids poultry runs.

In Russia the jungle cat's mating season is in February or March, and at this time the voice of the male, not unlike that

The jungle cat inhabits dense cover in the Middle East and Asia.

of the domestic cat but deeper and louder, is often raised in amorous dispute. The females have between three and five kittens in April or May in a dry den under the ground. Often the unused home of a badger, fox or a porcupine is pressed into service. The entrance to the den is usually well camouflaged.

The Chinese Desert Cat

The Chinese desert cat (*Felis bieti*) was first discovered only toward the end of the nineteenth century, and very little is known about it even today. It is about the same size as the domestic cat and appears to inhabit dry grasslands—perhaps semideserts would be a better description—in Mongolia and the Chinese provinces of Kansu and Szechuan.

Like many mammals from dry areas, it is rather light in color, the back being grayish-yellow, the flanks a little darker, and the undeside lighter. The rear part of the body and the face are lightly marked with broken bars. The tail has several dark rings and a black tip. The light coloring of desert animals serves as camouflage and may also assist in reflecting the sun's heat, rather than absorbing it as a dark coat would.

The Chinese desert cat is a little-known cat inhabiting semidesert regions of the Far East.

The Leopard Cat

Small spotted cats are found in most tropical countries. It is unlikely that they all evolved from a single ancestor; their coats, which are light in color with rows of dark spots, have developed similarly to protect the animals in their various habitats. These habitats vary from forests and light jungle to open woodlands and grassy plains, but these cats are all much alike in appearance and habits. One of the most common is the leopard cat (*Felix bengalensis*). This cat is the most common wild cat of southeast Asia, where it is found in Burma, the Malay Peninsula, Sumatra, Java, Borneo and some of the Philippines. Its range also extends to northern India, Tibet, China and eastern Siberia. It is about as large as the domestic cat, and being heavily spotted, it has a superficial resemblance to a very small leopard. However, the spots are not grouped into rosettes as are those of the leopard. The color and spotting of the leopard cat are very variable, as is often the case with a species which has a wide range. A typical specimen from Sumatra has fewer markings than those from the mainland of Asia, while

The leopard cat is the commonest wild cat of southeast Asia.

Javan specimens have brighter, orange-brown fur, and those from Bali are duller. Individuals from the Philippine Islands are altogether smaller.

The leopard cat lives in hilly areas and secondary jungle, avoiding the thickest forest, and climbs actively. Its prey usually consists of large birds and small mammals up to the size of squirrels and hares, but it may occasionally kill a small deer. In India the young are born in May. There are usually three or four of them, and they are nursed in a den inside a cave or under fallen rocks.

The Rusty-Spotted Cat

The rusty-spotted cat (*Felis rubiginosa*) replaces its slightly larger relative, the leopard cat, in southern India and Ceylon. It is rust-colored with lines of brown blotches along its body. This cat frequents long grass and brushwood, sometimes hiding in the undergrowth around ditches in the middle of open country. It never penetrates thick jungle. The young, if taken early enough, can be tamed more easily than those of some other wild cats.

The rusty-spotted cat is found only in southern India and Ceylon.

The Flat-Headed Cat

The flat-headed cat (*Felis planiceps*) is one of the smallest of the family, weighing about 4½ pounds. It inhabits the Malay Peninsula, Borneo and Sumatra, but is nowhere common, or if it is, the fact has never been reported, for it is nocturnal in habit and could easily escape observation. The color of the fur is more or less uniformly brown, darker on the back and shading to white underneath. Many of the guard-hairs are white-tipped, and this gives the body a silver-gray appearance.

In relation to the size of the body, the legs are shorter than those of any other cat of the Oriental region. The tail is rather short too, being only about a third of the length of the head and body combined.

In Borneo it stays close to the banks of rivers; fish and frogs form an important part of its diet, but it also occasionally eats birds.

The Bay Cat

The bay cat (*Felis badius*) has a very restricted distribution, coming only from the island of Borneo. That little is known of its habits is not surprising, for until relatively recent years zoologists concentrated on dissecting dead animals, collecting their skins and bones, and classifying them. The study of animals in the field, especially rare and furtive ones from remote parts of the world, is very difficult, and many animals, including the bay cat, have never been the objects of such a study.

For information about their habits we have to rely on the anecdotes of hunters and casual observers, and even those are scanty.

The bay cat has fewer traces of dark spots or stripes than any other cat of the East Indies, although there may occasionally be faint stripes on the face. The back of the ears is black with a white spot, and there is another patch of this color on the underside of the tail tip. Not for the first time, it will be noticed, the pattern is most marked on those parts of the body which function as signals between members of the same species. The fur of the body is yellowish-brown, often with a red tinge. The bay cat is a little larger than the domestic cat.

The flat-headed cat from the Malay Peninsula,
Borneo and Sumatra is a relatively rare species.

The rare bay cat
lives only on Borneo.

The black-footed cat is a wild cat of
southern Africa. It is named after the
black fur on the underside of its feet.

The Black-Footed Cat

The black-footed cat (*Felis nigripes*) is an African species
with a range which includes the Kalahari Desert and other
parts of southern Africa. It is not a common species anywhere in this area. This is yet another species which has
been known to crossbreed with the domestic cat, although
the black-footed cat is slightly smaller in size.

This cat is pale tawny-brown, shading to white underneath and on the insides of the limbs. This very common
type of coloring is useful as camouflage. The colors cancel
out the effects of shadows when light falls from overhead,
thus making the animal appear not rounded, but flat and
insubstantial. On the neck and shoulders there are darker
lines, and the body is spotted.

The Caracal Lynx

The caracal lynx (*Felis caracal*) has the tufted ears and short tail typical of the lynxes and to some extent replaces the larger northern lynx in warmer parts of the Old World. Its range extends from the deserts of southern Russia to northern India, the Middle East, Arabia and many parts of Africa. It is found in dry regions from the desolate and wind-swept plateaus of Asia to the mountainous semideserts of Africa, whether they are open or densely covered with bush. It is lightly built with a short 8-inch tail. The head and body together usually measure just over two feet long.

It is agile, and speedy over short distances and puts this ability to good use in hunting. Bursting from cover it hurls itself toward the prey. If this prey is a bird which attempts to fly away, it can leap into the air, grabbing it with its forelimbs. In Asia its prey consists of doves, hares, pikas (small mammals related to rabbits) and ground squirrels, while in Africa it is known to kill small antelopes and birds of all kinds. It may even attack eagles if it can surprise them when they are roosting at night.

The female usually has two or three young in an underground den or a hollow tree.

The caracal lynx has exceptionally long ears, ending in long tufts of hair.

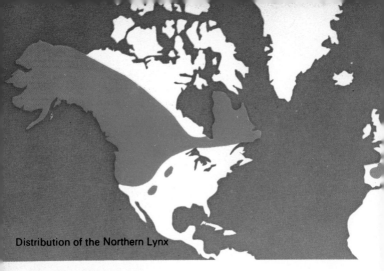

Distribution of the Northern Lynx

The Northern Lynx

The northern lynx (*Felis lynx*) has a range which originally included all the temperate forests of the Northern Hemisphere. The advance of civilization has resulted in the disappearance of the lynx from many of its former haunts, but in Europe they still exist in Spain and Portugal (where they are, however, in great danger of extinction), parts of Scandinavia, Poland, parts of the Balkans and Sardinia. Slightly different types of northern lynx exist, but all are regarded as a single species.

The lynx is a powerfully built cat with very sturdy limbs. Its tail is only about 4 inches long. Over short distances it can move very fast, although it lacks staying power and quickly tires. At lower speeds, it can cover long distances. It is an expert climber, jumping from one tree to another with ease and often hiding among the branches.

The lynx is cautious and cunning and moves quietly. Its high-pitched soft voice is seldom raised. In remote areas it is quite often active by day, but in the vicinity of man it becomes more wary, hunting mainly by night. Animals the size of roe deer and grouse, or in America snowshoe hares, are the normal prey. Unlike many cats, it will never eat carrion, and despite its size and power this lynx rarely attacks man.

The northern lynx lives in dense forest or in thick bush on mountain sides.

The bobcat lives in North America and Mexico.

The Bobcat

The bobcat (*Felis rufa*) is closely related to the lynx. Its range extends from southern Canada to southern Mexico. A full-grown male bobcat may weigh eighteen pounds and is smaller than a lynx. The two species therefore illustrate Bergman's Rule, which states that animals from warm climates are in general smaller than related animals from cooler regions.

The bobcat inhabits more open country than the lynx, preferring scrub, thickets and undulating ground. Hunting mainly at night, it preys on rodents such as mice, wood rats, chipmunks, pocket gophers and squirrels, as well as rabbits and birds. Occasionally it goes after bigger game, hunting white-tailed deer or birds the size of a turkey.

The majority of bobcat litters are born in the spring. The gestation period is about fifty days and two or three young are the usual number. Youngsters born in the spring can fend for themselves by the time their first winter arrives, but they may stay with their mother until they are a year old.

Pallas' Cat

The Pallas cat (*Felis manul*) owes its name to Pallas, the man who discovered the species in 1778, rather than the goddess Pallas Athene. It was first found among stony, steppe-like country, although it also inhabits woods from east of the Caspian Sea to Persia, Tibet, Mongolia and western China. Possibly this is the species which replaces the European wild cat, living very much the same life as its relative but in these different regions.

The basic coat color is orange-brown, but the white and black rings around the eyes, the gray forehead with black spots and the white chin make this one of the most handsome of the small cats in appearance. The small, rounded ears are set well toward the sides of the head and are yellowish-gray, and the hair on the sides of the face is long.

It hunts partridges, pikas and small rodents such as voles and mice.

Pallas' cat lives in central Asia.

The serval (*left*) inhabits bush country in Africa. It prefers areas where the bush is not too thick, and although it is occasionally seen at the edges of forests, it is never found in very dry regions or very far from water. The marbled cat (*opposite*) of Asia is seldom seen, partly because it is shy and nocturnal, but also because it is rather rare and inhabits forests, where cover is plentiful. Its fur is very long, and the markings vary a great deal from one individual to another.

The Serval

The serval (*Felis serval*) is a slenderly built, medium-sized cat which weighs about 34 pounds. It has rather a small head surmounted by very large ears, long slender legs and a short tail only about a foot in length. It is an inhabitant of bush country and is found over a wide area of Africa south of the Sahara Desert.

Although the ears are not tufted, this cat shows some resemblance to the lynxes and, like the caracal, it sometimes slinks toward its prey and then, breaking cover, sprints over the last few yards. In this way it often captures medium-sized birds, such as guinea-fowl, and mammals, including hares and duikers. Good eyesight is vital to the success of this method of hunting, and it is hardly surprising that the serval is often seen hunting by day. It also eats rodents, sometimes digging them from their burrows.

After a gestation period of about 70 days the female usually has three young, either in a nest among the dense, dry grass, or in a den underground. Often the discarded burrow of an aardvark is used for this purpose.

The Marbled Cat

The marbled cat (*Felis marmorata*) is very similar to the clouded leopard in appearance, but is smaller, being only a little larger than the domestic cat. Its range extends from Nepal and the slopes of the Himalayas, through Burma and the Malay Peninsula, to Sumatra and Borneo. It is a rare animal.

This cat is said to hunt on the ground in clearings and along river banks, but in view of its resemblance to the clouded leopard, which often climbs, this is by no means certain. It may well be that the marbled cat is less likely to attract attention when it hunts aloft, where its lighter weight would be supported by even more slender branches than those used by the clouded leopard. A long tail is an asset to a climber, being a useful means of adjusting weight distribution and therefore assisting balance.

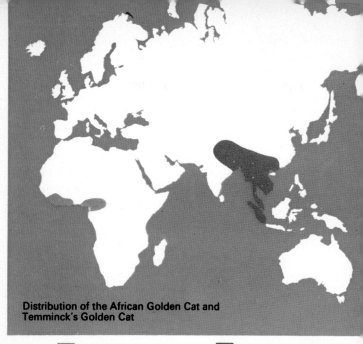

Distribution of the African Golden Cat and Temminck's Golden Cat

■ African Golden Cat   ■ Temminck's Golden Cat

Temminck's Golden Cat

Temminck's golden cat (*Felis temmincki*), which comes from Tibet, southwest China, northern India, Burma, the Indo-Chinese region, Thailand, Malaya and Sumatra, is often confused with the African golden cat. Not only do the two species look very much alike, but the true facts are even more confusing than is usually realized. The African golden cat was first described and named by Temminck, a famous naturalist of the early 1800's who was the author of a monograph on the cats. The other species of golden cat had not then been discovered. Later, in 1827, a member of the Asiatic species turned up as one of the very first inhabitants of Regent's Park Zoo. It was named by two Fellows of the Zoological Society and, in naming it, they decided to honor Temminck. Temminck's golden cat is accordingly the species which Temminck did not discover.

Both species of golden cats are probably very closely related, and this explains their great similarity of appearance. Temminck's golden cat is slightly the larger of the two. It is also a rare animal, but it is said to live among rocks in tall forests.

The African Golden Cat
The African golden cat *(Felis aurata)* is a handsome and rare species from western Africa where it inhabits high, deciduous forests near the coast from Sierra Leone to the north of the Congo. It owes its name to the golden-brown color of the short and very lustrous fur. Some members of this species are much more gray in coloring, and this is not entirely a matter of heredity, for one zoo specimen once changed from one color to the other. The back is usually a slightly darker shade, and darker spots are visible from the flanks downward. The tail bears no spots or stripes, and the backs of the ears are almost black. The head and body combined are about 28 inches long, and the tail is 16 inches.

The African golden cat much resembles Temminck's golden cat of southern Asia.

The fishing cat lives in marshy land in southern Asia and is believed to hunt fish as well as small mammals.

The Fishing Cat

The fishing cat *(Felis viverrina)* is heavily built and rather short-legged. Although the head and body together are about 32 inches long, the tail measures only about a foot. An average specimen weighs about 17 pounds.

Its Bengali name was 'Mach-bagral' and to this it owes its English name, which is an accurate translation. However, there is some doubt as to whether the species is as fond of fish as the name suggests. Some experts say that it has never been seen catching or eating fish, but others believe that it does do so occasionally by scooping them out of the water with its paws.

It is usually found near water, for it inhabits low-lying, swampy forests in Ceylon, India, former Indo-China, Thailand, Malaya, Java and Sumatra. It is quite common in some places. Its spotted mouse-gray or tawny-gray coat is one of the most harsh in texture to be found in the cat family and, to give support to the theory that it really does fish, the toes are very slightly webbed. It is certainly a bold and intrepid hunter and has been known to attack goats. It has even been said to carry off human babies.

The Ocelot

The ocelot *(Felis pardalis)* is nocturnal in areas where it is frequently disturbed by man, but otherwise it hunts both by day and by night. It lives in forests and thick vegetation where the stripes and spots of its fur blend well with the leafy shadows, providing excellent camouflage. It occurs rarely in the southern United States, but is common in Central and South America, being found as far south as Paraguay.

A large male may weigh as much as 34 pounds and measure 4½ feet overall, one third of this being the tail. Because of the handsome markings of the coat, the fur has commercial value. These markings vary a great deal from one habitat to another, lighter forms being found in more open country.

Being a good climber it often spends the day asleep amongst the branches of a tree, but much of its hunting is done on the ground. It eats opossums, small and medium-sized rodents up to the size of the agouti (a favorite prey), peccaries and small deer. It rarely eats birds, but tackles reptiles including fairly large lizards. One ocelot is reported to have killed a boa seven feet in length.

The ocelot is known for its beautiful marked fur, which has commercial value.

The Margay

The margay *(Felis wiedii)* or Wied's tiger cat is a close relation of the ocelot and has very much the same distribution,
being rare in the southern parts of the United States but
more common in the forests of Central and South America.
It extends as far south as Paraguay and Argentina. The head
and body of an average specimen are just under two feet in
length, and the tail adds just over another foot to this.

The soft fur is yellow-brown, being darker on the back of
the body and grayer on the head. The top of the head and
the cheeks are deeper yellow in tone. Between the cheeks
and the eyes there are conspicuous white markings. The
whole animal is marked with prominent black lines and
spots. Toward the tip of the tail the spots join together to
form complete rings.

Little is known of the habits of the margay in the wild.
Perhaps, being smaller than the ocelot, it spends more of its
time in trees hunting birds. The fact that the tail of the margay is relatively longer than that of the ocelot lends some
support to this view.

The Tiger Cat

The tiger cat *(Felis tigrina)* is sometimes also known as the
American tiger cat to distinguish it from the African tiger cat,
another name for the African golden cat. A species of animal
may have a number of common names, but names of this
kind have no scientific value. Scientific names are another
matter and are subject to strict rules. A species is only allowed
to have one scientific name. By definition a species is an
interbreeding population of organisms distinguishable from
other such populations with which there is no interbreeding.
In practice, however, criteria for this definition are hard to
establish, and as new facts are gathered, species classification changes. The range of the tiger cat overlaps that of the
margay and the ocelot, and it is often difficult to know which
species is referred to in accounts of spotted, forest-dwelling
South American cats. Also such accounts are scanty for, zoo-
logically speaking, South America is the least well known of
the continents.

The tiger cat inhabits forests and woodlands from Costa
Rica in Central America to northern South America. It is
a good climber and hunts birds and small mammals.

The margay (*top*) resembles the ocelot in appearance. It is usually smaller in size, although an exceptional animal may be almost as big as an ocelot. The tiger cat (*below*) is also known as the American tiger cat and as the little spotted cat. Both cats inhabit South and Central America, and margays are occasionally found in the southern United States.

The Mountain Cat

The mountain cat *(Felis jacobita)* is sometimes also known as the Andean cat. This is yet another species which is only found in South America. The various cats of this continent are all descended from North American ancestors but have evolved into very distinctive species.

The mountain cat lives in the mountains of Chile, Peru, Bolivia and Argentina. As it comes from the cooler heights where a bright orange-brown coat would be conspicuous, the fur is a brownish-gray with darker markings on its sides and rings on its tail. The head and body together are about 30 inches long and the tail about 18 inches. It hunts small and medium-sized rodents, including the wild relations of the guinea pig.

The mountain cat is one of the many unusual cats of South America. For most of its history, the Neotropical Region has been completely cut off from other regions by the sea, although land bridges such as the Isthmus of Panama have periodically risen above the waves. Because of this long isolation, the cats only reached South America from North America some two million years ago.

Geoffroy's cat hunts birds and small mammals, often plunging from low branches onto its prey.

Geoffroy's Cat

Geoffroy's cat *(Felis geoffroyi)* is named after Geoffroy Saint-Hilaire, a French naturalist who lived in the nineteenth century. The range of this species extends from Bolivia in the north to Patagonia, southern Argentina.

Like the mountain cat, Geoffroy's cat is usually found in cool and steeply sloping upland areas, but Geoffroy's cat is perhaps more often an inhabitant of the foothills than the mountains themselves. Being an excellent climber, Geoffroy's cat does not venture too far from trees and is not found above the tree line.

The Jaguarundi

The jaguarundi *(Felis yagouaroundi)* has a maximum length of four feet, and 18 inches of this consists of the tail. This is perhaps the most surprising in appearance of all the cats. Most of the family bear a strong likeness to each other, whatever the differences in size and markings may be, but the jaguarundi in some ways resembles an otter, or at least some other member of the weasel family, rather than a cat. Its body is graceful, but rather long and sinuous, and this effect is increased by the shortness of the legs. Despite its length the jaguarundi is a lightweight animal, weighing twenty pounds.

Gray and brown jaguarundis (*below*) belong to the same species.

For a cat it has rather small ears and an unusual snub nose. The fur is uniform in color, but there are two different color varieties. At one time it was thought that the reddish-brown individuals, known as *eyras,* belonged to a different species from the grayer jaguarundis, but we now know that they all belong to the same species and that the different colored varieties are not found in different parts of the animal's range. Normally the coloring of a wild animal is related to its mode of life, being adapted for survival. The reason for these different color phases in some species of the cat family is unknown.

At all events the jaguarundi is obviously a highly individual species of cat, different in every way from the animal with which its name might be confused, the much larger, heavily spotted jaguar.

The jaguarundi is found from the Argentine and Paraguay in South America to southern Texas in the United States. It is often spoken of as a forest-dwelling species, which is scarcely what would be expected of a plain-colored animal, but it also seems to frequent open glades and clearings on the forest fringe. It is found in bush country and is also abundant in the open on some savannahs.

This cat is equally active by day and at night and is an excellent climber, often traveling large distances through a forest entirely by way of the branches, although it can also move with considerable speed on the ground. The suppleness of the body adequately compensates for the deficiencies of the legs when running to an even greater extent than in other members of the cat family.

Jaguarundis hunt on their own, catching ground-living birds such as tinamous and trumpeters, small mammals and perhaps some frogs and fish. One very reliable observer has reported seeing them climbing high up in fig trees and feeding on wild figs in the company of howler monkeys. If this is true it is the most surprising thing of all about these unconventional cats. As a family, the cats are the most purely carnivorous of mammals and do not normally eat fruit.

The female usually has two or three young after a gestation period of up to 70 days. The young are slightly spotted at birth and, as is frequently the case in the cat family, the father plays no part in rearing them.

The kodkod inhabits woodlands in the foothills of the Andes in Chile.

The Kodkod

The kodkod *(Felis guigna)* lives in the foothills of the Andes in Chile. Although this is still part of the Neotropical region, it is effectively cut off by the long mountain chain so it is not surprising that in such isolation yet another South American species of cat should have evolved.

The kodkod is quite small, the head and body together being about 18 inches long and the tail another nine inches. The gray-brown fur is handsomely marked with rows of darker spots, and the tail is encircled with black rings.

This species normally inhabits woodlands, hunting small mammals such as rodents, but has been known to raid domestic poultry runs. The raiders were said to have come in parties. If this is true, mothers and their growing families may have been involved, or alternatively this species may be more social when hunting than any other species of cat, except for the lion.

The Pampas Cat

The pampas cat *(Felis colocolo)* is another species about which very little is known. It is to be hoped that more will be learned of it before it is too late, as the pampas cat is in some danger of becoming extinct. But little time may remain, for this species like so many others cannot cope with the disturbance caused by human civilization and is much less common now than it was a hundred years ago. It was then widespread in Argentina and Uruguay, occurring not only in grasslands, as its English name suggests, but also amongst reeds in swampier conditions.

It is about as large as a domestic cat and has a relatively long tail. The fur is gray, becoming lighter under the body, and it has brown markings on the body. Along the back is a distinct crest of longer hair. Hunting is said to take place mainly at night, and the prey consists of small birds and mammals. There are normally from one to three kittens in a litter.

The pampas cat is one of the rarest of the wild cats.

The Puma—appearance and distribution

The puma *(Felis concolor)* is considerably larger than other members of the genus *Felis,* but is nevertheless a true member of the genus. Like the smaller cats, it purrs both as it breathes in and as it breathes out—a feature which is a direct result of the structure of the larynx (or Adam's apple) and typical of the genus. The cry is also a typical, throaty, high-pitched

'yowl' rather than the roar of the big cats of the genus *Leo.* The puma's affinities show in other ways, too. In proportion it is more like the smaller cats, the head being relatively small in comparison with the body. In feeding, the puma, like the domestic cat, makes little use of the forepaws, which are placed firmly on the ground as the animal squats over its food. In contrast to this the big cats usually rest on their elbows, holding the food with their paws. In every way then, the puma is most like the smaller cats rather than the larger ones in spite of its size.

Many species of animals have more than one common name, but few have so many as the puma. In the United States alone its names include 'cougar', 'mountain lion', 'catamount' and 'painter', but its range extends far more widely than this and covers as wide a range of climates as that of any other kind of mammal. Formerly it was widespread in North America, but with the advent of civilization its range has been reduced. It now occurs in the Rocky Mountains extending as far north as western Canada. In the south its range includes plains and forests as well as deserts, and it extends through

The puma usually has a litter of two or three kittens, but up to six may be born.

Central America and South America to Patagonia, though it is not common in equatorial forests.

Not surprisingly, with a range like this, the puma is a very variable species. Individuals from populations in cooler climates are, on the average, larger than those from the tropics. This is another example of Bergman's Rule in action. The males are usually bigger than the females, and the head and body of a large male would measure about five feet with the tail another three feet long. The weight of an animal this size could be 260 pounds. A small male, on the other hand, might weigh only 80 pounds. Pumas vary in color from light brown to, in a few cases, black. Little wonder that some people who have studied them think that more than one species is involved. Even so most experts think that the puma is a single species, although one zoologist held the extreme view that there were at least a hundred different species of puma.

The Puma—behavior

Being one of the larger carnivores of the Americas, the puma naturally concentrates on hunting fairly large prey. On the whole its range coincides quite closely with the range of deer of such species as the white-tailed deer and the mule deer, and there can be little doubt that these provide the chief prey. In the United States it has been found that, on the average, the puma kills one deer each week, although the record seems to be held by a bloodthirsty and successful individual which killed a total of seven deer in ten days. Having made a kill and eaten its fill, the puma hides the carcass, often dragging it for some distance and covering it with sticks and leaves. Having done this, it may come back to feed again later. One such kill is known to have been revisited ten times.

Other animals killed by pumas include peccaries, pacas, agoutis, spiny rats, iguanas and, in Patagonia, young sea-lions. In Peru they hunt vicunas, which are fleet-footed relatives of the camels. Pumas have been known to tackle even animals as large as horses, but they rarely attack man. Bearing in mind that they are such large animals and often hunt in the open, pumas are seen relatively rarely. This is because they are cautious and shy and are most often active at night.

Although they keep to a more or less fixed territory, they are great wanderers within this beat which may extend for over a hundred miles. Having made a kill, the puma may lie up in the same district for a few days, but it soon moves on to another area.

After a gestation period of about 14 weeks the female Puma gives birth to a litter of usually two or three kittens, although exceptionally there may be as many as six. At first the kittens' coats bear prominent dark spots and the tail is ringed, but these are lost later, although the dark spots on either side of the muzzle remain throughout life, and dark hairs also remain at the tip of the tail. The kittens soon become very active and playful and are weaned at ten weeks old, although it takes two years for them to become fully grown. Although they grow up more slowly than domestic cats, pumas live no longer than the tame species, and few of them reach an age of fifteen years.

White-tailed deer are the usual prey of the puma. On the average a puma kills one deer every week. Pumas will attack mammals as large as horses, but they rarely go for human beings.

The Clouded Leopard

The clouded leopard *(Neofelis nebulosa)* is in some ways intermediate between the larger cats *(Leo)* and the smaller cats *(Felis)*, and for this reason some experts feel it best to place the animal in a genus of its own, *Neofelis*.

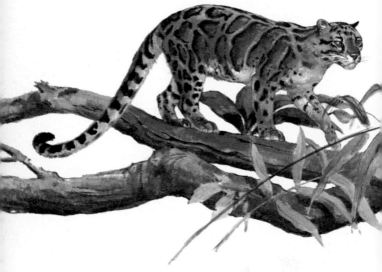

The species has an Oriental distribution, being found in Nepal and northern India, Burma, former Indo-China, southern China (including the islands of Hainan and Formosa), Thailand, Malaya, Sumatra and Borneo. Ever since being discovered in 1821 these animals seem to have been rather rare, or at least to have been seen rarely. Perhaps they are not uncommon in certain places, but of all the cats of Asia, clouded leopards are found in the thickest jungles. As they are great climbers and spend most of their time concealed in the leafy seclusion of the branches, they must often remain unseen.

The head and the body of the clouded leopard are three feet or more in length. The long tail, which is a useful adaptation to a climbing life, adds another 30 inches, but despite its length the clouded leopard is not very heavy. It has rather

The clouded leopard is a great climber, spending most of its time in trees.

short limbs and a graceful slender body, and the only recorded weight—44½ pounds for an adult male—is surprisingly light. Of course, in trees weight can be a disadvantage, for lighter animals can venture along thinner branches. Among the shadows the beautiful blotches of the coat with their less intense, 'clouded' centers, provide excellent camouflage. In elderly specimens—and clouded leopards in zoos have lived to be sixteen years old—all of the coloring in the center of the blotches tends to disappear leaving only the broken, black margins.

Clouded leopards hunt mainly at night and are presumed to prey on birds and small mammals, although they have been known to attack domestic sheep, pigs, goats and dogs. Nothing is known of their breeding habits in the wild, but in zoos litters of from one to four cubs have been born.

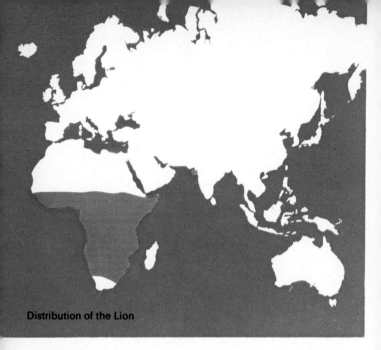

Distribution of the Lion

THE BIG CATS (GENUS LEO)

The Lion—distribution and appearance

In prehistoric times and even slightly later, the lion (*Leo leo*) had a continuous range, which included southeast Europe, the Middle East and India, as well as Africa. Inevitably the interests of such a large and predatory animal clashed with those of man, who wished to preserve his flocks and herds of domestic animals, and the lion, despite its power, was no match for the cunning of his human adversary. Lions have now dispersed from much of their former range, and, in the process, their distribution has become divided up into separate pockets.

The European lions were first to go and then those of Asia started to disappear. Today it is just possible that a few remain in Persia, but the only lions that certainly remain on the Asian continent are those that inhabit the Gir Forest near the northwest coast of India. At the last count there

Lioness

Lion

were 285 of them in an area of 483 square miles, and they were holding their own, preying mainly on domestic cattle. About a hundred of these Asiatic lions are killed by man annually, but such is their birth rate that their numbers remain roughly constant.

By the beginning of the twentieth century the lions of North Africa had gone too. At the other end of the continent, those of southernmost Africa came under human pressure and disappeared. Most of the world's remaining lion population is, accordingly, in Africa south of the Sahara. In western Africa, lions occur as far west as Liberia, but most of the species live in eastern Africa where some of the large herds of ungulates upon which they depend for food still remain.

In appearance lions are a very variable species. As is well known, males have a mane of long hair on the head, shoulders, chest and elbows, and this is an especially variable feature. Some manes are a light, tawny-brown and others are black, and the distribution of the hair shows equal variation.

87

A lioness usually has two or three cubs in a litter, but up to six may be born.

Perhaps several subspecies of lions do exist, but if so they can only be identified after examining a whole series of individuals and finding out the average typical of any particular area. For example, compared with African lions, most lions of Asia have a scantier mane on the head, but more profuse tufts on the elbows, chest and tail, whereas the coat itself grows rather more thickly. In size there is little difference between the lions of Asia and those of Africa.

The Lion—size and breeding

The average male is just under nine feet long overall, and ten feet is quite exceptional. An average weight would be 350 to 400 pounds, although higher figures have been recorded. Lionesses are usually smaller—perhaps eight feet long and with an average weight of 300 pounds. Of course individual variation occurs, and there is some overlap between the measurements of a small lion and a large lioness.

Perhaps because of their greater size lions mature more slowly than do lionesses, which are sufficiently well developed to bear their first litter when they are between three and four years old. Although they may in some parts of their range show a tendency to breed mainly at a certain season, lions can breed at any time of the year. The most likely mate for a lioness will always be the largest, fiercest and most mature lion in the pride of which she forms part, but sometimes several adult males gather and clash for her favors. At such a time serious fights may occur.

After a gestation period of about 108 days, the cubs are born. There are usually two or three of them, but there may be as many as six. Their nursery will be among bushes in order to provide some degree of security, for although the cubs are born with their eyes partly open, they cannot see well until they are at least a week old and are at first helpless. Their fur is prominently marked with clusters of spots, especially on the head, which fade gradually. Indeed traces of spots can usually be found on the underside and the hind legs of even a mature animal.

The cubs are gradually weaned at about eight weeks. As they gain in strength they play vigorously, but they are not capable of killing their own prey until they are about two years old. Until this time they are dependent upon their mother and other members of the pride.

Lion cubs are playful creatures, remaining dependent on their mothers and the others of the pride until they are two years old.

The Lion—lifespan and hunting

A lion comes into its prime at four to five years old and is past its prime at the age of ten. We have little knowledge of the lifespan of wild lions. Undoubtedly, lions have a high death rate during their first year or so, and if they survive this period they will still be unlikely to reach old age. Wild animals rarely do, for life in the wild is hard and death from starvation, disease or the results of an accident is common. Zoo lions, which lead sheltered lives, may reach old age. One specimen in the Dublin Zoo lived to be twenty-five.

Lions hunt a wide variety of prey. They have been known

The tawny-brown coat of the lion acts as camouflage among the open grasslands, where it preys on herbivores such as antelopes.

to kill animals as small as rats and mice, and they are very fond of domestic chickens. They certainly feed on carrion, especially when game is scarce. Nevertheless, they are primarily adapted as hunters of large herbivores such as antelopes and zebra.

Lions often hunt by day, especially if they are undisturbed by man. Sometimes they work on their own, stalking their prey as any other cat would and then seeking to surprise it by covering the last few yards in a few bounds, reaching speeds of up to thirty miles an hour in the process. Alternatively, lying in ambush by a waterhole may sometimes yield results. Methods like these are of most value when the prey is isolated and not a member of a large herd, as is often the case with those large herbivores that still survive in western Africa.

Other methods are needed to kill an individual from a large mixed herd of gnu and zebra such as is found in eastern Africa. Sometimes the males, being the more conspicuous animals, act as beaters, trying to drive the prey toward the smaller but just as deadly females, who lurk in hiding. Under these conditions it is the lionesses who are most likely to make the actual kill. However, once the prey is frightened and on the move, anything can happen, and the males often get their chance.

The Lion—making a kill and feeding

Lions use both their teeth and claws when making a kill, but their weight can also play a part. Sometimes the prey is bowled over by something like a flying football tackle before being dispatched. A single blow from a lion's massive paw can easily bowl over a medium-sized antelope. Larger prey is rarely attacked from the front, for lions are not invulnerable and have a healthy respect for butting heads and jabbing horns. In cases like this, they prefer to attack from the rear, clawing at the legs and thus disabling their prey before making their kill.

Once the kill has been made, the members of the pride lick up any blood which may have been shed and then disembowel their victim. The entrails are pulled out and put to the side and then the choicer morsels are eaten first.

Lions prefer kidneys and liver and then eat the thigh muscles, followed by the ribs. The tougher parts of the head, neck and back are left until later. Naturally not all members of the pride are equal in status, and high-ranking animals feed first and get what might, in other circumstances, be called the lion's share.

Unlike other wild cats, lions hunt together and feed together. The highest-ranking animals in the pride feed first and get the choicest morsels.

If times are good and game is plentiful the pride may well be unable to eat all the food that is available. If this is so they may return later for another meal, although if the kill is in the open they will find little left, for such scavengers as the vultures, jackals and hyenas will have made the most of their opportunity.

Exactly how often wild lions kill and feed has been the subject of much discussion and little agreement. Probably it varies a great deal, according to the circumstances. However, it is certain that once the opportunity arises, a lion makes a huge meal and may consume forty or even sixty pounds of meat at a sitting. Meat is a very filling food and requires thorough digestion, particularly as it is swallowed in large chunks. A single large meal may therefore be enough to satisfy a lion's appetite for up to a week. On this basis one kill every six or seven days would suffice to keep a small pride well fed.

Zoo lions feed more often than wild ones do but get smaller meals and so eat about the same total amount of meat. A meal of ten or twelve pounds of meat a day for six days, followed by a day's fast, is the rule in the lion houses of many zoos.

Lion Behavior

Lions have little to occupy themselves with between meals. By nature they are lazy animals and are content to spend much of their time resting. It is rare for adult animals to indulge in exercise for its own sake, and in the few cases where it is reported, it may well be that what has been seen has been misinterpreted. As has already been pointed out, every feature of a wild animal is adapted and geared to the need to survive. Unnecessary expenditure of energy would be inefficient and lower an animal's capacity for survival, and it is therefore unlikely to occur. Lions get enough exercise when hunting or when forced to move to another hunting ground because game is scarce or because they have been disturbed.

Although the lion has few natural enemies other than man, it has rival hunters to contend with. The presence of human competition in the form of big-game hunters can cause lions to desert an area. For this reason some of the

A pride of lions has a leader who will drive away rivals and fight intruders.

hunters of the past who amassed huge totals of 'trophies' were relatively unsuccessful as lion killers. Similarly, lions slink away when a roving band of hunting dogs arrives on the scene. These dogs belong to a wild species and, although they are smaller and less powerful than lions, they are socially more highly developed and are better able to coordinate their attacks upon their prey. As hunters, many who know these packs of hunting dogs fear them more greatly than the big cats, and they have certainly been known to take on and overcome solitary lions.

Apart from disturbances of this kind, however, a pride of lions keeps to its own familiar territory. A pride seems to be basically a family group, consisting of a fully grown male and his harem, accompanied by cubs of various ages. A large pride may consist of thirty animals, but such a large unit is only likely to occur when game is exceptionally plentiful.

The chief male in a group does not easily tolerate mature rivals and may sometimes fight to the death with intruders. Young males are driven away as they grow up and often hunt for a while in small groups of three or four on their own. Probably because they must face the world on their own without the support and experience of the pride behind them, young males have a lower chance of survival than females. At birth the sex ratio of males to females is roughly equal, but in the Gir Forest of India, for example, there are four to five lionesses to every lion.

Lions and Man

Man has always both feared the lion as a source of danger to himself and his herds and respected the lion for its strength and bravery. Some people who are familiar with lions in the wild have argued, perhaps with some reason, that lions are not particularly brave, but simply are successful carnivores which have a well-developed sense of self-preservation and will flee from trouble as readily as any other animal. The fact remains, however, that the hunting lion, or even the frightened lion, often *seems* to be brave and this alone commands respect.

Man has thus two motives for killing lions: he can eliminate a troublesome predator, or alternatively he can overcome an exceedingly formidable adversary and thus enhance his own self-esteem. Primitive herdsmen could achieve both of these objects at once. It takes considerable courage for a group of men armed only with spears to surround a lion and wait for it to make an attempt to dash through the cordon to safety. However, for hunts of this kind the economic motive was probably the important one, and to this day some lion hunting takes on the aspect of pest control. Troublesome lions in India are usually killed by poison.

Lion hunting became popular as a sport at the beginning of the twentieth century, but it occurs much less nowadays. In the nineteenth century, big-game hunting was done mainly for profit.

With the invention of firearms, lion hunting became easier and rather less praiseworthy as a feat of arms, but the practice was continued as a sport. Some of the inhabitants of Abyssinia had to prove their manhood by killing a lion single-handed, shooting it at close range from horseback. The best-known European hunters in Africa in the nineteenth century had other motives and shot game largely as a business proposition. Lion hunting was therefore not of great importance to many of them, although it still took courage to use firearms that were liable to misfire and took some time to reload.

Lion hunting as a sport for Europeans became really popular at the beginning of the twentieth century. This was the period when a man disappointed in love was supposed—if he could afford it—to redirect his resentment toward the fauna of Africa. It was usually eastern Africa, for by this time the large herds of hoofed animals upon which wild lions depend had already vanished from other parts of the continent. This was the period when the successful hunter took pride in being photographed with one triumphant foot planted on the corpse of his victim.

Lion Taming

An alternative way in which man could show his superiority over the brute strength of wild beasts was to tame them. The idea is an old one, as the story of Daniel in the lion's den proves, and to this day the lion tamer remains an impressive figure. To most people, lion taming is one of those incredible feats which can be believed only if it is seen. That it can be done is obvious, but the precise scientific basis upon which it stands is a matter for argument.

What is involved may be all a matter of the distortion of ordinary social behavior. Animals which live in groups naturally have a relationship with others of their kind. They may, as a result of fighting or of bluff be of high caste, lording it over their fellows, or they may lose the contest and adopt a subordinate position. If forced into proximity with one or more mem-

A lion tamer gains the respect of his lions by bluffing his way into a dominant relationship with them. The relationship is a personal one; the lions would probably attack anyone else who entered their cage.

bers of another species, a social animal sooner or later starts to treat them as if they were members of its own kind. This sounds improbable, but we have only to reflect that a pet dog living with a human family speaks to them in dog language, wagging its tail or perhaps snarling, while its owners address it in their own tongue. Before long each party understands enough of the other's language for harmony to prevail. Ideally the pet dog should be in a subordinate position and do as it is told, but like any other social animal it will dominate its fellows if it can. We have all known examples of dogs which dominate their owners, who have put themselves at the disposal of their canine's every whim.

A lion tamer, then, insinuates his way into a group of lions, being accepted by them as one of their own kind.

The famous lioness Elsa, although a wild animal, became tame in captivity with Joy Adamson. They became good friends and Elsa always greeted Mrs. Adamson with pleasure, even when she later returned to the wild. Their relationship was a strong personal one and shows that animals should be respected for being what they are.

He can do it gradually, getting to know them while first protected by the bars of the animals' cage. Consciously or unconsciously he must learn to read the mood of each animal from the signals it makes, and at the same time he must impress on it that he is the superior animal. When the time comes for him to step into the cage, there must be no doubt. He must be dominant, and he must have established his position by bluff, for in actual combat he would certainly stand no chance at all.

On this basis the lion tamer uses skills of the same type as those used by a teacher, who is able to quell a rowdy class with a glance. In neither case is the physical strength of the parties particularly relevant. However, a lion tamer must be able to understand an alien language, and the penalty for failure is much higher than it would be in the classroom.

Undoubtedly showmanship plays a large part in lion taming. Risks must seem to be taken, but often the danger is greater in those parts of the act that look safer. The lions with which the tamer works will not all be equal in status. Some will have high rank and will be the leaders in the absence of the trainer. These individuals will be the most likely to attempt to enhance their status by taking on their only superior and must therefore be allowed no liberties. If these animals are kept in order the rest will give no trouble. With low-caste lions the tamer can safely afford to take more liberties, turning his back for long periods and at times encouraging them to snarl and appear more aggressive than they are.

It should always be remembered that 'tame' wild animals are never truly tame in the way that some domesticated animals are. Some domestic dogs, for example, are friendly to all people unless they are given very good cause to behave otherwise. No wild animals can ever be trusted to such an extent. When wild animals are tamed, it is in a much more limited sense. They are trustworthy with some people whom they know but would show no such respect for strange humans—any more than they would necessarily show respect to strange members of their own species. Behind the showmanship and bluster, a lion tamer must earn the respect of his lions and must respect them, in turn.

A tiger's stripes blend well with the shadows of tall grasses.

The Tiger—size and appearance

The tiger (*Leo tigris*) is almost the same size as the lion, to which it is quite closely related. Because of this there is no simple answer to the frequently asked question 'Which is the larger, a lion or a tiger?' They vary among themselves and it all depends which particular specimens one is talking about. Many tigers have been measured by sportsmen in the past, but not all of the figures given can be relied upon. For example, if you want to know how long the tiger that you have shot happens to be, you can stretch it out and measure the distance between nose and tail tip in a straight line, or alternatively you can measure the same distance over the curves of the body, and this will give a higher figure for the same animal. If you skin it, stretch the skin and then measure it, you will obtain a still higher figure. Often we do not know which of these three methods was used in a particular case.

Probably the average male tiger is about as long as the average male lion—just under nine feet including the tail. It may be slightly lower at the shoulder than a lion, but if anything the body is more powerfully muscled. Certainly the tiger's back is slightly arched and looks stronger than the level back of a lion. Possibly the average tiger is the stronger of the two, but this cannot be proved.

That tigers are brown with black stripes is very well known, but few of those who have not had it pointed out to them realize that tigers have much white fur as well. In addition to white markings on the face and prominent white spots on the otherwise black backs of the ears, tigers are white with black stripes under the throat and body, and on the insides of the legs. This is countershading, a pattern which helps to cancel out the effect of shadows, making an animal appear to be flat and insubstantial. The tiger's stripes when seen in a zoo can give the animal a garish, yet beautiful appearance. The tiger has been well described as 'Death in a fancy dress'. Yet in the wild these same stripes blend well with the dark shadows of tall grasses or of the leaves of jungle trees.

The tiger is perhaps the most fearsome of wild cats to look at. Its brown and black striped coat camouflages it well in the wild.

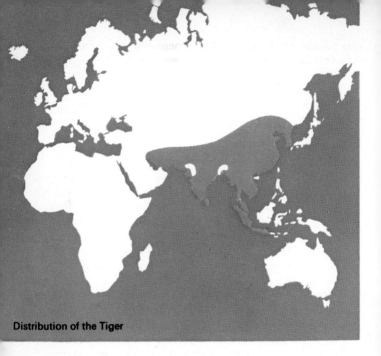

Distribution of the Tiger

The Tiger—range and variations in appearance

Tigers are often thought of as inhabitants of steamy tropical jungles. This is only partly true, and it seems likely that once it was not true at all. Fossils dating from some hundreds of thousands of years ago suggest that the ancestors of today's tigers lived in northern Asia, and from there the species has spread southward. Even today some tigers inhabit fairly cool parts of Asia, for the range of the species extends from central Asia and northeast China in the north, includes Persia, parts of India (but not Ceylon), Burma and the mainland of Asia, to the Malay Peninsula, as well as Java, Sumatra and Bali in the south. In most parts of this range tigers are declining in number, and those of Bali, for example, are rare. As usual, man is the culprit.

Although some tigers have lived in the tropics for thousands of generations, the species is still rather imperfectly adapted to the heat. The fur is thick, and it is very noticeable that tigers kept in zoos seem to revel in cold weather but dislike the heat. In countries where summer temperatures get very high, zoo tigers have been seen to immerse themselves in water so as to make a hot day more bearable.

It is only to be expected that a species with as wide a range as the tiger should show some variation in size and appearance in different areas. On the whole the tigers of the north are a paler brown than those of the south. This is presumably a matter of adaptation. In the less intense sunlight of cooler climates a paler color provides better camouflage. But there is no definite division between the lighter and darker forms. Just as the climate changes slowly as one moves from north to south, so the tiger population becomes slightly darker. Gradual adaptive variation of this kind occurs in many animals, and to describe it Sir Julian Huxley has coined the word 'cline'. Where a population of animals forms a cline, the typical animals from the extreme ends of the range may differ from each other considerably, but it is nevertheless difficult to divide the whole population into subspecies, for this means separating one group of animals from their very similar and closely related neighbors.

Similarly, tigers show a cline in the matter of size. Larger animals are found in the north, and smaller ones are found in the south. Once again this cline is adaptive, for larger bodies retain heat better than small ones do.

The striped pattern varies a great deal from one individual animal to another, but here, too, it is sometimes possible to distinguish between the inhabitants of different areas. With such a range of variation it is not to be wondered at that a number of subspecies of tigers have been named. Some of these, especially the island forms, are valid, clear subspecies which differ from their nearest neighbors.

Subspecies have a third scientific name added after those of the genus and species. Thus you will sometimes read of the Sumatran tiger, *Leo tigris sumatrae,* which is relatively small, very fully striped, has reduced white markings and a rather flat skull; you may also read of the Caspian tiger, *Leo tigris virgata,* from central southern Russia, which is medium-sized and has a long dark coat with many closely set brownish stripes. Many other examples could be given.

Wild tigers seem to be happy only where there is cover to hide them. They usually hunt by night, their dark stripes mingling with the undergrowth.

White Tigers

Of course, any population of animals can occasionally produce freak offspring, and this is what 'white tigers' are. One of the more common types of freak, found in many species, is the albino, which lacks normal dark pigments called melanins. White tigers are not true albinos, for they have some dark pigmentation, although only in a reduced form. They have dark brown stripes on almost white fur, ice-blue eyes and their noses and the pads of their paws are pink. White tigers have occasionally been glimpsed in the wild. In 1951 a young male white tiger was captured in the state of Rewa, India, and from this animal, mated to one of his own normally colored daughters, a number of white tigers have been bred in captivity, including the fine pair now to be seen in the National Zoo in Washington, D. C.

The Tiger—prey and hunting

Wild tigers normally live in remote areas where game is plentiful. Those of central Asia live among thick reeds or in bushes at the bottoms of river valleys. In summer they sometimes move to cover on higher ground, although they are never found above the tree-line in the mountains. In warmer climates tigers often inhabit mixed forest, preferably interspersed with rivers and outcrops of rock. They are sometimes also found in reeds and grass jungle where the vegetation may be over ten feet tall.

Although they are often forest dwellers, adult tigers rarely climb trees, probably because they are too heavy. Young tigers, however, quite often climb. Adults are usually solitary, although there are some reports of tigers hunting in pairs. They are mainly nocturnal, moving silently through the night in search of their prey. They can keep up a steady speed effortlessly and can easily cover fifty miles in twenty-four hours.

The prey hunted varies from one region to another. In Russia, tigers have been recorded as hunting wild boar, roe deer, elk, musk deer and even wolves. A wide variety of domestic animals are also taken when the opportunity arises, and these include dogs, cattle, horses, donkeys and camels. In the more southerly parts of Asia, tigers kill wild boar, deer of various species, antelopes such as nilghai and sometimes go in for even bigger game. It is estimated that in

White tigers (*right*) are extremely rare. They are not true albinos, which have totally white fur and red eyes, but their coloring is reduced below the normal range.

some parts of Burma one young wild elephant in every four is killed by tigers.

Tigers do not usually tackle full-sized elephants, for these may weigh between four and six tons and could easily crush a tiger. Even baby elephants are not easy meat, for the mother stays close by her young and is often accompanied by another female. For the tiger to be successful, the attention of both adults must be diverted before the young elephant can be killed.

In cases like this tigers usually get their prey on the move before attempting a kill, but against lesser opponents they more often steal in silently before bounding rapidly over the last few yards so as to take their prey by surprise. They sometimes kill by smashing the neck or skull of the victim, but they often make good use of their canine teeth, which are very long and powerful.

No doubt tigers' appetites vary, but it has been estimated that an adult tiger may kill in the course of a year about thirty victims, each with an average weight of 200 pounds. Obviously then, tigers eat meat when it is bad, for their kill will rapidly putrefy in the warmth of the tropics. Having made a kill, a tiger normally carries it off into thick cover, beyond the sight of thieving eyes, thus setting up a store of food which can be returned to again and again. A tiger in Burma once killed five bullocks, one after the other, and carried them off to form a really substantial larder. If anything, it almost seems that tigers prefer their meat partially decayed, and such is the tiger's strength that a bullock can be carried with ease.

When game is scarce a tiger will normally eat carrion. A dead buffalo, elephant or rhinoceros is very likely to attract its attention, especially after putrefaction has set in. If even this source of food is absent, then the tiger makes for some other part of its vast territory, covering distances of up to 250 miles. The tigers that roam the most are probably those of the more northerly regions where game can be hard to come by, especially in winter.

The Tiger—breeding
There seems to be no particularly favored breeding season. Like other cats, the female tiger is in heat periodically

and attracts the attention of males by means of her scent and her voice. The young are born after a gestation period of about 105 days, the nursery being any very secluded spot, such as a crevice among rocks or a cave, or in dense bushes or reeds. Up to six cubs can form a single litter, but between two and four is a more usual number, and not all of these cubs are certain to live for very long. Whatever size the litter was at birth, quite often only two youngsters survive to be weaned.

When they are just over a month old the cubs start to follow their mother as she hunts, although they are unsteady on their feet at first. As they grow, the area hunted by the family gradually increases, although they remain in the vicinity of each kill for several days. Eventually the young ones are able to play an increasingly active part in making the kill, but they do not become completely independent until the group breaks up, by which time they are between two and three years old.

In zoos tigers have been crossbred with lions. The offspring are known as *ligers* if a lion is the father, and *tigons* if a tiger is the father. Like mules, they are usually sterile, but not invariably so.

Tigers attack large prey, such as a water buffalo, on the move, but they often approach smaller mammals stealthily, taking them by surprise. They use their long, sharp canine teeth to kill large victims.

Man–Eating Tigers

Of all the predatory mammals, the tiger has the biggest reputation as a man-eater, and this reputation is not entirely unjust. Some tigers do, indeed, kill and eat man. Naturally, these occurrences are not as common as they once were, because tigers themselves are less common, but in the nineteenth century 148 people in one year and 131 in another were reported as having been killed by tigers in Java alone. No doubt many such deaths went unrecorded, and as Java forms only a small part of the range of the species, it is reasonable to assume that tigers were causing far more deaths than, for example, air disasters do today.

It has been suggested that man-eating tigers are usually elderly individuals, who are too infirm for the pursuit of more active prey, and this may sometimes be true. Man, after all, is a fearsome animal in his own right and is very properly shunned by the great majority of wild animals. Only a desperately hungry tiger, it might be thought, would so far abandon caution as to hunt such an opponent. However, some suspected man-eaters when shot have turned out to be in their prime, and evidence as to their former feeding habits in the form of cloth or the skin from the sole of the human foot, which is very resistant to the digestive process, has been found in their stomachs, proving the case against them beyond all doubt.

Undoubtedly man-eating is a habit which is retained once it has first been acquired, for deaths due to tigers do not occur singly and sporadically. Once a man-eater gets to work the human inhabitants of quite a large area can understandably become terrified, as the roll of casualties mounts and the killer becomes bolder.

The first few victims may have been struck down as they moved unwarily along paths at night, but as the tiger gets more daring, acts of startling boldness follow. In nineteenth-century India, it was not unknown for soldiers to be carried off from their encampment, under the eyes of sentries. At about the same period at a place called Hurdwar, a tiger sprang from the concealment of a barley field in broad daylight, dashed in among the crowd and killed a trader who was peacefully occupied in chopping up spice.

Man-eating tigers are usually desperate, hungry animals. However, even when hunting is good, a tiger may not identify its prey as a man, and, having made as easy a kill, become a confirmed man-eater thereafter.

The tiger was a wary and worthy opponent for hunters who enjoyed the thrills of danger.

Tiger Hunting

The activities of man-eating tigers drew the wrath of man down on them, but tiger hunting was also a sport pursued for its own sake in colonial India. Two methods were used.

A buffalo, elephant or some other game animal could be killed as bait in an area known to be inhabited by a tiger. From a platform constructed in a conveniently situated tree, the sportsman could then keep vigil for several nights in the hope of a shot at a hungry, scavenging tiger. Some sportsmen preferred a more social and active method of hunting which could take place in daylight. The tiger was flushed from its daytime cover by a line of armed sportsmen mounted on elephants. This method was best employed in tall grass rather than in tree jungle. One such hunt in Burma a hundred years ago was well described by Colonel F. T. Pollok.

Pollok was hunting with some other officers when, in the middle of the afternoon, they received a message that a tiger was surrounded by beaters on elephants close by. Mounting his own elephant, Pollok was soon rewarded by

the sight of a charging tigress, which he shot at and wounded in the foot. Another shot had little effect and the tigress hurled herself at Pollok's elephant, which recoiled, throwing her off to the accompaniment of another fusillade, as a result of which she retired into cover. Again the hunters went after her, whereupon she sprang at Pollok's elephant, clinging to its face, mauling it with her teeth and claws.

In an effort to throw off his adversary for the second time, the elephant dropped to his knees, throwing Pollok to the ground with a gun still clutched in his hands. Picking himself up, he found it impossible to shoot at the tiger as it was too closely engaged with the elephant, and he therefore retreated to mount another elephant. This mount, too, was mauled as it advanced. Darkness was then closing in, and the sportsmen withdrew to tend the wounded elephants and a mahout who had also been bitten.

The following morning the tigress was found on her back dead, bearing wounds from thirteen bullets.

The Leopard

The leopard (*Leo pardus*) is another species with a very wide distribution in the Old World—indeed it has a wider range than any other big cat. In size it is smaller than either the lion or the tiger, but it is hardly any less redoubtable than its larger relations.

A good-sized leopard would have a head and body about 4½ feet long, and a three-foot-long tail. This makes a leopard only a little smaller than a lion—perhaps 18 inches less over-all—but the leopard is more finely proportioned, being not only shorter but also lower at the shoulder. A greater part of the leopard's length is made up of tail, and as a result it is very much lighter than a lion. Although leopards weighing 200 pounds or so have been recorded, most males weigh less than half this figure, and 70 pounds is a fair weight for a female.

The leopard's spots are clustered together, each cluster being called a *rosette*. There are no spots in the middle of the rosette. The brown fur is very much lighter on the under-

parts, so once again countershading aids concealment. Like the other big cats, leopards have prominent markings on the backs of their ears, which are used as social signals.

Undoubtedly the leopard's pattern is camouflage, well designed to aid concealment among vegetation, and it is therefore surprising that leopards without this camouflage are not uncommon in some areas. As we have seen before, oddities can occur in any species, but if they are less well adapted than normal animals they will not usually survive to breed their like, and will tend to die out. It is therefore strange that unusually colored leopards are not rare.

The animals referred to are the darkly colored or melanistic leopards known as 'black panthers'. These are not members of a different species as is often thought. 'Panther' is simply an alternative name for the leopard and is quite commonly used in Asia for the species as a whole. Black panthers are simply leopards that happen to have very dark brown hair.

Distribution of the Leopard

Black panthers are most commonly found in the more humid parts of the leopard's range, and it has been suggested that the hereditary factors causing the dark color also adapt the animal to hot and sticky conditions, although it is not clear how they do so. As a black leopard is not so well camouflaged as its lighter brother (and both types can occur in the same litter), there must be some advantage they enjoy which would explain their survival in some numbers.

The Leopard—range

Leopards are quite widespread in Africa, although they have disappeared from the well-populated parts of southern Africa and are becoming quite rare in northern Africa. Elsewhere they are still numerous though their numbers are tending to decline, as they are shot for their coats which men or, to be more accurate, women covet. This is not a new trend introduced by Europeans, for there is in existence a ceremonial cloak from western Africa made from the skins of the tails of scores of leopards. Also just plain leopard cloaks were used by native Africans.

116

In Asia, leopards occur from Asia Minor in the west to China, Korea and Japan in the east. In the south their range includes India, Ceylon and southeast Asia as far as the islands of Indonesia. It is in India and southeast Asia that black panthers are especially common.

It would be expected that a species with a widespread distribution like this should show regional variation, but strange to say very little occurs. This is particularly surprising as leopards tend to stay close to their own territories and to breed with their neighbors, and as a consequence any one local population would be expected to be rather inbred. Such a breeding pattern is almost guaranteed to throw up local varieties and races, and yet with leopards this just does not seem to happen. Certainly a number of subspecies have been described and named, but there is little apparent difference between them, and a leopard from southern Asia looks very much like one from Africa.

Perhaps the most obviously distinct leopards are those of northern China which belong to the subspecies *Leo pardus japonensis*. These are larger than average and have extra long fur. No doubt both of these features are useful adaptations to cooler climates. Chinese leopards are also particularly handsomely marked, having large rosettes.

Like tigers, leopards keep to the cover of thick plant growth whenever possible. In Asia, where the ranges of the two species overlap to a considerable extent, this does not mean that they are in competition to any marked degree. The tiger, by virtue of its superior size alone, is able to tackle prey that a leopard would choose to avoid, while the leopard has abilities which mean that it can succeed in hunting where a tiger would fail. Because of its lesser weight and graceful form the leopard is, for a big cat, an excellent climber. It can move along surprisingly thin branches, unseen by all but the most keen-eyed observer below. The branches also provide a refuge from danger and sometimes a peaceful sleeping place during the heat of the day. The long tail is valuable as a balancing organ when its owner climbs. Of course, it would be unreasonable to expect the leopard to be as superb a climber as the lighter, and very agile, monkeys, but for its size it is a very good performer.

In Africa, leopards are most common in bush country where the cover is good, but they sometimes also venture into forests. In tropical Asia they prefer the same conditions. Further north they seem to like inaccessible forests on the lower slopes of mountains, living at altitudes between 3,000 and 10,000 feet above sea level. Here they rarely descend to the foothills and are never seen on the plains, although they are common enough on plains elsewhere, as long as there is enough cover.

Even among the cats, leopards are exceptionally secretive. They are rarely seen unless they themselves choose to make an appearance, and they do most of their hunting under the cover of darkness. In rocky areas they often spend the day in the cool comfort of caves. Apart from courting couples and mothers with young, they are solitary by habit.

The Leopard—prey and hunting

At dusk, when it is hungry, the leopard starts to roam in search of its prey, moving wraith-like through the shadows. Once game is detected, usually by sight but sometimes by smell, it moves in softly and poises itself before springing to make the kill, usually by means of a bite which can easily crush the neck of the victim. Alternatively, the leopard sometimes lies in wait on an overhanging branch, coming down heavily on any animal that is unwary enough to pass below. It is difficult to obtain accurate figures for such happenings, but it is sometimes suggested that in Africa leopards kill more men than lions do, and if this is true it may well be the result of this habit of ambushing the incautious traveler. Humans may be attacked and killed before they are identified as such.

Leopards do not invariably leap for the throat of their prey. When attacking a substantial opponent such as a warthog, which is well armed with sharp curved teeth, a leopard will often prudently attack the hindquarters first, seeking to disable its victim before finishing it off.

Leopards hunt a wide variety of game. Antelopes, such as impala and waterbuck, are commonly taken in Africa, along with smaller animals like baboons (a favorite food in rocky areas), other monkeys and large rodents. Many travelers have written of the leopard's fondness for domestic

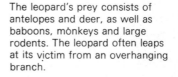

The leopard's prey consists of antelopes and deer, as well as baboons, monkeys and large rodents. The leopard often leaps at its victim from an overhanging branch.

119

dogs, and wild African hunting dogs may come into the same category, as long as they are not part of a pack. In Asia, deer form an important part of the diet.

Having made a kill, the leopard, like the lion, first rewards itself by licking up any blood that has been spilled. The carcass is then dragged into hiding before being disemboweled. The entrails are buried in a shallow grave. The meal then begins with those delicacies that leopards appreciate most highly—the heart, liver, nose and tongue, followed by the haunch.

Long before morning, repletion is reached and then, if circumstances permit, the remains of the kill are seized bodily and, with a bound, carried up to a fork in a tree well above the ground and securely balanced. This habit of leaving the remains of the kill in a tree is a valuable one to the leopard, for it is thus removed from the reach of such nonclimbers as jackals and hyenas. No doubt the vultures and other feathered scavengers can get a share, but their appetites are relatively small. Like the tiger, the leopard may return again and again to the same kill.

Leopards often store the remains of their kill in trees.

The Leopard—behavior and breeding

Leopards are usually silent creatures. Females are sometimes vocal when they are searching for a mate, but males may give a coughing roar at any time. It is thought that they do this for the same reason that birds sing—to establish their presence in their territory and warn off intruders of the same species. The voices of the other cats probably serve the same function, except for the lion, whose roar may be a means of keeping the members of the pride in touch with each other rather than a warning and a threat.

Wild leopards seem to have no particularly favored breeding season. The gestation period is about 92 days. There are usually between one and four cubs, three being the most common number at birth, although it is rare for the whole litter to survive to maturity. Adult leopards often breed more than once during their lives and, as the number of leopards in the world is declining, it follows that the chance of survival of any particular newborn cub is not very high. And if it is not going to survive to breed, an animal is always most likely to die very young.

Children have been carried off by leopards, never to be seen again.

Leopards and Man

Apart from man, leopards have few enemies. In the wild they die of starvation when food is scarce, from disease and as a result of accidents. Drowning is unlikely to be included in the last category for, like most other mammals, leopards swim well, and have been known to reach islands in some of the African rivers in this way. Colonel Stevenson-Hamilton has described seeing a lion in pursuit of a leopard on one occasion, and leopards certainly take to the trees when a pack of African hunting dogs makes an appearance.

Leopards sometimes attract the wrath of man by carrying off his domestic animals and sometimes, as has been mentioned, by making direct attacks on man himself. Because of its secretive and nocturnal nature, a leopard can easily remain concealed in the vicinity of human settlements, obtaining easy prey and causing widespread terror. In Algeria a hundred years ago, leopards were not uncommon, and sometimes caused havoc among flocks of sheep and goats. Men were less commonly attacked unless they provoked attention. A cornered leopard is always very dangerous— after all, even a rat will fight if it is cornered. During the day it is always possible for a man to blunder too close to the lair of a sleeping leopard.

Children are more likely to be attacked by leopards than are adults. Being smaller they may appear to be easier prey. More modern examples could be given, but let us complete the picture of nineteenth-century Algeria in this respect. A woman was working in a field, and she had left her baby on the ground nearby. It began to cry, and perhaps it was this that attracted a leopard which was lurking in a neighboring thicket. It dashed from cover, seized the infant in its jaws, and made off. The mother saw what had happened and set off in pursuit, but in vain, for she never saw either the leopard or her baby again. At about the same time in the same country, a boy of twelve was tending a herd of goats when he was attacked by another leopard, which wounded him so severely that he died of the injuries he received.

Leopard hunting

Because of the leopard's shy nature, nocturnal habits and its preference for killing its own food, the classic method of shooting leopards is to sit up at night, watching over a bait in the form of a tethered domestic animal, such as a goat. Some hunters keep vigil over the live goat, but this requires immense patience, for there is no guarantee that the leopard will deign to make an appearance. Bombonnel, a nineteenth-century French leopard hunter once spent thirty-four nights in succession in this fruitless manner. On the thirty-fifth night his luck changed and a leopard attempted to make off with the bait. Wounded by two shots, the animal sprang at the hunter and a desperate struggle ensued. Bombonnel was forced to let his gun fall, and was badly bitten about the face and left arm as he groped vainly for his hunting knife. At last, with a supreme effort he threw off the leopard and, picking up the knife, he staggered in pursuit. Fortunately for him, the leopard had made good its escape.

An alternative method of hunting is advocated by some other sportsmen. Once again a live domestic animal is tethered as bait. No further action is necessary until the leopard has made its kill. Being unable to drag the prey away, the animal will probably return to it, and this can provide the hunter with a chance. From a hide in a tree, preferably about thirty feet from the kill, he can then await his opportunity.

Colonel A. E. Stewart, a former officer in the Indian Army, has described his experiences of hunting in this way. Once in his hide he used to wait with his rifle ready from about three in the afternoon — the earliest possible time at which a leopard might be expected — until about 9 p.m. The leopard's approach, he says, was a silent one. Sixty yards from the kill it would halt and survey the surrounding area with suspicion. It might then take half an hour to cover the remaining distance, so great was its caution and so frequent the pauses. At this time the slightest move on the part of the hunter would send the quarry sprinting for safer cover.

Leopard hunting is carried out using a live tethered animal, such as a goat, as a bait for the leopard.

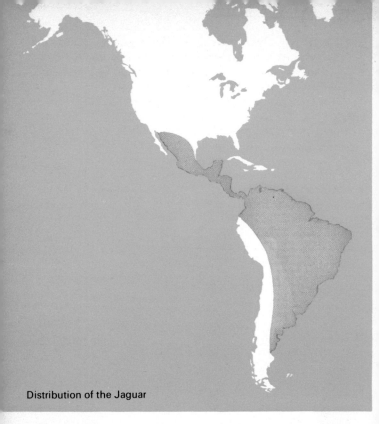

Distribution of the Jaguar

The Jaguar

The jaguar (*Leo onca*) is the largest of the cats of the New World. Only the lion and tiger are heavier. Although the jaguar was first reported at least as early as A.D. 1540 when the explorer Coronado came across the species in what is now New Mexico, relatively few jaguars have been weighed in the intervening centuries. One large male which was shot in Brazil scaled 290 pounds, and weights of over 200 pounds cannot be uncommon for males. Females are appreciably smaller and may weigh between 160 and 200 pounds.

At first sight the jaguar looks to be no larger than the leopard, being six or seven feet long overall, of which about two feet represent tail. However, in shape the jaguar differs considerably from its Old World cousin. The leopard is a graceful, beautifully proportioned animal, but those who know more about motor cars than they do about animals may be surprised to learn that the jaguar has a rather clumsy appearance. Certainly no member of the cat family can be downright clumsy, but the jaguar very nearly is. It has a rather large head, a tubby-looking body and a tail which is relatively short in proportion to the rest of the body. It walks with a bustling, almost rolling gait. This characteristic alone makes it easy to distinguish between the two species in zoos.

Another method is to examine the pattern of the coat closely. Both species are spotted, and in each case the spots are clustered into rosettes of various sizes. However, leopards have no small black spots in the middle of each rosette, but jaguars almost invariably have one, two or more small additional spots there. Of course, it is only in a zoo or a museum that confusion between a jaguar and a leopard could arise, for leopards inhabit only Africa and Asia, whereas jaguars live only in America.

The jaguar's range extends from the southwestern United States southward to include Mexico, Central America and South America as far as northern Patagonia.

The jaguar is the largest American wild cat. Only the lion and tiger are heavier.

As is usually the case, slightly different types of jaguars inhabit different areas, and various subspecies have been described. The Central American jaguar, *Leo onca centralis*, for example, is said to be smaller than average. However, individual variation among a single population is often considerable.

One form of individual variation which is quite common in some areas is shown by 'black' jaguars which, like black panthers, are in reality very dark brown so that the darker rosettes scarcely show. Presumably melanistic animals like this are the result of a hereditary factor like that which causes red hair in humans, which tends to run in families. The jaguars of any one region will tend to be more or less closely related and will tend to resemble each other more closely than jaguars as a whole. Some years ago black jaguars were said to be particularly common in some parts of Costa Rica. Of course, as with the black panther, it is surprising that black jaguars, which are poorly camouflaged, should be as common as they are. There must be a reason, but we do not know what it is.

The name 'jaguar' comes from a South American Indian name for the species—'Yaguar' or 'Yaguara'—but throughout its range the jaguar is usually known in Spanish as 'el tigre', which obviously enough means 'the tiger'. Why this name was ever applied is another mystery.

The jaguar and the leopard are reasonably closely related species, being descended from a common ancestor that crossed a prehistoric land bridge between Siberia and Alaska. Once the connection between the continents was broken the two populations became more and more distinct until the present separate species came into being.

Jaguars are most often found in thick forests. Often they keep close to rivers in lowland areas where, in the tropics, the heat and humidity can be intense. However, in the Argentine they sometimes inhabit more open country, concealing themselves among reeds and thickets. In the southwestern United States, where jaguars have been very rare for many years, they have been reported in forested, rough mountain country about 9,000 feet above sea level. In Colombia, too, jaguars are sometimes mountain dwellers.

Jaguars are most often found in thick forest.

The Jaguar—breeding and hunting

In the northern part of their range jaguars are usually said to breed in January, but elsewhere they seem to have no fixed breeding season. Certainly in zoos, births may take place at any time of the year. The gestation period is between 95 and 105 days, and there are usually from two to four cubs, although exceptionally there may be only one. The young are at first very dark in color, for they are heavily marked with solid black spots which are only slightly paler at the center. Each of these spots later forms a rosette. As is normal in the cat family, the father plays no part in bringing up his offspring. They mature at about the same speed as the other big cats. One male which was hand-reared in an American zoo weighed 165 pounds at just under two years old and obviously still had quite a lot of growing to do at that age.

Jaguars hunt by normal feline methods. With care they stalk their prey through the undergrowth before launching

a final, lightning, close-range attack. Over short distances they can run swiftly, but they lack staying power. Sometimes they lie in ambush and wait for likely prey to pass close to them. They rarely launch an ambush from trees for, unlike the leopard, the jaguar does not take to the branches unless it is forced to do so in self-defense.

Jaguars hunt deer, large rodents such as capybaras and agoutis, the pig-like peccaries, and they are even said to tackle tapirs, which must weigh as much as fair-sized ponies. They are not narrow in their choice of diet, for they quite often eat fish which they scoop from the water with their paws and have even been seen to dive into the water in order to attack fairly large alligators. Despite popular belief, not all cats dislike water, and of course, most jaguars live in regions where the water is comfortably warm. On the beaches of Central America jaguars sometimes dig up and eat the eggs of turtles.

Jaguars swim with ease and often take to the water in pursuit of the capybara, a large water-loving rodent.

A jaguar is quite able to swim whenever it is necessary.

Jaguars and Man

As to the effect that jaguars have on domestic animals, reports differ. Some say that jaguars rarely kill man's livestock, but others give the impression that it happens not infrequently, and one jaguar in the southwestern United States killed seventeen calves in quite a short period.

There can be no doubt that as the numbers of men in the Americas have risen, those of the jaguar have fallen. In the seventeenth century, 2,000 jaguars were killed every year in Paraguay alone, but now, although jaguars are still far from rare in some areas, this would be considered a huge total in any part of the range of the species. Exactly how numerous jaguars are it is impossible to say, for they usually remain well hidden. Where the hunting is good they stay inside a fairly small territory, but when times are hard they roam widely, and at such times jaguars are likely to be seen in areas they do not usually inhabit.

Despite its size and undoubted strength, the jaguar rarely attacks man, and it is not as greatly feared as the other big cats. As an illustration of the jaguar's attitude to men the events near Center City, Texas, one night in 1903 provide a fair example. A party of boys out walking with their dogs discovered a jaguar, which promptly took refuge in a tree. One youth who was armed with a revolver shot and wounded it, and seeking safer cover it dived for the ground and took refuge in some bushes nearby. Here it was quickly surrounded by men who had been attracted by the commotion. Despite its desperate situation the jaguar did not indulge in any leopard-like sorties toward its human attackers. It mauled and killed one dog and meted out the same treatment to a horse which somehow became involved in the melee, but despite the confusion and the cover of darkness it made no attempt to attack any of the men before it was finally shot and killed.

However, one can never be quite sure how wild animals will behave, and occasionally jaguars have caused surprises. In 1825 a jaguar was living on a low, bushy island in a tributary of the Rio Grande in what is now New Mexico. The river became swollen by flood water and the jaguar had to swim for its life, coming ashore in the garden of the Convent of San Francisco in Santa Fe. Seeing an open door it sought sanctuary inside the convent where, entering the sacristy, it was immediately confronted by a lay brother (it was a convent for men) who was returning unexpectedly from confessions. The jaguar killed him, and afterwards killed three more men one after the other as they ran up to help. The survivors closed the sacristy door, imprisoning the man-killing jaguar. They then proceeded to make a loophole in the woodwork. Once this was completed, a gun was obtained and poked through, and the jaguar was shot before it could do more harm.

THE SNOW LEOPARD (GENUS UNCIA)

The common name of the snow leopard (*Uncia uncia*) is rather misleading. It is not an ordinary leopard of any kind; and it does not always inhabit regions of perpetual snow. Big cats feed on herbivorous mammals, and no herbivore can get a living under such conditions. Besides, where canivores do live among snow, as the polar bear is able to do because it feeds chiefly upon seals, they have white camouflage as is only to be expected. The snow leopard has some white fur, but it cannot be described as a white animal. No, the common name of this species is not particularly satisfactory. The snow leopard, because of its distinctive anatomy, has been placed into a genus of its own—*Uncia*.

There is an alternative common name, the 'ounce', but it rarely seems to be used these days. This may be due to the feeling that 'ounce' is rather a lightweight name to give a cat which is not only beautiful, but also quite large.

The head and body of a snow leopard together measure about 52 inches, and the tail adds another 36 inches to this total. At the shoulder the height is about two feet—about the same as that of some leopards. Perhaps the weight is about the same as the leopard's too—few snow leopards have been weighed, and it is difficult to be certain. As compared to the leopard, the snow leopard has a smaller head and the body looks longer in relation to the legs. Here the comparison is made difficult by the length of the snow leopard's fur which is only just over an inch long on the back, but which reaches a length of two inches on the tail and nearly three inches on the underside. Because of this extremely soft, luxuriant coat, the snow leopard appears considerably larger in body size than it actually is.

The winter coat is appreciably thicker than the summer coat, and is slightly grayer in tone, but the basic color is always gray-brown with perhaps a tinge of yellow in places. Countershading is present, so that the underside is almost pure white. The body is patterned with large black rosettes which tend to be rather indefinite in outline. The tail, which looks enormous because of the length of its fur, has dark markings. The backs of the ears are dark at their bases.

The snow leopard's fur
is valued highly for its
warmth and is more
valuable than that of the
leopard. A few snow
leopards are trapped for
their fur in some parts of
Russia.

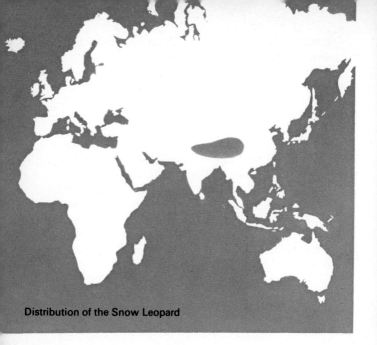

Distribution of the Snow Leopard

The Snow Leopard—range and breeding

Snow leopards are the least well understood of the big cats because they inhabit sparsely populated mountainous regions of central Asia. It is possible that there may be a few as far west as northern Persia and there may even be some in southern Persia, for it seems that perhaps they once lived there. Buffon, the famous French naturalist of two centuries ago, said that in Persia they were partly domesticated and trained for hunting, but perhaps he was confusing the snow leopard with the cheetah, which was often used for coursing (hunting). No other author seems to have referred to domesticated snow leopards, so there is considerable doubt.

Even today the range of the snow leopard is poorly known. It occurs in the mountain ranges of central southern Russia, such as the Pamirs, and from there eastward to Tibet and the Himalayas. Further north it extends to the Altai and Sayan Mountains and into Mongolia and into western China.

Although nowhere does it live in very northerly latitudes, the snow leopard lives at high altitudes and often encounters conditions which are cool or even downright cold. Accounts differ as to exactly how far up the mountains the snow leopard goes. One writer has mentioned an altitude of 20,000 feet in the Himalayas, but this figure seems a little exaggerated. A Russian zoologist who studied the species in Turkestan was probably nearer the mark when he said that it was usually found between 4,500 feet and 10,500 feet above sea level, with occasional forays to 14,000 feet.

Of course, like other mountain animals, the snow leopard migrates with the seasons, moving uphill during the summer and coming down for the winter, when it may even come down to 2,000 feet. In some areas it is said to live at this level the whole year round but even so, it must encounter some cold weather, for the interiors of large land masses have extreme climates, and there is no land mass larger than Asia.

The snow leopard is well adapted to resist the cold, for its coat provides excellent insulation and it has small ears, which are less likely to suffer from frostbite than large ones. Even the long tail—an appendage which is very liable to become chilled in some other species—is turned into an asset. When the animal curls up to sleep the tail is used as a perfect muffler to protect the bare nosetip.

The life cycle is also adapted to the climate. Tropical cats often have no very fixed breeding season, for to them all seasons are equally suitable for raising a family, but the snow leopard has a clearly defined breeding season. It would not do for the female to give birth to her young under icy, winter conditions. Mating occurs in late winter or early spring, and after a gestation period of 90 to 100 days the young are born in April, just as the days are getting warmer and the hunting is getting easier. There are usually from two to four cubs in the litter, and at first they stay in the den, often in a cave or a rocky cleft, although cases have been known of snow leopards making use of the huge nests constructed by vultures among the branches of low juniper bushes. By July the cubs start to follow their mother on her hunting trips, and they remain with her at least until the end of the following winter, when they are ready to hunt and find mates for themselves.

The Snow Leopard—prey and hunting

As might be expected from its spotty camouflage, the snow leopard often hunts amongst the dappled shadows of the juniper bushes and the spruce and birch forests on the mountain slopes. However, although the long tail would make an excellent balancing organ, there seem to be no authenticated reports of snow leopards climbing trees to any marked extent. Usually they inhabit more open country, lurking among rocky outcrops on the fringe of the mountain pastures.

Snow leopards are sometimes active during the day, but seem to do most of their hunting at night. Sometimes they go after quite small game, such as birds, ground squirrels, and pikas, which are related to rabbits, but they are capable of tackling much larger prey. They kill deer and mountain goats and sometimes manage to take gazelles by surprise in the foothills. On occasion they will even take on the wild boar, which is a very formidable opponent.

If game becomes scarce they may travel great distances in search of it. Their migrations may follow quite a regular pattern, for Ionov, a Russian observer, noticed that after a

Snow leopards often lurk among rocky outcrops, leaping out on to prey such as mountain goats and gazelles.

heavy fall of snow in winter or heavy rain in summer one particular snow leopard left its normal hunting ground and crossed a deep valley to reach another. A few days later, when the weather had improved, it returned by the same route.

Where their territory borders on pastures grazed by domestic flocks, snow leopards can become something of a pest for they frequently kill sheep, especially in winter when other game is scarce. They also take domestic goats and even cattle. In 1927 a snow leopard even succeeded in killing a horse belonging to the nomads of the Kirgiz Steppes of Russia, but this was a rare event. Horses are rather big game by a snow leopard's standards.

The method of attack used is either that of ambush or of stealing quietly toward resting or grazing animals. Quite often the last few yards separating the hunter from its prey are covered at a single bound, for snow leopards are superb jumpers. S. I. Ognev, a Russian zoologist whose word is to be credited, tells how he saw one clear a crevasse almost 50 feet wide.

Snow Leopards and Man

So far as is known the snow leopard does not attack man. At least, if it ever has no one has ever reported the event, which in some circumstances is a possibility, bearing in mind the lonely regions inhabited by this species of cat. However, without attacking man, snow leopards were once actors in a drama which has caused some excitement among the human population of the world.

For many years there have been persistent reports from the Himalayas of a strange creature which, from its description, is ape-like with human affinities. That these reports caused great excitement can well be imagined. The Yeti, or Abominable Snowman, caught the public's imagination. However, reports are one thing and concrete evidence is another. Apart from descriptions given by eye-witnesses—

Strange footprints found by explorers in the Himalayas and attributed to the 'Yeti' were probably bear prints.

descriptions which may have been garbled as they were passed on and translated—there were three additional pieces of evidence.

European climbers had seen footprints, made by what appeared to be bare, almost human feet, in the snow high in the Himalayas. One monastery had as a prized possession a hat, said to be made from the skin of a Yeti. And in addition to this there were strange roaring noises to be heard echoing round some of the high valleys.

An expedition went to the Himalayas to investigate and succeeded in borrowing the 'Yeti-skin' hat so that it could be brought back to Europe for investigation. The results were disappointing, for experts agreed that the skin was nothing like that of an ape and was probably that of a kind of Indian bison. The footprints also proved inconclusive, for although they could have been those of an ape or an ape-man they could equally well have been made by a bear—a much more likely possibility. But the roaring noises still required explanation. No known animal of the region was thought to have such a voice.

Now the snow leopard rarely roars and is, indeed, sometimes said never to do so. However, when angry it has a loud roar, as is only to be expected from such a big cat. Once this fact is known the evidence of the roaring could be explained. The snow leopard was providing the Yeti's voice.

So none of the evidence for the Yetis stood up to close examination, although this does not prove that the Yeti does not exist. Lack of evidence can never prove that.

THE CHEETAH (GENUS ACINONYX)

The cheetah (*Acinonyx jubatus*) is the oddest of all the cats and most certainly deserves its place in a genus of its own. Sometimes non-zoologists express doubts as to whether it is a cat at all but, although its running ability and methods of hunting are superficially dog-like, there can be no doubt that it belongs to the cat family. Even the method of hunting, when closely examined, turns out to be a variation on the cats' usual theme. Certainly the cheetah has evolved in such a way that it has come to be distinct from the other cats, but animals are classified by their ancestral relationships, and the cheetah evolved from the same ancestors as the other cats. It is not nearly as closely related to the dogs.

In its outline the cheetah is quite a large animal. The head and body are about 4½ feet long, and the tail another 2½ feet. At the shoulder it is sometimes three feet tall, but despite these dimensions the cheetah is very lightly built. The head is small and rounded, the jaws being much less string than those of a leopard or jaguar. The

The cheetah is also known as the 'hunting leopard', a misleading name for it resembles the leopard only in being a spotted cat with a range that includes parts of Africa and Asia. Otherwise it is quite different. The adjective 'hunting' probably refers to the fact that cheetahs have been tamed by man and used as allies while hunting.

neck, loins and limbs are powerful, but slender. Like all animals, cheetahs show individual variation in weight, but the normal weight range of the species is between 110 and 145 pounds.

The fur of the cheetah is a rather light yellow-tawny shade and is marked with spots in a manner which is unique among the larger cats. It will be recalled that in the leopard and the jaguar the spots are grouped to form rosettes which may or may not have additional spots in their centers, depending upon the species. The jaguar has these extra spots and the leopard does not. In the cheetah the spots are not clustered into rosettes at all but are scattered equally on almost all parts of the body. Toward the end of the long tail the spots run together, forming complete rings which encircle it. The short ears have dark backs but are lighter toward their tips. A dark line runs from the forehead, through the eye, and down the side of the face. On the nape of the neck of both males and females there is a patch of longer hair, forming a small mane.

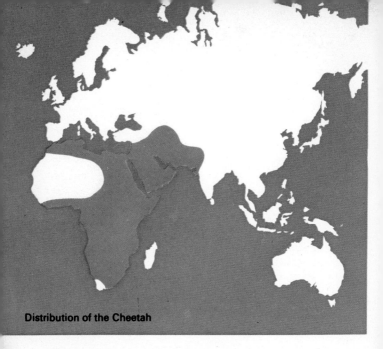

Distribution of the Cheetah

The Cheetah—range and subspecies

Formerly the range of the cheetah seems to have been much the same as that of the lion. It was found all over Africa wherever conditions were suitable, and also in the Middle East and a large area of Asia as far eastward as India. Today, because of the advance of civilization and the decline of the animals that it hunts, it has vanished from many of its former haunts.

In many parts of Africa, particularly in the north, it has become quite rare. Almost certainly it is extinct in Arabia and Jordan, and it has not been seen in Israel for over a hundred years. In India, it used to occur from the Ganges to the plains of the central Deccan, but none have been seen there since three were shot by one man in a single night some twenty years ago. The only cheetahs in Asia may now be in Persia, where there are perhaps a hundred of them; Turkmenistan in Russia, immediately to the north; and in Afghanistan.

The species is usually regarded as containing two subspecies, *Acinonyx jubatus jubatus* of Africa and *Acinonyx jubatus venaticus* of Asia, but there is no sharp difference between the cheetahs of the two continents. There is no agreement as to which of these two subspecies the few remaining cheetahs of Africa north of the Sahara should be placed in, and it may well be that they are of an intermediate type. If they are of the Asiatic subspecies it would not be altogether surprising, for the animals of northern Africa are in many ways more like those of western Asia than they are like those of the rest of Africa. After all, northern Africa is connected to Asia, and the Sahara Desert is a formidable barrier for animals to cross.

In 1926 a most unusual cat was trapped not far from Salisbury in Rhodesia. Its coat was not spotted but bore long dark stripes down the middle of the back and had exceedingly handsome, irregularly shaped dark blotches on the flanks. At first the animal was thought to be a hybrid between a leopard and a cheetah, but further examination proved beyond all doubt that it was simply a cheetah, typical in all except its markings. Inquiries soon brought to light the existence of other animals of the same type. At first it was thought that a new species of cheetah, named the king cheetah (*Acinonyx rex*), had been discovered, but nowadays these animals are regarded as unusually marked specimens of the ordinary cheetah species.

The king cheetah is an ordinary cheetah with unusual markings. It was discovered in Rhodesia in 1926.

The Cheetah—prey and hunting

Cheetahs avoid both thick cover and mountainous areas, preferring open sandy plains or gently rolling landscapes. Often they inhabit arid semideserts where luxuriant vegetation cannot grow but where there is just sufficient rainfall to support some wiry grasses, which provide food for the cheetahs' prey, and a few stunted bushes which provide cover for the cheetah when hunting.

The prey is usually said to consist of fleet-footed hoofed mammals, such as Thomson's gazelle of eastern Africa, the goitered gazelle of the Middle East or the Indian blackbuck, but there is no doubt that cheetahs sometimes take smaller game. Sometimes they kill hares, and they do not consider birds as small as larks to be unworthy of their attention.

Unlike so many of the cats, they do all of their hunting during daylight. To avoid the heat of the day they are most active in the early morning and in the evening, but not before sunrise or after sunset. They could not operate successfully in the dark, for they need to be able to see their prey from a distance.

That the prey will not be close to the cheetah is almost inevitable, for gazelles and other inhabitants of the cheetah's territory seem to appreciate full well the risks attendant upon venturing too close to bushes, and they stay well out in the open. On sighting the prey the cheetah sometimes walks slowly but purposefully toward it, moving up-wind so that its scent does not provide a warning. Gradually it accelerates until it is hurling itself at full speed toward the potential victim. More often, however, it crouches, flattening itself and inching toward the prey before suddenly unleashing the final assault.

In either case the cheetah must be able to cover a considerable number of yards in a short time to achieve success, for the prey is wary and will be off at the first hint of danger. Some gazelles can run at fifty miles an hour and, if they have a reasonable start they will have every chance of escape. Indeed, they often do escape. Sometimes, though, the cheetah is lucky and, catching up with the prey, succeeds in bowling it over with a single blow of its paw. Alternatively, it may fly straight at the jugular veins of the throat, obtaining a death grip with its powerful jaws and teeth.

Cheetahs are unsystematic feeders, often leaving choice tidbits instead of eating them first as a lion or tiger would.

147

The Cheetah—running ability

In order to have any hope of success in hunting, the cheetah must clearly be able to run faster than its prey and, indeed, it can do so. The cheetah is the fastest animal on four legs. Over short distances it can outrun gazelles, or if the opportunity presented itself it could run rings round racehorses or greyhounds, for the cheetah can attain speeds of up to 65 miles an hour. However, its stamina is poor and it cannot maintain such a pace for many hundreds of yards. It is only a sprinter, and if it does not reach the prey within seconds it gives up that particular hunt.

When the cheetah's method of hunting is seen in this light, it becomes understandable. Like the other cats, it pounces upon its prey, but the conditions under which it operates force it to pounce from a distance, and this is why it has become adapted as a sprinter. It is the cat that springs the furthest.

Its light build and the length of its legs are adaptations for speedy running, and even the long tail provides a useful weight which can be adjusted during cornering if the prey twists and turns in a last effort to escape. However, it is remarkable that the cheetah should be able to outpace gazelles and blackbuck, for they, too, are adapted for running and are in one respect still more perfectly adapted for the purpose. In effect, hoofed animals run on their toenails, for that is what hoofs amount to, and along with this the leg becomes as long as anatomically possible. The cheetah runs only on tiptoe. It is not the perfection of its legs which makes it the fastest of all runners.

The secret lies in the waist region. In galloping, a cheetah does not merely swing its powerful hind legs from the hip, but, by arching its back, it is able to swing them from the waist. This is the secret of its success. Studies of slow-motion film of running cheetahs have led one American expert to suggest that a theoretical cheetah with no legs at all could reach twenty miles an hour, humping along like a caterpillar.

As compared to those of other cats, the cheetah's feet are also adapted for running. Although young cheetahs can retract their claws to some extent, this ability is soon lost as they grow older. The adult cheetah's claws are permanently extended and enable the feet to grip the ground as they thrust the body forward.

The cheetah is the fastest animal, attaining speeds of 65 m.p.h. It gains its power by swinging its legs from its waist. It grips the ground firmly with permanently extended claws and with special pads on its feet that are ridged rather than rounded.

Cheetahs and Man

Of all the wild cats, cheetahs are the most easily tamed. Cubs which are caught when young and comparatively helpless are likely to grow up to be reasonably docile, and even animals caught as adults can very often be tamed. It might be thought that to catch an adult cheetah would be a rare occurrence, but this is not so. The cheetah's lack of stamina makes capturing it a relatively easy feat. A man on horseback or, nowadays, in a motor vehicle, can easily catch up with a cheetah.

Because it can be tamed and because of its speed, the cheetah has been used by man as an ally in hunting for many centuries. In India and Persia it was once almost commonplace for a wealthy potentate to have a string of cheetahs for coursing. One Mogul emperor in India four hundred years ago was reputed to own a thousand cheetahs

Hunters carried their cheetahs blindfolded to the hunting ground, unhooding and releasing them when game was sighted.

all at one time. It is not so well known that cheetahs were also kept in Russia, far from the present range of the species, and here they coursed game on the plains near the city of Kiev.

Cheetahs caught as adults were always found to be more efficient as hunters than young animals. Apparently the running ability of a cheetah is inborn, but its know-how in making a kill may be partly taught by its mother, and a natural upbringing is therefore most likely to produce a good hunter.

Sometimes the sportsmen were mounted on horseback, the cheetah being carried or conveyed in a special carriage with its eyes blindfolded. Once game was discovered, the animal was unhooded and the prey was brought to its attention. When the cheetah saw the game, it stalked it carefully before making a final dash. If it was successful it was rewarded with food and blindfolded once more. As an alternative method of hunting, beaters drove the game toward a line of men with cheetahs which were released as the prey came into sight.

The cheetah was not the only cat to be tamed for the chase in India. The caracal lynx was sometimes used in the same way.

Cheetahs in Captivity

The cheetahs which are to be seen in zoos are quite often fairly tame. This is because they are usually specimens which were born in the wild, orphaned or abandoned by the mother, and taken into human protective custody while very young. Of course, they are not tame in the sense that domestic cats are. Although they can often be taken for walks on a leash or even with no restraint at all, they can be very stubborn and it is not unknown for them to sit down and refuse to be led anywhere. More than this, beneath a bland and apparently docile exterior they are still wild animals at heart. Their actions are never entirely predictable. For example, for a man to seem to run away from even a tame cheetah might be a great mistake. The sight of something behaving like the natural prey might well trigger off the normal reaction of pursuit. Even domestic dogs' behavior cannot be guaranteed in circumstances like this.

Although cheetahs are often to be seen in zoos, they have always been regarded as the most difficult of cats to breed in captivity. That there should be difficulty is not surprising. Even lions, some of which have been bred in zoos for generations, do not always breed when they are expected to. There is more to it than keeping a male and a female in the same cage. Sometimes the conditions may not be quite right. Sometimes one of the pair may be sterile, or sometimes perhaps the animals concerned may just not like each other well enough to mate. Nevertheless, although disappointments occur, cats of most species breed reasonably freely in zoos. The cheetah has always been the notable exception.

The reason for this is unknown and this poses very many interesting problems. Despite their long history of association with man, cheetahs had never been bred in captivity until 1956, when a female in the Philadelphia Zoo in the United States gave birth to three cubs. They were raised to the age of three months before they died of feline distemper. In 1960, the Krefeld Zoo in Germany achieved the second success when two cubs were born. This litter was reared successfully, although bottle feeding was necessary. A few more cheetahs have been bred since then, but a litter of cheetahs is still cause for celebration among professional zoo keepers.

It may be that the limited success which has been achieved is the result of improved animal care, for the standards of the best zoos are continually rising. Perhaps diet is the most important factor here, for the first cheetahs to breed had been given a vitamin supplement in addition to their normal diet of meat. Other factors may be involved too. Research is beginning to show that for some mammals a natural upbringing for the young is essential if they, in their turn, are to make good parents. For the reasons already given, most zoo cheetahs do not have a normal start in life.

The gestation period of the cheetah is about 95 days. The cubs are born with their eyes closed—they open at just over a week—and at first a mane of long silvery-gray hair extends all the way down the back. This is lost at about ten weeks, although one tuft of longer hair remains on the nape of the neck throughout life. Until they are ten weeks old the cubs can retract their claws.

Cheetahs are sometimes kept in captivity.

WILD CATS AND ZOOS

In a way the animals in a zoo are ambassadors for their kind. It is true that we cannot see them doing all that they would do in the wild. The cats are not allowed to kill their own food, for example. If they did they would probably do it quickly and without fuss — the domestic cat is the only feline species to toy with its prey — but some of the public would hate the spectacle, and it is possible that one or two others would enjoy it too much. The meat is given already dead to zoo cats, and this helps most of us to keep up the pretence that meat-eating has nothing to do with killing. We like to keep butchery in the background, and we too easily forget that hunting is a natural way of life for some animals.

In every other respect, though, zoo cats lead lives which are as full and as contented as those of their wild relatives. It is true that they are not free to go where they choose, but this is only one freedom amongst others. They are free from starvation and fear and as free from disease as modern science can make them. Wild cats do not enjoy these freedoms. Zoo specimens on the average are larger, have glossier coats, and live longer than their wild relatives do.

Wild cats take exercise only when they must and spend much of their time doing nothing. Zoo cats take little exercise not because they cannot, but because they do not have to. In the large cages of some modern zoos the cats have room to run, but they rarely do. True, they pace up and down by the bars, but this is not an attempt to take exercise. Their one frustrated instinct is the instinct to stalk and to kill. The people beyond the bars become the prey, and the big cats move toward them as far as they are able.

No, zoo cats are not free to kill — few would suggest that they should be — but otherwise they are content. Often their contentment shows. They purr as often as wild cats do. And we, restricted in only slightly different ways by the restraints of our civilization, can see them and understand them better, and thus understand better the living world of which we are a part.

The pacing of a caged tiger is an attempt to stalk prey.

BOOKS TO READ

There are a few books that are solely concerned with wild cats. These
include:

Cats of the World. Armand Denis. Houghton Mifflin, 1964.

Born Free. Joy Adamson. Pantheon, 1960.

The Bobcat of North America. Stanley P. Young. Stackpole, 1958.

The Puma, Mysterious American Cat. Stanley P. Young and Edward
A. Goldman. Dover, 1946.

Simba. C. A. W. Guggisberg. Chilton, 1963.

The World of the Tiger. Richard Perry. Cassell, 1964.

Most general and regional books on the distribution and habits of mammals include information about cats. Some titles of this nature are:

Mammals of North America. V. H. Calahane. Macmillan, 1947.

Biology of Mammals. Richard G. Van Gelder. Scribners, 1969.

The Natural History of Mammals. F. Bourliere. Knopf, 1954.

A Field Guide to the Mammals. W. H. Burt and R. P. Grossenheider.
Houghton Mifflin, 1952.

The Mammal Guide. Ralph S. Palmer. Doubleday, 1954.

Wild Animals of North America. The National Geographic Society, 1960.

The Book of Indian Animals. Stanley H. Prater. Bombay National History Society, 1943.

Animals of East Africa. C. A. Spinage. Houghton Mifflin, 1963.

Mammals of Eastern Asia. George H. H. Tate. Macmillan, 1947.

Mammals of the U.S.S.R. and Adjacent Countries. S. I. Ognev. Israel
Program for Scientific Translations, Oldbourne, 1962.

The Terrestrial Mammals of Western Europe. G. B. Corbet. Foulis, 1966.

PLACES TO VISIT

Wild cats can best be seen in game reserves in their countries of origin. However, most people are only able to see these animals in zoos. A few of the zoos where these very popular animals can be seen include:

Bronx Zoo, New York City
Staten Island Zoo, New York City
Franklin Park Zoo, Boston, Massachusetts
Philadelphia Zoo, Philadelphia, Pennsylvania
National Zoological Gardens, Washington, D.C.
The Brookfield Zoo, Chicago, Illinois
San Diego Zoo, San Diego, California
San Francisco Zoological Gardens, San Francisco, California
Crandon Zoological Gardens, Miami, Florida
Cincinatti Zoological Gardens, Cincinatti, Ohio
Milwaukee County Zoo, Milwaukee, Wisconsin

Many of the rarer and sometimes already extinct varieties or species can be seen only as museum specimens. Museums where exhibits of recent cats, fossil cat ancestors and cat anatomy can be seen include:

American Museum of Natural History, New York City
United States National Museum, Washington, D.C.
Field Museum of Natural History, Chicago, Illinois
Carnegie Museum, Pittsburgh, Pennsylvania
Milwaukee Public Museum, Milwaukee, Wisconsin
Los Angeles County Museum, Los Angeles, California

INDEX